I wrenched my eyes away and lunged. He was fast enough that his throat wasn't pierced cleanly, but the wound looked like a woodcutter's first chop—and was just as bloodless. He hissed, dashing into the wall and up, his claws not even marking the faded floral paper. I sliced the sheet covering some wall hanging. Suddenly the surface he clung to was sliding. He scrambled, then hit the ground solidly. I delivered the woodcutter's next strike.

The body burst into a cloud of pyre smoke. My sword screeched across the floor, momentum thrusting my face into that blast of dry death. I twisted away, grimacing as I regained my balance. I hated that smell. The young ones smelled wet, the old smelled dry, but both had that throat-clogging bitterness.

Like a shadow given shape but not substance, the smoke fell but refused to disperse. It pooled across the floor, seeking cracks in the boards, trying to seep into the dark below. I hadn't ended the stranger—his head hadn't severed cleanly—just panicked him. Instincts were powerful things, even more so when immortality was at stake. He'd search out a dark place to recover, but he wouldn't be bothering me again soon.

I scanned the room for whatever he might have been looking for, but the woman caught my attention.

The cloth I'd cut from the wall revealed a portrait of a noble family: two arch-looking young women in matching floral dresses, plus a mother and father. My slice had cut a mortal wound across the chest of one daughter, but it was her near-twin who caught my attention. Red strands strayed from beneath her broad sun hat. The traumatized canvas distorted her face, but it was clear she was a fragile thing, with her father's calm expression.

I raised my hand to the portrait. Something about that woman seemed . . .

I pinched the limp canvas back into place.

It was me.

The Pathfinder Tales Library

BLOODBOUND

F. Wesley Schneider

A TOM DOHERTY ASSOCIATES BOOK
New York

FAN
Schneide

This is a work of fiction. All of the characters, organizations, and events portrayed in this novel are either products of the author's imagination or are used fictitiously.

Maps by Crystal Frasier and Robert Lazzaretti

A Tor Book
Published by Tom Doherty Associates, LLC
175 Fifth Avenue
New York, NY 10010

www.tor-forge.com

Tor® is a registered trademark of Tom Doherty Associates, LLC.

Library of Congress Cataloging-in-Publication Data

Schneider, F. Wesley.
    Bloodbound / F. Wesley Schneider.—First edition.
        p. cm.—(Pathfinder tales)
    "A Tom Doherty Associates Book."
    ISBN 978-0-7653-7546-9 (trade paperback)
    ISBN 978-1-4668-4733-0 (e-book)
1. Vampires—Fiction. I. Pathfinder (Game) II. Title.
    PS3619.C44686B58 2015
    813'.6—dc23

                                                                    2015023321

Our books may be purchased in bulk for promotional, educational, or business use. Please contact your local bookseller or the Macmillan Corporate and Premium Sales Department at 1-800-221-7945, extension 5442, or by e-mail at MacmillanSpecialMarkets@macmillan.com.

First Edition: December 2015

Printed in the United States of America

0 9 8 7 6 5 4 3 2 1

Dedicated to Marie E. Ritter,
for whom there was never any doubt.

Inner Sea Region

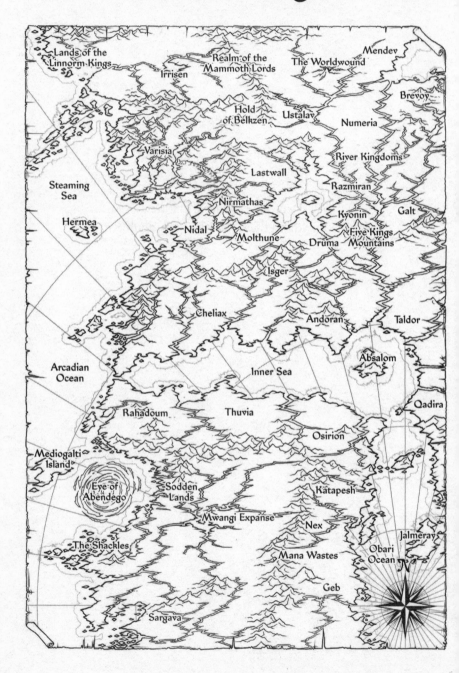

Southern Ustalav

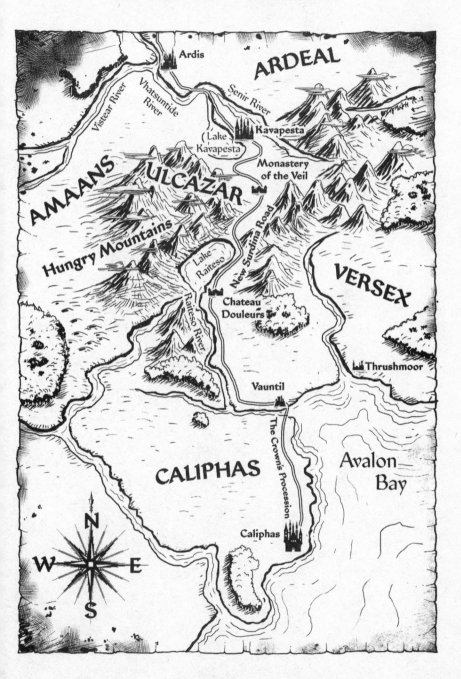

1

DESERVING VICTIMS
LARSA

Both were victims.

She ground against him, forcing hips away from the soot-smeared stone of the alley wall, hands grasping, mouth gnawing.

His breath came as a gasp but left as a growl. Hands struggled with her dress's collar. Hairy fingers dug in her skin.

Had I been a passerby, glimpsing them sidelong from the street, I might have been envious. Even knowing what they were, some voyeuristic urge stopped me on the slick shingle overlook. The appeal of hard and soft flesh aside, I wondered which of the pair was more the monster.

Clothes fell away, hardly barriers at all, the straps of her provocatively innocent dress following his tailored coat. Peasant cloth dangled from her waist, skin milky in the alley's slats of mist-webbed moonlight. He barely spared a hungry glance before diving back to her kisses, a coarse hand pinning her shoulder to the bare brick. Her own light touch played him like the moist rim of a wine glass, the results just as audible.

I couldn't hear their words, but the timbre of their murmurs gave away a predictable script. Gravelly whispers threatened plea-sures. Feigned naivete filled her response with blushes. His hand slipped behind him, reaching for the grips of the tool jammed in the back of his belt, no longer hidden under his big coat. The steel of workman's shears scored the gloom—shears that had, in preceding weeks, pruned at least four similar alley flowers. Her slitted eyes didn't see, her head falling back under an assault of bruising kisses. The blades came up.

Here it was.

Like a whip crack, the motion was too fast even to blur. With a snip and splash the shears clattered to the boggy cobbles.

There was no pleasure in his second gasp.

Pale arms that had strained to enfold him a moment earlier now bit into his skin like viciously pulled reins. Her kiss on his neck was deeper now, sharper and hungrier. He struggled, but only now, with jaws at his neck, did he realize that he wasn't the predator.

A shame. I'd hoped she'd be the one surprised. Few humans could match her experience, though—she'd likely been hunting in the city for decades. She might have continued, too, if she played by the rules. Now she'd become a problem.

My problem.

I dropped from my vantage. Heavy with the night's cold mist, my cloak slapped the stained cobbles. Her eyes were on me even as her mouth worked her lover's neck. Greedy thing, she was more chewing than drinking—obviously not of the sort of stock anyone taught manners. I straightened and pulled my sword, its silvered length catching a glimmer of moonlight through the dull haze.

Her eyes locked on mine, watching but obviously not considering me enough of a threat to risk losing her meal. The struggling in her grip was weakening, the man gradually accepting a warm, lethargic futility—the best part. I closed cautiously.

She came up, as if for the air she didn't need, gasping lewdly as she did. Sweat and blood trailed from her mouth in ribbons. She'd been sloppy, blood coursing down her jaw and chest. Daintily, she touched her hand to her lips, stained fangs glistening behind her fingers. A practiced pout poured over the shoulder of her current beau. "You can be next."

Very sloppy. My blade leapt up, obviously faster than she'd expected. A slender white digit arced into the air and plunked into the mud. It didn't bleed.

Her scream was not that of a blushing maid. Shrill with shock, it cracked, reaching a pitch like a shrieking hawk. Her lover barreled into me, thrown backward as she extracted herself from his embrace. I spun out of the way, surprised to hear him grunt as the muddy cobbles met his face.

My sword came back up for the milkmaid. The alley was empty. My eyes went higher, and so did a missile from my belt. The dart sounded like a wasp for the instant it flew, jabbing its silver stinger into a blood-drenched neck. She'd leapt up one of the alley's crumbling tenement walls—an elementary trick.

"Bitch!" Pain growled through the word. She sprang. I slid back. Even with a belly full of blood she was likely faster than I, but I was still quicker than she thought. Nails like claws sliced past my face, digging into filthy alley stone. It wasn't a jarring miss, though—she landed like a bounding cougar and pounced again.

My sword was between us, its hilt wrapped with the copper chain of an angelic ankh—the holy icon of Sarenrae, goddess of the sun. She skidded and reeled, expecting the symbol to flare with divine light.

"You are forbidden to hunt in this part of the city." I brandished the talisman as though I had faith in it. "Explain yourself."

"I have refined tastes." Even stained and exposed, she postured. "I hunt where I choose."

"You hunt where your master allows. You hunt where his truce isn't threatened."

She tittered, again raising a coy hand to her mouth. It came back wet. "I have no master."

"Your arrogance threatens more than you understand."

"You mean we threaten you mortals." She started to circle me. "Had that old coward not betrayed his kind with his truce, the only humans in this city would be mindless casks, waiting to be drained."

"Overestimation is a disease of the lowborn."

She sneered. "Your end could have been pleasant, had you the sense not to insult your betters."

It was my turn to laugh. "You had to trick a human into an alley. He wasn't under your control—he was planning to kill you. Was his mind too difficult to overpower? Or perhaps your will was too weak?"

Her eyes smoldered in the gloom. "How dare—"

"Speaking of control, not even a rat has come to your aid. Where are your minions, mistress?" I produced a match and ran my nail across its head, the crisp white flame dramatically lighting her snarl. She was ready to pounce.

"But most pitiful," I dropped the match into the muck between us, "is that."

On the ground between us lay her dainty, mud-stained digit.

"There's no magic in this blade, Your Ladyship. So apparently you're still mortal enough to be cut up by our weapons." I leveled the sword at her face. "You're not my better. You're hardly even fit to call yourself vampire. You're just some bored immortal's stray spawn."

Baring her fangs and screeching, she rushed me, crushing the match underfoot.

She wanted me dead. Good. There'd be no tricks now. She might not be a true vampire—at least, not as the full-bloods would consider it—but she was still deadly enough.

She lashed out wildly, claws blurring. I kept ahead of her, scoring several nicks across her forearms. The bloodless wounds knitted shut with unnatural speed, but her reckless rush gave me plenty of opportunities to make more.

Her chirping laugh echoed off the alley walls as I gave ground. A stroke across her stomach killed the noise, the gash deep enough to make her gush blood that wasn't her own. With a sound more gurgle than growl, she grabbed the blade as it freed itself from her midsection. The silver bit deep into her grasp. I thrust to impale her, but the sword didn't budge. Death lent her unnatural strength, and she yanked the blade from my hands. It clattered down the alleyway, toward her forgotten meal. My emptied hands snapped up, one covering my heart, the other reflexively trying to hold her off as she came. She slammed into me, pinning me against the wall just as her lover had trapped her moments before.

She locked her nails around my neck. "Scream!"

The chill of her hands caused my breath to catch. Death, palpable and endless, washed over me, an arctic wave seeking to erode my soul. While blood kept vampires fed, the chill of their lifeless essence leeched mortal life, freezing a living spirit to death.

Fortunately, I liked the cold.

"What?" She blinked, baffled as to why her touch wasn't sapping my life. I flashed her a smile, and in that last moment she understood.

I twisted, pulling a hawthorn stake from my bandolier, then lunged. The sharpened wood drove home, her weak, wet skin splitting like a reptile egg. A rigidity more appropriate to the deceased seized her body, freezing her face in a look of wide-eyed realization.

I pushed, and black locks trailed her stiff fall. She struck the stone with hardly a thud. The stake quivered, but stayed firmly planted through her heart.

She wasn't dead—or, rather, she wasn't destroyed. The stake would hold her paralyzed and unaware so long as it remained in place. A final destruction required a bit more effort.

At the other end of the alley, I was surprised to find the big man weakly struggling to pull himself against a wall, blood oozing between thick fingers clasped to his neck. I paid his groans no mind and retrieved my blade.

Back with my quarry, I performed the necessary field dressing—removing her head. It was a practiced grotesquery, and I hacked through the cold meat with a butcher's half attention. A trickle of gore—none of it her own—reminded me why I hated doing this right after the creature had fed. Finishing the work, I dragged the decapitated corpse to the alley's eastern mouth, propping it against a wall sure to be hit by the morning sun. The dawn would reduce the vampire's body to ashes, assuring no second resurrection.

A whimper drew my attention back to the bleeding man. Dropping the vampire's head into the stained sack I used for exactly that purpose, I turned back to the would-be murderer.

Past him, a carriage soundlessly pulled up at the far end of the alley.

I didn't hold back any of the curses that leapt to mind.

Stiff black clothes held a stiff-backed driver, a human in his late fifties who regarded the bodies and incriminating stains with disinterest.

"He's expecting you," he said in his perpetually bored voice. Despite the formality, I knew it was an order.

Damn. This was sure to further ruin an already perfectly unpleasant night. "I'm almost done."

The driver's expression didn't so much as twitch, yet I could tell he disapproved.

To hell with him.

I retrieved the bleeding man's heavy shears and knelt at his side. He couldn't resist me pulling his hand away, uncovering his torn neck. The spawn had been brutal, but he'd survive.

He let me scrutinize the wound closer, obviously mistaking my intentions. He hardly whimpered when my mouth clapped over the deepest wounds, fangs tearing the tortured flesh back open. I pressed his arm against the wall and drank fast, draining him like I was throwing down a shot. I didn't like sharing from the same flask as my quarry, but if the evening was taking the turn I feared, I wouldn't have another chance.

Anyway, he deserved it.

2

TRANSGRESSIONS
JADAIN

The goddess teaches us to recognize suffering, to minister to victims of all sorts—of fate, of tragedy, of violence. But the worst are victims of hope.

He was one of them.

He was kneeling upon the sanctuary's black-and-white marble while I attended midday prayers. He kept his place through the afternoon chorales. Even as I finished reading the evening inevitabilities, he knelt there still. If he'd been an old man, a bandaged leper, an expectant mother, I would have let him be—for those at the brink of life the goddess isn't always as silent as she appears. But he wasn't one of the common lot who came to Maiden's Choir seeking answers.

Perhaps the goddess had left him waiting there for me.

The last beams of dusk slipped through the cathedral's stained-glass depictions of watchful psychopomps and ascendant souls, bruising pale stone violet and blue. The colors shrouded one of the smaller statues of Pharasma—our goddess of birth, death, and the unknown—secluded within one of the vast sanctuary's peripheral shrines. Here, the goddess worked the wheel of fortune like a spinning wheel. Hundreds of purple prayer candles surrounded the statue, but only one nearly exhausted flame lit her toil.

Uncut, sun-singed hair and grass-stained clothes suggested the youth worked on the city's fringes, maybe still someone's apprentice. He rocked slightly upon his knees, hypnotically repeating a familiar mantra. "Mother of mystery, guard my path, and grace my death as you did my birth."

A dozen more repetitions passed. I settled my fingers upon his shoulder. "You know she's heard you."

His voice caught mid-word. He looked up dazedly, blinking as he came back to the world. "I'm—I'm sorry, Mother. I—uh. I didn't realize it was late."

"It's fine. You're welcome to stay as long as you like. You've been here for some time, though. Is there anything you need? A drink of water, perhaps?"

"No—no, thank you, Mother."

Among the servants of the goddess of birth, "mother" is a revered term, whether literal or honorary. I hadn't earned either yet.

"Please, just *sister*—or Jadain, even. I'm not old enough to be anyone's mother." I grinned, repeating a rote quip every Pharasmin acolyte learned.

His eyes went wide, obviously not understanding. It wasn't just awkward humor that unsettled him. With our black nails and the spiritlike spirals covering our robes, my order wasn't known for comfort.

I smiled as warmly as I could muster. "You've sacrificed nearly a whole day to the goddess. Are you always this devout?"

"Umm . . ." He searched me for accusation. "No, Sister?"

I seated myself on the alcove's cherrywood bench, its seat worn smooth by countless past penitents. "Well, if you've already told her everything on your mind, perhaps you'd like someone else to listen?"

He twisted to look out over the rest of the sanctuary. No more than ten others were wandering the temple's columned nave—mostly supplicants busy with their own prayers or acolytes polishing flagstone grave markers. He looked back to me, unsure.

I didn't push him. "If you think it might help."

"Well." He swallowed hard. "Her name's Marisia."

Of course. I pinched back a smile.

"Her family's been neighbors with mine for—for forever, and . . ."

I nodded.

"And during the Prince's name day last week she . . ." He blushed.

"She . . ." I prompted.

Out it tumbled. "She took my hand." His shy eyes fell. "Just on the walk home. But she'd never done that before."

"Did she?" Adorable. "What do you think that means?"

He pondered the memorial blocks etched into the floor.

"She . . ." His tongue was pinned under the unfamiliar weight of the words.

I gave him a moment.

He wrestled with the words. "She . . . loves me?"

I was sure my loathsome dimples were showing, but pressed on. "Is this about her?"

He looked back up, as wide-eyed as the hundreds of sculpted skulls around us.

"Isn't it more about how you feel? About finding the boldness to ask a very little question?"

He blushed, looking away again.

This was good. Simple. Uncomplicated in a way few things were or would be in his—in anyone's—life. I envied him his moment, his innocence.

"Maybe," he whispered to the stones.

"May I ask what you were praying for?"

He didn't answer.

"It's okay. I'm sure she heard you." I patted his shoulder. "But the Lady doesn't work in miracles. She's too old and wise for silliness like that."

Concern filled his face.

I was glad he had come here and not to some optimistic Shelynite street preacher. He might have come just because our cathedral was the largest in the city, but here we'd tell him the truth—that there were no sure things.

"Don't worry. She heard you, and if you and your friend's fates are intertwined, be sure she'll guide the two of you together. But you have a part to play." I lowered my voice, letting him think I was giving away a secret. "Your urges, your instincts, all the voices inside you—those are all messages from the goddess. Listen to them, weigh your choices, but then act. Our lady is the goddess of all existence's wonders, and rewards those who willingly travel the roads she sets before them. Consider carefully, but remember that the goddess doesn't have time to prod us down life's paths. We need to walk them ourselves."

Brown eyes sparkled at me from beneath that dusty mop. He was unsure, but inspired. I imagined him holding his tongue for the rest of the week, then making a bouquet of dandelions and gushing out his heart. It'd be in the goddess's hands from there, but whichever path she chose, he'd be on the road rather than halted here at the crossroads.

I smiled, and he allowed himself one, too. It was times like this that I most felt the goddess in the shadows around me.

"Sister." The voice came as cold and scrupulous as ceremonial silver.

I started. "Lady's curls—" The floor of my stomach dropped as I turned and glimpsed that crimson hem.

"Don't blaspheme further, Sister." Steel and solemnity reinforced accusing eyes, the relentless gaze of one of the order's inquisitors. Bloody from brim to trim, the saying went, referring to the holy hunters' broad hats and bold red robes. They barely hid the iron beneath, reminders that our goddess was the usher of both life and death.

"High Exorcist. I apologize, I didn't see you—"

High Exorcist Mardhalas's eyes fixed on the boy, petrifying him. "What are you telling this child?"

"To put his faith in the goddess, nothing more." I simplified carefully. The inquisitors were zealous literalists, prone to upholding the harshest interpretations of Pharasma's dogma. While my position as a priestess typically lent me authority in interpreting the goddess's will, Zetiah Mardhalas was commander of the cathedral's martial arm, and indirectly—but absolutely—my superior.

"Then clarify a point for me." Her sights retrained on me. "Is the throne of the goddess ensconced within every urchin's loins, or just this one's?"

My chest seized. "Excuse me?"

She nodded toward the adjacent shrine, the sanctuary's darkest, rearmost enclosure. "I overheard your whole private sermon, Sister. So tell me, what about this boy's lust makes it worthy of the goddess's attentions?"

This was a clear theosophical trap. I framed my response carefully.

"The goddess walks with us all upon life's paths, no matter how trivial. The route of a young man's first love is no different from any other. We should all make ourselves receptive to her guidance, no matter how she might veil it."

The boy was doing his best to make himself small, fixing his eyes intently on the statue's sculpted toes.

"You expect a child to distinguish between the voice of the goddess and every other base whisper? You've given this youth permission to indulge his fancy, be it today's infatuation or tomorrow's lechery. If it's all the goddess's will, why shouldn't he take whatever he sets his eyes upon?" Her stare pummeled the youth. "Get up, boy."

He'd been on that hard marble for at least half the day. His bruised knees wobbled and failed, sending him sprawling sidelong into the High Exorcist's armored shins.

She backed away, letting him scramble beetle-like upon the floor. I went to help him, purposefully bowing between him and Mardhalas. Standing slowly, I lifted him with me, whispering as I did. "I'm sorry for this. It's late now, run home, and good luck."

He took a faltering step—obviously full of pinpricks—swung wide around the inquisitor, and was off, run-walking with no thought for solemnity.

The High Exorcist let him pass, then shifted to fill the entrance to the shrine's enclosure. Posture stiff, shoulders broadened by armored robes, she seemed much taller than I knew she was. It felt like she was looking down from a pulpit.

I crossed my arms, wearing my disapproval. "You terrified him."

"Perhaps that will make more of an impression than your coddling."

"What would you have told him? To fret? Worry? Do nothing?"

"Find the goddess in the goddess. Forsake paths away from her throne. There need be nothing more." Her words sounded like responses to a sergeant's command.

I shook my head. "The goddess expects us to live. She doesn't demand we all fill the ranks of her army."

Mardhalas straightened, not used to being argued with. "Some go astray, but it's flawed evangelism that sends the wayward back into the storm. You've promised that child nothing. You've told him to make himself vulnerable. To follow whispers he can't understand."

"I don't apologize for encouraging a child to enjoy the goddess's gifts." I clung to my indignation, a replacement for courage in the face of the High Exorcist's chastising.

Her palm fell upon a nearby pillar. "These stones hold back many terrible things, Sister. Beyond there are more voices than just the goddess's. Vices we can't all have cathedral walls to protect us against."

"I know that," I shot back too fast.

"Do you truly?" Skepticism traced every slow syllable. "Then tonight you'll prove it." Mardhalas stepped out of the shrine's frame. "Go prepare yourself and return in one hour. You will attend me in this evening's work."

My mouth opened as a dozen defiances vied for voice. I snapped them back.

She noted my hesitance. "You are a priestess, prepared to do the goddess's work, are you not?"

"I will go where the Lady leads me." I did my best to sound bold. "Where are we needed?"

The edge of the High Exorcist's lip twitched. "Havenguard Lunatic Asylum."

3

BEHIND THE THRONE
LARSA

I'm waiting."

The door in the cluttered basement of Whiteshaw—headquarters to the Caliphas Department of Constables and Investigators—didn't obstruct the voice's bored annoyance.

I hadn't knocked.

Inside, hundreds of candles crawled across tables and heavy stone shelves, tiny lights that illuminated but spread no warmth. Fire and paper called truce here, with thousands of books, miles of maps, and countless pages rolled or filed at deliberate posts. Statuettes, key rings, tiny cases, gaudy baubles, and more adorned the repurposed storage room, but none were simple display pieces—all had some tagged and documented use. The musty air, the flames, the crude furnishings, and the cluttered curiosities made the space feel like a cave—the dwelling of some savage wise man, not the office of one of the nation's highest officials.

Diauden, Royal Advisor to Prince Ordranti, looked like some manner of old gray chameleon, frowning and alert, thin but tough. Standing at his tall desk, he directed an endless line of ink across stark white pages. He only paused at the end of a sheet, setting it atop a stack bulging with official seals.

I pushed the door closed. It locked, unbidden. The old man didn't acknowledge me, responding to some calamity with a legion of tiny, proper letters.

drifted toward a table covered by a map of the principality, s of fine demarcations dividing the nation into a jigsaw of nail-d fiefdoms. Clusters of flickering votives lit places of particular erest on the map, but offered no clue as to their significance. he country's name, Ustalav, spilled across the map's border in laborate calligraphic barbs.

I would have taken a seat, had the old lizard believed in such things. Idleness and simple comforts had no place in his work—or, by extension, the work of those who served him. I read every name on the map and he still hadn't finished. The flame in the crown-shaped votive illuminating Caliphas, our city and the nation's capital, flickered as I blew a thin breath. I imagined the moon outside wavering, unnoticed by anyone who'd ever be believed.

"Please stop," he said without turning.

Apparently he wasn't totally ignoring me. I came around into the periphery of his vision, pulling something from my belt. "Remember those stabbings in Leland—mostly sailors and barmaids? The killer the amateurs upstairs are calling Mister Scissors or something?" I tossed the rusty shears. They skidded on the desk, leaving a trail of mostly dry alley gunk. "I took care of that."

A nostril twitched. "They call him the Shepherd."

"Yeah."

Wrapping the shears in the sullied top page, he shifted them off the desk, letting them clatter into a spotless wastebasket. "He was not your objective."

"Yeah, I got her too."

"Anyone of consequence?" He was already starting work on a new page.

"Just some stray spawn."

"You're sure?"

"Yes. Totally unmannered. No noble would let a servant embarrass them like that." I smirked. "She also didn't seem to recognize me."

"And you thoroughly dispatched her?"

I cocked an eyebrow. "I've done this a time or two before."

His eyes rose, serious as a judge. I met them, but not for long.

"Ashes at dawn," I said, looking away without meaning to. Something about his eyes always unsettled me, and not much did.

His ebony quill clinked in the inkwell as he turned back to the page. "Good. More to report?"

"No."

"What of this Shepherd?"

"Just a victim."

"Then you're available for what's next." It wasn't a question.

"No." I tried to cloak my displeasure in formality. "I haven't reported yet." I had to constantly remind the old man that I wasn't one of his messengers—at least, not entirely.

"The matter is one of some urgency. Your visit to the Old City can wait."

He was overstepping his bounds. I sighed my disapproval. "Siervage won't be pleased."

"He won't know."

"That's quite an assumption." I folded my arms. "I won't start lying to him now."

"You don't need to lie. Your expertise is required. The matter outweighs the urgency of a report."

"I doubt he'd agree. You know how seriously Grandfather takes—"

"He won't jeopardize the truce."

"Like you're doing by assuming that?"

He half turned his head to me, casting a look of droll patience. "It depends entirely on how the matter is presented to him."

"You're leaving me to shoulder this?"

"Yes." The whisper of a nail creasing pages lent finality to the word. He withdrew a loop of small keys and fitted one into the desk, piercing some hidden lock.

"Why?" As if I didn't know. It was a subtle snub against my other master, the freshest discourtesy in a campaign of unacknowledged insults.

"It's an unusual situation. One related to your post." Reverently, he lifted a seal of bone and steel from the hidden drawer. A hollow needle extended from its grip.

"Then I assume that letter is for him, requesting his consent."

"No." Dark wax pooled, and he positioned the seal. He pressed down, impaling his thumb upon the needle. A single blood drop mingled with the wax. "It's almost dawn. They won't be trapped there during the day. You'll have to hurry if you're to meet them."

"Meet who?"

"Just outside the city is an estate called Thorenly Glen. The Thorenlys are all but extinct. Lord Blake Thorenly has auctioned nearly all his title's holdings. Bankrupt, Thorenly and his wife took on boarders. Recasting his desperation as charity, he's hired two nurses and opened his house as a final retreat for aging nobles. His wards, most being only slightly older than he, pay what they can for the estate's doubtful amenities, bartering heirlooms to cling to illusions of privilege. It's a place to be ignored and forgotten. At least, by the living."

This had become a briefing.

He lifted the stamp from the page. The seal wept another drop of blood upon the stamped emblem. I couldn't see the impression, but knew it well: a tower with a star-shaped window at its height.

"Thorenly's wife, Lady Ellishan, was found on the Crown Road after dusk, babbling and wearing only her nightclothes. Aside from scratches, she was unharmed, but even the night air can be dangerous to one of her age. Rightly, the constables who found her took her directly to Havenguard. Her hysterics were largely unintelligible, but the situation is strange enough to warrant investigation."

"To warrant *their* investigation." I nodded toward the mostly empty floors of the constabulary above. Let the humans deal with their own daylight problems.

"The officers heard enough of blood and teeth to start rumors."

"Damn." That was starting to sound like my sort of problem. "Can't you—"

"I've delayed the inspection of Thorenly Glen until morning, but at first light two detectives head into the country. I expect them to find something terrible. I expect you to go and make sure they find the mysterious *remains* of something terrible, not something terrible still at work."

"This could be anything."

His narrow breath blew over the cooling seal of wax and blood. "There are vampires at Thorenly Glen."

"You're basing that on a mad woman's ranting. Certainly none of Siervage's clan would make such a flagrant attack, and I doubt that even any spawn loose in Caliphas would lay siege to an estate so close to the city."

"They're not local." He tucked the letter into a sturdy leather case. "But I believe they're here to meet with Siervage."

"That doesn't make any sense. If they were here for Siervage, they would have just gone through the sewers into the Old City. Where do you think they're from?"

"Ardis."

Ardis—former capital, before the royal court relocated to Caliphas a half-century ago. Already the short-lived humans referred to the crumbling shell as the Old Capital, not knowing that the true seat of power had already lain under Caliphas's streets for centuries—the immortal court of Grandfather's Old City.

"I assume Grandfather's grip on Ardis is as strong as ever. What makes you think they're here to meet him?"

"Eight days ago, three individuals left Ardis in a coach bearing Siervage's crest. My messengers marked that same coach leaving

Vauntil along the Crown Road at dusk last night. It has not yet entered the city walls."

"They might have avoided the gates."

The old man barely wasted a condescending glance. We both knew Siervage and his people relished the concessions their pact with the nation's royalty quietly granted them. Markings upon their coach would grant them unimpeded passage through any of the capital's gates, a luxury not even the nation's human nobility enjoyed. Even the least arrogant vampire would be hard pressed not to indulge the novelty.

"I'm expecting guests. Now I hear my neighbors have unwelcome visitors." Diauden took up the leather case and finally faced me. "If these callers are one and the same, then our guests are proving themselves dangerously rude. All parties will prefer if it's you who doles out a lesson in civility, should one be necessary. I believe such is within the scope of your responsibilities."

He extended the case to me. "Dawn is in three hours. I don't expect these strangers to tarry for an entire day, so time is already against you."

"Fine." I snapped the case away from him, knowing the missive within bore the seal of the Royal Advisor, a mark that bore the authority of the prince himself and was reserved for dire royal business. "These are my orders and a report to Siervage, then?"

"No." He was already turning back to the desk and taking up his pen. "They're for Agent Vashalnt. Deliver them to her on your way out."

I was through the door before the old man's papers slapped the floor.

4

PROCESSION
JADAIN

High Inquisitor Mardhalas ushered me into the cathedral's somber black coach as though I were a convict, watchful for any signs of escape. I climbed past her, summoning what indifference I could muster.

Inside, greasy lavender curtains and the smell of joyless bouquets betrayed the coach's typical use, ferrying mourners to and from funeral services. It felt like I was being forced to attend such a service, and I could only think of one type of funeral-goer who never attended by choice.

The High Inquisitor took the bench opposite me and pulled the door firmly closed. The last of the lantern light clung to her robes, filling the space with their crimson in the moment before it fell into mostly darkness.

She was watching me then—and for the next hour, every time we passed a lamppost or lantern, she was watching me still.

I considered meditating, but feared Mardhalas would mistake that for sleeping. So I spent the time listening, folding my hands upon my lap as if in silent prayer, charting our path through Caliphas's streets by the clatter of the wheels and the feel of the turns. I didn't fare well, becoming lost soon after passing from the cobbled streets into the city's outer quarters. Eventually we slowed, turning onto a gravel drive. I allowed myself to part the curtains and look out.

"Impatient," came Mardhalas's judgment, hardly muffled by the rasping gravel. I ignored her.

There was little to see, the moon a faint haze through a veil of heavy clouds. A processional of lonely trees marched past the window, beyond which a slope dropped away toward nothing at all. The ground fell away into a ghost world, a ragged acre or two of fields and the hint of a distant hedgerow fading into the fog.

Several long moments passed. Then we turned, and the coach ground to a halt. Sensing my anticipation, my desire to escape the dark, judgmental silence, Mardhalas didn't make a move. The seconds stretched before the coachman opened the door, letting lamplight spill into the space. I didn't wait or spare a look for Mardhalas, and made my small escape.

I almost reared back into the coach with my first step.

Havenguard Asylum was an old, hungry-looking place. Batlike, its body rose high, dark and furred by mosses. Its eyes were an array of dark windows under sharp gables, ears twin pointed towers bent to the dark, mouth a hollow portal atop a veined tongue of cracked marble stairs. But most prominent were the wings, multistory arms sprawling away from the central structure, symmetrical and marked by hundreds of tiny windows. In either direction, they swept on, eventually dissolving into the dark. I'd never given the city's infamous asylum much thought, but certainly hadn't expected something so palace-like in its size and imposition, or that rivaled Maiden's Choir's oppressive presence.

It was the latter that had nearly driven me back. The place had an unmistakable pulse. It thrummed with the breath of hundreds of residents, but also something else. In much the same way one could stand in the goddess's sanctuary and almost hear the marble echo past prayers, so did this place resonate. Instead of chants and sermons, though, the asylum stones restrained a more discordant choir.

The High Inquisitor prodded me less than gently from behind. I stepped aside. She fired a few curt orders to the coachman, then strode up the front steps. As she banged on the battered door, the coach followed the circular drive and was soon claimed by the fog, marooning me here with a zealot.

As Mardhalas's knocking drifted away I noticed the distant breathing. Rush then fade, rush then fade; it was the sound of water, of surf on rocks. Powerful but repetitive enough to be relaxing, it was strangely apropos, capable of masking any number of sobs and moans.

"Remember," Mardhalas only half turned her head to look back at me, "you are here to assist me. Do nothing—say nothing—without my permission."

My jaw tightened.

She looked down from the entryway. "Do you understand?" It seemed as much insult as a question.

"Yes, High Inquisitor." I didn't bother to keep the resentment out of my voice.

She opened her mouth to say something more, but the asylum door opened. A surprisingly warm light spilled into the night, holding within a slight woman in stark white. A long coat hung open over a well-fitting buttoned shirt with suspenders. The straight lines made her look tall, an impression sharp features and posture reinforced.

"You're somewhat early." She spoke swiftly, her words peculiarly clipped.

"My message said we would arrive prior to midnight." Mardhalas, too, seemed uninterested in pleasantries.

"Yes, but the last three times you've called you arrived between a quarter to midnight and a quarter after. It's currently thirty-four minutes before midnight. Compared to past averages, you're early."

Mardhalas took a moment to acquiesce. "So it seems."

"So it is." The woman looked at the inquisitor expectantly. A moment passed in strained silence. "Come inside," she finally chirped.

Mardhalas entered, and I moved to follow, but found the asylum woman standing in the doorway.

"Yes?" she asked plainly, as though I were some solicitor.

"I'm Jadain Losritter, a priestess of the Lady of Graves." My nod was a little bow. "A pleasure to meet you Miss . . ."

She didn't budge.

"She's my assistant for tonight," Mardhalas explained from inside. The inquisitor stared at me again, blaming me for the holdup.

The woman regarded me, her eyes moving slowly over my purple vestments, seeming to follow every swirl and twist, embellishments suggestive of Pharasma's holy spiral.

"You've never required an assistant before." She was speaking to Mardhalas despite not turning from me. I didn't like the way this was heading, and certainly didn't relish the idea of spending my night waiting outside an asylum.

"I do tonight," Mardhalas said flatly, not offering that she was using the outing to flex her ecclesiastical authority.

"Why?" the tall woman absently pressured.

"A precaution, should some aspect of the exorcism go awry. Can we get on with it?"

"So then your past work has somehow been unsafe?" The woman leaned in uncomfortably close, scrutinizing the holy symbol hanging around my neck. So close, I could make out rusty spatters flecking her starched coat.

"No," Mardhalas snapped. "Do you have need of our services tonight or not?"

The casual inspection continued.

I tried to reassure the asylum's gatekeeper. "I promise you, miss, I'm quite capable—"

"Doctor," she corrected, stressing the title. "Linas." Her name came almost as an afterthought.

"Doctor," I amended. "I'm quite capable of assisting the High Exorcist and providing an additional degree of protection for both her and the asylum's residents."

"Patients," she corrected again, but with no hint of arrogance.

"Of course." I nodded. "Please consider my participation evidence of the importance the faithful of Maiden's Choir place on our relationship with Havenguard's healers—an additional blessing on your continued good work."

She looked from me to stoic Mardhalas, then back.

"Ceremony. Of course." She turned and began walking away.

Stepping out of the night into the asylum was a matter of stepping from one chill into another. The entry was not what I might have expected, with dark wooden paneling and polished doors giving the hall the look of some welcoming noble estate. Solid waiting benches lined the walls, interrupted by cases of the metal and leather curiosities of those who healed with intellect rather than faith. A carved lion silently roared at the base of a narrow stairway's banister. At a broad landing above stood an array of thick glass windows, each pane thoroughly shattered but still balanced in its frame.

Doctor Linas ascended the stairs two at a time. I moved to follow, but the High Inquisitor didn't budge. As I passed, she fell in one uncomfortably close step behind me.

Taking the steps, I realized as we approached the landing that the windows there were not shattered. Rather, dark molding created an elaborate fractured design that, upon taking in the whole series, created a subtle but predictable pattern. It was clever, but still unnerving. I could imagine such being a theme here.

The doctor led us to an equally well-decorated second-floor hall, tiny metal plates on the doors suggesting administration and record-keeping. We turned through a pair of swinging doors and the decor changed, taking a dramatically utilitarian turn. Two large men in coats similar to Doctor Linas's lounged at a stained table, its wood an antiseptic white that repeated upon the walls. A dented metal door hunched behind the attendants. Despite its fortress-like bulk, someone had still reinforced it with a second swinging door of crossed bars.

One of the guards practiced balancing a heavy leather baton upon a finger. Noticing the doctor, he gripped it seriously, and the other stood from his chair, both adopting sober expressions. "Good evening, Doctor," they stammered in unison.

The doctor ignored the men's inattentiveness. "I am escorting the exorcists to Cell 18. We will return in . . ." She looked to the High Inquisitor.

"Within the hour," Mardhalas said.

"Forty minutes," Doctor Linas amended. "I will be ignoring the standard prohibitions on visitors and weapons on Doctor Trice's authority."

Both nodded, one rattling keys while the other unbolted the grating on the sturdy door. The metal squealed as it opened, even the door's lock screeching at being turned.

The guardroom's creamy shade spilled down the hall beyond, covering brick, tile, and doors cushioned with yellowing pads. Dim lanterns interrupted the mirrored march of doors with tiny windows, every frame distinguished by a number on a crowning metal placard. Distant waves whispered calm through the corridor, but even they weren't enough to completely drown the din of snores, sighs, and faint whimpers. The hall bent some ways ahead. From beyond echoed sharp but quickly smothered giggling.

It wasn't a prison, but if there was mercy in this collection of bars and locks, I didn't see it. I patted the sheath hanging from my belt, the curved dagger—as much for ritual as defense—lending some comfort.

The door whined behind us, boomed to an echoing close, and not a resident seemed to care.

I glanced at the nearby placards, both in their fifties. "Cell 18?"

"The numbers begin at the far end of the men's wing." Linas walked calmly on, not bothering to take a lantern. We followed.

Occasionally I caught glimpses through the doors' tiny windows, silhouettes or following eyes proving more than one cell occupied. Somewhere in the forties, fingers stabbed into the hall, wiggling obscenely, while another room seemed filled with hissing prayers. I found my opinions changing rapidly in this place. Perhaps it was a prison after all—one of the most important kind. I stopped looking into the cells.

I came alongside Doctor Linas. "It seems like you're an important doctor here."

"All of the doctors are important here," she said flatly.

I nodded, not really having expected Linas to be one for small talk. "But you were the one who met us tonight. Why you and not one of the guards?"

"I am Doctor Trice's assistant. He requires I oversee those matters of asylum maintenance for which he has no time. Orderlies have other responsibilities" We turned into a new length of one of the building's batlike wings.

"I see. I could tell the guards—the orderlies—respect you."

She didn't acknowledge. We walked on past another dozen cells.

"You're a lesser priestess."

Her statement surprised me. "I've been an ordained priestess of the Lady of Graves for almost five years now. I'm not one of out faith's leaders, like Mother Thestia—the head of our cathedral—or the High Exorcist, but I minister to any who would explore the mysteries of mortality."

"Then explain your decoration." She gestured to my robes.

"Oh. Well, the High Exorcist and I are of different orders within the church. While her robes suggest the blood sometimes spilled—"

"No. Your symbol."

My hand went to the sign of Pharasma hanging from a simple braid of thread around my neck. Reflexively circled its spiral design.

"Yours is wooden," she clarified. "Hers is silver."

"Ah. Yes." I chose my words delicately. The clergy of Caliphas inwardly enjoyed the benefits of their congregation's wealth, but outwardly denied any undue luxury. "I started my service to the Lady of Graves in Barstoi, at a particularly poor church. I received this symbol when I began studying the Lady's mysteries. I've kept it ever since, to remind me of those studies and my simplicity in the face of Her grand designs."

The answer seemed satisfactory to Linas, who didn't delve further. The High Exorcist, however, proved impossible to please.

"We should all be humble in our service, Sister. This is a state of being, not of fashion. If your spiral has become more a symbol of yourself than the goddess, you'd do well to cast it away."

I looked back to Mardhalas's prominent symbol of silver and lapis. It and her eyes glimmered in the dull light.

A click, and a door squeaked open.

Doctor Linas returned her ring of tiny keys to her coat. "This is the concern."

Matters of interpretation put aside, we gathered close, looking into the shadowed cell. Padded white walls, a dark window too thin to squeeze more than a hand through, and nothing else. The cell was empty.

"The patient died more than a week ago—choked to death after swallowing his own tongue." Linas sounded clinically detached.

I looked at Linas dubiously. She'd seemed quite competent. "Is that possible, Doctor?"

"He severed his tongue with a sharpened spoon, gagging after swallowing it. The patient believed his dead brother was haunting his tongue, making him say wicked things. I am investigating how he came to have a utensil in his cell and have relieved three orderlies for the oversight."

I swallowed the lump in my throat, being particularly aware of my tongue's motion in doing so.

"Yet he's not vacated the cell," Mardhalas said.

"Indeed." Linas scanned the room, just as I did. "Four, including myself, have heard his distinctive raving since his death."

"Only in this cell?" the High Exorcist asked.

"Yes."

"What was his name?" I asked.

"Wintersun, Elistair." Linas said it like she was reading a file.

"Sounds Kellid." Mardhalas made the name of the northern people sound like a slur.

"It is," I said, ignoring her prejudice toward my mother's people. "One of the old Sarkorian clan—"

"Sister Losritter. See what the goddess reveals to you." It was an order, but it was the first time the High Exorcist had addressed me without contempt. If not polite, at least she was professional.

I strained my eyes, staring into the cell's shadows. The darkness collected at every corner, but nothing so much as shivered within. "I don't see a thing. Perhaps more light . . ." I reached for the lantern by the cell door.

"Inside," Mardhalas ordered.

I looked at her, incredulous. "Me?"

"You're not here just to observe. Go inside and tell me what you feel."

I looked to Doctor Linas for some sort of support, hopeful that she'd advise against such a course. She considered me calmly, but offered nothing. She might as well have been observing one of her patients.

Fine. I took the lantern from beside the cell door and, not sparing a look for Mardhalas, held it before me as I took a tentative step inside.

Once my younger sister, Sylvie, got stuck in the middle of a frozen lake, her sled taking her farther than she'd expected. She wasn't able to do anything more than sob as the ice around her cracked and popped. Taking that first sliding step onto the ice to drag her back in was the most frightening step I'd ever taken in my life.

Stepping into that cell, I longed to creep back onto the ice.

As I lifted the light to the corners of the room, the last sputters of the cell's former resident revealed themselves upon the walls and floor, a spattered array of scrubbed brown stains. Nothing unnatural made itself known, but still the feeling was here. The passage of death resonated in the space, the clinging sense-echo of a tragedy.

Placing the lantern carefully in the center of the room, I took a deep breath, closed my eyes, and ran my hands over the always cold, smooth wood of Pharasma's holy symbol. I whispered a prayer, letting it touch every corner of the cell. The power in the goddess's words reached through padding and stone, searching for affronts to the goddess's will. A moment later, they murmured back.

"He's close."

The door squealed and slammed shut behind me. High Exorcist Mardhalas looked through the tiny cell window, eyes hard.

I stifled my shout when ink burst upon the interior of the cell's door, blooming from its padding. I wasn't sure what I was seeing. The black stain spread fast, pressing into the air of the chamber. As if through soaked satin, a sagging face pushed forth, writhing and seemingly trapped within the liquid dark.

I tripped back, the edges of my holy symbol biting into my hands. The stained thing fixed me with what would never again be eyes. What served as a jaw fell away, spilling putrid drops. Thought-breaking babbling followed, boiling into the air, the frustrated railing of a soul still shackled to madness in death.

As its insane song rose, I added my scream to the chorus.

5

UNWELCOME GUESTS
LARSA

The night's fog was already retreating by the time I reached Thorenly Glen, withdrawing as the first shades of daylight bled over the distant tree line. The walk had taken considerably longer than I'd expected. The city's constables would be on their way soon, following up on Lady Thorenly's distress from the previous night. I wouldn't have much time to investigate without interference, or to deal with what would assuredly ruin a couple of guards' morning.

The blanket of mists receded slowly, and its removal wasn't flattering. A manor house rose across a lake of weeds and shapeless hedges. Porch sagging, windows blinded by shutters, roof shedding shingles like an old man's hair, Thorenly Glen lacked anything in common with the pastoral haven its name suggested. A road-worn coach rested in the weedy turnabout just before the mansion's cracked steps. Whoever the estate's guests were, no one had bothered to prepare for them.

I circled the manor at some distance, following a line of knotty trees. Unbelievably, the estate was putting its best face forward. The roof over the house's back porch had collapsed, blocking doors and windows and burying much of the rear in splinters. Ivy crawled through the ruins. The damage was far from fresh.

Lady Thorenly had been discovered raving along the road leading south. Had she actually been living in this wreck? Even more outrageously, had she and her husband actually been charging others to board in their ruin? "Retreat for the aged" indeed.

The baffling nature of what nobles would pay for aside, the house was too still. Were Lord Thorenly, two nurses, and some number of boarders in residence here, there would be some sign—the flicker of a light left burning overnight, a window left open a crack, servants preparing for the day. But instead, nothing. With every window shuttered or boarded over, not even a rustle of curtains or a passing silhouette suggested the manor was anything but abandoned.

I slid out from behind the shell of a disused shed, approached and listened under the windows. There was briefly something inside—an unexpected tromping on the floor above. Booted steps, perhaps. It swiftly faded.

I came upon a servant's door, its threshold at waist height. A soggy barrel and mismatched crates formed makeshift steps. I skirted them and was headed back to the front when a wordless roar burst from within. Somewhere glass shattered. It certainly wasn't the sound of a retired landlord turning down his morning tincture.

It also wasn't anywhere near the servants' door. I carefully scaled the crates to the entry. No one had bothered to lock the door.

The cramped kitchen within was surprisingly clean, a busy array of pans and cooking implements hanging over well-scrubbed countertops. Several tea services stood ready, but the fireplace's hearty kettle wasn't growing any warmer over the ashes. The tromping was louder now, boots practically tumbling down nearby stairs. They passed close by, rattling the cups and saucers. Somewhere a door slammed open.

Someone was in quite a hurry.

I cracked the kitchen's swinging door enough to see a sliver of the hall beyond. Threadbare carpeting stretched to an open door at the end of a gallery of faded portraits. Beyond, a cast-off sheet twisted in the air, sprawling across a floral divan. Stomping and clattering continued inside.

I slipped out, checking the hall in the opposite direction—doors, bad art in cheap frames, blood. Upon steep stairs, a mass of wrinkles and shredded robes hardly recognizable as a man no longer bled. I ignored it for now—it was one corpse I didn't expect to be a threat. I moved on, the clamor from the hall's end covering the complaints of crotchety floorboards and the hiss of drawing my blade.

A brass candelabrum skipped across the floor as I reached the doorframe. The room had been closed up early—or never opened at all—its furniture, paintings, and fireplace all covered in linens. Stale air suggested it hadn't been used for some time—and even then it surely hadn't received the rough treatment it was getting now.

At the opposite end of the room, a figure in a coal riding coat pulled the covers from a pair of mismatched bookcases. With one swipe, he scattered a shelf's contents to the floor. Delicate figurines and silhouettes in tiny frames cascaded down amid an avalanche of decorative tomes.

I stepped into the room, trying to start things lightly. "I don't think the owners would appreciate their—"

"Where is it?" He spun with inhuman speed, his dry lips cracking with the shout. Before I could reply he stormed toward me. His fingers shriveled into claws, already stained from feeding.

Only half surprised, I brought my blade up. He swiped for my gut, but I slid aside. "Is this how you treat your elder's agent?"

That should have slowed him down, but it didn't.

"You're not him." His claws came up for my face. My blade slapped his forearms but the blow pushed me back, heels and spine slamming against the hearth. Who had he been expecting?

I made a show of it, my sword slicing a broad warning between us. Having no clue what he was talking about, I bluffed. "Plans changed."

"Liar!" His rage surged between us, red thoughts roiling at the edge of my sight. Like most of his kind, his consciousness wasn't entirely fettered to his mind—something in death had jarred it free. Now it scratched at the corners of my own. Few humans know what it is to have their thoughts invaded, but once you've been a captive inside your own head, you recognize trespassers.

I wrenched my eyes away and lunged. He was fast enough that his throat wasn't pierced cleanly, but the wound looked like a woodcutter's first chop—and was just as bloodless. He hissed, dashing into the wall and up, his claws not even marking the faded floral paper. I sliced the sheet covering some wall hanging. Suddenly the surface he clung to was sliding. He scrambled, then hit the ground solidly. I delivered the woodcutter's next strike.

The body burst into a cloud of pyre smoke. My sword screeched across the floor, momentum thrusting my face into that blast of dry death. I twisted away, grimacing as I regained my balance. I hated that smell. The young ones smelled wet, the old smelled dry, but both had that throat-clogging bitterness.

Like a shadow given shape but not substance, the smoke fell but refused to disperse. It pooled across the floor, seeking cracks in the boards, trying to seep into the dark below. I hadn't ended the stranger—his head hadn't severed cleanly—just panicked him. Instincts were powerful things, even more so when immortality was at stake. He'd search out a dark place to recover, but he wouldn't be bothering me again soon.

I scanned the room for whatever he might have been looking for, but the woman caught my attention.

The cloth I'd cut from the wall revealed a portrait of a noble family: two arch-looking young women in matching floral dresses, plus a mother and father. My slice had cut a mortal wound across the chest of one daughter, but it was her near-twin who caught my attention. Red strands strayed from beneath her broad sun hat.

The traumatized canvas distorted her face, but it was clear she was a fragile thing, with her father's calm expression.

I raised my hand to the portrait. Something about that woman seemed . . .

I pinched the limp canvas back into place.

It was me.

Somehow, impossibly, the other woman seated in the picture was unmistakably me. The dress was some pampered socialite's, the hair impractically styled, and the scene's other occupants utter strangers. But everything else was absolutely me.

The creak on the steps brought me back to the moment. Down the hall, another man in a dark coat and hat peered from the stairs. He'd already seen me, and maybe the last wisps of his companion settling into the floorboards. Our gazes barely met before he launched back upstairs.

"Damn it." The portrait's eerie occupant would have to wait. I vaulted the banister, swinging myself over the bloody mess staining the steps. Battered doors and artless decorations lined the upper hall. The houseguest was nowhere in sight, but most of the doors were open.

Inside the nearest room spread remnants of a gory debauch, a slaughter framed in nurse's white. The resident was in but wouldn't be receiving guests, butchered in what she must have known would be the last bed she'd ever own. Nothing stirred. I moved on. Each room presented a similar tableau, though the framing was different in each—a hunter, a debutante, a collector of glass figurines sprawled amid his shattered collection. Despite myself, my tongue was starting to feel dusty.

The last door was open only a crack, though the wood around the lock had been shattered. I checked behind me, then pushed into what was clearly the master bedroom. Dawn's light drowned beneath thick, sea-foam curtains, casting everything in shades of sunken green. A bulky vanity lay wrecked against one wall, its hinged mirror shattered. There was certainly truth to the vampiric aversion to mirrors, but few knew how personally some took their weaknesses.

A lavish mahogany box sat open upon the bed, brass clasp gleaming. Inside, white satin cushioning and nothing more.

I smelled him the instant before he struck. Rolling across the bed corner, I rounded on him, sword still in hand, my back to the window. He was already on me, fangs like a snake's striking for my face. He was too close. I dropped my sword and grabbed the loose flesh of his forearms. My grip did little to slow his charge, a power stronger than death driving him on—but I didn't have to be stronger.

Adjusting my footing, I pulled him to me, adding my weight to the force of his rushing frame. We toppled back. His wide hat shadowed his face except for bloodless lips. They twisted into a smile the moment before the glass shattered.

We crashed onto the sloped porch roof, glass and loose shingles slipping beneath us as our bodies slid on the tearing curtain. His victorious expression vanished and I rolled hard, forcing him beneath me. He shrieked and flailed his arms in an attempt to simultaneously throw me off and slow his slide into the dawn light.

The smell came first, appropriately like sulfur and burning garbage as his fleshier features charred.

We hit the edge of the roof. I let my body go limp, crashing upon him as we hit the ground. His chest gave way, crackling like a bundle of brittle twigs. Ash and the echoes of another shriek burst into the air. As flesh or as smoke, for him this was immortality's end.

He burned quickly.

Standing, I brushed ashes off of my hands. The house and drive were still, looking far less ominous without their veils of morning fog. Whippoorwills warbled in the distant trees.

A shadow settled near the stranger's cinder-filled coat. His traveling hat landed gently, a wide-brimmed slouch common to the riders of Amaans. Supposedly the horsemen wore them to keep the sun out of their eyes when riding valley trails.

"Huh. Not your worst idea, friend." I tried it on.

I checked the height of the sun from under the shady brim. The city constables were already late and might arrive at any moment, but I still had questions. Questions with answers I might learn from a torn canvas, or from a coward hiding in basement shadows. I started back toward the manor's front door, pulling a sturdy stake from the holster on my thigh.

6

THE EXORCISM OF ELISTAIR WINTERSUN

JADAIN

Pain pierced my fear, forcing me back into the moment. Still the essence of the asylum's insanity bled into the room, babbling its shattered psyche as it reached for me. My amulet, slipping in my grip, forced the edges of the goddess's spiral into my palm.

I thrust the holy icon before me, nearly plunging it into the core of the shrieking thing.

"Get back!" I poured my swallowed scream into my words, lending them something like force. "In Pharasma's name, get back!"

A measure of conviction, of my faith in the goddess, must have shone through my words. The carved image of the Lady's spiral shivered to life, its cold radiance washing over the blot of murmurs and shadowy limbs.

The stray soul refused to be lit, but its inky mass diminished, flagging in the goddess's light.

I sought sanctuary in remembered lessons, but a chorus of uncertainty drowned out most of those teachings. Was this literally a stray soul? As a servant of the goddess, wasn't it my duty to banish the remnants of just such a thing? Was my fear nothing more than a novice's unease? Could all hunters feel such dread upon first drawing their bows?

The High Exorcist must have been watching me through the door—testing me.

I raised the icy blue spiral, letting its radiance fill the room. The apparition withered, and I addressed it as I knew a Kellid would prefer. "Elistair, son of Clan Wintersun—your gods and ancestors wait for you."

The thing shuddered upon hearing the name. The babbling slowed, features congealing in the blot's depths.

"Leave here, son of the North. The Lady of Graves waits for you. You'll not travel the River of Souls alone."

Eyes, lips, hands strained from the oily dark—signs of reason. The features of an aging northman fought for form beneath unlife's stain.

"Join your lieges and the spirit of the land that once was. Your path—"

Shrieking, its form tore back open. The tarry pollution of soul surged, consuming any semblance of sanity. A lash of intangible dark defied the goddess's light. Before I could jerk away, a corrupt limb boiled over my holy symbol. In an instant-eternity, insanity stronger than the grave filled my mind. A chorus composed of a single fractured voice drowned out my thoughts, the unhinged ensembles spanning registers from terrified to furious. The goddess's symbol fell from my trembling fingers.

"No," I whispered.

As the icon slipped, so did the goddess's light. Shadows crashed back into the room. The madness that was Elistair Wintersun filled the cell. I groped after my holy symbol, trying to keep my desperation separate from the insane jabbering forcing itself into my head. The cell was not large—the thing was over me. Desperate hands scraped over stone encrusted with the madman's blood. In the blackness, I found nothing of the goddess.

Lightning flashed. The spirit's shriek clawed to unearthly pitches of pain. In the moment my body was still my own, I scrambled away, slamming into a wall. The flash came again, fast and limned in crimson. Behind it was the hint of the cell door, the screeching of its opening lost amid the howling. An ember-colored cloak and a glowing blue blade flared. The stained soul twisted, its shadows weakening before this new vicious light. Its song shot through every pitch of confused pain. Dark tendrils whipped toward the dancing blade only to be cut away. With every slash, the black madness lost form. Seeking to escape, it surged upward, soiling the ceiling.

High Exorcist Mardhalas stepped beneath it and plunged her cold blue longsword up, skewering the shadow and impaling what remained. A thousand franticly babbling voices gasped, the form shuddering as the sword's glow burned through.

"Go," the High Exorcist commanded. "And be damned."

What remained of Elistair Wintersun burned like a page cast into a bonfire. The ashes of shadows scattered, rained down, and faded away.

Next, the exorcist came for me. She reached down.

"Thank you, Sister," I practically panted. My head pounded, my fractured thoughts slowly recrystallizing. "I don't—"

A rough hand clamped around my throat. The sound I choked wasn't a word. My hands sought to loosen her grip, but years of flipping hymnal pages made my fingers poorly suited to breaking a soldier's grip. My heartbeat pounded in my neck, frantically trying to break the High Exorcist's hold from inside.

She released me. My effort to tear away threw me back, knocking my head soundly against the wall and shooting sparks across my vision.

"Lady's tears! Have you lost your mind?" I rubbed my throat against the sudden hoarseness.

Mardhalas looked down at me unapologetically. "Your heart still beats. As poorly as you handled that, I couldn't be sure it hadn't drained you and left something else."

I was dimly aware of Doctor Linas entering the room behind her, holding the other lantern.

"Had it been a living thing, I might have let the goddess take you." She retrieved my holy symbol, inches from my foot. I snatched for it as she stood, missing thoroughly. "But stray souls are not of Her nature."

She held my simple amulet before her eyes, examining it suspiciously. "Bringing you here confirmed my suspicions, though. You're too weak and sentimental to serve the goddess."

Another cold wave crashed over me. I mouthed a word, but the sound didn't come out.

"The cycle of life and death isn't your rosy path of hope and wishes. It's cold and brief. You can tell yourself otherwise, but such fairy tales have no place tainting the Lady's teachings. I had hoped to show you that here tonight, but the lesson almost cost you your life."

She twisted the twine holding the amulet, setting it spinning. "I know you don't accept it yet, but deep within, you agree. You know you're not fit. In the face of that abomination, your faith proved wanting. The goddess's own mark abandoned you."

She tossed the holy symbol onto my lap. "A true priestess wouldn't be separated from this, no matter the cost."

I swallowed deeply, mining whatever stone I had to buttress my voice. "I know I'm not a warrior like you, but I *am* a servant of the goddess." Still my words cracked. "I'm every bit as devoted as you."

Somehow she took that as an insult. "You think I've ever shrieked and fled? Begged an abomination to leave by the whim of its blasphemous soul? Cowered?" She laughed—actually laughed. "No, Miss Losritter, you and I do not share the same devotion."

The High Exorcist turned.

Doctor Linas had been watching intently. "This is not a usual part of the exorcism."

"No. But we're done here." Mardhalas's words seemed as much for me as the doctor. I struggled to my feet, a challenge with trembling legs and one hand still numb from the spirit's attack. I gripped my holy symbol. It felt tepid.

"Good," Linas said. "Should we take any special precautions before assigning this room a new occupant?"

"No."

"Excellent. I'll have your payment sent in the morning—or donation, whatever your order prefers to call it." Linas stepped back into the hall, ready to show us the way out.

"That will be fine." Mardhalas followed without looking back.

We returned to the asylum's entry in silence. Even the lunatics seemed more subdued.

Only once the door was in sight did the High Exorcist acknowledge me. "Miss Losritter. Upon returning to the cathedral, I'll be leaving a message for the Holy Mother. In the morning, I will discuss with her the unsuitability of your performance and advise we dismiss you from the order. Whether this means relocation or excommunication will be her decision, though I will make my recommendation plain. Expect a summons to interrupt your afternoon routine." Her words were casually formal, as though she were discussing the weather with a respectable stranger—not promising to shatter a life. "Now go fetch the coach."

"No." The incredulous word escaped before I could think better of it. The idea of sharing the ride home with this vicious woman, of enduring her company a moment longer, twisted my stomach.

She looked back, frowning. "This sort of behavior certainly won't encourage the Holy Mother to look upon you more favorably. Go get the coach."

I ignored her, turning to Doctor Linas, who'd paused upon the front steps. "Doctor. Does the asylum have a shrine or other place of worship?"

Her brows lifted. "Yes."

"Might I make use of it?"

"For what?" The words were clipped and clinical.

"I find myself in need of the goddess's counsel, and feel the need to pray for temperance."

Mardhalas scoffed.

The doctor considered over the course of several slow blinks. "Through there." She pointed to a pair of sliding wooden doors, just off the foyer.

"Thank you, Doctor." I said it as politely as possible, restraining the slurry of emotions roiling in my stomach. Something boiled over, though. I turned on the High Exorcist. "And thank you as well, Miss Mardhalas. I don't—"

The slam of asylum's front door cut me off. The High Exorcist had left, taking with her my life as a priestess.

7

EXPERT WITNESS
LARSA

Iloathed Caliphas's rare, cloudless days, but my new headwear was already proving worth the price. My eyes, though excellent at night, were poorly suited to the day's glare. Normally they'd force me on a course ducking from awning to alley. This morning, I angled the hat brim against the dawn and chose a route based on expediency rather than the sun. Cutting through the city's cluttered outer districts, I passed from one outlying community to another.

The Thorenlys' surviving vampire visitor hadn't survived for long. He'd been of little help, and violent enough that I had to drag him into the light without learning much of use. He was from Ardis and, along with his compatriot, was delivering a message for Grandfather. A message that he'd somehow managed to lose during their gory debauch at Thorenly Gardens. As for whom the message was from or why they had stopped outside the city, he refused to say. I didn't give him the time to think better of it.

The constabulary arrived at Thorenly Glen over an hour later than I'd expected. Aside from dealing with the house's last guest, it gave me the opportunity to take another few moments with the sitting room portrait. My painted twin wasn't exactly identical. Aside from the simple fact that I'd never sat for that painting and had little clue as to whom the other occupants might be, there were flaws in the details—a freckle here, something that might be a scar there, her pierced ears. Regardless, it fell far outside the realm of coincidence.

I considered visiting the Old City and asking Grandfather what he knew, but there were still avenues that might hold answers—answers to both the portrait's occupant and Thorenly Glen's ruin. I also wasn't in any mood to deal with my extended family's tedious criticisms. Returning to Whiteshaw and Diauden seemed little better—he'd doubtlessly have some other priority of national concern to distract me with. No, I'd pursue my own answers while there was still an obvious path to follow. Even if it did lead to one of the more unpleasant addresses in Caliphas: Havenguard Asylum.

It was a prison. Certainly the guards and warden of the place didn't refer to it as such, but whatever they chose to call it, walls and bars made it a place to forget the bothersome and unwanted. I'd heard plenty of stories that painted the asylum as something worse, and maybe it was, but what humans did with their own didn't concern me. The city guards who'd discovered Thorenly Glen's only survivor, Lady Ellishan, had taken her here.

It was nearly noon when I banged on Havenguard's iron-banded doors. I explained my reason for coming to the brute in white who answered. He didn't look like a doctor, especially with a scuffed baton dangling from his belt, but he asked after my relation to their patient. I had none, of course, and he tried to close the door on me. My boot held it open. His hand went to his baton. Mine nearly went to my sword's grip, but instead I gave him the least sour smile I could muster and retrieved my iron badge. On it glimmered a variation of Ustalav's national emblem, but rather than sixteen stars surrounding the royal tower, a lone ruby star glimmered from the tower's height.

In shades of royal purple, this was the mark of the Royal Advisor—a post of authority that Diauden had held through the reigns of three monarchs. In black alone, though, as my badge was, it was the mark of the Royal Accusers: the noble ignoble, the untitled to be obeyed, the gilded knives—in short, the Royal Advisor's agents and sometimes assassins. Few beyond the capital's constabulary and nobility across the country would have any reason to recognize the difference, but for the common folk it rarely mattered. Everyone in Caliphas knew someone who knew someone who had impeded an agent of the court and was never seen again, or who gave assistance and found all their problems mysteriously solved. We low-blooded agents rarely did either, but the wariness served us—and those we dealt with—well. Diauden didn't select for patience, after all.

The burly guard's gin blossoms faded several shades toward matching his coat. He threw the door wide, muttering apologizes and promises to fetch his superior—promises he promptly fulfilled, disappearing up a stairway. I waited. The glass eyes of a lion sculpted into the stair's newel followed me as I made a circuit of the room's displayed torture devices and meaningless accolades.

They kept me waiting longer than most would. At times like this, my annoyance made me realize I'd grown accustomed to certain perks of my position—like not waiting on commoners. Or was it waiting on any human? Maybe I had more of my grandfather's blood than I liked to think.

My frown wasn't entirely intended for the prim woman descending the stairs, but that changed as soon as she matched mine with her own. Buttoned from collar to waist, her narrow coat fell without a wrinkle. Every tightly pulled charcoal hair seemed as deliberately placed as the thin glasses resting high on her nose. She held herself too stiffly. Halting on the last step, she stood just above eye level.

"Your insignia, please."

I searched for insult or arrogance in her quick, level words, but didn't find it. Her insistence wasn't unreasonable. Still, I didn't like being given orders. Pursing my lips, I retrieved my badge and stepped close enough to hold it out to her. She reached to accept it, but I didn't release it. She hardly glanced at it. She was staring at me.

I lowered my brows. "Is there a problem?"

"You're not human."

I matched her stare, consciously seeking out the weight of the weapon at my hip. For the lack of surprise in her tone, though, she might as well have been noting the weather. If there was a judgment in her words, she hid it expertly.

"No." I didn't normally acknowledge my mixed heritage to strangers—anyone for that matter. Of course, they typically didn't notice. "Is that a problem?"

"I've yet to decide. What is your business here?"

This wasn't going the way it usually did. "I'm investigating a matter of importance to the Royal Advisor. Who are you?"

"Doctor Linas, assistant administrator."

The doorman brought me an underling? Bothersome. "I'll see the administrator, then."

"That won't be possible." Still, no pride—no emotion at all—tinged her words.

She certainly couldn't say the same of mine. "Why?"

"Doctor Trice is in surgery for the majority of the day. Interrupting him will jeopardize lives. I am authorized in every capacity to act in his stead. I can assist you in whatever business you have."

I wasn't accustomed to dealing with someone's second, but she certainly seemed capable enough.

"What is your business?" She did know how to push.

I relented only as much as I needed to. "A woman was brought here last night—Ellishan Thorenly. I need to speak with her."

"Do you intend to drink her blood?"

Her question pierced my gut, and something hot and red welled up there. I twitched and restrained it. The question had been as concisely blunt as every other statement, but that didn't make it any less outrageous. Never had a human asked me such a thing—at least, not without tears or other blathering.

"Excuse me?" I responded slowly, careful not to let anything boil over quite yet. I'd see how far down this path she'd tread.

"You're a dhampir. You need blood to survive. Have you come here to drink this woman's blood?"

Dhampir: it wasn't a word I heard often. Most humans didn't know it, or conflated it with a host of other bogeymen. Most full-bloods prided themselves on more creative slurs. In any case, it meant half-vampire—one born with a measure of a vampire's poisonous power. Being born, and thus being alive, made dhampirs distinct from spawn—individuals killed and made the undying slaves of full-blooded vampires.

And the doctor was correct in her observations.

I held her gaze. If it had borne even the hint of a judgment—of an attack—I wouldn't have bothered restraining my temper. As it was, she seemed earnest and utterly naive. I didn't imagine her patients typically valued etiquette.

"No." I answered clear and unmistakably.

"I don't—" she didn't finish her reply. Her eyes wandered away from me, some thought having interrupted her. After a moment they returned. "This is a matter of state business, then?"

"It is."

"I can't allow you to interview the patient alone."

"Is this a rule you enforce on all visitors?"

"Yes."

Fine, then. "Lead me to her."

"Wait here." She'd already shown me her back, moving down the hall to a pair of sliding wooden doors. She slipped inside and closed them behind her. Only the stairwell's lion heard my annoyance. Was it roaring or laughing?

Ignoring the obnoxious sculpture, I paced the room, counting the wasted moments, eventually turning enough laps to forget I was counting them.

When Doctor Linas returned, someone who certainly wasn't another doctor followed. The woman lagging behind sniffed and swallowed hard, adjusting robes spiraling through a spectrum of bruised shades. She wore an askew amulet: a wooden whorl, the emblem of Pharasma, goddess of common deaths. Soft layers of mousy hair fell past her chin, ending in jags like the tail of her cometlike symbol. They framed a face that looked too young, her nose an upturned button, her eyes a matching her hair. Black enamel covered her nails.

"Is this also an asylum rule?" I didn't hide that I was insulted. Pharasma was hardly friendly to the living, but stirred her followers in open crusade against the undead. That left me—straddling the border between life and undeath—at the crux of an awkward theological question. Thus far I'd avoided learning the church's official stance, as well as the silver blades and searing divine magic I expected accompanied it.

"No." Linas either didn't notice or didn't care that I'd taken offense.

"Just for me, then?"

"Yes." At least she was honest.

The priestess brushed a wave of thin hair from her flushed face, avoiding looking at me with eyes still moist at the corners. Fantastic. What was she, some mourner?

"You're here to make sure I don't hurt anyone?" I glared at her, suddenly very aware of both her and Linas's exposed necks and wrists.

The priestess opened her mouth, failed to speak, and promptly shut it. She was more successful on the second try. "I don't know anything about that," she said in a mostly steady voice as she shot Linas a glance. "The doctor only asked me to assist her. Should I be concerned?"

"I'm not. But I suppose we'll defer to the doctor's professional opinion."

"Indeed." Doctor Linas barely paused in the entry, hand touching the wooden lion's upraised paw as she started up the stairs. "Please, follow me."

The asylum's lacquered wood facade dropped away soon after we reached the top of the stairs, but hardly proved all the stories of the place true. Past heavy doors and a checkpoint of toughs dressed as doctors we entered the wing for female inmates. I'd expected a cacophony of screams and hysterics. Instead, whispers and only an occasional whimper crowded a hall of bars and padded stone. The anticipated tangles of naked halfwits and throwbacks were also nowhere to be found. Instead, things appeared quite orderly. Tiny windows on evenly spaced doors looked in upon patients reading, praying, or calmly at work on simple flower and yarn crafts.

Zigzagging through the angled hall, Doctor Linas ignored the nods of several men and women in coats matching her own, eventually bringing us to a door with the number 72 embossed in brass.

Doctor Linas unlocked the door. "While the patient has suffered only minor cuts and bruising, her age and lifestyle left her quite unfit for such exertions. The effort, night's exposure, and shock of whatever initially set her upon the road have left her physically and mentally exhausted." Turning to us, she held the door's handle. "I've imposed no safety restrictions upon the patient, but do nothing that might upset her or force her to further exert herself. You will have to keep your interview brief—ten minutes at the maximum. However, I cannot promise she will be able to answer any questions you put to her."

"You'll be waiting here, then?"

"Miss Losritter and I will accompany you. I cannot leave a patient unsupervised."

I thought to argue—something about royal security—but relented. Who knew if anything would even come of this? And even if anything did, who did a doctor and a priestess have to tell?

I nodded, and she pushed upon the door.

Wrinkled sheets and loose gray features lay seamless and still, crushed beneath a pile of starched blankets. A mostly hollow mouth leaked upon the pillow. If breath still passed the old woman's colorless lips it was drowned by the sounds of surf through the curtained window.

The living fear and hate my people because we are touched by death. Some who call themselves my aunts and uncles recall when Caliphas's walls were still made of wood—and Grandfather was old when the forests that furnished that wood were nothing but saplings. But never have I known any of my kind, even the most starved and feral, to be as ripe with death as a human giving way to age.

Doctor Linas knelt to touch the fragile form mummified within the bed. For a moment she almost sounded like a normal person, her curt monotone replaced by a breathy whisper as she repeated her patient's name. Against my expectations, the woman moved, deep creases unfolding to reveal glassy eyes. Confusion, panic, and understanding flickered across her face before it settled on indifference.

"Lady Thorenly, I'm sorry to wake you." Doctor Linas's whisper rose a deliberate step. "Someone is here to see you."

"My husband?" Her voice sounded like damp lace squeaking across dusty porcelain. She raised herself on shivering elbows.

"No, my lady, an emissary of the court."

"That's somewhat better, I suppose." The old woman squinted toward me, brushing flattened hair from her face. Her eyes and lips rose in a dreamy smile. "Ailson, I knew you'd come."

I looked to the doctor, then the priestess, but their expressions held the same questions.

"I'm afraid you've mistaken me, Lady Thorenly. My name is Larsa. I'm an accuser in service to the crown." I stepped closer so she might see me better.

She bobbed her head slowly, smiling on. "You always come when I'm in some sort of trouble. It's a good thing Father isn't here to see what a terrible older sister I turned out to be."

"Lady Thorenly, do you know where you are?" My hopes of learning anything useful from the old woman were swiftly deteriorating.

"You've changed your hair." She reached out weakly, her hand all gristle and bone. I recoiled without thinking. She frowned. "I don't like it. Makes you look like you don't know any better. And your clothes—what are you now, someone's driver?"

"My lady," I insisted, aware that both Doctor Linas and the priestess's eyes were on me. "I need you to tell me what happened at your home last night. Why you were found on the street, and all the details of the attack."

She blinked. "Attack?"

"Yes. Tell me what happened at Thorenly Manor last night."

She looked at me intently, but didn't seem to see. "Oh, is this another one of your adventures? Tell me, are you writing this all down? I haven't—"

"Lady Thorenly!"

She rambled on, ignoring my raised voice. If the doctor had some tonic or salts to reawaken reason in the aged, she didn't offer them.

Fine. I had my own methods. I reached to grab the old woman's shoulder. The priestess's hand was up and in the way, pointing, as if for a moment's indulgence.

"Lady Thorenly, it sounds as though you've had a trying experience." The Pharasmin spoke as if to a child. "How are you feeling this morning?"

The old woman squinted past me. "Like I've been left on the drying rack overnight. Is there a window open? It's so chilly and dry in here. Call the girl for some water, would you, dear?"

"Of course." Doctor Linas was moving before anything was asked, squeezing out of the small room to exchange whispers with some subordinate in the hall. The priestess waited. I indulged her approach.

A moment later Linas returned and a chipped ceramic cup passed from doctor to priestess to patient. Lady Thorenly drank slowly, one sip at a time lest she drown on a gulp larger than a raindrop. After minutes of slow slurps and gasps, she held the cup out.

The priestess put it aside. "Better, m'lady?"

"A bit." The noblewoman's voice was gaining a measure of the arrogance I expected from the city's wealthy.

"I'm glad." The Pharasmin squeezed past me, kneeling at the bedside so the patient could see her better. "We'll let you rest or help you ready for the day in just a moment, m'lady, but before that, I have to ask what you remember of last night. We—and your sister—are quite concerned."

"Last night . . ." She paused, her gaze wandering. "It's difficult . . ."

"Please try."

The surf gave several calming whispers.

"There were visitors. They came late—unannounced. An argument of some sort. Blake—Lord Thorenly—and I were already abed. There was shouting, and he went to see to the problem. Something shattered, thuds on the stairs, and more shouting . . . screaming. I went to the top of the steps to see about the commotion, to see if someone had fallen. And they were there. They were smiling, smiling like wolves. Fangs . . ." She looked at me, eyes as clear and sharp as I'd seen them yet. "It's all happening again, but it wasn't in the dark this time. I wasn't alone. They came back for me."

The priestess was quick with comforting platitudes, but I edged past her. "Who?"

Already, though, her expression was glazing over. I leaned in closer, speaking firmly. "Who came for you? Why is there a picture of me in your home?"

The dull confusion drained from her face, along with what little color clung to her cheeks. "You're not . . ." She rose up farther, palms slipping on the bedsheets as she struggled to push herself away. "You're not Ailson. You're one of—"

The priestess reached out a hand to calm her. "Lady Thorenly, please. It's all right. We're here to—"

A shallow gasp, then a scream as she slammed her pigeonlike back against the wall. Thin and painful to hear, it sounded like she was about to shatter. She thrashed, tangling herself hopelessly in the sheets, white hair whipping to keep us at bay.

Doctor Linas was there immediately. "Out."

The Pharasmin was already obeying, but I hadn't learned what I'd come for. I leaned in, pursuing. "Why?"

The shrill noises rose a panicked pitch.

"Out!" Linas demanded, her voice finally taking on some fire. She thrust a tiny envelope smelling of lemon toward the woman, weathering a lashing of hair and bony palms.

I was prepared to ignore her again, but something touched my shoulder. I jerked away and spun on the priestess. "Don't you—"

She cut me off. "I know who she thinks you are."

I pointed at the hysterical woman, eliciting a new round of pitiful sounds. "She's mad. Who cares who she thinks I am? She knows something, and I'll rip it out of her if I have to."

"There's another way, if you'll just come with me." The priestess was begging.

I looked back at the flailing old woman. Even with my back turned, Ellishan Thorenly was struggling to get farther away from me. I'd seen men and women terrified of me before, but every other time I'd purposefully put that terror there. Who or what did she think I was?

Doctor Linas tried to force me from the room with her expression alone. The noise was bothersome anyway. I followed the priestess into the hall, stepping out just in time to avoid being shouldered aside by two matronly orderlies rushing in. They closed the door behind them, muffling the whining within.

The Pharasmin watched me warily. I spread my palms to urge her on.

"You scared her."

"Good. I meant to. It's the second-fastest way I know to get someone to talk."

"No you didn't."

"What?" I wasn't growing less annoyed. First she presumed to put a hand on me, then claimed to know my mind. I was tempted to go back into that room and show her the fastest way I knew how to get the information I wanted.

"What you said didn't scare her. It wasn't until you got closer." She pointed. "She saw your teeth."

"So what? Plenty of you get scared when you see them. Even your cold-blooded doctor in there was scared. That's why she dragged you along."

"She thought you were her sister. Her sister turned into . . . something else.

I narrowed my gaze on her. "So she thought I was her sister. What of it?"

"I don't know what your business is with Lady Thorenly, but it sounds like you were investigating a crime at her home and found something strange?"

"Yeah." I almost left it at that, but she seemed headed somewhere. "A painting. One with someone who looked too much like me."

"So then it wasn't just poor eyesight or dementia, you actually do look like Lady Thorenly's sister. Ailson." Both voice and gaze drifted away.

"What?" I snapped.

Her eyes widened as she turned and started back down the row of cells. "Just follow me."

I didn't budge. She'd gone five or six steps before noticing and turning to look back. "There must be a records room. If they know anything about Lady Thorenly, it should list her immediate kin. It might say something about this Ailson." Her eyes urged me on as she edged farther down the hall. "Don't you want to know who you look so much like?"

I looked back at the cell, dismissing the fleeting idea of returning to the room. If I needed to I could always do so later . . . unattended.

Grimacing, I followed the priestess—the asylum's records surely couldn't be less lucid than its patients.

Nurses eyed us disapprovingly as we passed from the wing, Lady Thorenly's cries having broken down into the echoes of hacking sobs.

While the woman in the portrait unsettled me personally, my orders were to find out about the attackers—the vampires who seemed to be purposefully jeopardizing the truce between Caliphas's living and unliving populace. On that front, this diversion had been a pitiful waste.

Or maybe not. Something the old woman had said rang within her dwindling sobs. Something that, as I thought on it, began to feel like a stolen confession, a warning she thought she was giving someone else—her own blood.

"It's all happening again . . ."

8

MASTER OF KEYS
JADAIN

Gods be damned." Doctor Trice, the asylum's administrator, gaped as he fell into his tall desk chair.

I'd guessed that the doors in the asylum's wood-paneled upper hall had been record rooms and offices for overseers. I was right, but more so than I'd expected. When I'd knocked on the plain door at the hall's end, I was surprised that a firm voice bade us enter—perhaps just as surprised as the head of the asylum was upon finding two curious strangers trespassing into his office. I was only halfway through introductions, apologies, and explanations when I realized he was ignoring me, intently studying Larsa.

In a crowd, she'd be easy not to notice, just a traveling cloak beneath a hat that almost matched. Where the cloak parted, steel traced dark leather. The armor was easy to hide, but its repeating bands and long gloves hid her as well. Only her V-shaped face was exposed, just a narrow band between hat brim and high collar. Long, brick-colored hair fell aimlessly, drawing eyes up to a deep-set glare that made it clear looks weren't welcome. In different framing, I could have envied her strong features. As they were, though, she looked like a raven, and one large enough to decide what passed for prey.

"Doctor Trice?" I followed his look back across the crowded mahogany desk.

Trice wasn't an old man—though more than a little gray accented his untrimmed chestnut hair—but for a moment he wasn't there, his look blank, his thoughts astray. Hearing his name, he gestured to the chairs. "Please, take a seat."

Both Larsa and I accepted, though the big chairs were certainly not as comfortable as they appeared, their padding stiff and unyielding.

"I apologize for my rudeness, but I'm usually better informed of my appointments—and it's already been a trying day with the knife." He rolled his wrists in rough circles, popping them audibly. I tried not to wince. "What did you say your names were, again?"

"Jadain Losritter, and—"

"Larsa," she said curtly, busy examining the crowded, ceiling-high bookshelves. Trice raised thick eyebrows expectantly. It took a moment for her to notice. "Accuser Larsa."

"Hum." He sounded unsatisfied. "And you were looking for something?"

"My apologies, Doctor. That's my fault." Doctor Linas only entered the room far enough to close the door behind her. She was obviously ready to escort us out. "The accuser had business with one of our patients: Lady Ellishan Thorenly, a noblewoman committed only this morning. The accuser is a—"

"Quite," Trice interrupted, noticing Larsa's darkening expression. "Which is where a servant of the Lady of Graves might come into the picture. Good of you to come on such short notice."

"No trouble at all." I tried to be gracious. If I was going to be a trespasser I could at least be a polite one. "I was already here."

"Indeed?" he raised a curious eyebrow to Doctor Linas. "Are all our Wealdays so busy, Cereis?"

"I keep nothing from you, Doctor," her response came like clockwork. Admittedly, I was surprised to hear a given name—the "tick-tock" sound of "doctor" just fit her so well. "Miss Losritter has been here since last night. She was the exorcist's assistant."

He frowned. "I thought that nastiness dealt with."

I took it on myself to clarify: "It is, Doctor Trice. Elistair Wintersun is at rest."

"So . . ." he led.

I began carefully. "I . . . stayed . . . to assure that your chapel was appropriately consecrated and open to the goddess's attention. Since then I'd been praying for all who work and reside here."

"There was a falling out," Linas cut in. "She did not perform to the High Exorcist's expectations."

My stomach knotted as if I were once again a girl in seminary, caught in a lie before the Holy Mother. Doctor Trice nodded thoughtfully, fingers steepling over his mouth. The accuser was also looking at me, but I didn't turn enough to see her expression.

Trice turned to Larsa. "As the head of this institution, would I be permitted to know your interest in Lady Thorenly?"

"No," she replied, blunt as ever. The unshaven head doctor obviously didn't intimidate her. She cast a look back to Doctor Linas. "But, since your doorwoman will tell you everything she's overheard: I'm investigating the attack that drove Lady Thorenly into the night and ultimately here. Those involved could be enemies of the throne."

"There's a personal reason, as well," Linas started. "Something about a—"

"Yes, yes." Larsa raised her voice, drowning out the assistant's explanation. Trice's attention didn't waver from her. "I've investigated Thorenly Glen, Lady Ellishan's home, and found a portrait of someone I recognized."

When she didn't continue, Trice did for her, speaking through the cage of his fingers. "You."

Larsa straightened. "Excuse me?"

"The portrait in the Thorenly house. It was of or included someone who looked like you." He spoke as if pointing out the obvious.

"How—" Larsa started to rise, but snapped her mouth and body almost immediately back into place. "Explain."

The doctor pushed back from his desk, stepping to retrieve something from a cabinet of drawers. At the turn of a small key a long file clattered open, its length bulging with pages crammed into identical folders. He riffled through, tugged one loose, and frowned. The folder was old, bent and yellowed beyond the others, but thin—empty.

Trice gave a bemused snort. Heaving the drawer closed, he spun the folder onto the desk, letting it slide to Larsa's corner.

The accuser flipped the folder open. It was absolutely empty. She didn't look amused.

I leaned over. *KINDLER, A., 4657* was written in even, capital letters upon the reference tab. There was also something longer scrawled in a corner. I read the leaning, almost unintelligible cursive aloud as I deciphered: "You know more than enough. Anyone else can buy the book. —A."

"What's this supposed to be?" Larsa flipped the folder shut.

Doctor Trice reclaimed his seat, his fingertips lightly drumming his spotless desk blotter. "It's the treatment history of one of my patients. As you can see, our record-keeping has been somewhat lax in this case."

Larsa shrugged. "One of your lunatics? An escapee?"

"Ailson," I said. "Ailson Kindler."

Trice gave a disbelieving smile. "You know the lady?"

"Only by reputation. Almost everyone's at least heard of her stories."

Larsa arched an eyebrow at me. "I haven't."

"She's an author of mysteries and frightening tales. She's quite good, and very popular among those who read." I nodded my personal recommendation.

She narrowed her eyes. "I read fine."

"Oh, I didn't mean to imply . . ." I trailed off as she waved her hand.

"In any case." I turned back to Doctor Trice and gestured at Larsa. "Lady Thorenly called her 'Ailson,' and seemed to think the accuser was her sister. Is Lady Thorenly really Ailson Kindler's sister?"

"She is," Trice confirmed. "Miss Kindler is also an old colleague of mine."

Larsa acknowledged the folder. "Looks more like she was a patient."

"Among other things. But most of her records predate my practice. Be that as it may, I would like them returned."

"That sounds like a problem for your bookkeeper." Larsa slid the folder away from her side of the desk.

"Maybe. But, at present, my bookkeeper isn't the one looking for facts about the Thorenlys and their relations."

Larsa frowned. "I'm not interested in the history of a stranger's chills and sprains. If you suspect your records contained something relevant, just tell me."

He gave the barest shrug. "I can't say for sure."

"You understand that my investigation is backed by the Royal Advisor? Withholding information from an accuser has penalties somewhat steeper than ducking some dockyard constable."

"I certainly do," Trice replied coolly. "But I'd be remiss in my civic duties were I to provide you only with memories and hearsay when verifiably records lie within reach. I also don't suspect your Mr. Diauden would appreciate seeing his most trusted medical consultant thrown in a Whiteshaw cell."

I only faintly recognized the name "Diauden"—some member of court. For a moment it looked as though Larsa might storm from the room, but a gradual sigh marked her concession. "So you keep copies of your files? Or do you think your Miss Kindler still has it?"

"Sadly, Ailson retired to Ardis many years ago—that's probably when she collected her records. But I suspect she only pilfered my files, not the originals." His attention settled back on me. "Before Havenguard opened its doors, those with disorders of the mind—afflicted spirits, as they used to be called—were either put into the streets or taken to Maiden's Choir." His fingernails absently traced the salt-and-pepper stubble across his cheek. "That only made sense, as the clergy's power to perform healing miracles is well known—even if it is frugally used."

I didn't think he was deliberately baiting me, but he obviously knew something of my order's philosophies. Pharasma's mandates might not be as popular as those of deities who openly coddled their worshipers, but I wasn't ashamed. "My order certainly *can* call upon the Lady to perform wonders, but as the weaver of fate she has reasons we will never understand. She teaches us to accept our lots and find our own solutions to life's challenges, especially the painful ones. Therefore, we see her plan in even our hardships, and don't call upon her wonders as frivolous charity. Even so, for a time Maiden's Choir did maintain a shelter where the afflicted could pray, reflect, and beg for the money to pay for costly rituals. They're called 'lamentations'—many of the Lady's houses have them. The cathedral's was closed before I came to the city, though."

The doctor didn't seem impressed. But after all, part of faith is being willing to believe, and he seemed like someone who relied overly much on his own senses.

"So as a mercy, they let them suffer." He ignored my frown and I didn't bother trying to further enlighten him in his own office. "Maiden's Choir closed its shelter about fifteen years ago, after some ridiculous court ruling. The Pharasmins turned more than a hundred patients out onto the streets. Some found places with charitable families, others found jail cells, many didn't last through the winter. I made a place for about a third of them here—we were much smaller then than we are now."

"In the transition, I discovered that Pharasmins make excellent bookkeepers." He waved an open palm toward Larsa. "Although their records dealt mostly with births and deaths, their shelter maintained detailed admittance and observation reports. For bureaucratic reasons I've given up trying to understand, they refused to turn those records over to me, but they did allow us to make copies." He picked up the folder. "This, along with years of irreplaceable notes, was one of those copies. It could be that Miss Kindler was part of the reason for the problem at Thorenly House." Trice pointed at Larsa with one of the folder's wrinkled corners. "This might have confirmed or dismissed my suspicion."

"What's your suspicion?" Larsa pressured.

"I work in evidence, not feelings. And I want my file back. I suspect Maiden's Choir still has the original copy."

That last part had been a question for me. "Our library's records date back centuries. If it happened under our steeples, I suspect documents about it are still there." I eyed him warily, knowing how preciously our librarians guarded the cathedral's holdings. "But fifteen years doesn't mean much to our order. If they didn't grant you the records when they were most necessary, I can't imagine them parting with them now."

"But it's not me asking." Trice flung the folder toward Larsa's lap. "One of His Majesty's accusers is requisitioning them on national business."

Larsa's hand snatched the file, stopping its spin midair. "This better be worth my time."

"Well." Trice grinned. "We won't know until you get it for me."

An unusually bold sun lit colorful leaves and weedy flowers across the asylum grounds. If it weren't for Havenguard's grasping shape dominating the field, it would have been pleasant—especially with the endless thrum of churning surf. We were higher than the city here, and through distant branches slipped the somber sails of ships in Caliphas's Outer Harbor.

I was still blinking against the light when the accuser paused with me at the bottom of the asylum's steps. She was looking at me, even as she squinted and angled her black hat against the morning light. Her headwear reminded me of that worn by the inquisitors of my order. The High Exorcist's face sprung to mind along with the thought. I wondered if Havenguard might have need of a resident priestess.

I offered a noncommittal nod.

"You're headed back to Maiden's Choir?" she asked.

"Yes." I tried to sound more confident than I was.

"Good. Then I'll ride there with you."

"Certainly," I chuckled, "if I had ridden here."

Her lips thinned. "Priests usually travel by coach. You didn't?"

"Oh, I did. But . . ." I let the reason trail off, not eager to share my humiliation with a stranger.

Larsa nodded and didn't press the topic.

"You didn't ride?" I knew what a walk it was back to the city. I hadn't been relishing it either.

She looked about the institution's empty drive, obviously taking stock of her options. "I don't ride animals."

"Really? I'd have thought the court would give you any training you needed, especially with as much traveling as you must do."

"No. Animals don't agree with me—it's mutual. And I don't travel."

Now that was interesting. I didn't know much about the accusers, just that they were royal agents entrusted with matters regarding the nation's nobility. They were the ones that made the highest nobles' problems go away, and if a noble had too many problems, they might make *him* go away. Supposedly there weren't many accusers. So why would her business keep her so close to the throne?

"Hey!" Larsa snapped, though fortunately not at me. Doctor Linas was still standing in the asylum's entry, probably assuring we didn't slip back in to snoop around anymore. "Your boss said to see us off. We're having some trouble with that. Have anything to help us out?"

"Doctor Trice said nothing about additional allowances." Linas had a right to be annoyed with us, but if she was, it didn't reflect in her tone. She was perfectly professional. Larsa cursed under her breath anyway.

I tried a more delicate route. "I know Doctor Trice didn't request the accuser's return by any specific time, but I'm sure he expects some haste." I nodded toward a gravel path leading from the drive around the side of the asylum. "If the asylum has anything, even a cart for deliveries, Miss Larsa could probably return before dark. If not . . . well, I can't speak for the accuser, but an errand like this might take me some time."

Linas looked at me blankly, calculating.

"Wait here." She shut the fortress-like door behind her.

"Do you think she's going to ask permission?" I gave a little chuckle. Larsa shrugged, her attention clearly elsewhere.

I followed her eyes. A mossy birch tree stood outside the men's wing of the asylum. It was thin and far enough away from the building that, even if a patient were to get past his barred window, it wouldn't help an escape. But she seemed fixated.

"What?" I asked, only to be ignored. She started walking toward it.

It really wasn't any of my business to follow her, so I didn't. But then my curiosity got the better of me. I had just bargained a ride into the city for her, so she couldn't get too upset.

I had only just come up behind her when she whipped the small crossbow from her hip, loaded it expertly, and fired. My heart jumped, and for half an instant I was sure I'd somehow surprised her and she'd shot me dead. But she hadn't turned, loosing the quarrel into the tree's pale branches. Something launched off, a thin chunk of white wood.

"Shit!" She reloaded and brought the crossbow up again, swinging toward me.

I cursed and half-ducked, giving her and the loaded weapon room. She was aiming, but not at the tree, following something in the air—the ribbon of bark she'd shot free. Then it flapped.

"A bird?" I asked, as if that might explain her behavior.

She lowered her weapon. "A bat."

It was already disappearing into the distance, flitting toward the city. A moment more and it was gone.

"A white bat?" I asked.

She nodded, starting back toward the drive.

"Are those . . ." I tried not to sound totally ignorant, but was at a loss, "somehow dangerous?"

"Dangerous?" she scoffed. "Someone would like to think so."

"Who?"

She didn't answer.

Clattering interrupted before I could press further. The noise echoed off the asylum's brick facade as a wagon pulled by a dappled gray mare rocked into view.

This time, I shared in Larsa's exasperated sigh.

Sturdy and windowless, this wasn't some delivery wagon—or at least, it wasn't for the deliveries I'd imagined. It was a repurposed constable's wagon painted in white. If I'd had to, I would have guessed it was padded on the inside like the asylum's cells. It slowed in the drive and Doctor Linas descended from the passenger's seat while an orderly held the reins. The doctor recited a litany of restrictions and expectations on how we were to treat asylum property.

"Think I could steal a ride?" I said, already climbing onto the bench. When the accuser frowned, I added, "I can show you the cathedral's library. A few thousand years of birth and death records aren't something you'll want to navigate alone."

I didn't add that I much preferred the idea of returning to Maiden's Choir with a purpose rather than slinking back in shame.

"Fine." Larsa took the driver's place. "But I've got a stop to make along the way."

She cracked the reins before Linas finished.

9

BLOODLINE

LARSA

Welcome home, madam," trumpeted one of the legion of nearly identical porters stationed outside the Majesty Hotel. He smiled like he knew me and tugged open a door of glass panes and brass ivy leaves. I tamped down my first urge and ignored him, being painfully aware of the results of throttling members of the hotel staff.

One of the tallest buildings in Caliphas, the Majesty rivaled the size and luxury of even the royal palace. A prince's ransom in gilded tiles, crystal chandeliers, conclaves of wide-seated furniture, and imported flowers—freshened hourly—ringed the concierge's desk at the lobby's heart. Polished to a dazzling sheen, every bit of the place, from the mosaic tiles to the heights of a forest of pillars, tempted visitors to stay just a moment more, a day extra, a week longer.

The staff, used to fulfilling the impossible demands of the highest nobility, proved endlessly attentive. Beyond the vanguard of doormen bustled a battalion of hosts, hostesses, housekeepers, valets, unobtrusive musicians, and courtesans—the latter discrete in every sense and changed more regularly than the flowers.

"Home?" The Pharasmin Jadain gawked. "You live here?"

I cringed, not having noticed the priestess following me into the lobby.

"Wait with the—" I started, but it was too late. Behind her two valets were unenthusiastically leading the ominous wagon away. I grabbed Jadain by the arm, pulling her alongside a garlanded pillar.

"No, I don't, I just . . ." I whispered swiftly, heat rising to my cheeks. "I just sleep here."

"You keep your coffin here," she said matter-of-factly, eyes tracing the lobby's faux woodland decor to the gilded boughs above.

I nearly choked. "I don't have—I don't *need* a coffin!"

Her attention jerked back to me. "You actually have a coffin?"

"I'm not discussing this."

"I thought I was joking. So are all the stories true? We crossed running water on the way—can you even drink water?"

I stared down a stranger who looked our way, then pulled the priestess into closer confidence with the column. "Careful."

She shut her mouth, but her questions still practically hummed on her tongue.

"I didn't choose this. It's part of my work."

"For the court?" she dared, dubious. "They put accusers up like this?"

"No. They don't."

"So you're rich, then?"

"So it's none of your business." I pressed my fingers into her upper arm and twisted her toward a circle of throne-like seats. "Now be quiet, sit, and wait here." I ignored her tiny yelp of surprise. "And if anyone offers you anything, you can't afford it."

She scowled, but I left before she could protest.

I approached the lobby's central desk, an altarlike ring of marble polished to a glassy sheen. I knew the concierge's name. The well-pressed Mr. Still was, as always, at his post.

"The Jalmeray Room. Is it empty?"

"Never, madam." He answered almost before I'd finished the question, confident and in his usual peculiar accent.

We exchanged nods and I headed up the grand stairway.

The crowd thinned away from the lobby, as did the assault of light and decadent decor. A small maze of halls wound between deserted salons and quiet clubrooms, finally turning into a blind alley of somber wood paneling and discreet lighting. Dignified brass placards shone upon each of the otherwise identical double doors, every one naming off some distant land: *Taldor*, *Sargava*, *Thuvia*, and second from the end, *Jalmeray*.

During the walk, I hadn't been wholly aware of my rising annoyance, but it all boiled up as soon as I hit the door. It crashed inward.

The Majesty's lounges were not themed, but the Jalmeray Room had been redecorated to match the humor of its exclusive resident. The gaudiest slice of some cut-rate bazaar had been emptied here, hiding stately paneling behind a gallery of snarling masks, garish weavings, stunted tropical trees, and a haze of licorice-infused smoke. Around a low central table, two men and a young woman sprawled across battered wicker chairs. All were stylishly dressed, but utterly ignorant of how to wear their clothes, creasing and stretching their costumes as they slouched, limp and distant. All were forever away, but the thin tails of the table's vermillion hookah tethered them here.

"Pathetic," I said, booting a discarded tea service. No one noticed the clatter. I navigated heaps of beaded pillows and more dishware. The girl was closest. I knocked the hookah's hose from her hand and yanked her to her feet. She squirmed in her under-filled emerald gown.

"Isn't she a bit unripe?" I didn't have to fake my disgust, looking into eyes darkened by more than mascara. "Even for you?"

The girl choked, her surprise stuttering in her throat even though I wasn't talking to her. I dropped her back into the chair, where she exploded in raspy laughter—a boy's wild laughter. At second glance, she was more clearly a pretty boy enjoying the novelty of a corset. Around me, his fellows followed his lead, tittering through lazy breaths.

I considered hurting these pets—that would surely get some attention. Rather, a quick kick to the table upended the waterpipe, spilling burnt flayleaf and filthy water. The laughing stuttered out as each of the addicts noticed in their own blunt time. I ignored their sleepy curses.

More than just the mood of the room fell. A tendril of the smoke clinging to the ceiling began to settle. Crossing to the fireplace, I snatched for what was inside vapor.

Amid the smoke condensed a thin form, revealed as if fog had rolled back from a sculpture that'd been standing there the whole time. Pale skin and rich clothes constituted themselves, a cardinal vest with gold brocade hanging open over a wine-stained ivory shirt. His feet were bare, but at least he was wearing pants this time. A tousled mess of short auburn hair covered his forehead and hid the tips of slightly pointed ears. Algae-green eyes and perpetually bemused brows were among the last things to materialize. As soon as the cool, strangely loose flesh of his neck settled into my grip, I dug my nails in.

I kept my message simple, stating it slowly: "Stop following me."

Considine opened his mouth, making a show of gasping. Red stained his fangs—unusually slender, even for a full-blood. No words escaped. He needed air more than most vampires—not to breathe, but to blow away the endless stream of unrequested opinions that crowed his tongue.

"No." I shook him. "We agreed. That means your pets, too." I shot disdainful looks to his clique of guests, then to a covered birdcage in the corner. "All of them."

He pursed his lips in something between a scowl and a pout.

"We're still agreed then?" I squeezed my nails deeper.

An assortment of frowns complained on his lips, but eventually stilled. Closing his eyes, he nodded once.

"Good." I released him and backed away a step.

He rubbed his neck—entirely for show—firing me a practiced half-smile. "I sense I've somehow offended."

"I saw your chimney rat at Havenguard."

"Oh? Is that all? What a coincidence." He crossed to the sequestered birdcage and lifted a corner of the cover. An albino bat dozed inside. He cooed to the disgusting thing incomprehensibly.

"I'd never purposefully break my word to you," Considine said over his shoulder. "You can't really consider Vris a pet, though. He's practically family. That puts him outside our agreement."

"The hell it does. I don't care what you call the thing, I don't need checking in on."

"I do wish you two could put this silly feud behind you." I couldn't be sure if he was talking to me or the damned bat.

Considine's guests were starting to squirm, having sucked the last wisps out of their pipes. "Do we always need an audience?"

"Aw, these pretty things? They won't be able to gossip." He chuckled. A few slow looks passed between the vampire's company—did they even know? Considine bent to right the hookah, then added something less suggestive of impending murder. "After all, I only buy the best."

With a word and a snap of his fingers, the burner relit—an unnecessary display of the eternally youthful vampire's knack for magic. He smiled conspiratorially to the group who, had he been anything near the age he appeared, could have been his school-mates. Recovering pipes, they smiled back, all three faking that they were in on a joke only the vampire knew.

I shook my head. There would always be prey too dumb to even acknowledge that predators existed.

His guests attended to, Considine turned back to me, straightening his vest.

I looked only slightly down on him. "If I see it again, I won't miss."

"Miss?" He caught my meaning an instant later. His look flashed to Vris's cage then back, turning wounded. "Cruel."

He circled the lounge, then closed the door and crossed to a sideboard jumbled with dirtied salvers, champagne flutes, and a silver serving dome, idly straightening them.

"And unnecessary. I've held to the letter and intention of our agreement. I haven't been following you, and neither have any of my usual connections. You can't expect me to be responsible for every coincidence—same circles and whatnot. Truthfully," he cast a sidelong smirk, "the only way I can absolutely ensure that none of my associates cross your path is to track your whereabouts at all times. I can arrange that, if it would suit you?"

I looked at him flatly.

"I thought not." He shrugged. "Then you might have to occasionally suffer spotting me and mine as we go about our business. I'll be sure to tell my favorites to cover their faces if they see you coming.

"You had business at Havenguard this morning, at exactly the same time I was there?"

"Yes." He didn't miss a beat.

"What?"

"A social call on an acquaintance." He flipped a hand.

"Do you often send your familiar to pay visits to lunatics?"

"I do when this turns up in one's home." He lifted the serving dome without flourish and immediately dropped it. His guests looked only well after it clanged back to the platter beneath. In the second before, though, I'd seen all I needed. The woman's severed head resting in a nest of her own tangled gold curls, thrusting her stately nose into the air.

"Who—" I hardly began.

"Yismilla Col. Surely you remember—or perhaps she was before your time." He delighted in reminding us both of my relative youth, at least by the standards of beings who counted age starting from their moment of death. "Supposedly she's a traitor, one Grandfather ordered executed, but who managed to flee to Ardis."

"Supposedly?"

"That's the story he tells the rabble. Actually, she's his executor there. Grandfather fabricated her betrayal and flight to ferret out traitors some half a century ago. She's served in the Old Capital ever since, an imaginary rebel who reports on full-bloods moving against him."

"Seems like someone thought they were doing Grandfather a favor."

He creaked out a dubious hum. "I don't think so."

"Why?"

"Because it was delivered, and he had me meet the messengers. They arrived on the outskirts of the city last night and made quite a mess—"

"Thorenly Glen. I know." I spoke over the sigh he gave upon being interrupted. "Diauden sent me there just before dawn. Someone's spawn had ripped the place apart and killed everyone. It seemed like they were looking for something."

"They were looking for her." He nodded at the covered salver. "I prefer not to deal with slaves, especially poorly mannered ones—you saw the mess they'd made. They were too busy lapping stains off the floor to know I'd even arrived, much less that I'd received their message."

"They were in a panic when I showed up," I said. "They'd obviously noticed their parcel had gone missing by then. I tried to get an explanation out of them but it didn't go well."

"Oh good." He pointed at my headwear. "I'd hate to think *those* were coming into fashion."

I ignored him. "If someone thinks they've done Grandfather a favor by killing a fake traitor then flagrantly violating the capital's truce, they've penned a rather elaborate suicide note."

Considine blew out a lazy breath. "I get the feeling they're not overly interested in your truce."

"It's a truce that's given Grandfather a reason not to add your head to his collection. If I was in your position, I'd take the situation far more seriously."

"Oh. Thank you for the sisterly advice," he said as though I were a horse-kicked child. "I see how seriously you take it—you do fantastic work out in the gutters hunting wild spawn every night. Sometimes it makes me jealous. But, alas, orders. I'll just keep dealing with any humans who get the notion they're not the only ones living in this city. And those who do and want to do something about it can find me right here."

I looked to the three humans only a step away. None of them seemed to be following the conversation. "How many of them have you protected your family from so far? One? Three? In all these years."

He gave an exaggerated shrug. "It's not a contest, dear."

I rolled my head, my neck muscles suddenly tired. Hopeless. "So, you got your message. What's it tell you?"

"The parcel? Well, I'd say a severed head sends a pretty clear message, wouldn't you? Especially when that head used to sit upon the body that controlled Ardis's underworld." He crossed his arms, posing with a finger upon his lips. "It's hardly the most interesting part."

"Something has you interested?" I honestly marveled.

"I know. The world surprises me still." Both his voice and eyes were flat. "Far be it from me to presume to know our illustrious grandsire's mind, but you know my relationship with Grandfather is . . . strained."

That was beyond an understatement. Considine held his position because he'd displeased Grandfather some years ago.

"As much as I've enjoyed the last three years of dangling myself close to the light, waiting for whatever would-be avengers the rabble works up, I don't think Grandfather's reconsidered banishing me to the surface." He tapped his lips. "So then I'm sure you were only slightly less surprised than I was to learn that he chose me to accept a message on his behalf."

I hadn't considered it when he mentioned it earlier, but he was right. "That doesn't—"

"Precisely. He has favorites for that." He cast me a look, but seemed far from jealous. "Grandfather's not exactly the change-able sort. So, of course, I expected that I was finally being sent off for my much-delayed murder. Since that sounded far more interesting than my usual routine, I took Grandfather's errand in the country. Disappointingly, though, I found what I found." His knuckle struck a tinny note on the serving dome.

"He's not giving you a second chance." I was mostly thinking out loud. Both of us knew Grandfather wasn't the merciful sort, either.

"Certainly not," he snorted. "I had my whole unmurdered trek back to think on that little riddle. You're going to love the answer I came up with."

"What?"

He looked proud of himself. "Now I'm no expert on how ancient lunatics amuse themselves . . ."

I hurried him on with a wave.

"It's simple. Who's the last person I'd want to collect a message from? You as well, for that matter—I might have done you a favor."

It wasn't a philosophical question. I bit the inside of my cheek, a bitter heat welling up. "Have any proof?"

"Not a jot, but can you think of anyone else who'd be so bold and who Grandfather would want to flaunt me in front of? Makes me glad the messengers never even saw me—not that it sounds like they'll be reporting back after your meeting."

This wasn't real evidence. I wanted to smack Considine's simpering face for even bringing the idea up. It did make a sort of sense, though. "Last I knew, Grandfather's hunters were tracking him in the mountains, but there were rumors from as far away as Lepidstadt and Vigil. That he'd show up in Ardis, that's . . . unexpected."

"Unexpected, and bold, and poignant, all traits of a fine rebel. Revealing himself and challenging his father from the Old Capital, there's more than a little poetry to that. Add to it that he's making things a pain for me and it sounds exactly like Rivascis."

I strained to keep my teeth from grinding together at hearing his name. Even then, I was suddenly aware of the hundreds of old scars—old blames—hidden beneath my clothes. *Rivascis.*

Considine's lips pursed as if he fought back a smile—as if he knew everything going on in my mind.

I pretended not to notice. "You, of all people, should know to be careful about that kind of talk." Grandfather had forbidden anyone from so much as mentioning his wayward son, and that went doubly so for Considine. Rivascis had turned Considine into a vampire, after all. That fact alone went far in winning Considine his current outcast status.

"My dear, I assure you, I am the picture of restraint." His right hand fell upon the head of one of his guests, massaging the addict's hair like a dozing cat. "But you . . ."

"I'm fine."

"You don't sound fine. You sound pained . . . maybe even a little eager. I've heard addicts with that tone." This smile wasn't wide enough to show his fangs, but somehow he still looked like a snake. "What's it like, after all these years, to have—"

I half drew my blade, enough to let the silver glint in the flickering light.

"Fine, fine—always so dramatic." He rolled his head along with his eyes. "Put it away. We both know it's not good for anything more than slicing up spawn."

He was obnoxiously right. The blade didn't bear the magic necessary to do lasting damage to a true vampire like him. Just another reminder of the leash Grandfather kept me on.

"It's still sharp enough to take your tongue—even if only for a moment or two. Is that the only way to convince you that I'm not discussing this?"

He raised palms shaking in mock fear.

I wasn't going to get anything better. My sword clicked back into its scabbard.

"Still, I have to wonder," he couldn't help himself, "does Grandfather still make it a point to remind you how he left you?"

"Enough!" I'd obviously have to change the topic myself. "There wasn't anything else with the . . . with Yismilla, was there?"

"Her?" He looked over at himself, reflected in the silver dome. "No, nothing. They were lugging her around in a common chest. I tried to give her slightly more tasteful accommodations and a bit of privacy."

I imagined Yismilla Col's dead gaze—now truly dead—piercing the serving dome, burning into Considine. "What's next for her?"

"I'm expecting one of Grandfather's couriers promptly at dusk. It's for him to deal with."

"That's all?"

He looked about. "Should there be something more? I've done my part, and—most importantly—I've done it in a manner that I don't believe will give our grandsire a reason to collect my own head. I've had more than my fair share of dealings with our stray prince as it is. I think I've earned a bit of a reward." He plucked a straw-colored hair between strokes. If the youth noticed, he didn't complain.

I rolled my eyes. "Then you're washing your hands of the matter?"

"Just another errand well done in the name of our honorable ancestor." He nodded sharply.

"Then why Havenguard?"

He tried to keep his face blank, but he couldn't hold back the crack of smile for long. "Like I said, just checking in on a loose end."

"Horseshit," I said plainly. "Diauden told me Ellishan Thorenly survived the attack. What's your interest in her?"

"Ooh, quite the detective you're turning into. I bet you could find work with the Sleepless Agency if this whole Royal Accuser thing ever goes sour."

I waited.

"You know me, endlessly curious. Grandfather was quite particular about when and where to be. A random noble's home seemed like a strange—and unusually messy—meeting place. Unless, that is, it wasn't at all random."

"Grandfather chose the meeting place?"

"Well, if he didn't, our—"

"Don't."

The beardless trio looked to Considine. He smiled, gesturing with a finger that he'd need only a minute more. That finger then tapped the nose of the concerned blond head looking up at him.

The vampire's attention drifted back to me. "One of them did."

"Any idea why?"

"Certainly not for the decor. You saw the place."

I nodded. Thorenly Glen wasn't the site of a random vampire attack, then. It had been deliberately chosen, either by Grandfather or his damnable son. I almost asked Considine about the painting there, but there was no way he'd seen it. I also wasn't eager to confide in him about something so unusual. Not while I might get answers from Doctor Trice, at least.

"Are you planning on visiting Ellishan Thorenly again?"

"I heard the gist of your interrogation." He nodded toward the birdcage. "I trust that if there was anything useful to learn you would have coaxed it loose."

Vris's reporting must not have been terribly thorough—a relief to hear. I'm sure Considine would have been eager to needle me over the old woman's misidentification and my futile questioning if he knew the details.

"So that's it? What happened to your curious streak?"

"There's lots I'm curious about." His fingers wound through the blond's hair one last time as he stepped away. "Bad memories and old women aren't high among them."

I sniffed. "Living among humans hasn't diminished your aristocratic streak one bit."

"Thank you, dear. In celebration of a job well done, I think I'll have something to drink, see what distractions flit by, and continue to enjoy my exile as a prince among sheep." He flopped into an empty wicker chair and crossed his bare feet on the table. His hollow smile beamed up at me. "After all, chasing bogeymen, that's your job. I'm just a lonely shepherd, making sure my flock doesn't wander too near the wolf den."

"You know what they say about sheep and lonely shepherds."

"We all have our vices." He grinned around him.

"I thought I knew yours, but every time I come here I'm more convinced that it's actually self-pity."

"I keep a diverse portfolio." He saluted with the hookah pipe he'd collected. "What you call pity, though, I call patience."

"You're not doing yourself any favors by just rotting here. You're letting him forget about you."

"At the moment, I'm perfectly happy to be forgotten." He refilled the bowl of the hookah from a small pouch.

I almost felt sorry for him—as much as I might for some wolf pup kept in a prince's kennel. "Does that even work on you?"

He puffed, then released. The smoke split into two streams around his canines. "No. I just enjoy the sensation."

I moved toward the door, flattening the brim of my hat. "I'll give Grandfather your regards."

"Rather you didn't." His voice slipped from around the ridiculously tall wicker chair.

I didn't close the door behind me as I left.

In the lobby, a gesture attracted a valet's attention and a word sent him off to bring around our wagon.

I found the priestess leaning over the side of an overstuffed lounge chair, pointing at a page of sheet music as one of the house musicians nodded. ". . . it's really just the hymn "In Her Voice," with a faster tempo. You'd be surprised how many songs start as devotionals—especially bawdy ones."

"We're going," I interrupted, immediately turning for the door.

Jadain caught up to me outside, just in time to watch two resentful hotel footmen slow the rickety asylum cart. "So, who did you have to visit?"

"A dead man." I accepted the reins from one of the servants, ignoring his outstretched palm. "What's the fastest way to Maiden's Choir?"

She gave simple directions as she circled to the passenger's seat and climbed up. "Your dead man have anything interesting to say?"

"More than I expected. Now I know who sent Ellishan Thorenly to Havenguard."

"Oh? Who?"

I whipped the reins, bound for the cathedral of Pharasma. "My father."

10

DEATH'S RECORDS

JADAIN

I usually imagined Maiden Choir's gigantic blue-and-purple dome as some great eye, staring through the clouds, watchful for signs from the goddess—a towering emblem of the vigil the faithful kept through our prayers and meditations. Today, the Grand Cathedral looked like a blister, a swollen thing due a terrible diagnosis.

Maiden's Choir numbered among the oldest and largest buildings in Caliphas. I remember being awed upon first laying eyes upon it, almost falling backward in an attempt to take it all in. Before it stretched the Waiting Yard, a plaza of black and gray flagstones circling lethargic fountains. Polishing the stones was a common punishment for the seminary's inattentive acolytes, but fortunately only the darker stones required cleaning. While the gigantic mosaic's inky surfaces were kept polished to a glossy sheen, the gray stones were left with all but the most offensive stains of everyday life. The tiles of familiar grit lay alongside the lustrous black ones, together reflecting a distorted view of the cathedral in a gigantic, embellished interpretation of Pharasma's holy spiral.

Maiden's Choir itself grew from amid a forest of shadowy buttresses, a monument not just to the goddess, but also to ages of her devout. Generations of faithful had created countless whip-poorwill-haunted gargoyles of saints and psychopomps. Hidden spouts channeled mist and rain through the eyes of sculpted mourners, while an endless stone pilgrimage wound its way into the Great Beyond. It was breathtaking and impossible to ignore, but I understood why most passersby didn't linger.

I pointed out a series of posts hidden between two buttresses and Larsa steered the wagon into their shadows. Once the cart had stopped, we dropped from the bench and set to tying the horse's reins to a convenient hitching post.

"Bitch!" Larsa shouted, jerking her hand away from the horse's bit. Her curse repeated off the cathedral's walls.

I shushed her firmly, imagining the word passing through the stained glass, its echoes scandalizing some senior priestess at her prayers.

"What? The bloody thing bit me." She punched the mare in the neck. It snorted dismissively.

"I'll do it, I'll do it. Just keep your voice down—and civil."

Larsa repeated the mare's snort.

By the time I tended to the horse and turned to lead Larsa inside she was already headed toward the Waiting Yard. Strangely delayed, her curse echoed inside my head one more time. I had to run to catch up to her and clapped her arm as I came up from behind.

I might have grown up tugging at stubborn vines, but most of the muscle I earned on my father's vineyard stayed back in Barstoi. So when Larsa whipped away, then turned on me with a look like hot steel, I immediately shrank.

"Sorry! Sorry," I apologized before she even opened her mouth. That seemed to placate her for the moment, and while it didn't extinguish her look, I had gotten her attention.

This wasn't how I wanted to broach this topic. I hadn't come up with a polite segue all day, and only a few dozen steps from the cathedral's doors seemed like the last opportunity.

"I need to ask . . ." I tried to choose my words carefully. "Are you particularly religious?"

Her brow tightened as she searched for my intention. "I don't need a sermon."

"No, that's not what I mean." I didn't know how to put this delicately. "But, have you ever . . . actually been inside a temple?"

She looked puzzled, an expression bordering on annoyed.

I blurted it out. "Holy ground. The cathedral is holy ground. Can you even go inside?"

She sighed. "I've been in temples before. All the singing and wishing in the world doesn't make a stack of stones any more than a stack of stones. Don't worry about me."

"I'm not." In truth, she was only the first of my concerns. "My goddess's faithful, however . . ."

"You expect me to hurt someone?"

"No! Not at all." I hoped my honesty showed in my shock.

"Then what?"

"The goddess's word on . . ." Again, I searched for the tactful turn of phrase, "your condition." I immediately winced.

Her litany of curses was blessedly far enough under her breath that the particulars didn't echo this time. "My 'condition'?" she finally asked. "What, exactly, is my 'condition'?"

I squeezed my eyes shut. "An extraordinarily poor choice of words. I am so sorry."

She made an indignant noise and was halfway up the stairs to the cathedral's doors before I caught up to her again. Panels depicting veiled, motherly figures covered the entryway, half holding quiet children, half swaddling raucous corpses, all with their eyes cast in reverence toward the spiral of stained glass above. Like the gate of a fortress, the doors were large and sturdy enough to either admit or deter an angry giant. Hinged panels created a smaller door within the towering gate. To either side, priests in deep purple robes stood in mock meditation, their hoods pulled low. Voluminous sleeves hid their folded arms and hands near long silver daggers, weapons that all the goddess's servants were trained in wielding.

My stomached tightened as Larsa approached, still a stride or two ahead of me, her scabbard plain upon her hip. I almost called out to alleviate the concerns I imagined the guards having, but she was already doffing her hat and passing between them. The priests didn't budge. There were those who would certainly reprimand the sentries if they discovered the half-dead had been admitted into the cathedral, but I surely wasn't one of them. Just one more reason to keep our visit brief and quiet, lest I draw others into a debate I wanted no part of.

Larsa had stopped just inside the narthex. The day's grayness dulled the mystical hues of the sanctuary's stained glass. In the dimness, the vaulted ceiling, already suggestive of an elaborate ribcage, looked distant and dusty. Representations of past church leaders, some sculpted as they appeared in life, others as skeletal as they must be now, stared down in judgment from columned aisles. Fortunately, none immediately sprang to life to shout down condemnations, thus preserving the pious murmur of parishioners and shuffling acolytes.

"Which way?" Larsa asked brusquely.

I took the lead. "Follow me."

My heart lurched at the flash of crimson. A neglected pair of candles backlit the red of a temple inquisitor, waiting in a nearby prayer alcove. I recognized him, but didn't know him personally— one of Mardhalas's students, but not the High Inquisitor herself, as I'd momentarily imagined. He nodded as our eyes met, watching as we passed.

He hadn't been praying.

I looked back after a few steps more. The inquisitor was walking away, crossing the sanctuary toward the south wing— where the clergy's senior residents quartered. My heart didn't quite settle back into its usual comfortable place.

Larsa followed my look. "What?"

"Nothing. But let's get this over with quickly."

More so than glory or love, birth and death occupy the minds of the living regardless of race, age, nation, or creed. It also occupies their pens more than any other topic, as evidenced by Maiden Choir's three floors of books and records. Iron railings twisted into steep spiral stairways, clinging only tenuously between whole floors sagging under the weight of bookshelves. Several priests— mainly those aged enough to be absolved of daily chores—bent over the main floor's long wooden desks, suffering uncomfortable benches as they pored over yellow pages or marked fresh parchment with fine lines. A slightly elevated desk rose at the back of the room, where the assistants of the cathedral librarian made themselves available to facilitate official requests.

Fortunately, any request made by an ordained priestess was considered official enough. For records, we were pointed toward a small door nearly hidden between stacks of thick reference volumes.

The room was so cluttered I had no sense of its actual size. I felt as though I were breathing through a handful of dusty pages, the walls mostly hidden by workbenches, shelves, and pegboards cluttered with bookbinding tools and fabrics. Past the workspace, rows of old and poorly repaired shelves bowed under the weight of tightly crammed white and black folios, each marked with a concise row of stamped numbers—year, month, volume.

Larsa pulled a black tome from the nearest shelf, flipping it open to reveal a spectrum of yellowed pages. "What are these?"

"Death records." I laid a respectful hand upon a shelf of spines. "Many are copies from civil and family records, but the majority are created here with reports from local graveyards and whatever other details we can piece out."

She flipped though idly, the pages wildly inconsistent in size, color, and quality. "Why?"

"To honor them, to note their lives and their passing. Think of these as books of gravestones."

She looked at me with raised eyebrows and closed the folio. "That's morbid."

I shrugged. "'Morbid' suggests unhealthy. We don't fixate on death, we celebrate it." I pointed to the book next to the one she was replacing. "And not just death. The white ones are birth records."

Larsa scanned the stacks. "The black ones are thicker than the white ones."

"Yeah. People are quick to note deaths and mourn passings, but life isn't celebrated nearly as reliably."

She gave a little hum as she moved deeper between the rows. "It would have been 4657."

"What?"

"The date we're looking for." She didn't look back. "Will hospice files be in with the births or deaths?"

"No, they'll be different, if they're on these shelves at all." I headed down the row next to her, scanning the spines.

It was several minutes before a thin folio sailed through a gap between the shelves, fluttering open and smashing its pages upon the floor. I frowned.

"Something like that?" Larsa's voice came from the adjacent aisle.

I retrieved it, doing what I could to flatten the crinkled pages. It was bound like the death records, but was thinner, with a date stamped in gray. Inside, the records varied: lists of symptoms, treatment methods, feeding schedules, all roughly organized by patient name and admission date, though the system was by no means consistent. These were definitely notes from the lamentation.

Having an example of what one compilation looked like made finding its siblings easier. It wasn't long before we were riffling through records for the year 4657. That period alone spanned multiple shelves, with some months occupying multiple volumes. Larsa started at the beginning of the year, I from the end, pulling volumes, thumbing through the flaking pages, reshelving them in something close to order. Fortunately, it didn't take long.

"'Kindler, A.,'" I read aloud. "'Admitted 18 Lamashtan, 4657. Exhaustion. Malnutrition. Physical abuses.'"

The file wasn't long—nothing compared to some of the repeat patients or unfortunates unfit for life outside institution walls. Only nine pages with the admitting sheet, the record compiled the notes of multiple councilors and nurses, most written in tight, nearly illegible hands. Certain words rose amid the scrawl, made obvious by their repetition: nightmares, paranoia, nyctophobia, uncooperative.

At my intrigued hum, Larsa snatched the file. I held tight, fixing her with one of the patiently bemused looks I recalled from many a seminary instructor. Not interested in actually provoking a fight over common courtesy, I released the book to her as soon as I was sure she'd noted my irritation.

Her own annoyance cooled as she took the collection and verified its contents. "This is what Trice wanted." She snapped the folio closed and folded it under her arm. "Let's get back."

We left the records room and not an eye rose to acknowledge us as we passed through the library proper. Normally there were limitations on what books might be taken from the collection, by whom, and for what purposes. I didn't expect anyone would miss such a specific record, but I quietly promised that I'd see the file back to its proper place.

Obviously eager to leave, Larsa strode ahead of me, retracing our steps through the airy temple passages, strident despite the gaze of sculpted souls that followed us from every column and rib of the vaulted corridors. She didn't seem at all unnerved by the grim decor. Perhaps already being half-dead dispelled some of the mysteries of death. Perhaps she'd simply seen worse.

We passed back into the sanctuary and Larsa halted. The solemn sound of murmured prayers and soft footsteps were gone, replaced by agitated muttering and the rustle of robes. Several of my brothers and sisters had gathered in the nave, acolytes and my fellow priests in the somber shades of the priesthood, but grim crimson flashed among them.

"Sister Losritter." High Exorcist Mardhalas's voice rose above the assemblage, laced with sardonic sweetness. "I've heard there's a new convert you'd like to introduce."

The crowd parted. Mardhalas was attired just as she'd been the previous night, her bloody robes open over a chain shirt and an array of tools designed to hasten the end of Pharasma's enemies. Her silver holy symbol shone bold and bare. Had she not changed since the asylum, or had she prepared for another exorcism?

I stepped past Larsa, swallowing the ball of tension rising in my throat. "High Exorcist. I regret to say you've been misinformed. The *accuser* is here on a matter of state, not spirit." Murmurs rose and several heads lowered at the mention of Larsa's title. "Though I think I might be convincing her to consider her soul's final condition."

Links of chain slithered across one another as Mardhalas approached. "An agent of the crown?" She stopped almost on top of me, staring through me at Larsa. Any courtesy evaporated. "Prove it."

With calm disinterest, Larsa produced a dark iron badge. It was similar to Ustalav's national crest, which united black antlers, a pointed tower, and sixteen red stars upon a field of Pharasmin purple, yet all the stars had fallen except for one, which alighted upon the tower's high window.

Mardhalas barely looked at it before turning to me. "Escorting an agent of the court is above your station, Sister Losritter."

She was right. I opened my mouth, hoping a defense would spill out.

"I requested Miss Losritter's assistance," Larsa interjected. "My time is short and the matter is beneath the high clergy's concern. This seemed the most expeditious course."

"Is your matter of such great secrecy that it demands theft from our library?" Mardhalas's eyes fixed upon the folio slung under Larsa's arm.

"It's not my place to advertise the will of the crown. I assured Miss Losritter that the records would be returned undamaged. As a dutiful citizen, she has trusted me to uphold my word."

"It was my intention to inform the high priestess as soon as the accuser has no further need of me." I tried to sound as sincere as possible. "But I'm lucky to find you here, High Exorcist, so one of the cathedral's elders can grant her blessing."

Mardhalas's eyes narrowed on me. Her reputation for distinguishing lies and extracting confessions was infamous, both within Maiden's Choir's walls and beyond. I hoped I hadn't pushed my luck.

"Why her?" The question summed up the inquisitor's estimation of me.

"We both had business at Havenguard. She was on hand and proved useful." Larsa glanced at me. I don't know if she saw something in my face or if she spoke honestly, but she added, "I won't require her assistance much longer. Till the day's end at the latest."

Mardhalas frowned. "What assistance do you still need? I'm sure one of our more experienced sisters would be better suited to your work."

"Sister Losritter will be fine, thank you. I don't wish to advertise the crown's business any more than necessary."

The inquisitor's stare made her suspicion clear. It passed from Larsa back to me. "She already has her claws in you then, Sister?"

My heart lurched. She knew. "High Exorcist, I don't . . ." My lie was plain.

Rather than condemning me, she leaned toward Larsa, her whisper loud enough for only the three of us to hear. "I smell what you are. Agent of the crown or not, I look forward to putting you back on the right side of death."

Larsa didn't blink and didn't lower her voice. "Thank you for your courtesy, High Exorcist. I look forward to it." She stepped around the inquisitor and headed for the door. "Please join me, Miss Losritter."

With a deferential bow, I hastily followed.

"Sister," Mardhalas called after, "I have spoken to the high priestess on your behalf once already today. Now I will a second time. She wishes to speak with you . . . should you ever rejoin us."

I turned back to her. What was that last comment? What did she think I'd done? My eyes felt suddenly wet. Mardhalas, and behind her several of my sisters, stared, their eyes as cold as the statues around them. I blinked tightly, made a quick bow, and followed Larsa from the sanctuary.

"You've given me a new reason not to bother with religion," Larsa said, climbing onto the wagon.

I gave a polite little laugh, focusing on untying the anxious mare.

Several moments later, when I pulled myself onto the driver's bench, Larsa was watching me.

"That was about to be worse than it was," she said.

I nodded.

"They knew about me?"

"I . . ." I'd tripped over this topic once already, trying to be sensitive about Larsa's state. "I don't think so. Mardhalas did. I think she wanted to be dramatic—to unmask you."

I clicked to the horse and set the cart in motion. I felt like I was fleeing—probably because I thought I was.

"Unmask me? How?"

"By announcing to the others that you're a dhampir."

"Why would she need to? You're all Pharasmin priests. I figured nearly everyone we passed in there noticed."

"Why—no. Not at all." I looked over, just enough to give her a glimpse of my surprise. "Most probably didn't. Certainly when we met I wouldn't have."

"Wouldn't have?" She matched my surprise.

"Doctor Linas told me in the chapel. That's the only reason I even knew. If she hadn't, I probably wouldn't. Even when Lady Thorenly went into hysterics."

I steered the horse across the Waiting Yard, hastening it out of the cathedral's shadow, imagining some acolyte might race out to fetch me at any moment, so long as we remained within its shade. I could feel Larsa's frown.

"My parentage doesn't seem to matter to you," she finally said.

"No." I didn't think about it, just answered. It was mostly honest.

"But it does to your High Exorcist." If there was any emotion in her voice, I didn't hear it.

"More than it should."

"Why?"

"I suppose it's complicated. More complicated than it should be." I sighed. "The goddess teaches that life follows a never-ending spiral, a river that begins in the unknowable, then passes through the gateway of birth, the challenges of life, and the mystery of death, inevitably flowing back to the goddess so she might direct each soul to its place in her design, continuing the spiral into the ages. Thus deviations from the goddess's plan are, to her and her servants, not just abominations, but blockages, dangerous to the entire river's continuation."

I didn't mean to start sermonizing, but it seemed natural—comfortable, despite feeling like I'd just been exiled from the church. Larsa wasn't watching, but she was listening. "Blockages," she repeated.

"The church teaches that the undead are corruptions of Pharasma's plan. Maybe more like stagnant points in the river, where souls become obsessed with life and so don't continue in the stream. All of the goddess's priests, and to an even greater degree her inquisitors, are dedicated to freeing souls that become stuck at the transition between life and what lies beyond. The Lady's will is clear on this matter, but there are debatable nuances.

"Many take a particularly rigid view of the goddess's will. If undeath is an abomination, then so anything touched by the undead must be unclean. By that reasoning, the goddess demands we destroy not just the undead, but anything associated with them. There is a measure of prudence in this, but as with any rule there may be room for exceptions."

Larsa leaned onto her knees, pulling down her hat's brim as we emerged into the sunlight. "Exceptions, like the living offspring of the dead?"

I didn't immediately answer. Many among my faith wouldn't call a dhampir an exception.

Larsa took my silence's meaning. "I see."

"It's . . . difficult. For many of my faith, it's all philosophical. They only know about spirits and undead things from their readings. There's a mathematical simplicity to their judgment, but ultimately it doesn't matter to them. The closest they'll ever come to a vampire is in midwinter stories, and many probably have never even heard of a dhampir."

She looked over. "Your High Exorcist noticed, and likely so did whoever fetched her."

"They're trained to. They see sin in everyone, and in almost everything. Most Pharasmins wouldn't even think to note the sharpness of someone's ears and teeth. Even if they did notice such a peculiarity, though, I doubt they'd leap to vague stories of half-vampires. You're hardly a common lot. The inquisitors, though, they're suspicious of everything."

Larsa nodded. "Good, then. I'm not used to people just *noticing*. Especially as many as have today."

"Try not to worry about it. Except for obviously walking corpses, most of my order would have to rely on the goddess's power to identify a vampire. I'm sure they'd never guess that you're one."

"I'm not." There was a shortness in her voice. I though I'd offended her again, but then she saw fit to explain. "There are vampires—the full-bloods—the old, greedy things from story-books. Then there's their spawn, their tools and playthings. They're like full-bloods, turned through death and draining, but they have only a fraction of a true vampire's power. Sometimes they get loose. When they do, most act little better than stray animals, hunting where they shouldn't and endangering their betters. Tracking and getting rid of those feral things makes up a good bit of my job."

She hesitated, and I thought she might leave it there. "Then there are dhampirs. We're the sad stories that vampires tell, born from unions between vampires and humans. We're cursed with their hunger, but lack their power, trapped between life and undeath. And when full-bloods are forced to accept that we're not just stories, they certainly don't call us vampires.

"But we're also not humans. So we're neither—we're nothing."

I spared a look over at her. She was intent on the pages in her lap. "That's one of the saddest things I've ever heard."

A dismissive humph was her only response.

Moments passed. The cart pulled onto the cobbles of the city street. I resisted the impulse to look back at the cathedral, just in case someone was trying to catch up to us.

Eventually, Larsa gave a mean little snort. "So how would your exorcist 'unmask' me?"

"Many like Mardhalas only see in black and white. Sadly, some of my sisters might not see any difference between you and—I'm sorry to say—some shuffling zombie."

"And you do?"

The comment surprised me. I couldn't blame her, though. She didn't know me or how I'd been raised. One of my order's heads had just threatened her. Why wouldn't she be suspicious?

"I don't." I thought a moment longer. "I know you don't have any reason to believe me, but from what I've seen so far, you'd make a poor story—even for vampires to tell. You're just a person."

She sniffed, but the brim of her hat bobbed in a little nod.

"It's easier to adopt others' opinions than it is to come up with your own. If Mardhalas had announced what you are, I don't really know how the other clerics would have reacted."

"But you don't expect well."

I shook my head. "Especially in the church, it's easy to become a zealot. It's also easy to use zealots. And zealots tend to be far louder than philosophers. I think if Mardhalas had called out what you are, the zealots would have shouted down calmer heads."

She stared calmly ahead.

"That's why I announced that you're an accuser. Maiden's Choir is the royal cathedral. Mardhalas might eagerly 'exorcise' a dhampir in the goddess's sanctuary, but an agent of the crown? That would certainly have unwanted repercussions."

"It certainly would." Larsa's comment sounded like a threat.

I didn't add fuel to the flame.

The accuser idly flipped open the folio in her lap. "You might want to pray for your sisters, at the very least for them to learn the difference between being faithful and being asses."

I couldn't help but chuckle. "Our goddess is the Lady of Mysteries. Many philosophies ebb and flow among her servants. Like a good mother, she allows each of us to make our own interpretations. I think her church is strengthened by a diverse array of views rather than a single, inflexible creed . . . but I agree, arguing can be damned frustrating sometimes."

"Well, you didn't have to throw your calling away on my account."

Her comment wrenched my attention from the road. "What?"

"You said anything touched by the undead was unclean. If I'm unclean, and you've taken to assisting me, then to an ogre like your High Exorcist . . ." She trailed off, her point clear and attention elsewhere.

I didn't bother to answer. Hearing the concerns I'd been tamping down all day laid out so matter-of-factly, and from a stranger, stirred the snake pit of worries in my gut. I felt nauseous, and suddenly steering the cart required a great deal of focus.

Larsa didn't notice.

Several blocks passed before the accuser made a sound. "That bastard!"

At her outburst, my grip tightened on the reins. The cart jerked.

"What?" I split my attention between her, the knotted feeling in my chest, and the agitated horse.

"Get us to Havenguard." She slammed the folio shut, seething.

"What is it? What'd you find?"

She didn't answer. I looked over, then quickly away, avoiding the sneer cementing itself upon her face. Though her lips remained tight, her tongue ran across her teeth, lingering on sharp canines.

In my head, I heard an echo of what I said about her not being a monster. I wondered if I'd spoken too soon.

II

FAMILY DEBT
LARSA

The black-bound hospice records skidded across Doctor Trice's desk, upsetting his inkwell, smudging whatever he'd been writing, and cutting off his meaningless greeting. I shouted as I crossed the office. "You think she's my *mother*?"

His lips disappeared as he looked down at the folio that had just slid into his chest. He lifted it deliberately, moving it out of the way of the pooling ink, and set it aside. He fixed me with a clinically calm expression. "Yes. Though, of course, I can't yet be sure."

I reached the opposite side of the desk and stared down at him, tempted to reach across and grab him by the collar. "I'm not one of your patients. I didn't come here so you could run some experiment to satisfy your curiosity. If you knew that portrait actually was of me—of her—why didn't you say so?"

The door gently clicked shut behind me. Jadain was trying not to intrude.

"It would have been irresponsible. You might look like Ailson Kindler, particularly as she did in her youth—enough, at least, to confuse her delicate sister. You might even sound like her, but . . ." He righted the inkwell and dabbed at the stain with a handkerchief. "The coincidences may only be skin deep."

"I came here about the Thorenlys, not so you could try nailing branches onto my family tree."

He slid his attention to the folio, flipping through, speaking as he skimmed the pages. "You weren't entirely clear what you were here about. The two of you wandered into my office, unannounced, leaving me at something of a disadvantage. Since then, Doctor Linas has related the details of your interview with Lady Thorenly. It doesn't sound like you're investigating an attack by particularly bold brigands."

Presumptuous little . . . "An agent of the crown requires your cooperation. That's all that need concern you."

"Oh, but it's not." Trice flipped pages idly, pausing to skim passages throughout the folio. "'Fangs,' I believe Miss Thorenly mentioned, and multiple killings. This doesn't sound like a raid by your usual housebreakers. Rather, it sounds like a matter someone like you might have unique insight into. And one that affects both a patient in my care and an old friend."

Jadain shuffled into the periphery of my vision, perusing shelves covered in dense medical tomes and morbid anatomical representations. She wisely kept out of the crossfire.

"It's a state concern." I crossed my arms. "Such incidents are dealt with discreetly."

"Dealt with by you?" He sounded almost flippant.

"Doctor Trice." I tried to restrain myself, but certainly wasn't accustomed to being questioned on my responsibilities. "Your service to the crown and the Royal Advisor have put you in a certain favor, but I assure you that whatever concessions you enjoy end far short of details on accuser duties and assignments—particularly mine."

He looked up from the record, his expression combining a boyish grin with dark, calculating eyes. "Fair enough."

Several moments passed. He read a page in its entirety, then another. "The year's about right, I assume?"

"For?"

"The records are marked 4657. I believe that could be about right for your birth year."

Jadain made an amused snort, not taking her eyes from the shelves. "I'm going to bet you're not married, Doctor."

I ignored her. "It could be."

"What?" Jadain's head whipped around. "Come now, that's fifty-five years ago."

"Fifty-six," Trice offered.

"Something like that," I confirmed.

Jadain gaped. "There's no way you're that old. That would make you more than double my age." She chuckled awkwardly. "You couldn't really be more than . . . what, twenty? Twenty-two?"

"Time doesn't grip her as tightly as it does us, Miss Losritter," Trice explained. "There's less for it to cling to, less for the years to strip away."

"That's a prettier way to put it than I've heard before." I examined my hand on the arm of the chair, thin blue veins visible snaking their way through skin a shade I'd only ever seen on the oldest or sickest humans. "You could also say that since death already has a hold on me, it's not in an awful rush to collect."

Jadain stared, but in a low voice finally asked, "Really?"

I met her eyes, not answering or shaking my head either way. I'd appreciated what she'd said in the cart, about me being a poor storybook monster, despite sounding utterly naive. Now, she seemed to be understanding just how naive. She looked like she had just come upon a stray dog and was trying to decide whether it'd be prudent, ridiculous, or dangerous to bolt.

I looked away.

"Kindler would have been in her twenties at the time," Trice went on. "The record lists numerous physical abuses: various minor fractures and scarring, repeated punctures on the neck and wrists. They don't suggest a cause, but that might have been a mercy by her physicians—the victims of vampirism often face certain stigmas. They also note similar repeated but smaller wounds upon the chest." He forged on with scientific indelicacy "She was likely feeding something, and not just blood."

I felt like I was being accused of something.

"This, of course, isn't absolute evidence of your relationship, but in combination with your similar features, it starts building a convincing case."

This attention was making me uncomfortable. I'd never expected this to get so personal. This morning it had just been an attack by rogue vampires. Now it was a message for my grandfather left in the home of . . . what? Supposedly my aunt? An aunt by way of a famous mother who was still . . .

"Kindler." I looked up at Trice. "Where did you say she retired?"

"Ardis." He sounded unsure if he should tell me.

I could feel Yismilla Col's eyes on me, staring through the serving dome on Considine's sideboard. Yismilla Col, Grandfather's former agent in the Old Capital, murdered by my people's most notorious traitor, a man who also happened to be my father.

I spoke warily, still adjusting the pieces in my mind. "Would anyone have any reason to want Miss Kindler . . . harmed?"

Doctor Trice's gaze lowered. "Oh yes," he said gravely.

"Who?"

"It's not as simple as that."

"What's not? Either you know or you don't."

"Earlier Miss Losritter mentioned Ailson's stories." He nodded at Jadain. "But her stories aren't merely fiction."

"Certainly," the priestess said somberly. "Some of the terrible things she writes about are all too real—the walking dead, were-creatures, spectres . . . vampires."

"I don't mean her subject matter, I mean the stories themselves. Most of them actually happened." Deliberateness crept into his voice. "Most of them actually happened to her."

"So they're memoirs?" I asked, but Jadain cut in.

"Wha—" she started incredulously. "*Hunter's Moon*? *Case of the Dreaming Dead*? *Feast of the Nosferatu*? Are you saying those all happened?"

"More or less." Trice nodded. "Her characters are typically based upon herself and her colleagues. I have a copy of *Steps Upon the Sanguine Stair*, over there." He gestured at a low corner shelf. "It's my strange honor to be the inspiration for the character Quintin."

Jadain moved to find the book, but Trice didn't wait for her comparison. "In actuality, though, for all the dread and dark things in her stories, they're typically rosy variations on the truth."

"So she was what? Some sort of adventurer?" I asked.

Trice grimaced. "She was a lot of things, but adventurer doesn't quite reach far enough. She was obsessed. She traveled across Avistan, learning all she could about terrible things. For a while she did it alone, but eventually she fell in with the Pathfinders."

"Really?" Jadain asked from a crouching perusal of Trice's collection. She sounded legitimately surprised. "It seems like every time they show up in her stories, they're either the cause of the problem or incompetents who get themselves killed."

"Yes, well, she had a falling out with the Society," Trice said flatly.

"I've heard constables around Whiteshaw talk about the Pathfinder Society. They're some kind of thrill-seekers or something?" I asked.

"It's a group of explorers, largely dedicated to learning from the past to help create a better future. There are thousands of members, active across the world, organized so they can share their findings, learn from each other's discoveries, and call for help if need be."

"Sounds impractical."

Trice frowned. "Kindler didn't think so. She was one of the Society's foremost experts on unnatural creatures, particularly the undead. I doubt even she could say how many abominations she put an end to, and the accounts she shared with the Society surely saved scores more." A somber look settled over his features. He suddenly looked much older. "I must have written her a dozen times begging her not to leave, but she always was a stubborn one."

"So you're one of them?" Jadain stood with a flimsy crimson book in her hands.

By way of response, he reached into his drawer and produced a fist-sized bauble of dark metal, etched with intertwining lengths of thorny vines. He set it upon the desk and flipped it open, revealing a bejeweled compass face inside, a tiny arrow twitching toward an ornately painted N. Worked into the lid's interior was a symbol like a road stretching to the horizon, lit by a gemstone star.

"So you doctor by day and by night . . . what? Hunt monsters?" I said it like it was preposterous, but I'd just described something close to my role as an accuser. We likely defined "monster" somewhat differently, though.

"No, my days of uncomfortable traveling and tomb-breaking are behind me," he said with an obvious tinge of wistfulness. "Now my role is mostly administrative. I've set aside a house on the asylum grounds to serve as a lodge for Society members in need of a place to work or plan upcoming journeys. But Caliphas isn't exactly a hub of activity for the Society. Most members only pass through on their way north or west to wilder places. Things are usually pretty tame here, which is fine as the asylum demands almost all of my attention."

"Do you think anyone in the Pathfinder Society would want to harm Miss Kindler, then?" I asked. "Perhaps for leaving?"

"Certainly not." Trice didn't give it a moment's thought. "Not only is that not how the Society operates, Ailson Kindler left a hero. Her departure was a major loss and widely mourned, but not resented. Even now I occasionally send Society members passing through Ardis to call on her with news of interesting findings and maybe a few trinkets. She never admits them, but she usually shouts them off loudly enough that at least we know she's doing well."

He grinned, but it swiftly faded. "No. But there are still plenty who might prefer to see her dead. As effective as she was at putting an end to terrible things, her record wasn't flawless. More than once something slipped away or she put an end to a symptom without ever discovering the cause. I trust that even now she can look after herself, but sometimes I do worry that something with a long, bitter memory might come out of the past, seeking revenge."

"When was the last time you checked in on Miss Kindler?" Jadain asked.

"It's been some time." Trice closed his compass. "But after a vampire attack on her sister a visit is certainly in order. While you were collecting these records I asked a visiting Society member to make preparations to travel to Ardis and make sure everything's okay, both with her and with our other people in the city."

I started to open my mouth, but my lips tightened, balking at sharing any details of my discussion with Considine, especially after chiding Trice for asking after details of my assignment. I wrestled with my pride, but pushed past it.

"You're right that vampires attacked Thorenly Glen, but it wasn't random," I blurted. "They were sent by another in Ardis, a rebel named Rivascis."

Both looked at me expectantly, but I'd shared nearly all I was willing. "I met with an informant on our way to Maiden's Choir. I trust his information."

"What do you mean 'rebel'?" Jadain asked cautiously. I shot her a glance, but didn't answer. She let the matter drop.

"Ailson mentioned the name 'Rivascis,' before. Not often, but I know she was tracking him. She never said why, and she never used Society resources to pursue him—she claimed groups were too vulnerable. Every few years, though, she'd get a lead from here or there and immediately head off. She always returned disappointed, and more than once she went off with help and came back alone."

I was surprised that Trice recognized the name. "What was he to her?"

He shook his head. "A bogeyman? I asked more than once, but she never said."

The words echoed through my head: *He's my father.* They were so loud I thought for a moment that I might have spoken them, but I pushed them back. I'd already said too much. This further battered any doubts I had about my connection to Kindler—whatever it might be. A relationship between her and my father, even one that sounded purely antagonistic, couldn't be a coincidence.

"If you're sure this vampire is in Ardis, it's my duty to send Ailson warning and any help I can. Tomorrow morning my agent leaves for Ardis." Trice spoke gravely, falling easily into his administrative role.

He turned to Jadain. "Miss Losritter, I have an agreement with Maiden's Choir granting the asylum priority attention when it comes to exorcisms and related supernatural concerns. I could make the argument that, as Miss Kindler is a former patient, this is a matter of asylum business. As you're practiced as an exorcist and know the details of this matter, I would request you to accompany my agent to Ardis. In return, my contribution to the cathedral will be twenty times the usual donation. Is this something we can reach an agreement on?"

Jadain stammered and blinked several times. "Well, I don't know how practiced I really am as a . . ." She obviously thought better of continuing, choosing not to mention that she'd earned the ire of one of her faith's leaders. She quickly altered her stance. "I will of course have to get the Holy Mother's permission. If she grants it, I can be ready in the morning."

"Good." Trice nodded, then turned to me. "I can also assure you that this is a matter the crown should take an interest—"

I didn't wait. "I'm going. Not because of any of this foolishness about my mother, though. My superiors have their own reasons for wanting Rivascis, and if anyone's going to take his head, it's going to be me."

I turned for the door, not giving them time to ask after my motives. If everything I'd been told in the Old City had been true, if everything I'd learned in my years as an adopted daughter of the dead meant anything, if Rivascis really was my father, then I had more reason than anyone to want him dead.

12

CONFESSION

JADAIN

The Holy Mother would speak with you," Brother Lheald reported, his voice little more than a whisper in the shadowed sanctuary. I glanced at the statue of Pharasma, silent and ominous at the chapel's center. Her eyes were only stone.

I'd only just returned to Maiden's Choir, having walked back to the city from Havenguard. Despite the miles-long hike I'd taken a less than direct route, choosing a path through several of my favorite gardens and quiet avenues. The sun had set some time ago, but it had still taken a couple hours before the cold fog finally drove me back to the steeples and spirals. Lheald, the Holy Mother's aide, had obviously been waiting.

I followed the bald priest, expecting his careful steps to eventually led us to the Holy Mother's chambers. Instead, we reverently approached the altar. Parishioners, mourners, midwives, and all the others who so often sought the goddess's blessing were gone for the day, their prayers lingering only in a few dwindling votives flickering from alcoves and wall-mounted grave markers. There was still a head bowed in the front pew, though, a fragile frame bent under the weight of a long life and an impressive coiffure of snowy ringlets. The Holy Mother was praying.

Lheald halted a respectful number of pews behind the head of our order and gestured to the bench beside her with a liver-spotted hand. I reverently found my place.

The Holy Mother's hands were folded over her heart, a gesture of prayer performed in life and repeated in how we laid corpses in their coffins. She didn't mutter her prayers like some—her lips were still, and her eyes, if they were open at all, were lost in the dimness.

I followed her lead. Being one who too often whispered her words for the goddess aloud, I deliberately kept my lips sealed.

Practiced verses and personal appeals tripped over one another in my mind, a silent prayer-jumble I hoped the goddess understood. It might have been a dozen slow breaths, it might have been an hour, but by the time the Holy Mother lowered her folded hands to her lap I had repeated my prayers at least twice and was struggling with wakefulness. I was still alert enough to follow suit, though, tracing the spiral of Pharasma over my heart with my thumb and dropping my hands.

We listened to the deep silence of the cathedral for several minutes.

"Tell me." Her request bore no judgment or hint of what she might or might not have heard.

I told her everything.

I told her how the High Exorcist requested my assistance, of my failure at Havenguard, of Mardhalas's threat of dismissal from the order. I told her of my anger, certainly at Mardhalas for her harshness, but more at myself for flinching when faced by a soul lingering in blasphemy but also in need of guidance in passing on. Before I realized what I was saying, I was giving words to feelings that had been strangling my heart the entire day. Confusion, hurt, indignation, and worse, more than a little directed toward the goddess herself—in part for abandoning me when I needed her protection, in part for leaving me to wonder if that were actually the case. Had she spurned my faith? Had my faith always been lacking? Was Mardhalas right? Was the goddess something else than what I'd always believed? Was my faith really just imagination?

Between philosophizing and self-criticism, I related the rest of the day's details: meeting the Royal Accuser and hearing of the violence she was investigating, Doctor Trice's request and the visit to our own library, again meeting the High Exorcist, and the discoveries upon our return to the asylum. I concluded with Doctor Trice's second request: that I travel with his emissary to Ardis. It had been an eventful day, but I struggled not to miss any detail, doubling back on my story several times as I recalled this or that detail. I didn't try to hide Larsa's *condition*.

I was exhausted by the time I couldn't think of any more to say. Unburdening myself of so many weighty feelings left ample room in the pit of my stomach for anxiety regarding the Holy Mother's reaction.

"You should go," she said flatly. Though her voice was nothing more than an old woman's whisper, it fell upon me like the cathedral toppling. She wasn't even turned toward me; she just stared at the altar, her expression as craggy as the stone martyrs surrounding us in the shadows. A cacophony of emotions sounded inside me, each with its own question. I opened my mouth, but choked. Heat rose in my face and something stung my eyes.

Then it was all gone.

I stood stiffly and heard my sandals on the stone—echoing, final, and distinctly out of place.

Something cold brushed my hand and I ignored it. When it clamped upon my wrist and spun me around, I looked down into the face of the Holy Mother, standing next to me beneath the statue of the goddess.

"You should go to Ardis," she clarified, only somewhat. Her eyes were as cold and colorless as gravel on a rainy drive.

"Faith can be your life, or it can be your tomb." She squeezed my hand, her grip cool and startlingly strong. "We share the goddess's words, repeat them as they've been taught to us. Even when we offer them in comfort, are we actually speaking in the goddess's name, or are we repeating what we've been trained to say—or what we'd hope the goddess would tell us in our suffering?

"The goddess's voice is not made of stone. It grows and varies, whispering through the spiral and finding its way to all of us. We must always listen for her voice, and recognize it from among all the others, even from the voices of her other servants, even from our own voice."

With her free hand she gestured to the choir, totally hidden among the sanctuary's darkened buttresses. "Amid the chorus, who hears the voice that cracks? Does the song lose its meaning with one stray note?" She placed my hand over my heart, releasing it there.

My jaw was trembling. I couldn't make it stop. "Am I dismissed, Holy Mother?"

"No," she said softly. "But you are free to leave the choir for a time. Sometimes it's better to listen than to sing."

I wasn't sure I knew what she meant, but I nodded like I did. "What about the High Exorcist's recommendation?"

"Faith is Sister Mardhalas's dagger. But faith can be many things—even imperfect things. I have considered her words, and I have considered yours. This is my decision."

I bowed my head graciously, but I felt more shame than gratefulness. "And when my journey is at an end . . ."

"Then you will do as the goddess wills." She glided past me, moving as she always did, with a silent grace greater than her small steps would seem to allow. "As do we all."

I was somewhat startled to discover myself in my cell, my feet having delivered me back to my quarters without my mind's participation. I'd always thought of my room as lavish, as I didn't share it with multiple others like I had during my training back east. In truth, it had exactly enough room to hold my narrow bed, a battered writing desk, and a short chest of drawers. Tonight, though, filled up with the chill dark slipping through the open window, it felt as vast as the sanctuary's airy hall.

Or perhaps I was dwindling.

The Holy Mother's words repeated over and over in my head. With every repetition I tried to recall her tone and expression, searching for intention behind the words. I didn't truly think that she had hidden exile in her meaning—if she wanted to be rid of me she had no reason to flinch from saying so. Yet her words were also far from comforting.

Lighting the desk's dented lantern, I surveyed the room I'd slept in every night for the past two years—the room I wouldn't be sleeping in tomorrow night. It seemed like the moment should feel auspicious. It didn't.

I looked out the narrow window, another luxury of my cell being an impressive view of the cathedral's entry and the Waiting Yard's fountains.

A rider was waiting at the cathedral steps, his sooty horse looming at the border between the brazier light and Caliphas's notorious fog. Though he was as silent and still as a gargoyle, the traveler's broad hat and deep crimson clearly marked him. It was well past midnight, but such was the time our hunters were often forced to act.

I watched. Certainly he was uncomfortable and tired. Surely something distant and dark lay on the path between him and the warmth of his bed. Perhaps even his death was close at hand. If any such concerns wore upon his mind, though, they hadn't deterred him thus far and didn't undermine his confident posture. No matter what forced him into the night, faith was certainly his dagger.

My resentment surprised me.

The sanctuary door opened and High Exorcist Mardhalas stalked down the steps, her cloak a crimson wave behind her. She was too far away to hear, but it didn't seem like her mouth moved, she merely stabbed a rolled parchment into her underling's hand. The inquisitor and his steed launched into the fog, darkness and mist muffling the sound of hooves upon the plaza stone.

I followed the shape until it vanished, and the galloping pulse until it faded into the sounds of the city.

When I looked back to the stairs, the High Exorcist's gaze was on me.

13

SCARS
LARSA

"Shit." The blood smear high on my cheek was visible even in the mirror across my suite. Hopefully to anyone who might have noticed in the hotel lobby it just looked like . . .

Like what? Like I'd cut myself shaving my eyelashes?

Well, hopefully it didn't look like I'd just torn open the wrist of a Virholt Street pickpocket and drained him to within a few drops of his life. How did it even get there anyway?

Scratching the scabby smear off my cheek, I threw my drenched cloak over the half-back of a ridiculous chaise lounge I'd never sat in—its elaborate damask of storks and golden leaves ruined by countless past soakings. I usually didn't bother with candles, seeing almost as well without them as with, but they made certain things easier, like using mirrors and writing. And I had two letters I didn't want to write.

Though my suite had an adjoining office—and servant's room, kitchen, and dining room—I carried a twisted brass candelabrum into the master bedroom. It was probably the first time in over a year that light spilled into the room, and the musty shadows seemed reluctant to part. It wasn't that the room was designed to be cavernlike—quite the contrary, in fact. Elegant glass doors covered the dawn-facing wall, beyond which opened a balcony on the Majesty's penthouse floor. If I recalled correctly, it presented an impressive view of Restoration Park and the spidery towers of the royal palace beyond.

Now, though, the many-pillowed layers of a decadently over-sized mattress slumped against the curtained windows. Blankets and rosy veils that once also covered the nobly banistered bed joined the upright mattress in reinforcing the drawn curtains, creating a barricade against even the most insistent daybreak.

The bed frame remained, displayed at the room's center like the skeleton of some primeval beast. I hadn't left it entirely unused, though. Filling less than a third of the space meant for the repur-posed mattress lay a coffin of plain pine.

It was the reason I'd replaced the apartment's lock with my own, after having to improvise an awkward and utterly unbeliev-able explanation to a particularly insistent maid—even after my multiple and unmistakable requests never to be disturbed. Not that I needed a coffin, like a true vampire did. In the Old City beneath Caliphas's streets, coffins were synonymous with rest. Being raised there as Grandfather Siervage's ward, my resting place was no different. Even when I was old enough to learn of the differences between the Old City's residents and those living above, beds were something I still didn't feel like I fully grasped. I eventually overcame my fear of rolling out of bed, but still always felt strangely exposed sleeping in something without solid walls. So when, at Grandfather's command, I was forced to make these apartments my home, I insisted on one luxury.

I sat my light on the brow of the bedroom desk and slid open the roll top. Although I'd never used them, the hotel-provided quills were sharp, the stoppered ink only slightly crusty, and the paper woven with enough linen to be pleasantly soft. The first message came easily.

Sir,

Resolving our business demands I pursue avenues beyond the capital. I will report in person when practical.

Accuser L.

Diauden would want more details, but between what his informants had already or would soon report, he'd have enough to deduce my destination and general purpose. Since it had sounded like he and Doctor Trice were acquainted, the old spymaster could even ask after the particulars at Havenguard. The note was merely a formality to reassure the Royal Advisor that I was keeping his interests in mind.

The second would not be so easy.

Grandfather,

I snatched the sheet and chewed it into my palm, spitting it into a wastebasket embossed with laurel leaves. Too demure—I wasn't asking permission.

Your Grace,
    As you surely know, your agent Yismilla Col has been fatally removed from her position in Ardis. Evidence suggests that the traitor Rivascis is responsible for this disrespect. Anticipating your response, I am already en route to the Old Capital, intent on assessing the situation there and putting an end to whatever rebellion I discover. Necessity and the need for haste prevent me from personally seeking your counsel in this matter, a discourtesy for which I beg forgiveness. I hope that my success in expunging this disgrace from our family name will redeem me in your regard.

                                Dutifully,
                                L.

I read it over a dozen times, making minor corrections and subtly refining the tone. It committed at least three blasphemies:

presuming to know Grandfather's will, acting without his leave, and blatantly lying about my reasons for not consulting him.

My message was nowhere in the words I'd written. As was everything with Grandfather, it was all subtext and suggestion. He would know that I knew his mind better than I demonstrated— even as his pride bristled. He would know that I knew he had deliberate plans when it came to Rivascis. He would also know my urge to avenge myself against the one they called my father, to simply act, to speed to Ardis, blade bare the entire journey. Yet he'd have to acknowledge that I still paused to write, that regard and duty still tempered my action, even as I disobeyed his unspoken demand.

Or he'd set a dozen deathless slaves on my heels and they'd take my head before I ever neared Ardis.

Was it worth the risk?

I pulled back my sleeve. Scars without a hint of pigment criss-crossed my pale forearm, following the faint blue trails of my veins. A map of Caliphas's slums would have been less chaotic. Most of the marks were tiny nicks, just enough to make the blood flow. Others were longer trails, languorous, deliberate slices that had, for a time, split my skin into yielding lips. The worst were a pair of savage gashes that had dug indulgently deep, almost crippling my arm. I hadn't inflicted even one of the marks upon myself— though I'd considered it often enough.

I hated them. Looking at the ugly marks turned my stomach. Sometimes I almost forgot about them, my leathers proving quite effective at simulating a second skin. Invariably I'd catch some glimpse, though—along my wrist, at my ankle, slipping from under my collar. When I did, every track, every crime across my body caught fire. I could feel them all—ghosts of violence that never faded. Memories of the nightmare that was my youth. The life he—they—had made for me.

It wasn't easy to decide who I hated more. Luvick Siervage, the vampire I and dozens of others called "Grandfather," was an obvious target. The ruler of the Old City, he was easily the eldest and most vile creature dwelling in Caliphas—and he claimed I was one of his favorites. He proved it by calling me "Granddaughter," a title he foisted upon few. Even still, there was no question that I was just one of his pawns. Certainly any favoritism he felt was for the novelty of my dhampiric existence, not for me personally. I was a tool, one he saw myriad uses for. Today, it was as an operative among the Royal Accusers, one who could walk among the living and serve as a bridge between his dominion and that of Diauden's prince. Yet before, it was merely as a thing that bled.

What I'd had of a childhood was a blur of cold and darkness. He raised me and those few like me among the dead, in the lightless, reeking depths of the Old City. His kind knew nothing of cold or discomfort, and mocked us when we were hurt or sick. We learned to fear our own blood and those barely leashed undead that Grandfather had assigned as our protectors. When we disobeyed or performed poorly, Grandfather granted his other children their vices. "Don't mar the skin that shows"—that was his only order. That was the only mercy the vampires showed the half-blood children raised in their crypts.

Only the strong survived.

Those of us who endured eventually became too valuable to waste on feeding thirsty corpses. The most terrifyingly joyous day of my life had been when Grandfather had moved me to the Majesty Hotel, assigning me to work among the living for as long as he willed. Yet dread hung over every moment of near-freedom, as I knew that, at any time, he might yank back my chain. I'd dreamt of a thousand ways I might disobey him—that I might escape if his order came. Realistically, though, each ended with death. There was no way I could escape the sire of a hidden vampiric nation. It might take years, but Grandfather could not allow a slight to stand, and would not be disobeyed.

I hated him, but he had my respect. He was a monster, but one I understood. Deliberately, in all my youth, he'd never raised a hand against me—not personally. That wasn't mercy, but it assured that, somehow, something frail in me loathed him less than the others. Grandfather was the nightmare I recognized, the thing in the dark that I knew well enough to give a name.

And for my entire life, he ensured I knew one other name: Rivascis.

I'd never met the man, but Grandfather had told me a great deal about him. In life, Rivascis had been an actor who'd charmed courts across the world. In death, he'd been Luvick's favorite, so much so that the vampire lord had called him "Son." Supposedly it was a great thing to be deemed heir to Grandfather's nation—a position so vaunted, so rare, that none had held the title in my life. None spoke of it in the Old City, but when Rivascis betrayed Grandfather, it had stung.

I didn't know the particulars, and none of Grandfather's slaves jeopardized themselves by sharing—not even Considine. All I'd gleaned was that Rivascis had fled the Old City against Grandfather's wishes, spoiling some scheme that had amused Luvick at the time. When he did escape, he'd done so alone—despite the fact that I'd been born just months before. Although it was forbidden to even speak Rivascis's name in the Old City, its residents—my nightmarish aunts and uncles—and even Grandfather himself, made it clear that I was the daughter of a traitor. Worse than being a half-breed, I bore the sin of my father's betrayal, making me a convenient outlet for countless slights and vague revenges. Some who bit me claimed they could smell my father in my fear or taste his cowardice in my blood. And when I lay weak from bleeding and sore from the wounds of arrogant leeches, I'd hear Grandfather's voice through the dark: *If you must blame someone, blame your father.*

And I did.

I'd never met the man, but I hated him still. Intellectually, I knew it was just another of Grandfather's manipulations, a life-long ploy to turn me into a weapon against his treacherous son. I was too willing to play along, though. I didn't blame the snakes for their bites, I blamed the one who threw me into their pit.

Every one of my thousand scars, I blamed on him.

I read my letter once more. It felt more juvenile, more obvious with each line—especially as its recipient was more than a thousand years old.

I crumpled the page, flicked a candle off its setting, and kicked the wastebin blaze into the bedroom's immodest fireplace.

Grandfather be damned. If I was to be killed, let me get killed doing something for myself.

I was parched again.

Snatching my still-damp cloak, I headed back out. If I was lucky, I knew just the place off Virholt Street with a few drops still untapped.

14

FINAL PREPARATIONS
JADAIN

Y ou're late!" I shouted, teasing Larsa as she came through the asylum's gardens.

Havenguard presented an ominous facade, but the grounds behind the institution's stone and bars had been lovingly cultivated into a series of precisely arranged flowerbeds. Some were little more than dirt patches, plump with nearly ripe vegetables, while others were dance floors for flowered lattices and decoratively sculpted trees. It was only moments after dawn, and already a handful of doctors and distant orderlies had led freshly dressed patients into the open grounds. Some talked in small groups, others drifted to visit their favorite plants, and a few took up wooden spades to mulch and replant as needed. Over it all repeated the soothing lapping of surf upon the nearby cliffs.

It was difficult not to compare the peaceful, even idyllic, therapies here to the struggles common to the nearby city. Perhaps we should all be committed every once in a while.

The morning haze blessed the sun with a soft, golden aura as it rose over the water. Larsa obviously didn't share my appreciation—her hat was lowered as if against a midday glare.

"Late?" she asked irritably, approaching the half-loaded cart I leaned against.

I retracted the joke. "Nothing."

She eyed the already loaded packs and cases. "It's hardly a fortnight's journey. Is all of that yours?"

"Nope." I toed my reliable rucksack. "Just this."

"What's all that then?"

"Trice insists on outfitting our trip."

She cocked an eyebrow, but something past me caught her attention. I looked over my shoulder at the modest cottage backing up against the sea cliffs.

"Well, that's what he said." I nodded at the man coming through the cottage door, bearing a third matching wooden case toward the wagon.

It was obvious he wasn't from Ustalav. Our people were known for their icy paleness or drained olive hues—with those of less seemly Kellid ancestry, like myself, having ruddier traces. A hint of bronze underlaid his skin. That same metal seemed to sharpen most of his features. With his slightly hooked nose and round chin, his face had an openness to it, undisguised by a head of dark scrub. He wasn't old, but I couldn't honestly tell if he might number more or less than my twenty-six years. Although he didn't seem to be hiding his foreign heritage, he wore local dress, a dingy vest and jacket common to many of Caliphas's working sorts. A sunny scarf peaked from beneath his cloudy coat, daring just at bit of color.

He grinned as he approached and gently set the box on the back of the wagon. It wasn't a large case, but he was hardly some dockworker—there was a compactness to him, like someone used to running. He slid the baggage into place with the others.

"Good morning," he said cheerily with a bow of his head.

I gestured to him. "Larsa, this is Tashan Essesh."

"Miss Larsa." He bowed to Larsa again, this time more deeply. His voice had only the barest accent, something charming in the "R" sound. I pinched back a smile.

He straightened. "Venture-Captain Trice bids me travel with you to Ardis, as our interests cross there."

"Venture-Captain?" Larsa asked.

"Doctor Trice's position within the Pathfinder Society. He's a senior official for the region, and I'm honored that he's chosen me to assist in this business." Tashan practically beamed.

"Has Captain Trice explained our business in Ardis to you?" Larsa hardly sounded as friendly.

"Miss Jadain is an official of Pharasma's church. You are an official of the nation's crown. Our concerns are complimentary, but distinct." He spoke like a soldier. "That's how he explained the matter to me, and that's all I need know."

"And what's your business in Ardis?" she asked.

"I'm planning an expedition to Sarkorian ruins in the north. Ardis is on my route, so I don't mind familiarizing myself with the way, especially with company."

Larsa's eyes fell upon the wagon's load. "All this is yours, then?"

"Provisions committed to our travels." Tashan gestured to the assortment of cases and packs. "Food, cooking supplies, dry wood, blankets, tents, hunting and fishing gear, various tools, emergency supplies."

"Ardis is fifteen nights off, by road the entire way. It looks like there's enough here to keep us in the wild for a month."

"Venture-Captain Trice has been generous." He gave an excited smile. His enthusiasm was adorable, but I agreed with Larsa that the preparations seemed a bit excessive.

Larsa lifted one end of a wooden pole out the wagon's bed—it was easily ten feet long. She raised a brow dubiously.

"You never know." Tashan shrugged. Her doubtful expression didn't change, but she dropped it back in place

"There's more?" She marched toward the cottage door.

I chuckled, having played the same part in exactly the same scene just moments before Larsa's arrival.

"Oh no, Miss Larsa, I'll take care of it. If you'll wait with Miss Jadain, we'll be ready to leave soon." He smiled with proud politeness, like a young noble showing off his manners before company.

Larsa scoffed and marched on.

Tashan jogged after her. "Miss Larsa, please! If my mother knew I'd let a woman load her own bags, she'd never speak to me again." His hand went to her forearm, no more than a gentle touch.

I cringed.

Larsa wheeled on him, smacking his hand with a solid crack.

"Your mother isn't going to make me another moment later to Ardis than I already am. Now help, or stay out of the way." She spun, red hair slashing behind her. She disappeared into the ivy-covered cottage, but her voice emerged a second later. "And if I hear you say 'miss' again, I'll throw you over those cliffs."

Tashan looked back to see me covering my smile, his eyes wide. I nodded a warning, followed by a shrugged secondhand apology. Summoning back his boldness, he followed Larsa inside.

I didn't join them, happy to let Tashan have his way. He had changed our long walk to Ardis into a long ride, after all. It seemed like the least I could do.

Larsa and Tashan made a few more trips back and forth from the house.

"That's it," Larsa said, dropping a dusty burlap sack. She drifted away toward the cottage's shadiest corner.

Tashan was several minutes following, eventually emerging with his personal baggage: a dingy white pack, an unsheathed sword with a polished bronze blade, and an elaborate contraption of twisted red glass. He loaded them carefully into the wagon, opening a padded case and carefully placing the vase-like glass device inside.

I asked about it, as much with my expression as words.

"A hookah. A water pipe, for smoking . . . whatever have you. They're terribly relaxing. I'll show you when we make camp tonight."

I made an interested noise and nodded politely, having no actual intention of taking him up on his offer. Once his effects were stowed, he jogged off to fetch our packhorse—eager either to finally get underway, or to prevent Larsa or me from claiming the errand for ourselves. He pretended not to hear my offer to help.

I joined Larsa in the shadow of a grizzled chestnut tree shouldering the cottage's eastern face. She was watching the white-clad forms drift through the gardens—peaceful, but more than a little eerie. Two in particular had captured her attention: Doctor Trice and, a half step behind him, Doctor Linas in a fresh white coat. They followed the mossy flagstone path toward the cottage, their interest obviously not entirely on the patients this morning.

"Ready to be off?" Doctor Trice asked once close enough to be heard over the surf. His hair was tamer than yesterday, likely owing to the morning's care. It looked like the weight of his work hadn't settled onto his shoulders yet this morning.

"Yes, sir. Just as soon as Tashan returns with the horse." My own words surprised me, sounding more enthusiastic than I'd meant them. Yesterday's troubles had unfolded so quickly that I hadn't realized just how honestly excited I was to get out of the city and see a bit of the countryside. The Old Capital as well, although I had no idea what might meet us there. Ardis was supposed to be an impressive, history-rich place, home to kings and queens—when we still had them. This might not be a holiday, but it was certainly a break from the prayers and tears of Maiden's Choir.

Trice nodded. "Good, good. You're all introduced, then."

"He seems young." Larsa didn't hide her disapproval.

"Tashan?" The doctor shrugged. "Maybe. He comes well recommended by my compatriots in Isger."

"You seem to be putting a lot of faith in a messenger you don't know."

"It's true I don't know Tashan well, but he's come a long way without much. In my experience, anyone who can make that claim knows a thing or two about getting along in the world. Also, if he's clever enough to earn himself a Society membership, he's done something right."

"You don't know what that something is?"

"He's been in the city less than a week and my schedule leaves little time for entertaining. So no, we're not on familiar terms." A touch of annoyance crept into the doctor's voice. "But whatever virtues my usual agents might possess, Tashan overshadows with presence. He is available, able, and ready—a perfect fit for the errand."

Larsa's brow arched. "And if it's more than an errand, he's expendable?"

"If it's more than an errand he'll have the opportunity to make good on his recommendations." He reached out a hand to Doctor Linas, who snapped a thin, tightly wrapped brown parcel into his palm. "I'm giving this to Tashan. It's a message for Miss Kindler, along with her file from Maiden's Choir."

He noticed my frown—the record was my order's property, after all. "I'll be sure to make an additional donation to the church, since their property was mislaid while in my care. Regardless, I'm sure Miss Kindler will appreciate putting hands on the last copies of these reports. Hopefully it will also make her more receptive to your visit."

Tashan was returning from the stables leading a speckled gray draft horse, a sturdier—and hopefully better-tempered—sort than the mare from yesterday. Between the less ominous wagon and the more impressive horse, I wondered if our prior travel conditions had been Doctor Linas's revenge for disrupting her peaceful schedule.

"As far as he's concerned," Trice said before Tashan entered earshot, "this journey is nothing more than an errand—one both crown and church hold interest in—but ultimately a page's work. He knows nothing of this parcel's contents or those involved."

His eyes locked with Larsa's. We both nodded as the Pathfinder led the horse to the edge of our circle. Tashan tried to match our serious expressions, but the way his eyes skipped from face to face belied his eagerness.

Trice greeted him in a language that seemed to use significantly more of his mouth than our native Taldane. Tashan smiled and repeated the words with a few variations.

The doctor winced. "When you return, I'll find the bottle of shedeh I've hidden away if you promise to point out some of the ways I've been butchering your language."

"Not at all, doctor. Your Osiriani is especially good for a northerner." Tashan grinned, though it was obvious his superior wouldn't be so easily placated.

Trice passed the tightly wrapped parcel to Tashan and moved on to business. "This package is for Miss Ailson Kindler and her alone. Although the contents are neither valuable nor dangerous, they are private. You will deliver it and convey the Society's esteem. Upon doing so, you are to respectfully indulge Miss Kindler's wishes and, should it please her, return any correspondence she might have."

Tashan gave a single solid nod.

"Do you have any questions about your assignment?"

"No, sir."

"Travel to Ardis, this time of year upon the Crown's Procession and New Surdina Road, should take about fifteen days. Allowing for about three days in Ardis, then your return trip, I expect to see you back in approximately a month's time. Understood?"

Tashan made some deferential acknowledgment

"Good." Trice turned to Larsa and me. "And do you have all that you need?"

Larsa snorted.

"More than enough, thank you, Doctor." I touched my amulet. "May the Lady bless you for your generosity."

Trice hardly spared Larsa a glance. "I look forward to hearing of your journey—I hope it goes as smoothly as possible. May fortune and your gods watch over you."

With that, he started back toward the gardens and the enfolding arms of the asylum beyond.

Doctor Linas didn't spare a look or word. We might as well be strangers—not that I'd expected heartfelt well wishes from the detached doctor. She fell into silent step behind Trice the moment he passed.

"Give me just a moment and we'll be ready to go!" Tashan was already moving, leading the colorless gelding.

I glanced sideways at Larsa after watching him go. She'd surprised me with how quiet she'd been. "Are you all set?"

"Except for disposing of some extra baggage." She was glaring at Tashan.

"He was just trying to be polite about loading the cart." I tried to play peacemaker, not relishing the idea of carrying disputes with us all the way to Ardis.

She shifted her glare. I grinned innocently.

"Trice seems to trust him," I offered more seriously.

"Trice trusts his club. He doesn't seem to know a thing about this one."

"Well, fortunately it's an easy trip. We'll be in Ardis soon enough, meet with Miss Kindler, then be on our way back."

"That's the story for the kid." She looked at me sharply, then away—considering. "And you'll be more useful prepared . . ." she muttered, more to herself than me.

When she looked back, there was a decision in her eyes.

"You know a part of the story—certainly more than you should." Her voice lowered. "I'm breaking a royal edict telling you this. I've silenced some who know less. But if you're going to walking into this, I'm not going to be the only one watching for the teeth of a trap."

I nodded, a part of me quite certain that I didn't want hear what she had to say. The apprehensions I already had about the accuser and this errand began multiplying.

"You know we're not just visiting Trice's old wet nurse. There's something gone wrong in Ardis, and it has to do with things old and terribly dangerous." Her gaze was intense— serious and a little sad. "Do you understand how much stronger I am than you?"

Her question was blunt, but it wasn't an insult. Of course, I had no idea.

"How much faster I am? How much longer I'll likely live? The only thing that doesn't make my blood a blessing is that your people call it a curse." She paused, blame in her eyes. "But then, so do mine. I can walk where they can't, pass as human in ways they can't, stand under the sun without being burned. But despite that, I'm a curiosity—a runt. I'm still one of them, but I'm not 'of the blood' in the way they are."

Despite the burden of her experience, her matter-of-fact tone was utterly detached, like a widow claiming she'll be fine.

"Because of that, when a bargain was made with the humans— when my people needed someone to work with our prey and their laws—I was offered up. They said it was because I could pass, but it's really because it's work too demeaning for any true vampire. So I serve among the Royal Accusers and help keep the nation's nobles in line. But rather than spying on mansions and attending masquerades like most, I skulk in alleys and sewers, making sure the most brazen of my people don't jeopardize the truce. I mind the affairs of my people to safeguard a land too terrified to even acknowledge our presence."

Disdain dripped from every word. I could practically see the fangs glinting behind her lips. A slow shiver crawled up my back.

For not the first time since I met Larsa, something in me acknowledged that she wasn't just cold and misunderstood.

"It's my duty to help the humans preserve their delusions of control. In return, my people live out of sight and feed only on those who won't be missed. It's not a flattering arrangement, but it preserves the lives of hundreds of vampires and countless humans."

I wanted to disbelieve. It'd be an easy thing not to accept, after all. The very idea of our crown allowing monsters to live among us, to feed on us, sounded crazy. My eyes inadvertently strayed to the asylum.

When I looked back to Larsa, she was staring, watching my thoughts play out across my face. What reason would she have to lie? Her skin seemed suddenly drained—unhealthy, bloodless even. Was she, a half-vampire, her own proof?

"Ellishan Thorenly," I cautiously ventured, choosing for the moment to accept her claim and racing to chart the implications. "She and her family would be missed."

Larsa nodded. "Not all of my people accept the truce with the humans. Every vampire has a prideful streak, but those who refuse to restrain themselves jeopardize us all. I track down any who break the terms of the truce and either report or put an end to them before too much damage is done." A humorless half-smile crossed her face. "It doesn't make me popular."

She was like Mardhalas, a hunter of the dead. The difference was that she was one of the things she hunted. It occurred to me how terrible it must be to work as an assassin against your own people. Terrible, but I was finding it more difficult to pity her.

Her grin faded. "Usually my investigations led me after reckless young vampires or arrogant foreigners, but that's not what I expect in Ardis."

"The one you mentioned to Trice—the one you said sent those murderers to Lady Thorenly's home."

She nodded. "Rivascis Siervage. He's old, and among my people, that means dangerous. We've pursued him for a long time. Now that he's come out of hiding, I plan to take his head." She removed her hat and pulled her scarlet hair back into a tight ponytail. "You're going to help me with that."

I didn't let her presumption rankle me. "You called him your father."

Her jaw tightened. "Yeah."

"Does that have anything to do with—"

"It's my duty to slay vampires who violate the truce. Rivascis has done that. I've never met him, and I'm not some human whelp he turned into a slave. He's nothing to me but an outlaw." She sounded like she believed most of that.

I gave a slow nod and didn't press. "Your people, they've been after this Rivascis for a long time?"

"Yes."

"I assume that hasn't gone well."

She replaced her hat, but didn't answer.

"Others have gone after him. Did any return?"

"None."

"It sounded like Kindler did."

"That's entirely why I plan to meet her. If she truly made a hobby of hunting Rivascis, I want to find out how she's still breathing."

That sounded thin. "So tips from a retired Pathfinder and my prayers are going give you your advantage?"

"We'll certainly see. Even if they don't, I don't have to play by the same rules as the other vampires we've sent after him. I know what he is and his weaknesses. That's an advantage."

It was still far from a plan. "I suppose we'll have plenty of time to come up with details on the road."

Something in her neck twitched. It didn't seem like she'd be asking for suggestions.

"Something about this one really gets to you, huh?" I knew I was walking on delicate ground. "If I'm to be helpful, I hope you'll come to trust me with why."

Adjusting her hat's brim, she started toward the cart.

I found my enthusiasm for the trip waning, especially if she thought I was going to be taking orders the whole way. "Remember, though, my church's arrangement with Doctor Trice is for me to see to Miss Kindler. That's my first duty."

"Fine." She slowed but didn't turn. "But you might want to hope that she's dead."

"*Honestly?*" That kind of lashing out seemed beneath even her cynical nature.

She gave a detached look over her shoulder. "Rivascis already struck Kindler's family half a nation away. If you're intent on being her new protector, then you're probably making yourself a target. Maybe you'll rethink how much you want to help me once the heroic sheen wears off your assignment."

She went to join Tashan, who was waving from the driver's bench of the loaded wagon, expression sunny and eager to be off.

15

EVIL'S MARK
LARSA

They left me on a hill.

Vauntil was the first burg we'd seen sizable enough to call itself a town, but that wasn't any reason to spend the better part of the day there. My companions didn't share my opinion, though.

They both assured me it was a lovely spot, insisting the surrounding lavender fields made it seem like the whole country-side was wearing the town's famed perfumes. They said my vantage ensured I'd see anyone coming up from the Crown's Procession—the highway we'd been traveling the past two days. They said they'd make a quick call at Pharasma's shrine to learn anything of interest.

They didn't say they'd be all day.

Something over a mile away, pale buildings and rooftop gardens spilled across a much broader hill than mine. Colorful and quaint, Vauntil was Caliphas's niece from the country. She was pretty in a naive way, and made a show of being carefree. Lazily rocking wagons heaped with like-colored flowers made their way up from the fields, as if the townsfolk had a diet far different from the cereals of most villages. The lazy course of the Raiteso River wound its way beneath the town, unburdening itself of cask-laden skiffs into the blue-black waters of Avalon Bay.

It was all something out of some too-idyllic scene from a lady's dressing chamber. In my experience, the most inviting faces were the ones hiding the most. Fortunately, I wasn't interested in making Vauntil my problem.

It was past noon by the time I picked out the slightly deeper twilight of Jadain's robes amid the wine stain of the roadside lavender fields—the trailing speck of Tashan's yellow scarf giving her away. She said her people had, amid the common traffic, noted a coach passing south several days ago, as well as one of her faith's inquisitors headed north a day or so earlier. The first I'd seen in the drive at Thorenly Glen. The second didn't seem relevant, but caused Jadain to frown—from our discussion at Maiden's Choir, I could see why. Beyond that, the local priests didn't have anything useful to add.

With no more excuses to tarry, we circled the town and headed west.

The New Surdina Road tracked the Raiteso River back to it distant mountain origins, winding through lands holding Caliphas county's rich wine country and the estates of many of its most influential nobles. Fortunately, like the Crown's Procession, regular travel warranted the road be paved and well maintained, and we made good time.

Over the course of the next two days we followed the Raiteso. From Vauntil, the Hungry Mountains were nothing more than misty shapes on the horizon, their snow-capped peaks easy to mistake for clouds in the distance. But every hour they grew more concrete, more formidable, and more obviously opposed to visitors. The even rise and fall between dales gradually gave way to a slow climb. Brooding clouds regularly bloomed amid the peaks, carrying short cold showers into the lowlands. Even the numerous hamlets and side roads winding off toward austere estates became rarer, as most settlers had the sense to heed the mountains' none-too-subtle warnings.

Or it might have been the guards.

Setting out from the capital, we'd passed several patrols of the Crown Guard. The tower and antlers of Ustalav's national seal proudly shone on their breastplates and the barding of their shaggy black fell ponies—the prided steeds of the riders of Amaans, horses renowned for sturdiness and bravery. After passing Vauntil, the patrols had changed. Gone were the simple dark breastplates and fur cloaks of the royal riders, replaced by crimson-clad soldiers that would look more at home on a parade ground than the road. Each group included a single lancer whose weapon flew an elegant red pennant bearing the silhouette of a hawk with sweeping antlers.

"Whose men were those?" Tashan leaned over to ask, but not until we'd rounded a bend in the road. They'd scrutinized us intently, going out of their way to split ranks and flank the cart as they passed.

"The countess's troops," Jadain said from the bench next to him.

"They don't look like the others." Tashan looked back to where crimson still peeked through the thin woods.

"Because they aren't like the others," I added from my uncomfortable lounge in back. "They serve the countess. The others served the prince."

"But the countess serves the prince." He sounded unsure.

Jadain snickered. "Not if she made the rules."

I turned just enough to see the look of confusion deepening on Tashan's face. "Formally, yes, but there's tension there. These are the countess's lands."

Tashan looked about at the drizzly woods. "Since where?"

"Did you cross Lake Encarthan to get here?" I asked.

"Yes."

"Then since you set foot in Ustalav."

His brows screwed together. "All of this, then? The city, too?"

"All of Caliphas county, including the city of Caliphas, are the lands of the Caliphvaso family—the countess's family."

"But then, what about the prince? If the capital is where the royal palace is, surely he must rule there."

I tried not to smirk. He was flailing over a system we Ustalavs took as second nature, despite its complexities. "The prince rules from Caliphas, but his home is in Odranto, much farther north."

Tashan pondered this. "So then who were the soldiers we passed before?"

"Near the capital? Members of the Crown Guard, our national army. Soldiers whose first loyalty is to the throne."

"So your prince allows his servants to keep their own armies, then rules from within their lands?"

I nodded.

"He must trust his counts a great deal."

I joined Jadain in laughing this time, the Osirian's innocent question made all the more comic by his clear bewilderment.

"What's funny?" A hint of frustration tinged Tashan's voice.

I stifled my laughter. "Given the choice, the prince would bed down with a pack of wolves before his counts."

"If they're disloyal, why keep them?"

"They're not disloyal. They just hate each other."

Tashan stared. "I don't understand."

"Let me try," Jadain said. "The prince rules the nation, yes?"

"Yes."

"And the nation is divided into counties, which are largely ruled by counts, yes?"

He was slower to answer this time. "Yes."

"But the prince and the counts, they're all just nobles, right?"

"I suppose."

"So what's the difference?"

He pondered. "Well, in my country, the family of the Ruby Prince was chosen by the gods and given the right to rule. Is it not so here?"

"No," I chimed in. "Ustalav's first royal family died out centuries ago. The Ordrantis were chosen to rule only because few other families were as old. They were just counts before that."

"So your prince—forgive me if this is insulting—is no different from your counts?"

"In all but title and tradition, yes." Jadain grimaced, as if revealing a dirty secret.

"Then what keeps them loyal? Why don't your other counts just call themselves princes and use their armies against him?"

"Tradition," Jadain offered with a shrug.

I added, "And the fact that they all hate each other too much to cooperate, even in rebellion."

Tashan's expression became distant. A moment passed before he asked, "And this arrangement, it works for your people?"

"Not in the least." Jadain smiled.

Tashan shook his head, still perplexed. He obviously thought he was missing a joke. But the only joke was that we acknowledged and more or less accepted our nation's baroque, utterly dysfunctional government.

Jadain offered him a pat on the shoulder. "My father told me there's a saying in Sinaria: 'A good heart rarely has a good name.'"

The foreigner stared at her for a long moment. "You Ustalavs, you are a strange people."

She shook her head. "My friend, just wait and see."

As night approached, Jadain noticed a weathered wooden sign etched with the words "The Trail's Tail." Turning the cart off the main road, we followed the arrow-shaped marker down an uneven wooded path only to find the charred shell of a building, its timbers scorched, its roof and porch collapsed. The destruction was years old, moss and ivy having done considerable work reclaiming the building. Broken glass still glinted in a few of the windows, reflecting just enough to suggest movement amid the shadows collected inside. Three splintered posts leaned before what remained of the front stairs.

Jadain stopped the wagon at the path's abrupt end and I hopped down. I knew the posts were grave markers before I even left the cart. I only bothered with them to see what was written on each.

Approaching, I could make out Pharasma's spiral on all three, crudely etched near the top, but in reverse. The backward mark wasn't a mistake; it was an insult to the dead, meant to confuse their spirits' paths and prevent them from finding the goddess's judgment. On each was a single word: *liar, eunuch, thief.*

I touched each post lightly. They were cool and damp.

"Wait here," I called back to Jadain and Tashan, still with the cart.

I circled the wreck, watching the darkened gaps. I could see through the shadows better than the humans—if there was something lurking just within, I'd notice. I could also see in a way they couldn't. To them, it wouldn't look like anything unusual. But for me, it was a cold kind of sight. It felt like reaching out with the empty places inside, willing the silence between my heartbeats to find like silence. I knew the sights and smells of death well enough, but what had saved me countless times was the ability to sense it, to feel death before it struck.

This place looked like death. It was old. Nothing unnatural stirred within now.

"We should camp here," I said as I came back around to the front of the inn.

Jadain stood before the posts, eyes closed and hands folded over her heart in prayer. I came up beside her as she finished.

"Really?" She opened her eyes, surprised.

I nodded.

"There's plenty of wood, shouldn't be too hard to get a fire started," she said. "And I'd be happy to cook again. Tashan, could you take care of the horse?" She started toward the supplies loaded in the back of the cart.

Tashan hadn't moved from the cart's bench and didn't budge now. His eyes were fixed on the ruin and its gaping windows.

"This place is not right." His voice was a dire whisper. "We should leave."

Jadain looked at me sidelong.

"It's fine," I repeated.

Tashan didn't move, and for a moment I thought he might be right. There was just a twinge . . .

"I'm not doing double the work just because in a few minutes you're not going to be able to see in the dark. Now get down and make yourself useful."

He tore his eyes away from the building. "Don't you see it?" He threw his palm toward the wreck. "This is a place of death!"

I sighed. "Yes. But that's past. It's fine now."

He looked at me like I was insane.

"We're staying here." I nodded to Jadain, who had started gathering some fallen limbs. "You can head off if you want, or you can stay with us. Your choice."

It didn't take him long to make a decision. Reluctantly, he helped us set up camp—though he never took more than one eye off the wreckage.

It was after supper before he asked.

"How do you know?" He was eyeing me suspiciously.

"How do I know what?" I wanted to hear him say it. I'd taken a seat with my back to the ruined inn just as purposefully as he'd taken the seat across our small fire from me. He'd spent the meal in silence, watching the firelight flicker off the charred porch banisters.

He nodded past me. "That it's safe."

"I never said it was safe."

His eyes bulged. "You said we should camp here!" He looked from me to Jadain, then back. The priestess raised an eyebrow at me, but took the opportunity to quietly collect the meal's dishware.

"Yeah," I said, purposefully sounding as nonchalant as possible. "We can't camp in the road. The clearing makes a good shelter, and any bandits who know the area likely give this place a wide berth."

"Probably because they have eyes to see this place is cursed!" He was whispering dramatically again.

"No more so than anywhere else." I retrieved a stick and prodded the fire. "You really mustn't let a few shadows bother you."

"That's more than a few shadows." His voice rose an octave. "Someone burned this place. People died here—died badly. Those posts aren't graves, they're insults. And you suggest we sleep here?"

"Jadain, how well do you know your history?"

She didn't look up from bundling the cooking gear. "Don't frighten him more than he already is."

"I'm not trying to frighten anyone, but it's better he knows. He plans to travel out here alone someday. Can't have him scaring himself to death."

She scoffed, obviously not buying my faux good intentions.

Tashan turned to his ally. "What's she talking about?"

Jadain put down her pots and spoons with a soft sigh, giving him a sympathetic look. "You've been places that feel . . . wrong?"

His nod was urgent. "We're in one of those places now."

I chuckled, first at Tashan and then at Jadain's scolding look.

"Yes," she continued. "But places that give you that feeling—they're rare, right?"

"Fortunately."

"Not here," she said bluntly.

He blinked.

The priestess continued. "Many, many generations ago, this land was conquered. Not by any army of invaders, but by the angry dead."

His eyes widened.

"The people were mostly slaughtered or forced to flee. A few managed to survive as slaves and sustenance for the leaders of the undead armies, but there was no resistance. The Kingdom of Ustalav was wiped out. The dead didn't only threaten our people, though. After Ustalav fell, other nations fought back against the unholy invaders and their necromancer king, the Whispering Tyrant. Over decades and at great cost, the armies of the living defeated the Tyrant, but even their greatest heroes were unable to destroy his evil. So they locked him away and set guards over his prison. To the east, those guards still remain, in the land of Lastwall."

Tashan leaned closer while Jadain spoke, like a youngster hearing a ghost story.

"But even after the evil was locked away, our land was not what it once was. The land had been tainted by decades of possession by the dead. Even with their master defeated, many of the Whispering Tyrant's minions were not destroyed. Some just found quiet places in the dark, where they lurk still."

Tashan didn't look reassured. "Why—" He stopped himself, trying again in a voice that was more than a whisper. "Why would anyone remain in such an accursed place?"

Jadain smiled. "Because this is our ancestors' home. Those who survived the wars had their homeland returned to them, to rebuild as best they could. The task was already beyond imagining—the cities were burned, the old kings dead, the land turned—but they weren't about to let a few lingering shadows deter them. Certainly you can still feel it in some place: the grave sense, the wrongness. But you can't give in to vague fears, or else it's like the dead still rule. These are our lands, our home."

He still seemed doubtful, turning to look at the shadowy wreck. "But how can you know there isn't something . . . waiting?"

"You can't always be. That's why our people have so many superstitions—gourd lanterns, lines of salt, garlic wreathes, unlucky opals, hawthorn spirals." She touched her amulet. "Many tie back to some legend, or magic, or charm against the dead. But most people don't believe so many strange things because they're sure to work. They believe because the traditions make them feel like they have a defense against the dark things, a recourse when they're afraid."

"So your people . . ." he spoke delicately, "make up tales to protect themselves from the evil things in their land."

I laughed, probably harder than I should have. "The weak ones do. They need something. But you don't have anything to worry about. Jadain's superstitions work just fine, and it's part of my job to put dead things back in the ground."

Jadain frowned. "Faith is no superstition. Not any more than your . . . insights."

Tashan's attention snapped to me. I rolled my eyes—there was no need to hide what I was from the foreigner. "What? Trice didn't tell you that one of your traveling companions was half-dead?" I smiled and leaned into the firelight.

I didn't understand his language, but I know what words go along with someone swirling Pharasma's spiral over their heart.

"Mother keep us." Jadain put her palms between us. "I see you're much less delicate about your heritage out on the road."

I shrugged. "He was going to have to find out sometime."

"Don't worry about Larsa. She's the same monster she's always been." Jadain tried to calm the Osirian, but his wariness had shifted from the burnt inn to me.

"This will take time to understand." He stood brusquely. "I will take our first watch. Sleep well." With that, he walked to the edge of the firelight and set his back against a tree, his bronze sword glimmering golden in the dark. A stylized eye adorned the weapon's pommel. It watched intently.

I prodded the fire again. "I think I scared him."

"I think you offended him," Jadain said, returning to cleaning up the meal.

"Offended him? How?"

"You're treating him like a bumpkin. He's not from here, but he's not an idiot. I don't think he's sure what he can believe about what we just told him, but he knows you're playing some sort of trick on him."

"Please. If he's going to act like a coward, then he should expect to get spooked."

"That's a pretty cold opinion. I suppose I expected you to know a little more about how hard it is being an outsider."

"Ugh." I blew out a long breath. "Fine. I'll try to take it easier on him. Will that make you happy?"

Her half-smile carried all the chiding connotations of a mother asking *What do you think?*

I shook my head, clearing away the topic. "Anyway, it's not me playing some sort of trick."

Jadain finished her chore and looked over at me. "Hmm?"

"Before, when I rounded the house. You seemed to know what I was doing."

She nodded. "Your people have a connection with the undead, can sense them. Right?"

"Yeah." I returned her nod. "And I did sense something. But not back there. It was when I came back around." I nodded at our guard. "It was when I was talking to him."

Her back was to where the Osirian had taken up watch. While her eyes shifted, she didn't turn to look at him. "What do you mean?"

"I don't know," I admitted. "It was just for a moment, and I haven't felt it again, but still . . ."

Tashan was watching us from the edge of the camp, the fire glinting upon the bronze of his eyes and blade. It made them both looked like they were smoldering.

"Our companion is hiding something."

16

BEHIND THE VEIL
JADAIN

"If you don't have an invitation," the lead red-plumed guardsman snapped in his gravely voice, "then you're trespassing. Move along, or else!" Behind him, his two doubles moved hands to sword hilts wrapped with ruby ribbons.

The flagstone road had turned abruptly and, following it, we found ourselves before a shining steel gate set within a wall of pale granite and spade-shaped finials. Dozens of sculpted, metal antlers locked together, forming the gateway, along with several metallic birds of prey that stared with dark stone eyes. At the center of each door, a circular shield bore the horned hawk of the Caliphvaso family and an ornate letter *C*. In the haze of misty rain, the ornate gate shimmered like silver.

I tried to be diplomatic, even as I heard Larsa standing in the wagon behind me. "Sirs. We're merely travelers headed north. It would seem that we've somehow lost our path. Would you happen to know the way leading into the mountains?"

"Back the way you came. You just missed it." The guard pointed to the bend in the road.

Admittedly, the weather that had left us all huddling within our cloaks certainly wasn't helping my sight, but it was clear that the road we were on led to a single destination.

"Sir?" I started, but he interrupted.

"Before the bend and north, past the paving's end." He stabbed with a red-gloved finger. "You won't be able to rely on the countess's graces from here on."

I squinted through the drizzle. Sure enough, the paving ended but there was a muddy opening between the trees that continued north. It was quite a change from the road we'd been traveling, so much that it was no wonder that we hadn't noticed it in the rain.

"Ah, I see now, sir, thank you. Might I ask, though, is that the only way into the mountains?"

"Oh, not at all, Your Grace!" He swirled his hand. "I'm sure your porter and lady-in-waiting can find you a silver-paved deer trail, and maybe even a team of stags to carry you along your way!"

"Ignorant oaf." Larsa's voice was less than a whisper.

"What did she say?" The lead guard took a step forward.

I shot a glare back at Larsa, but it was obvious she wasn't interested in being mocked by the countess's thugs. I had no idea what sort of jurisdiction the countess's guards might claim or how it compared to a Royal Accuser's, but I had a feeling that, out in the woods with no witnesses, steel and skill trumped official right.

"Only that we've taken up enough of your time. Thank you for the direction, gentlemen. Good day now!" I leaned over to Tashan, whose grip had never left the horse's reins, and urged him to turn the cart quickly.

A few minutes later we were clattering through bumpy ruts upon a muddy trail, the path already starting to climb. This was obviously the backside of the New Surdina Road.

"Why did the paving end back there?" Tashan asked after just a few moments' jostling. "It's clear the way isn't going to get any easier."

"You recognized the guards, right?" Larsa said. "Those were the gates to the countess's private estate, Chateau Douleurs. In fact . . ."

She trailed off as we crested into a cleared section of hill, one that allowed for a momentary view of the lands below. Silent avalanches of mist rolled between the hills, pouring over mossy cliffs and through the sparse woodlands in unpredictable courses. But the fog cascades dispersed before the banks of a great lake, its placid surface so gray that it might have been filled with that same mist. Gaps in the haze revealed the path of the paved road we'd just been bullied from as it made its way along one side of the lake. It wound through half-seen gardens and snaked amid the silhouettes of topiary figures before finally becoming lost in the spectral scene. Near where it vanished, six towers lanced through mist, their heights uneven but stained in matching rusty red, their gables as sharp as cathedral spires. Only the ridges of lower roofs gave any hint of the rose-colored structure hidden in the fog, a multitude of peaks and glass pinnacles suggesting rambling decadence.

"The road we've been following leads there." Tashan's tone made it not so much a question.

"No. Just the part that matters—straight to the countess's country estate." I shook my head, "I hadn't realized most of the New Surdina was nothing more than her manor's private drive."

"Wasn't so private this far," Tashan said.

"Guess no one of importance needed it to go any further." Larsa spat into the bushes. "Nobles."

"We can't keep on in this!" Tashan shouted against the winds, sounding as though he were under water, not just on the bench next to me.

"You think you can turn around here?" Larsa yelled from the back. Her sarcastic tone might have been lost to the storm, but the impossibility of the act wasn't. There wasn't anywhere to go behind us anyway—we had no other choice but to push on.

We'd been traveling narrow mountain paths for days now. Our maps and the occasional gray sign still marked our route as the New Surdina. Appropriately, none appended the word "road" to the name anymore. I'd stopped thinking the trail couldn't grow steeper or more narrow, as I'd been proven wrong each time.

On the third day of stone and cold, the clouds seemed to grow tired of our presence. They conspired against us, roiling and darkening, threatening us with some wordless language of the sky. It was about midday when the sun abandoned us, casting the mountains into an early dusk. Then the thunder peals began.

We'd all been looking for shelter, the need obvious enough that no one had even bothered mentioning it. The goddess wasn't smiling, though.

The path had narrowed once more, now barely a thread between cliff face and ravine. That was when the heavens struck. The storm brought all the tears and moans of a million mourners.

Small rivers coursed across the trail, eroding the already unreliable line between trail and endless plummet. More out of self-preservation than because of Tashan's cautious driving, the horse pressed its body against the rising cliff, accepting the pelting of rubble and small mudslides that washed across its back more than once. Locked to our path and blinded by shadows and water, we were trusting in the horse for every step. If any portion of the trail ahead had collapsed in the storm, I feared we'd only know in the moment between toppling into the chasm and being smashed upon the rocks.

With the realization of that quite real possibility, I bowed my head and began to pray.

"Can't your goddess do something about this?" Larsa shouted into my back. I ignored her, not willing to interrupt my appeal to the goddess with a theological debate. Of course she could do something, but Pharasma wasn't known for overt miracles. Even the magic she granted me was thoroughly outstripped by the storm's ferocity.

"I think she just did!" Tashan called, daring to take a hand off the reins to point ahead.

Looking up, two paths emerged out of the rain, momentarily rendered in stark grays by a flash of lightning and its immediate explosion of thunder. One branch continued around the mount we'd been following, while the other crossed a narrow ridge and wound higher.

"Which way?" Tashan struggled to out-shout the storm. The route we'd been following carried on, narrow and treacherous, while the side path promised much the same, along with the dangers of an uncertain ascent.

"Right!" I pointed down the somewhat-known path. "I don't want to risk it."

Again, lightning flashed, momentarily revealing just how small and vulnerable we were.

"There!" Larsa surged between us, pointing into the dark between the paths—a course leading directly into a fissure.

"Are you mad?" I yelled.

She kept pointing. "Look higher. Wait for the lightning."

Praying that the next strike wouldn't be the one that blasted us from the mountain wall, we stared into the dark.

When it appeared, it was nothing more than a collection of sharp peaks. But they were too severe, to similar to be natural.

"A castle!" Larsa confirmed that we'd all seen the same improbable vision perched on the mountainside ahead.

"All the way out here?" Tashan didn't believe his eyes so readily. "Impossible!"

It dawned on me that he was right. "Not a castle. A monastery. That must be the Monastery of the Veil. My brethren can give us shelter!"

No one cared to debate, and Tashan tugged on the reins to coax our steed toward the ridge trail and the salvation hidden in the dark. But the horse refused to move.

Lightning webbed through the sky, and for an instant it looked as though the clouds had shattered. There was something else, though. In that instant of sight, something in the path ahead had changed.

When I looked over, Tashan was already staring at me—he'd noticed, too. Neither of us spoke. Trying to overcome our blindness by force of will, we strained our eyes against curtains of stinging rain and darkness.

It took an eternity, but the merciless light blazed again. What it revealed was as unmistakable as it was impossible: A figure stood on the trail ahead, a soaking robe and deep hood masking any hint of his identity. He stood in the middle of the trail, head bowed against the rain, little more than a silhouette in the burst of light.

I raised my voice. "Someone's out there!"

"Another traveler?" Tashan asked, his doubt obvious even through the wind.

"Maybe a monk from the monastery. He might need help." I indulged my optimism. "Or maybe he's here to lead us to the refuge."

When the sky tore open again, the figure hadn't moved.

More glances passed between us, and a frozen weight not caused by the icy rain crystallized in my stomach.

"Larsa, can you see—" I stopped, as she was already peering past me.

"It's there." Her words slit through the wind.

Calling the man "it" wasn't reassuring. My hand slid to Pharasma's symbol, hanging from my neck. "Can you tell if he's . . . living?"

She nodded that he was. At least that was something of a relief.

"I'll see who he is. He must have come from somewhere, and might know where there's shelter." I tried pulling my soaked cloak and robes tighter, but there wasn't any warmth left in them. Climbing from the cart, I ducked into the wind. Every step was a struggle against the wind and the rain-slick trail, the elements conspiring to push me toward the ravine.

Another bolt, and still the figure stood unmoved. The storm appeared not to touch him, his posture seemingly bent less by the storm and more out of some silent reverence. He seemed totally unaware of my approach.

Although the trek was one of only a few dozen steps, that alone was more harrowing than our entire journey this far. I stopped several strides away from the ominous figure, coming no further than my shouts would need to carry.

"Sir!" I yelled into the shadows. "We have to get out of the storm! Do you know a safe place? Can we take you there?"

If the strange monk moved, it was entirely lost amid the shadows. It dawned on me that the only thing tethering me to the cart and the world beyond was Larsa's remarkable sight. Otherwise, I was completely alone in the freezing dark with this mysterious figure.

The idea chilled me, but the need couldn't be more urgent. I took a step closer. "Brother!"

Still not a twitch, so far as I could tell. I stepped closer, purposefully stopping just outside the stranger's reach. Again I yelled.

The figure's arm snapped up like a sapling released from bonds. A gloved hand jabbed from his robes, a single finger lancing out to point north—away from the monastery path.

I stumbled back, startled. Behind me I thought I heard a voice, but it was lost in the rain. "Brother! I am one of the faithful, traveling from our lady's monument in Caliphas." I proved my words by lifting up the wooden spiral around my neck. It seemed strangely fragile in this lost corner of the world.

His arm didn't fall.

"You're a brother of the Monastery of the Veil? We saw it through the storm. Please! Can you take us there?"

His posture didn't so much as tremble, his head still lowered. His gesture seemed like an exile.

Could this be some ritual, some ancient test of faith we were interrupting? If this were a monk of the cloistered order, I couldn't expect him to speak, but even for an anchorite at the world's edge this behavior was more than just discourtesy.

I backed away, skidding back to the cart as fast as my courage would let me. Tashan and Larsa were waiting, the Osirian shivering violently.

"He's a monk from the monastery, I think! But he won't acknowledge me, and he doesn't seem interested in moving. He pointed that way." I repeated the figure's gesture to the north.

"The monastery's right there!" Larsa shouted. "Tell him to take us!"

"I tried! But there's something . . . something wrong about him."

"There's something wrong about us dying on a mountainside! I'm not freezing just because some monks are afraid we might track mud in from the trail." She vaulted over the side of the cart. "Tashan! Bring the wagon. Jadain, come on!" She strode past me, into the dark.

"Larsa, wait!" I tried to yell through the gale, but either she didn't hear or she didn't listen—I had my guess at which. Something knotted in my stomach. "There's something wrong here! We should go!"

She was only a step away from the monk when I caught up to her, one hand smashing her hat to her head, the other gripping her cloak closed. Her mouth was moving, but her words were lost to the wind. I came alongside them a moment too late.

"Are you deaf as well as mute?" Larsa's voice tore through the rain, as did her hand, grabbing for the man's shoulder.

I started to shout, outraged at her lifting a hand against a brother of the faith. It escaped as nothing more than a shocked squawk, though, as in the same instant the monk faded away—or appeared to. It happened with such sudden smoothness that in the rain it took several blinks to realize he'd fallen back several steps. In his retreat, the wind caught his hood, throwing it back, releasing a tangle of knotted hair to lash over dark, lowered features.

Larsa's glance snapped to me, but then she was closing on him again. I followed a step behind, increasingly sure that he wasn't just some religious hermit.

He stabbed a finger north. As light and deafening thunder burst over us, he lifted his eyes, accentuating his silent command. For a moment the flash revealed his face—or what there was of one.

A savagely twisted whorl of flesh spun where there should have been a mouth. Instead of a natural gap, uneven knife-work and crude stitches carved away lips and nose, replacing them with a wound parodying Pharasma's holy spiral. His eyes were glistening flecks somewhere between the coils of skin and his sopping mop of hair, just two slightly darker pools amid the rivulets of water charting unnatural courses over his deformities.

The goddess's name was on my lips as I recoiled, but Larsa's sword was between her and the stranger who certainly wasn't a brother of my faith.

"Get out of our way!" Larsa shouted, seemingly unfazed by the man's vicious scars.

Still the figure didn't move. She advanced on him, and I found the cold grip of my own dagger hidden amid my robes. My training with the blade leapt to mind, as did the names and motions of a thousand different mercies. Before I drew, the stranger was once more replaced by darkness.

Both of us searched the storm futilely, Larsa turning quickly, trying not to expose her back to any one direction for long. Obviously her sight wasn't serving her any better than mine. I waited for the next flash of lightning.

When it came, the trail leading toward the Monastery of the Veil was empty. I looked to Larsa, but she wasn't looking down the trail, but up, seemingly into the storm clouds. Without turning to me, she pointed.

Lightning flashed again, and I realized I wasn't staring at the clouds, but rather the rocky cliffs above the trail. The stranger was there, a man-shaped silhouette staring from a higher ridge. He wasn't alone. At least nine other silhouettes joined him in looming over us.

Something hit my boot. I couldn't see what clearly, but it felt like a small rock, rolling against the wind. Then more came. Only for a moment did I mistake the rumbling that followed for thunder.

Larsa and I turned for the cart as one. Half-blind, we raced back, the trail shaking beneath us, threatening to buck us off the mountainside. Behind us it sounded like the mountain was moving, obeying the commands of its strange, scarred masters.

A cloud of dust and grit defied the storm and blew past us, reaching Tashan before we did. I could hear him coughing, then shouting my name and Larsa's. The sound of grinding rocks followed, a cacophony repeating in every crag and fissure. I barreled into the side of the cart, choking on rain and crushed stone. Larsa, only a step behind, crashed next to me, also struggling to breathe. Tashan shouted questions, but there was little to be said and less to be done. Nowhere else to run, we waited for the mountain's fist to fall.

The gnashing of ancient stones swelled. It rolled, so much like crashing surf. Then, finding no outlet for its anger, it grudgingly receded. Echoes carried the mountain's rage into the surrounding chasms, but soon the thunder and rain drowned them, too.

I gasped, not realizing I'd been holding my breath. It took several moments more, but when we were sure that rain and wind were again the only things threatening to kill us, all three of us approached the trail leading toward the Monastery of the Veil. We didn't need to wait for the lightning. It was clear the path had disappeared, transformed by the rockslide into a seamless slope of jagged rocks plummeting from the cliffs above into the ravine's impossible depths.

We stared, searching the dark for the ridge above, seeking out the mountain's jury of strange masters. When the flash came, the rise was destroyed, but a single cloaked figure still watched over us.

Larsa was moving before I'd done more than point. Her blade cut ahead of her as she charged up the wall of loose rocks. I shouted as she vanished into the storm, but she didn't listen. Neither Tashan nor I dared follow. I wondered if Larsa, who considered herself only half alive, considered her life to be of only half value.

When lightning flashed again, she was already climbing back down. The cloaked figure was gone, replaced by an uprooted scrub tree.

"What happened?" I asked as she returned.

She held up a tattered cloak, little more than rags. "Nothing. It was only this." It thrashed in her grip and she released it to the wind. The storm swept it up and the dark consumed it. "But I could see down the trail from up there. There's a light ahead." She pointed. "That way."

Her finger traced the path of the northern trail, just as the stranger had directed.

17

COLD COMFORTS
LARSA

We leave the monks be." Mrs. Saunnier handed me a thread-bare towel. "It's better for everyone that way."

The Slit o' the Sun had only been a short push from the turnoff toward the Monastery of the Veil and its freakish watchmen. Wind still tore through the mountains outside, shaking the roof and windows of this heap of old stones posing as an inn. Huddled in the corner of two colliding cliffs, the elaborate hovel and its adjoining stable dug into the rock as if fearful of falling into the ravine only a few dozen steps beyond its door. The place might not have much to recommend it, but it was reasonably dry.

The owners, the Saunniers, had been reluctant to admit us, but once Jadain displayed her holy symbol the door flung wide. A stringy pair with the same weather-beaten look as their establishment, the couple had seemed surprised to hear we were travelers. For a moment I thought they might try to throw us back into the storm, but, grudgingly, they had their son stir the fire in the taproom's chest-high fireplace—its strange design presumably meant to suggest a burning hollow in a tree of crudely carved stones.

I accepted Mrs. Saunnier's towel with a nod—Jadain and Tashan had already said enough "thank yous" to mark us as the most desperate sort of rubes. Not that we weren't. Leaning against the warm rocks of the fireplace was gradually returning feeling to my hands and feet, but had we spent much longer in the storm I doubted they would have ever thawed.

"Who says it's better?" I asked, squeezing half of the storm from my hair onto the increasingly muddy dirt-and-straw floor.

"I do." Mrs. Saunnier spoke like a woman unused to being questioned. Mr. Saunnier stood on hand, weary detachment plain on his long face. I don't think he'd spoken a word since we entered. "I suppose you'll be wanting something to eat, too."

"Anything warm would be a blessing," Jadain said. "Thank you again for your hospitality. We're so sorry to be a bother."

Mrs. Saunnier gave a stern harrumph, then shouted over her shoulder at her straw-haired son. "Kensre! Kick up the kitchen fire, too." The boy—actually near enough a man not to be jumping at his mother's orders—disappeared through a split orange curtain behind the row of tables that doubled as a bar.

Eventually Mrs. Saunnier sent her husband upstairs, charging the mute, post-still man with being too much in the way. We quickly covered the fireplace with every bit of drenched clothing modesty allowed. Modesty, of course, meant something different for each of us. Although I'd expected the opposite, the Osirian suffered the grip of most of his soaking clothes while the priestess stripped down to nothing more than her battered amulet and a drenched linen shift. Jadain didn't show the least shyness even though I could have counted the freckles on her shoulders for all her drenched undergarment hid. Part of me envied her for being so thoughtless of her body. I mentally inventoried every scar on my own, knowing that removing my hat and cloak hadn't revealed any of them, but unsure enough that I double-checked a moment later. When I realized my stare had been lingering on Jadain, I turned it on Tashan, mindful of where his eyes might stray. To his credit, he comported himself as a gentleman long before noticing my glare.

Supper arrived with a clatter, two bowls of thin broth drowning a few stringy pieces of nameless bird meat. Mrs. Saunnier dropped them on a table close to Jadain and Tashan, hardly pausing before she circled back to the kitchen to retrieve a third bowl and a handful of battered silverware. Though far from appetizing, the meal was hot, and I supposed that was all Jadain had asked for.

"So, do the monks ever come here?" I pressed after she'd returned to check the locks on the door.

"This isn't some big city where everybody makes everybody else's business their own," she said matter-of-factly. "You want to know about our neighbors, you go right out and ask them, but they ain't any of my concern." She moved on to check the fire. "And I'm not going to say anything more on that."

The wind rattled the building, confirming the finality of her words.

Always the peacemaker, Jadain was quick to chime in. "Forgive our curiosity. It certainly wasn't our intention to offend you, ma'am."

"Didn't offend me. That's just the way it is." She swept the straw around the hearth. I was impressed by the woman's resolve. I guessed you had to be stubborn to survive all the way up here.

I thought to test her stubbornness, but she beat me to the next question. "You'll be wanting rooms, 'less you're in a hurry to die out on the ridge."

She was obviously aware she had something of a captive clientele.

"How much?" I asked suspiciously.

She didn't disappoint. "Three gold." Then she took it a step further. "Each."

Tashan's eyebrows rose and Jadain's mouth was already open by the time I lifted a finger to restrain them. Guests probably paid several times that back at the Majesty, but this was more than several times less accommodating than that palace. "How many beds does that get us?"

"One." She didn't look up from her sweeping.

"Arrange it so we each get a bed, a hot meal in the morning, and our horse watered and fed, and we'll pay four—each." We obviously weren't getting out of here cheap, but I also wasn't particularly concerned about the money. Between my stipend from the crown, what Grandfather regularly granted, and what Trice had sent us with, our expedition was exceedingly well funded. Not that I'd let my traveling companions know that.

Mrs. Saunnier looked up from her floor, still looking slightly perturbed despite having transacted a deal only a half-shade from brigandry. "That's fine."

Despite my expectation, the rooms at the Slit o' the Sun weren't terrible. Modest to be sure, but better than the closets with flea-infested pallets that I'd expected. My purposefully poor dealings had bought us two rooms, one with beds for Jadain and me and another for Tashan. I couldn't help but note that had we pushed together all three beds the combined size would still be smaller than my unused mattress at the Majesty. After a week of sleeping outside, though, I wasn't about to complain about the amenities. The wooden second story of the inn didn't weather the wind and rain as well as the stone of its sunken ground floor, but any leaks were far enough from the beds to not be a bother and the thunder had receded to just an occasional rumble.

I snuffed the light as soon as Jadain got into bed. After the day's various exhaustions, it wasn't long until her breathing was deep and regular enough for me to venture changing out of my own still-sopping clothes. As soon as I had, though, the sound of the rain and the comforting stiffness of the bed was enough to lull me to sleep.

Screams woke me.

The faintest glow at the window suggested it was only just dawn. Jadain lurched upright in her bed. "Larsa," she said into what, for her, was still mostly blackness.

"I hear it." It, in this instance, was a woman's screeching. Mrs. Saunnier, I guessed.

Jadain fumbled out of bed and quickly dressed. She paused in the door. The weak yellow glow of the hall lantern seeped into the room. "Aren't you coming?"

"I'll be along." I didn't feel any particular rush. The shouting had already plummeted from the sound of immediate shock to a grief-ridden warbling. Since Jadain was accounted for and I doubted Mrs. Saunnier would be sobbing over Tashan, I wasn't in any particular rush to loiter over a stranger's grief.

Jadain didn't wait. As soon as she disappeared down the hall, I found my still more than damp clothes and shrugged on my cloak. Although soggy, it was heavy in all the right places, the weight of a dozen concealed pockets and sheathes reassuring me more than any armor. My hair, matted by sleeping on it wet, was another matter entirely, but one I and the world would just have to deal with.

The narrow hall was short, and once around the only corner it was clear where the commotion was coming from. Inside a room hung with ropes and climbing gear, Mrs. Saunnier pummeled the floorboards. Her husband, as still and aloof as before, stood over her, his face registering only a sad sort of quiet surprise. Jadain sat alongside the bed—Kensre Saunnier's bed, where the young man lay stock-still. Her thumb traced the spiral of her goddess's symbol endlessly as she muttered to herself. It was obvious from that alone that Kensre wasn't asleep.

Jadain looked up at me as I came to the foot of the bed, her eyes wide. My name was an accusation on her lips.

"What?" I dared over the lady of the house's sobs.

Jadain touched the youth's cheek, turning his stare toward his mother. She brushed away a shock of shaggy blond hair. Blood had dried into the collar of his bedclothes, collecting from two small rips on his neck.

I clenched my jaw, first to resist the urge to gape, then at the priestess's implication. This wasn't how I fed. Even though it had been more than a week and the urge gnawed at the back of my mind, I knew how to control it. The need to steal blood didn't compel me like it would a true vampire. Even then, this was reckless . . . indulgent.

"Bastard," I said in a moment of utter awe. The first time was under my breath, the second time less so. "Unbelievable bastard!"

Ignoring Jadain's glare, I was out of the room and down the hall. The door to Tashan's room was locked, but wasn't so strong that a solid kick didn't bust it open. He was still in bed, splayed naked amid a tangle of sheets. The door slamming against the inner wall roused him, and he lifted his head groggily. His hookah was set up on the bed stand, one of its hoses reaching toward his pillow like a limp arm.

I slammed the door behind me then kicked a piece of the splintered doorframe underneath, wedging it closed. It would hold well enough.

"Who?" I shouted, driving my heel into his ribs. "Who's commanding you?"

Pain drove the grogginess from his eyes and he rolled away. "Larsa? What?"

I kicked him again, aiming for the same spot. "Who?"

He threw his pillow at me and I batted it aside, but he was fast behind it, flailing to push me away. I caught his arm and dragged him out of bed, a tangle of thrashing limbs and sheets. His face slammed solidly into the floor and I ground it down. "Who?"

Tashan attempted several awkward, backward kicks, eventually managing to buck me off. He pulled himself completely onto the floor and twisted to get his legs between us. I moved faster than he could spin, getting around him easily. Forcing all my weight into my knee, I dropped onto his gut. Stew stunk in the rush of breath he gasped out. I shot past his flailing limbs and dug my hand into his throat.

He might not need to breathe anymore, but he still needed something to keep his head on. I tightened my grip and—

A pulse. So much for that theory.

With my free hand, I pinched back his upper lip. His teeth were normal. "Then how?"

I seesawed back onto my feet and stepped back, staring at the gasping man on the floor. He was breathing, deeply and desperately, but otherwise lay still.

I let my own breath slip away in a long, thin sigh, quieting the noisy thrum of blood. Something still and dark readily rose in the depths of my chest. I cast out with it, sending the dead part of me searching.

It swept first toward Tashan. Its thin fingers reached for him but instantly recoiled, flinching as if from a flame. He didn't show any signs of being a half-blood—an undead slave, a vampire spawn. I wasn't wholly surprised. I'd searched him for the taint of undeath multiple times since staying the night by the ruined inn. The night I knew I'd sensed death from him.

From him, but maybe not from inside him.

Turning slowly, I reached into the shadows of the room. If not him, then what? Some possessing spirit? Some hidden phylactery amid his clothes? The lingering taint of a previous brush with some damned soul? Whatever it was, my theory about Tashan being Kensre's killer was evaporating. Those shadowy fingers reached out through my gaze, blind but lusty, probing but rejecting everything I fixed my sight upon.

Then they snared the hookah, grasping, squeezing, seeking what was within.

I lunged for it.

Tashan made a hoarse sound. He tried to sit up but collapsed from the pain of his smashed innards.

I grabbed the ruby water pipe by its slender neck. Immediately it exploded in smoke, as if whatever pungent lump filled the thing had caught fire. I almost let it shatter to the ground, the thin clouds spilling out like a genie escaping a bottle.

As soon as I recognized the smoke, I did let it fall.

The vapor rose in an unnatural column, then retreated into nothingness, releasing a lean figure in a wine-colored vest embroidered with gold thorns.

Considine.

"I surrender." The vampire turned his palms to the ceiling, less the pose of a captured thief and more that of a child caught in the act.

I was gripping one of the daggers hidden in my cloak before I checked myself. My hesitation lasted only a moment, though. The silver-shod dagger flashed as I lunged. A too-familiar look of obnoxious bemusement flashed across his face as he flowed back from the blade.

"Dear, please don't tell me I've surprised you—not Grandfather's esteemed half-vampire vampire hunter. How could you have not known I—" A wild slash for his mouth momentarily halted his chuckling.

"Why did you follow me?" I reversed my blade, slashing across his chest. The point squealed across one of his vest's golden, bloom-shaped buttons. He flung himself back and looked down with the horrified expression of a gutted soldier. He threw up a hand, calling for pause, but I wasn't playing. My next slash crossed his extended palm, cutting a hollow streak across its width. The barest hint of blood that stained my blade was incidental—and likely Kensre Saunnier's. Considine didn't even flinch, mourning his scraped button.

"Only following orders, dear." He frowned over his shirt.

"Bullshit." I almost stabbed him again, but it seemed pointless. Not only wasn't he paying attention, but the gash across his palm was already knitting shut. In a moment, nothing but a smear of someone else's blood would mark the wound's existence.

"Oh, yes, you know how I've pined for the rustic comforts of the mountains. I've always been quite the outdoorsman." He frowned up at me, smudging the button with his thumb.

I snatched up a corner of the bedsheets and wiped off my blade. Tashan was still on the floor, but had scooted into the room's corner, quietly holding onto his guts at the end of a trail of sheets and blankets.

"Grandfather sent you after Rivascis?" I didn't believe it.

His elaborate snort proved he equally dismissed the possibility. "Afraid not, dear. No, I've been sent to assure that you do all you promised to."

"Promised to?" My brow knotted. "I didn't promise to do anything."

"That's not what I was told. Grandfather said you wrote him a whole confession—all strong words and apologies and must-dos." His hands crossed over his unbeating heart. "It sounded truly moving."

"I didn't write any—" But I had. And I'd burned it.

Considine nodded thoughtfully. "Hope you didn't think I was the only one who kept a concerned eye on you." He stepped around me, briefly touching my shoulder before retrieving the cracked but still mostly intact hookah. "You must watch what you jot down and where you do it. Otherwise, he'll find a way to make you into your own traitor."

It was my turn to scoff. "So what, then? You're here to help?"

He delicately set the hookah back on the nightstand. "Dear me, no. I'm merely on hand to make sure your hunt goes as you said it would. To make sure you don't accidentally trip into some sort of reunion with your long-lost papa."

"You think I'm doing all this just to meet my father?" Muscles tightened, both in my chest and around the weapon in my grip.

"Not at all, my dear, but Grandfather . . . well." He looked at me with something approximating sympathy. "I'm sure it's just that he hasn't felt anything for so long. Conviction must be a constant mystery."

"Shouldn't he be just as worried about you? Rivascis made you what you are, after all."

"Grandfather knows my loyalty to him has always been my downfall. Ratting out Rivascis when he fled the Old City was what permanently placed me in Grandfather's low regard, after all. Betraying my maker to serve my liege didn't go quite the way I expected." He tapped his lips, as if contemplating his old half-crime for the millionth time. "Still, exile as a traitor to a fallen prince has always sat better with me than death for disobeying Grandfather's will."

"I'm sure." I didn't sympathize. "So then you're just all wrapped up in this by coincidence?"

"Oh, not at all, I'm afraid. This is as much Grandfather's trick on me as it is on you." He perched himself on the end of the bed, near where Tashan huddled. "It's also this little desert mouse's fault."

I didn't bother to keep the incredulity from my voice. "Tashan's? How?"

"We've had an arrangement for a bit now. I pride myself on knowing when anything interesting washes up on the docks, and he was the first thing from Osirion I'd ever seen that wasn't bound for the Royal Archives." Considine grinned down at the young Pathfinder. "And since I'm one of the only people in the city who knows where to find decent shisha, we became fast friends."

"You dominated him, then?" Like the vampires I'd fought in Thorenly Manor, Considine could effortlessly force his will upon the living.

"No, no, no." That caught-in-the-act expression returned to Considine's face. "Well . . . perhaps a little at first, but just to lubricate our first outing. Beyond that it's been absolutely consensual."

If Tashan was at all bothered by the revelation, the grimace on his face disguised it.

"Then Grandfather enlisted you because he knew you had a Pathfinder in your pocket."

"That." He frowned. "And you didn't exactly give him much time to put together something else. By the time I received my orders, I had just enough time to stow away in Tashan's glassware before you were off."

"What about your coffin, then?"

"Oh, did you not notice a seven-foot-long box smuggled amid your luggage?" His sarcasm took on a nasty tinge. "Probably because Grandfather's command forced me to leave it back in Caliphas. A dark box and a piece of stained glass has been all there is between me and the sun for the past week."

To call the move reckless would be the grossest understatement. It would have been like walking into the desert with the hope of discovering water along the way. For every vampire, his coffin—not just any coffin, but *his* coffin—is a sanctuary. More than a resting place, as a vampire has no need for sleep, it serves as his connection to death, a focal point for the energies that keep him tied to this world. While a vampire doesn't need to rest in his coffin nightly, not doing so would be uncomfortable on a fundamental level. Beyond comfort, though, a vampire's coffin is the only place he can restore his body if mortally wounded. Relying on instinct and the draw of dark energies, the vampire flees, practically mindlessly, back to his coffin to regenerate. In Considine's case, though, his coffin was several days' travel away. If his body were destroyed and drawn back to his coffin, he would doubtlessly be caught under the sun, which would obliterate him utterly. Actually, it would be far less dramatic—reduced to nothing but a bank of mist by whatever attacked him, he would dissipate in the sun faster than morning dew. There would be nothing left.

He noted my sudden understanding. "It's no secret that I'm expendable."

I was incredulous. "You understand we're traveling with a Pharasmin priestess. If she discovers you, she'll be bound by her faith to destroy you."

His grin returned and he clapped me on the shoulder. "So we're traveling *together* now?"

I jerked away. "You haven't given me a choice in the matter. There's no way to send you back, and I can't leave you here with the—" In my shock I'd almost forgotten. "You idiot! The innkeepers' son! Why? Especially when this one's apparently so accommodating." I flung a hand at Tashan.

"If you don't mind . . ." Considine cooed over Tashan. The Osirian didn't seem to be in any condition to resist whatever the vampire had in mind. Considine pinched a fold of the sheets entwining Tashan and pulled deliberately. The cloth slid across the beaten Pathfinder's dusky leg, over his knee, and up an only slightly paler thigh, moving like silk across a harem dancer's skin. Across Tashan's inner thigh spread whole constellations of tiny, twin wounds. Piercings, tiny slashes, delicate perforations—the signs of repeated feedings.

The vampire sounded nonchalant. "You can't drink the same wine every day."

"Selfish letch!" I nearly shouted. "They're going to blame me for this!"

He threw the sheet back over Tashan. "Oh, did you tell the innkeep you're a half-breed with a taste for street folk? You're making confidants so swiftly these days, I can hardly keep track."

"Jadain! Jadain will think it was me. She already thinks it's me!"

A soft rap sounded at the door.

"Hum. Now that you say it, I can see how that would be your problem." He burst like a popped bubble, leaving behind a cloud of mist that quickly drew itself to the ceiling.

My frustration released in something between a growl and a sigh. Tashan stared up at me, jaw set with the pain of whatever I'd broken in his bowels. "You and I have more—" I started through clenched teeth, but settled with driving the point of my boot into his bare shin. He gave another yelp of surprised pain.

"We could hear shouting," Jadain said as I opened the door. She looked into the room, her face painted with confused concern. "What happened in here."

"I had to be sure he wasn't involved." I jerked a finger at the Osirian huddled in the corner. "I am now, but he'll need healing."

"And what about you?" The question sounded like an accusation.

"What about me?"

She reached out to my shoulder and wiped at something on my cloak, then presented the smear of blood that came back on her fingers. I cursed Considine a thousand times more.

Jadain searched my face so intently that she didn't notice the fine ribbon of mist slipping like some repulsive millipede down the wall of the room, over the doorframe, and out into the hall.

I met her gaze and spoke in a manner that made it clear I wouldn't be repeating myself. "I didn't touch him."

She nodded, but her doubt was clear. "Do you know what did, then?"

I slipped past her, leaving her to her next patient.

18

NOT FOR THE LIVING
JADAIN

I felt like I should say more. I'd repeated the blessings and offered all the usual condolences. Anything else I could think of sounded either trite or repetitive. It still seemed like I should apologize. Even though the church strictly taught us to never accept a stranger's death as ours to control, to never internalize blame for the goddess's will, my lips barely held back a flood of regret. The spiral of life and death was the goddess's alone, but even though I hadn't laid a hand on Kensre Saunnier, I couldn't help but feel like I'd brought death into his home.

The Slit o' the Sun huddled at the foot of the slope below us, still partially shadowed by the surrounding cliffs despite the sun's height in the sky. Tashan had loaded the cart and prepared the horse. He was already sitting in the driver's seat, obviously ready to leave. Larsa waited in the shadows of the kitchen doorframe. I couldn't see her face, but I knew she was staring up at me. She'd wanted to leave hours ago. Whether out of honest desire to be on our way or a criminal urge to leave the scene of the crime, I couldn't be sure.

Something had transpired between her and Tashan, something that had left our Pathfinder friend with three broken ribs and a belly full of blood. The goddess had seen fit to heal him, but despite my prayers his torso would be tender for days. I'd tried to get him to explain what had happened, but he'd said only that there'd been a misunderstanding, and then refused to elaborate.

I asked Larsa if she had confronted Tashan about whatever it was that killed the Saunnier boy, guessing the Osirian's wounds were evidence of very direct questioning. She'd confirmed my suspicions, but didn't elaborate, confessing that she'd been wrong and that Tashan hadn't been involved with the murder. When I pressed her on what had, she claimed she couldn't be sure.

I wasn't satisfied. The wounds on the young man's neck were too distinctive and too obvious. Even Mr. Saunnier had swirled his thumb over his heart when he noticed me examining them. I tried to assuage the parents' concerns, but any explanation I attempted sounded too hollow to even give voice. Only the stranger in the road seemed a possibility, with his scarred face. When I'd suggested that, though, the innkeeps shared a long look, then dismissed the possibility. I knew I wasn't being told the whole story.

My duties as a priestess swiftly overshadowed my attempts at investigation. Being so isolated, the Saunniers had no one to assist in their son's burial. Their fears about his manner of death lent haste to their preparations and Mrs. Saunnier demanded I stay long enough to preside over his burial. My unquiet conscience aside, I couldn't refuse.

Mr. Saunnier had climbed the slope near his home to a broad ridge where the innkeeps kept a row of dusty gardens. Among the struggling gray-green things he'd found an unused plot with a view of the inn and a vista of the dramatic, knifelike mountains beyond. When he couldn't dig any deeper, he collected heavy stones. In the end, it didn't look like a comfortable bed, but even without the goddess's blessings nothing was likely to rise from such a rocky tomb. I helped the vacant, voiceless man wrap the body in clean linens and what protective herbs were on hand—mostly rosemary, violet, and a small clump of mistletoe. Less than an hour later we laid our bundle into the ground and I watched as he and his wife said their unexpected, too brief good-byes.

The blessing for a stranger's son was far from the shortest of the goddess's burial rites, but too soon there was nothing left to be said. It wasn't my place to guide them back to their lives or put an end to their grieving. I bowed once more toward the cairn, circled it with one last solemn spiral of my thumb, and reverently made toward the path back to the inn. I passed close to the mourners, but respected their vigil.

Mrs. Saunnier's hand shot out, seizing my robe. Though her abruptness surprised me, I turned my calmest expression to her. She glared back. She looked older than the woman in her forties who had buzzed over us just the night before. The streams of tears had dried, but their paths were still etched upon her face.

"Your fault." Her words were a curse. "You brought this with you, and now my son—" She choked, momentarily unable to go on. "I don't know how, but never—never before . . ."

Tremors shook her, throttling me through her grip. I tried to pull away, startled not just by her hand on me but by her reckless expression—the look of a beaten child with her fingers around a bird's neck. She held fast.

Again I thought to apologize, but for what? I had only the barest hint of what had happened to her son. Would I beg her to forgive me for brining a dhampir into her home? Could I truly blame Larsa for the boy's death? Did I know the thing traveling alongside me at all? And what secret did she and Tashan share while I'd been consoling parents over the body of their son?

I gaped and tugged my robe from Mrs. Saunnier's grasp, tripping away a step. Something in me—a young faithless piece of myself—wanted nothing more than to run. I took another step away.

The woman's eyes flared, but Mr. Saunnier's hand was on her shoulder. Her jaw trembled and she bared her teeth. "You never come back here. None of you. If ever I see you again, I swear by all the gods of blood I'll . . . I'll drag you down. I'll drag you down with me if I have to!"

I swallowed my shock. I'd counseled dozens of grieving souls. I knew what close siblings anger and grief were. I'd even heard threats against the goddess herself. I'd never been personally blamed, though, and I'd never felt like I deserved to be.

I'm too close. The thought rang through my mind, though I wasn't certain if they were the words of my training or bodily fear. Either way, I bowed respectfully, as if heeding the woman's wishes, and walked swiftly away.

"You hear me!" her words followed. "I'll drag you so deep Hell will never find you!"

Her curses rang off the surrounding cliffs until they were nothing more than wordless echoes of rage.

"Is it done?" Tashan asked from the wagon's bench.

I only nodded.

"Are you all right?" he asked, his slow southern accent somehow making his words sound more sincere.

I looked up at him. "How did their son die?"

The honesty in his eyes faded. My jaw tensed in frustration. Was this why he and Larsa had come to blows?

"Tashan." I laid a hand on the knee resting almost at my eye level. "Please. I have to know we didn't do this."

Something flitted across his expression, perhaps a shiver of doubt, but he merely turned his eyes away.

"It's my fault," Larsa said almost nonchalantly, climbing into the back of the wagon and angling her hat's wide brim against the sun just climbing above the cliffs. She fixed her sights on me, challenging.

I accepted. "How?"

"Don't think I laid a hand on the boy." She sounded indignant. "I'm not a slave to any thirst."

"Who, then? Because the body in the ground up there says otherwise." I was past caring about insulting her.

"What you've read and a week of my company hardly makes you an expert on my kind. I don't kiss like that." She displayed her canines, more pointed than a human's, but not so prominent that they marked her as some monster. Still, they seemed plenty sharp to me.

If she expected that to spark some insight, I disappointed her.

"A vampire fed on your patient. The marks were obvious." Larsa tapped a nail against her tooth. "My fangs can't leave punctures that deep. If I want to drink, I have to tear. But that's not the case for whatever's been following us."

"What makes you think something's following us?"

"Aside from the dead man? You know I have a sense for the dead. The night we camped by the burned inn I sensed something. At first I thought it was him," she jerked a thumb toward Tashan, "but it was something lingering, something close by. Since then, I've caught hints of something shadowing us. If it's needed to feed, it's done so without us noticing. Last night there was only one hunting ground and only a few choices besides us. The local boy was obvious prey."

"Is that why you beat him bloody?" I gestured at Tashan.

"I suspected something else and was wrong." She gave him a sidelong glance. "We've made our peace."

Tashan didn't so much as nod, making me wonder if the sentiment was truly shared.

"It's not him, and it's not me, so it has to be something else. Something that's dead, and that bites. So I suspect a vampire from Caliphas—maybe a servant of Rivascis, I don't know. Whatever the case, it's following us."

"So we did bring it with us," I thought out loud.

"It's watching us, but I don't think it means us harm. It would have had plenty of opportunities if it did."

Larsa's nonchalant suggestion that a monster followed our
trail left me more angry than scared. "It just means those around
us harm."

She made a small shrug.

"You don't seem concerned."

"I'm not. If the time comes to deal with it, we'll deal with it.
Until then, nothing's changed."

I leaned forward, barely restraining the desire to scream into
her face. "You understand that whatever it is killed that boy last
night? We brought that death here."

"We didn't kill him and have no control over what did." She
closed her eyes, as though the conversation was over.

"Except to move on," Tashan chimed in. "Staying only threatens
these people longer. We should go."

He was right. It made me feel like a coward, and a guilty
coward at that, but he was right. The best we could do was get back
on the road where we perhaps jeopardized fewer lives, and where
we might be able to coax our stalker out.

I glared back at Larsa, but her face was hidden beneath her
hat's brim. With an annoyed grunt I set aside the matter for now
and climbed onto the bench opposite Tashan. He tugged the reins
and started the cart into motion.

The Slit o' the Sun had been a beacon that saved our lives the
night before. As we left, it looked abandoned, just a few stone walls
and timbers heaped amid the cliffs. Whatever light had been here
was certainly gone now.

I couldn't restore the Saunnier's son to them, but I could make
sure that whatever had killed him followed him soon.

"Are those tombs?" Tashan asked, his eyes fixed on the wall of
spines rising along Lake Kavapesta's distant bank.

"Worse." Larsa looked past him. "Cathedrals."

The Osirian marveled. "There are so many—like a city not for the living."

He was right, in a sense.

Not long after we left the Slit o' the Sun, signs of civilization had begun to appear. Gargoyles, their faces erased by age, watched us cross the defiant arches of the Senir Bridge. The ancient stones marked the border between the mountain county of Ulcazar and the vales of Amaans below. We were tempted to race across the lonely length, but crumbling gaps—some large enough to swallow a whole carriage—yawned along the bridge's edges. We passed cautiously, the winds from the Senir River below bemoaning a missed meal.

Scant miles beyond, a trail maker bore the name "Wait's Span," yet all we found were cold foundations and stones melted like wax. Again we hurried on.

Finally, we emerged into the northern hills, a country of thin fir trees and slow, freezing streams. The land felt somehow frail here. Cold mountain winds blew from our backs, sending dust devils flitting through the woods. Bare roots were a common sight, with whole groves of crooked trees having just given up their grips in the sandy earth. Birds and rodents seemed common enough, but I'd seen better-fed things in the gutters of Caliphas. From the crowns of some hills we could see through the spindly trees, glimpsing vast muddy waters beyond.

As we crested a bald rise, the cloudy expanse of Lake Kavapesta spilled before us. Countless islands of rotting wood and mossy scrub mired in the muddy shallows, obscuring any border between the lake and land. The winds barely stirred the murky waters, making it look like some great mud plain.

I couldn't imagine who would look at the stagnant lake, the loose earth, and the patchy plants, then willingly decide to raise a city here. The hills were only a step away from being a wasteland,

and we'd seen no sign of mines or their tailings along the path. The only reason was faith.

I answered Tashan's comment. "They call it the Holy City of Pharasma." I nodded toward the steeples, made ghostly by the distance.

Larsa scoffed. "Who does?"

"Mostly those who live here. Believers in the Pharasmin Penitence."

"What's that?" Tashan asked.

"Fanatics," Larsa oversimplified.

"Not entirely," I explained. "They're servants of Pharasma, but they hold strong beliefs about how the goddess expects us to live our lives."

Tashan looked surprised. "Members of your faith don't all believe the same thing?"

"We believe in the same goddess, the path from birth to death, and the mysteries along the way. But for members of the Pharasmin Penitence, that path is covered in thorns."

He looked doubtful.

I tried to explain. "They believe pain comes from Pharasma. That every hardship in their life, every sorrow and loss, is orchestrated by the goddess."

"They think their goddess is wicked?"

"They believe she tests them, that life is the strictest trial. They believe that in death, the goddess will weigh their hardships and tears and balance them with rewards in the afterlife. Those who struggle and suffer will find an eternity of comfort, while those who find fortune in life will pay for it in the life beyond."

"It's a delusion for slaves," Larsa said.

"It's a comfort for those born into hardship," I clarified, "and who have little hope of escape. Everyone wants to believe they have it harder than their neighbors, that their survival is somehow extraordinary. The Pharasmin Penitence lets its followers believe that every trial has a purpose, that the goddess is mindful of them—even if it's only to confound them—and that every loss is not just divine, but bears the promise of a future reward."

Tashan gave the distant city a suspicious look. "They sound like a joyless sort."

"Many are, but some of the most steadfast servants of the goddess I've ever met follow the Penitence."

"And they burn witches," Larsa threw in. I could hear an atheistic smile in her voice.

I began explaining before the furrows creased Tashan's brow. "The penitents believe magic is for the goddess and her servants alone. To them, those who can reshape the world with magic are sidestepping adversities meted out by the goddess. There have been *stories*," I cast a frown back to Larsa, "of evangelists of the Penitence dredging up tales of curses and crones, pointing at those who dabble in magic as allies of evils. In some more rural villages it has led to regrettable attacks on those who practice magic. In the worst cases, some outcasts have been burned as witches."

Tashan shook his head. "Foolish."

"These are extreme and very rare cases that the larger church certainly doesn't condone."

"So they're heretics?" he asked.

I paused to think how best to explain. "Pharasma is the goddess of mysteries. While she is very clear regarding some blasphemies, like any good mother she lets her children learn for themselves. Her holiest prophecies are among those that can be interpreted in the greatest variety of ways. So, as her servants, we endlessly seek meaning in her words, in the world around us, and in ourselves. In that way, on many matters, it's difficult to say that any one interpretation is right or wrong, or that there is but a single meaning."

Larsa scoffed. "In other words, your faith is fine with innocents occasionally getting burned alive, so long as someone can argue that it's in the goddess's name."

I disregarded her antagonistic tone. "Pharasma is neither a savior nor a murderer. She watches, and at the end of our lives she judges. We are responsible for those lives. The headsman, the fugitive, and the innocent are all judged alike."

She gave a nasty little chuckle. "Convenient."

"The people of Kavapesta, then, they think this way?" Tashan asked.

"The Pharasmin Penitence began there long ago. The faithful remain, both to honor the goddess, and because life here is so difficult."

"The place is cursed. It's a plague city," Larsa helpfully pointed out.

The Pathfinder's head shot around.

"Must you?" I asked with a sigh.

"It's true, isn't it?" She pretended at innocence.

I tried to sound reassuring. "The people of Kavapesta have suffered more than one plague, but the last was years ago, and they're much less likely this late in the year."

I could tell from the look on Tashan's face that I hadn't been especially successful.

"We're well provisioned and can stand another few nights camping. We don't need anything badly enough to waste time stopping there." He didn't sound like he wanted to debate. Even though his fear was misplaced, he wasn't wrong.

"I agree." Larsa's voice suddenly had a congenial ring to it.

Oh. I chuckled, realizing her scheme. Of course she didn't want to stop in a city full of Pharasmins. If even a few moments in one of the goddess's cathedrals had ended so uncomfortably, a night in a city full of the Lady's most fervent devotees could go far worse.

"If you were concerned about stopping here, you could have just said so."

She shrugged.

Avoiding Kavapesta proved more difficult than we'd expected. The trail rode the hills alongside the lake for miles, the city slinking toward us every time it fell out of sight behind a hill or grove of trees. Cottage farms appeared some acres back from the road. Occasionally, a somberly dressed traveler passed by. I didn't think much of it at first, but by the third time, I realized each passerby was going out of his way to meet my eyes, acknowledging me with either a nod or by making Pharasma's spiral over his heart. None spoke, though. They all seemed more interested in divulging their faith than making greetings.

Dusk fell over Lake Kavapesta in bizarre streaks of orange and magenta. As we crested out of the highlands, the city revealed itself again, smoke from a thousand chimneys drifting up as if from as many censers. Few buildings rose above walls so pale they might have been made from temple marble. Without, exception those that did were cathedrals, each marked with thorny spires or the goddess's symbol in colored glass. Even Caliphas held only one of the goddess's holy houses, but if Kavapesta's skyline was to be believed, the city was peopled by priests alone.

The course of the New Surdina passed near Kavapesta's gates, still miles away. Not far ahead, though, a road swept north, winding away into a land of brown grasses and tiny bridges over muddy streams. Tashan gave a nod as I pointed it out as the way toward Ardis.

By the time we reached the crossroads, the sky had succumbed to night. Traffic had thinned as the day came to a close, but still we passed locals with lanterns, mostly in small groups but occasionally a lone individual. No one seemed to be in any particular

hurry—a rarity with our land's countless tales and truths of disap-
pearances in the night.

We could have probably found a place to stay, even skirting
Kavapesta. Although the locals were likely just as wary of strangers
here as anywhere else, I suspected a flash of my holy symbol could
have bought us a warm meal and a dry barn for the night. But how
many Kensre Saunniers might be lighting candles in the home-
steads along the road? And was there even now something waking
into the night behind us? Something that would soon find us and,
after it did, turn its attention to its hunger? Better to sleep apart
from any innocent. Even if we couldn't prevent our stalker's hunt,
we could at least not condemn the guiltless for the sin of charity.

It was hardly the hero's option, but I wasn't trying to be a hero.
I just didn't want to feel like a murderer when I woke up.

A guard wearing chain armor over violet robes stepped onto
the road as we approached the fork leading to Kavapesta. He
wasn't alone. Several mounted figures bore torches against the
night, tarrying at the crossroads with their lights held high. They
bore emblems emblazoned with crowned skulls and Pharasma's
spiral, the crest of Kavapesta. Guards, except for the ones that were
clearly Pharasmin priests—not surprising if what I'd heard about
the city's near-theocratic rule held true.

I asked Tashan to slow the cart and was suddenly unsure of
how I held myself when I wasn't actively trying to look innocent.
The guard on foot approached my side of the cart and asked my
name. His fellows looked over the coach, scrutinizing us with
casual suspicion. Knowing that, realistically, I had nothing to fear,
I told him plainly.

A pike's blunt end cracked upon Tashan's jaw before any of us
realized what was happening. When Larsa moved, prayers washed
over her with holy fire.

19

BLOODY-MINDED
LARSA

A metallic screech brought with it a reminder of consciousness. In the dark, that relentless pounding battered every thought struggling to crystallize, an endless beating I'd lost any will to resist. My pulse rose in my chest, my face, my skull, every strike a soundless steady assault.

Realizing I was alive was a surprise, but also released a flood of awareness. It was warm and I was lying on something hard. Thirst assailed me. Even through the pounding pain, it gnawed for my attention—parched and bottomless, a well in the sand. Gods of Heaven and Hell, I wanted a drink, wanted it so bad I could feel the thirst in my teeth.

The pain, the craving, the dull cramps, the sense of falling—I'd been broken enough times to recognize them all. There was a snapping noise as well, something I couldn't account for. Drops, too, striking my face—too irregular for rain.

Opening my eyes felt like lifting my whole body, forcing myself up from an oblivion of calm dark and simple pains into a world of worse.

Fire rushed through the crack in my lids. It pierced, sharp and white, and my body knotted as if stabbed. I squeezed my eyes shut for a long while before trying to breach the world again.

The burning blur beyond didn't relent, but through slits my eyes adjusted as best they could. Even through the harsh light I could see the stone beneath me. Warm and reflecting the intense glare, sandy blocks spread like a sculpted desert, dust encrusting eye-level seams.

There was a snap. Something dripped on my neck.

Adjusting to roll some of the weight off my aching side was more difficult than expected. Something peeled, the wet rip of stickiness between me and the floor. Knives unsheathed in my side, scouring raw nerves. Slapping a hand to the stabbing sensation didn't help, but it was a relief to feel the numbness ebbing from my fingers.

Another tick. A drip into my hair.

Damp crust coated my clothes. Sweat? Blood? Had I been wounded? A crossroads, priests, their damnable chanting, fire that burned past flesh. I felt light. My arms and legs were bare. My gloves, cloak, leathers—they were all missing. The ugly scar-ladders climbing from my wrists and ankles tingled, taunting me, making me feel worse than naked.

"It's disgusting how much you bleed."

I started at the unfamiliar voice so close by. Instincts shouted to roll away, but without knowing how badly I was wounded, I didn't dare anything dramatic. I exhaled a slow, ragged breath, but that—and the thought that I'd be long dead if the speaker had wanted—did little to make me feel less like a caged dog.

"How much of that can you even call yours?" continued the arch, philosophizing voice. Another tick, then something struck my face. It bounced off and hit the slab floor, skipping to a halt under my eyes. Something black. I strained to focus.

A shell. A cracked sunflower seed shell.

Gingerly, I pushed myself off the floor, trying to keep the pain bearable. The dozens of knives stabbing my insides increased their attack, but didn't grow into larger, angrier blades. I was panting by the time I managed to sit up.

Tiny shells pattered upon the floor as I shifted. Some slipped down my shirt, more caught in my hair.

Light streamed into the room from every angle. There was no doubt it was a cell, but I'd never seen one so bright, or with so much glass. Polished manacles offered places for several occupants. Between each pair of restraints climbed a column of thick glass bricks, meeting above to create a clear, pointed roof. It was like the inside of a glass steeple, the crown of some temple for worshiping the heavens. Some of the glass squares were shattered, suggested that not all brought here worshiped willingly.

The room's pale stone tolerated no shadows, reflecting the harsh glare into every shallow corner of the octagonal cell. Even the single metal door was polished to nearly a mirror's sheen. For most it would probably be uncomfortably bright. For eyes like mine, born for shadows, it was like staring into the sun. It invaded through my cinched eyelids, filling my mind with a wall of white. I inched myself against one of the narrow windows, trying to block even a small portion with my body. It didn't help.

A glance through the windows revealed distortions of steepled structures hanging amid the blaring white. I was somewhere high, but had to turn from the blaze beyond before guessing more.

Another tick. It came from a man-sized silhouette, limned in white and drifting near the center of the room. Squinting, I made out a hint of red and the vague shape of a barrel-lid hat. A Pharasmin inquisitor.

"How many innocents are bleeding through you?" It was clearly a man's voice, deliberate and accusing, like a barrister speaking in court. Another shell hit the floor. "How many do you think? Six? Ten? Twenty?"

I swallowed as best I could, my lips cracked. I wasn't sure what I appreciated less: his sanctimonious tone or that the question make me even thirstier.

"I might remember better after I had a drink." My voice sounded raspy, grating in my throat.

A condescending little chuckle drifted through the light. "First thing on your mind. Sorry, but we don't feed our children to monsters here."

"Water would do."

He popped another seed. Fabric rustled and something hurtled toward me. I fumbled with both hands, jamming still-numb fingers, but somehow caught it.

Clear water sloshed inside the bottle, held in by a stopper etched with Pharasma's holy spiral. As tempting as it was, I frowned down it. A flask from a holy man's robes? There was no way it was just water. Holy water, likely, but it could also be some sort of healing draught. Blessed water drank just as well as any other sort, but the reaction my body had to Pharasmins' usual healing magic made me wary.

The pain flared as I thought about it. It came from all over, even from inside. The priests had called it with their prayers, the fire of their faith. To them—to the living—it was a warmth that healed. But not for those like me. For those who harbored death, it was a searing flame. A flame that consumed, that could even destroy. And it could take many forms.

I considered the flask. Fretting was only giving him what he wanted. I yanked out the stopper and sipped, prepared for another wave of that soul-searing burn. It didn't come. I gulped down the rest. Aside from being body-warmed and having a slight after-taste—likely never having been meant for drinking—it was plain water. I made a show of wiping my mouth. "Thanks."

I rested back against the wall, shading my eyes as best I could. "So how long do you usually hold kidnapped agents of the crown?"

"Not long. I'm aware of what you claim to be." Another seed cracked between his teeth then skidded across the floor. "We would have let the goddess's fire consume you if it wasn't for your enslaved priestess."

"Jadain?" A fresh stab of pain cut off my chuckle.

His voice grew sharp. "You will call her Sister Losritter."

"I'll call her half the pain in my ass and the reason I'm not in Ardis already."

"You planned to use her to sneak past the city's guards."

"Oh really?" I shook my head at the claim's self-centered idiocy. "Why? So I'd be on time for evening services?"

"I know why the snake seeks the nest."

"Of course you do." He started to ask something else, but I cut him off. "Where are Jadain and Tashan?"

He ignored me. "When did you take control of Sister Losritter?"

"That's ridiculous. As if I'd want to even if I could."

"Don't patronize us, monster. We know your kind better than we'd like."

"I bet."

He said he knew my kind, but I doubted he'd ever actually met another dhampir. In the bastard's mind I was already staked and burning in the sun.

He repeated himself. "You will tell me how long ago you enslaved Sister Losritter."

But he wasn't asking about me.

"If you're so interested in her, why not ask her directly?"

"We certainly will, once we're convinced your control has faded. This will be easier if you tell us what we want to know. I know your kind can still feel pain."

I'd seen dozens of vampires force their will upon humans, dominating weaker minds with the intensity of their presence. Although it would make my investigations endlessly less compli- cated, it was simply a talent my watered-down vampiric blood denied me. My jailer obviously didn't believe that, though. If I'd dominated Jadain, she was my victim. But if I hadn't, she was my . . .

He began some threat.

"In Caliphas, weeks ago. Who remembers." I tried to sound flippant.

"Accuracy will make this easier for you." He fished among the seeds in his palm, flicking out an unworthy or two. "Why her?"

"A priestess seemed like she'd make good bait. No one would question a holy woman asking them to step down an alley with her."

"But why *her*?"

I dared only the smallest shrug. "I passed her one night. I almost took her, then thought better."

"You've fed on her, then?" His disgust was apparent.

"Of course not. Marks could give her away." I tried to change the subject. Details were tripwires in an interrogation, and the more I laid the more likely I'd eventually stumble. "When am I to be executed?"

Again he ignored me. "You took her from Maiden's Choir?"

It was my turn to be insistent. "When?"

The silhouette hung silently for a long moment. "I can force you to answer."

Did he think I didn't suspect what his order had in store for me? I doubted I had much to lose. "Not if I bite my tongue off first," I said plainly. "We both know it won't kill me, but a few hours of silence is starting to sound real good."

He took a breath to consider. "You'll have another night."

With that, the figure drifted toward the door.

I laid my arm over my eyes, trying to ignore the feel of old scars in order to block out the relentless light. "I suppose I'll see you in the morning, then."

"Sooner than that. We wouldn't send you to the goddess unclean."

I doubted he meant some ritual incense-burning and cloth-waving. "Try. We can visit your miserable goddess together."

"Your kind always says the same thing, but we have our ways." I could practically hear his sneer.

"I'm sure."

"And in case those ways don't work on a thing like you . . ." He opened the cell's door, its hinges screeching. "The doses of calotropis oil you just drank should."

My arm fell from my eyes, a litany of curses and a sudden bitter taste crowding my mouth. Calotropis oil? Some kind of poison?

A crimson hem fluttered and the door to my gleaming prison slammed shut.

20

INQUISITION
JADAIN

The door to our dingy prison whined open.

I released Tashan's hand, having just pulled it away from his jaw to examine the plum-sized bruise fruiting there. It wasn't pretty, but it was far from life-threatening. Normally I wouldn't bother calling upon the goddess to heal what nature would tend to, but in this case I was tempted—one of my order had given him it, after all. Tashan gingerly reapplied his scarf, its dawn colors now stained with rusty red bursts.

My heart lurched at the sight of crimson robes. Heavy iron keys rattled as one of Pharasma's inquisitors stepped into our bare stone cell.

Only he didn't look like most inquisitors. The goddess's hunters were typically from the same stock as soldiers, severe types that didn't look comfortable without a weapon in hand. This was someone's grandfather. Thin-shouldered with a head of wispy, hat-flattened white hair, he looked more like a schoolmaster than an agent of divine justice—especially as he wrestled his keys from the stubborn lock. An amulet like mine, but cast in steel, bounced against his chest. He retrieved his keys with a jerk and squinted into the dim cell.

"Sister Losritter?" He sounded unsure. "And . . . attendant."

I exchanged a suspicious glance with Tashan. "Yes?"

"Yes. Good." The elderly man stepped inside, unarmed and leaving the door open behind him. "Terribly sorry, all of these chambers look very much alike."

"Where I'm from, cathedrals don't have dungeons," I said.

After we'd surrendered to the guards, they'd taken us through a gate attended by priests and crenelated with short steeples. A march through narrow, excessively well-lit streets led us to a tower sculpted with staring, masked psychopomps and, finally, to this cell.

"Oh, you're not in the cathedral." He said it like it was supposed to be reassuring. "Even in the Holy City we have places to attend to our more secular needs." He peered at a sheaf of papers in his hand, going on without waiting for an answer. "Conveniently, that brings me to my first question. Our records show you studied at the Chapel of Guilts yet were ordained at the House of Solace in Vische—"

"I never served at the Chapel of Guilts," I interrupted.

He gave a curt hum and tapped the page with a finger like a chicken bone. "But you served in Caliphas? At the royal cathedral?"

"I still serve there," I answered shortly. I shook my head, clearing the haze of bureaucracy. "Who are you, and why are we being held here?"

"My bones! Forgive me. I'm Brother Abelard, servant of the Lady of Mysteries and the high priestess of her holy city, Mother Ulametria." His tone turned gentle, even sad—a man giving a child serious news. "You're here, Sister, because you attacked a guard patrol alongside a devil in mortal skin."

Attacked! Devil?

"We didn't!" Tashan tried to yell, a thick noise smothered by the scarf balled over his face. The inquisitor looked mildly surprised.

I held out a hand and Tashan reluctantly slumped back into the corner. "Larsa? Where is she?"

They hadn't carried her into the city with us. Last I saw her she was lying limp in the back of the cart, overwhelmed by divine light.

He shook his head.

The followers of the Pharasmin Penitence were staunch traditionalists, obsessed with the soul's condition, but even they wouldn't have murdered Larsa outright . . . probably. "Brother, please. Is she alive?"

He frowned, staring. "Not as you and I know the goddess's gift, but in a manner of speaking. Until judgment is wrought, she's being kept in one of our sun cells. It's designed to hold things like her."

I didn't know what a "sun cell" was, but that she was alive was something of a relief.

Brother Abelard spared a glimpse at Tashan. "Does your man need healing?"

"I'm fine." The scarf covering Tashan's mouth did little to disguise the bitterness in his reply.

"What crime is she being charged with?" I pressed.

"Sister," he said with a father's firmness. "Please. You must forget her."

I tried not to rankle at his patronizing. "I have responsibilities in Ardis—responsibilities the Holy Mother of Caliphas gave her blessing. Larsa has a role to play in my work."

"What responsibilities?"

I saw no reason to hide our goals from him, and briefly explained Doctor Trice's concerns regarding Ailson Kindler's safety and the doctor's position as a healer and friend of the church. I certainly didn't understate Larsa's part in our venture, or her position as a royal agent.

He nodded as I finished, his thin white brows pinched together. "And your Holy Mother endorsed the half-dead's involvement in your work? She gave her the goddess's blessing?"

I sealed the truth behind a tight frown. No, of course she hadn't. While I hadn't lied about Larsa's involvement, Mother Thestia hadn't asked about her specifically, and I hadn't gone out of my way to bring up her heritage.

My pause was answer enough for the inquisitor. "I thought not. That does ease some of my concern about how far our southern brethren have fallen, though."

"What's that supposed to mean?"

He ignored me, considering a cell wall. "What hold does she have over you?"

"What hold? As in, has she hypnotized me or is she using some power to control me?" I scoffed. "No, of course not."

He looked back to me, his mouth a grim line. "Consider this well, Sister. The undead have many terrible ways. They can infect us, turn our own wills against us. Can you be certain she hasn't exerted some power over you."

Why was he trying to get me to confess against Larsa? Did they need crimes to condemn her as neatly as they wanted? Was her blood not crime enough for them?

I composed myself, speaking firmly and clearly. "Royal Accuser Larsa has no power over me. In fact, neither my training nor my experience give me any reason to believe she even has the ability to mystically influence other minds."

Brother Abelard made a short, disappointed sigh, shaking his head.

Somewhat heartened, I continued. "We know so little about her kind. The church teaches us not to fear death, but to see wonder in the miracle of being and the mysteries of the hereafter. Undeath is abomination, but those like her are as alive as they are undead. If life and mystery are holier to the goddess than undeath, why would we ever extinguish lives as tenacious and mysteries as deep as what she represents? The goddess brought her into this world. We must trust in the goddess's will and accept Larsa as one of her children."

Silence hung between us.

"This is what is in your heart? These are your words and no other's?" The inquisitor's face remained impassive.

I didn't hesitate. "They are."

Again he nodded. "Then I'm sorry, I had hoped it would be otherwise." He folded his papers, tucking them into his robes and drawing himself up.

"Jadain Losritter." His voice had changed. No longer the casual sigh of a bored clerk, every word became an accusation. "The inquisition of Cryptgate Cathedral, executor of Pharasma's law in her holy city of Kavapesta, accuses you of crimes against the faithful, the church, and the goddess herself. For willfully misinterpreting the Lady's creed and spreading blasphemy with the intent to disguise her enemies, I charge you with heresy in the second order."

The charge struck me like a slap.

"As a member of the inquisition, I confirm and second allegations brought against you and will recommend to the office of the Holy Mother that you face immediate excommunication. You will be held here to await the Holy Mother's verdict and then face trial for your crimes."

It felt as though I were underwater. My vision bobbed, I forgot how to breathe. Tashan was on his feet and at my side. He brought an arm around my shoulder, as if he thought I might fall.

The Osirian channeled my question, anger bringing out his accent. "What allegations?"

The inquisitor answered as though I'd asked. "We received word from your own church some days ago, informing us of your situation."

I drew myself up, pushing down a sick feeling. "What situation?"

"That blasphemous forces may have tempted you from the path of faith. It was only a suspicion, but one it saddens me to confirm."

"My faith has never faltered!" I gripped the wooden spiral around my neck. Immediately I looked down. I felt the grain of the wood . . . and that was all. The cold touch of Pharasma's presence, the comfort of that subtle chill, was entirely absent. Suddenly I was back in Havenguard, in cell eighteen.

He saw the concern in my face. "Your church's own High Exorcist saw this in you and warned us."

"Mardhalas?"

The rider I saw her send the night before we departed. The High Exorcist couldn't act against Larsa in her own temple, not without our Holy Mother's consent and not with the throne close enough to defend its agent. Here, with these zealots, though, all she had to do was raise the shadow of doubt. Or was I truly her target? Was my mercy really so unforgivable to her?

"I know our brethren in the capital think of the goddess as an absentee mother, but here we know her lessons and feel her guiding hand," the inquisitor said. "Here, when we stray, we feel the sting of her slap. I pity you, Miss Losritter. Your failure should have been noticed sooner, but it seems that many in your order are just as lost." He turned and laid a hand on the door.

I wanted to ignore him, to beg him to take it all back, to scream. "Wait!"

Over his shoulder he spared a look of waning tolerance.

"Regardless of my place in the church—"

"You have no place."

"Regardless, I'm still a witness to Larsa's innocence. Don't let the condition of my faith influence your ruling over her. She's no monster and deserves to be released."

"My dear, that creature's end was decided the moment she came within these walls. Our questions were only ever about you." The door swung. "And now we have none."

21

CAVITY
LARSA

The cramping came gradually, rising in my body as the sun rose above my glass cell. What there was of stone and steel fell away, replaced by relentless light and aching stiffness. The poison seized my legs and shoulders first, then seeped through the rest of my body. I stretched and twisted for hours, limbs knotting, screaming to bend even as muscles grew thick and tough. It was all I could do to bury my eyes in the crook of my arm, sealing out the bombarding sunlight. I could still feel the heat on every inch of my skin. Even through my arm and clenched eyelids I could see a glow like a hot iron.

My prison was a red ache, exploding with every pulse and forced breath. Never before had my heart felt tired. I tried not to panic, but with every beat it grew more exhausted.

At some point I broke. I screamed, but the poison denied even that release. A dry draft escaped the crack between my lips. I strained, but only managed a squeak. I doubt my agony disturbed even a dust mote.

The crash of the door against the wall pealed through my silent prison. I had no idea how long it had been. The heat on my body might have cooled, or perhaps my skin had blackened to nothing but blisters. Even if I could bring myself to dare the light, I couldn't force my paralyzed arm from my face.

Footsteps. The whisper of clothing, too, brushing the floor. My visitor returned.

"I tasted the oil myself once, when I was young and careless," came the familiar voice. "It was only a drop, but it felt like my muscles were going to crush my bones. I pitched for hours, broke two ribs in the process."

A prodding boot rocked my hip, releasing a burst of frozen pain.

"Making sure you're not asleep. Can't have you missing anything."

Metal struck near my head. I flinched, the jerk like a stab to the neck. A breath locked in my throat. My lungs strained, but my gasp was utterly silent.

I could feel the inquisitor close, kneeling down.

"I want you to know, I thought about having more conversations with you," he said. "I've interrogated several of your kind."

A cord loosened only inches from my ear. Muffled metal clattered and squealed, sounding like a sack full of silverware. Leather slapped upon the stone floor.

"They're always as arrogant as you—but they're usually more charming."

Metal slid across a soft surface, then delicately touched to stone.

"I spoke with your friend earlier today, and you know what I think?" He hardly paused. "I think you're a liar."

The soft clinking took up a slow, regular beat.

"It's a pity, because that makes your friend a heretic—but we know how to deal with traitors to the faith."

Jadain a heretic? She was certainly softer than most Pharasmins I'd met, definitely less dour and more concerned with the living. Could being too sympathetic, too alive, be a sin against the goddess of death?

"You, however, are a more unusual case." He let something heavier clatter to the stone. "The entire climb here I was wondering if I was wasting my time. I half expected to get up here and find nothing but a pile of ash. I should have known better. You're a stubborn one."

Another metallic clatter.

"And that's good for me."

Disgust rose simultaneously in my mind and the pit of my stomach.

"I've been afforded broad discretion in dealing with you," he went on, sounding increasingly self-important. "You being what you are, we don't have to make any show of a trial, you see. Your fate lies totally in the hands of the inquisition—and I suspect you can guess how the inquisition deals with things like you."

So I was being condemned for having one foot in the grave, while Jadain was being condemned for not. If this was going the way I expected, at least I'd soon have my chance to smack Pharasma for breeding a church full of hypocrites.

"I have to admit, though, I'm somewhat out of practice with things like this. I can't travel like I used to, and now I have a whole troop of zealous youngsters ready to leap at even the rumor of a sunken grave."

The clinking ceased.

"But the goddess smiles on the truly faithful. See how she brought you? You practically knocked on our door."

A frail hand lightly patted my shoulder. I tried to recoil, but my body was like wood. Fortunately, his touch didn't linger.

His voice turned wistful. "I remember what it was like. We were heroes—crusaders for the goddess. 'You'll find worms under every hearth,' they said, and we proved them right."

Was this his punishment—his "broad discretion"? A has-been's rambling?

"How many kept idols hidden in the shadows? How many signed bargains in blood? We tore their roots from the mud and dragged them to cathedral marble. That was always that. A warning to the people, a victory for the church . . . but don't you wonder what the inquisitor takes away?"

He paused, too long to just mock my inability to answer. Was he reliving his memories?

"The priests would say our reward was in the deed, in spreading the goddess's justice—but eventually the rhetoric wears thin. We're not man-hunters or sellswords; the church never paid a bounty on sinners. So we had to find our own rewards."

He dropped something by my ear, something hard that clattered but wasn't metal. A rosary perhaps.

"We went back into the mud for them. We called it purifying—it sounded good to the priests—but we all knew what it was. Sometimes we'd actually find something, a mark to scour clean or a fetish to hand over to the clerics. We were all looking for something different, though. It was never about gold—though Brother Markave did keep a chain of coins. It was about proof, evidence of victories, standing amid our ranks. We were champions of the goddess and her work was done, but we were soldiers, and every soldier takes trophies."

I had expected some kind of torture, or even outright murder, but I was realizing that this was something else.

"Our only rule was it had to be something different. If Teym was collecting locks of hair and Lorrimor had a pouch of bent spoons, you had to take something else."

The heap of pieces clicked together, the inquisitor fondling them.

"I was always proud of my collection, even if they were a pain to take. Got me reprimanded more than once. They were even confiscated—Old Rollenthol probably died thinking they were lost in his desk drawer. But they've been worth it. Even taught me a skill that made me handy at the barber." His chuckle was a dry stutter.

Collection? Trophies? I wasn't some rabbit to slice up for good-luck charms.

Barely perceptibly, metal whispered against stone. He'd selected something from whatever he'd arranged. Were they knives?

Suddenly all the cuts across my body cried out, the thousands of scars making themselves known. I was back in the Old City, frozen with fear, knowing something ancient, ugly, and old planned to make a meal of me. I tried to struggle, but was no more effective now than when I was a girl. Grandfather's voice was in my head: *If you must blame someone, blame your father.*

Rivascis. The curse I'd spat untold times felt empty now, tinged with regret. If this was the end, if this was my execution, then every night that I'd soothed my pain with vows to destroy the one who'd left me in the dark had been a lie.

The inquisitor's arrogant voice was even closer now. "We're taught the dead don't feel pain, but I've always wondered."

Without warning, a thin, dry thumb invaded my mouth, snaring me between my cheek and upper row of teeth. It tasted like dust. He wrenched upward. A spasm shot through my face. I screamed in my mind. I dared the pain, commanding my jaw to snap shut.

It amounted to nothing more than a quiver.

"I'd like to ask if that's true, but the calotropis oil will hold you well through the morning—and you've got a strict schedule to keep." His voice was above me, leaning in. "They're out there building your pyre right now, readying it for dawn. You'll have to burn fast if you're going to have your ashes scattered by noon."

Something metal forced its way into my mouth. His grip on it trembled. The scraping of steel on bone clawed through my head.

"But then, your kind always seem to go up like tinder." His voice remained infuriatingly calm.

The instrument split in my mouth, wresting my jaw open farther. It felt like a pry bar forcing apart a cracked log. The muscles of my jaw tore, the pain pounding a blood-red drumbeat in my skull.

Shuddering metal slipped deeper, grating my tongue. My throat quivered but couldn't even tighten enough to gag. A long thumbnail scraped my dry gum, gaining a better hold.

I could hear myself screaming. They weren't even words. Images exploded through my blindness, searing white and fierce. I was struggling, clawing, biting. I was back in the dark beneath Caliphas. Loose flesh split under my nails, and I tore and tore. Shrieking images burst one after another. Through pain and fear and desperation I screamed against my body's prison.

The instrument in my mouth adjusted, his hand on the handles brushing my cheek. Some rational reflex twitched amid my panic, an image of unassuming metal grips. I realized what he was after.

Pliers bit my canine and pulled.

22

HERESY

JADAIN

Tashan prowled the cell like exactly the sort of criminal you'd be a fool to let out. After his face stopped bleeding he'd looped his crusty scarf around his belt. It gave him the look of a fighting dog, blood on his muzzle and haunches.

I'd been ignoring him since Brother Abelard left. He'd said my name several times, asked if I was all right, put a hand over mine, but I couldn't accept his worry. At some point I'd wrapped my hands around my amulet, letting the rough wood of Pharasma's cometlike spiral dig into my hands. All I felt was wood, though, rough and warm from my grip.

Usually the goddess's icon was cool to the touch. Not a biting cold, but the chill of a night under the stars, of the dark beyond bedsheets, of bones in a stone crypt. When I touched my symbol I felt the mystery of the world and worlds beyond, and I knew I knew nothing. The goddess was there, though, and she knew, she would be my guide. Or that's what I'd always thought.

It had been one thing to disregard the accusations of a joyless termagant like Mardhalas, but a fatherly old man a half a nation away? They might have been of the same order within the church, but otherwise they couldn't have seemed more different—and I'd somehow convinced both I was unfit.

Excommunication. Spiritual execution. And what after that? What sort of life is there after the goddess of creation deems you unfit? And even beyond. Most souls are judged only once, but if I'd been found lacking in life, what did that herald for my ultimate judgment after death? Excommunication? What he'd really meant was damnation.

I squeezed my amulet, feeling only my pulse in the wood.

Tashan had halted. He was looking down at me. I continued to ignore him.

"Many worship your goddess in my country as well," he said. "In Sothis, the dead are honored, their lives celebrated. In death, they're sent to rest with treasures of a life well lived. The priests there pray to remind the Lady of Mysteries of the departed's deeds and virtues. Their temples are grand and bright, decorated with gold and the faces of the old gods of Osirion."

He crouched in front of me. "And Pharasma smiles on them all the same. If their path pleases the goddess, then certainly that inquisitor's way is not the only one."

I kept studying the stone floor before me, staring through him. I didn't bother to acknowledge him, but I couldn't say he was wrong. Tashan might be an outsider, unfamiliar with many of our nation's customs and ways, but he certainly wasn't a fool. I'd caught myself discounting some of his suggestions based on his ignorance, but in truth he'd traveled farther than I ever had in my life. It would be easy to dismiss his words as baseless optimism, but he probably knew more of the world than me.

I raised my head enough to look him in the face.

Keys rattled in the cell door.

Tashan was up, his back to me. His left hand reflexively grasped at the place where his absent sword would have hung. Disappointed, he clenched it into a fist.

The shadowy figure of a guardsman stood in the door, outlined by torchlight from behind. Possibilities—most frightening— flooded my mind. Were we being released, interrogated, separated, executed? I pushed myself up the wall, regaining my feet.

The guard just stood, bearing a lumpy bundle. Tashan rushed him.

I snapped my mouth shut on a cry, startled by his impulsiveness but dreading our options more. Tashan was on the man, yanking away the guard's load and at once drawing something from it. Metal caught the weak light and Tashan's sword made a familiar wheel, coming between its wielder and the soldier.

The room froze.

In fact, the guard didn't even twitch in surprise. He stood petrified, his arms still crooked, presenting his load.

A long moment passed before Tashan took a cautious step, waving his blade under the guard's chin. The jailer didn't move.

"What is this?" Tashan gave me a quizzical look.

I didn't answer. The same moment he'd turned away, a silhouette had congealed behind the guard. It hadn't come from either of the hall's directions. Instead, it rose as though the jailer's own shadow were defying its owner. Fingers coalesced upon the soldier's helmet.

Seeing my widening stare, Tashan whipped back. The guard's head jerked with the crack of a splitting branch. Dead flesh didn't muffle the sound of falling armor. The shadow remained standing.

I'd barely gasped when Tashan's bronze blade slashed for the door. The shadow vanished into the cell's gloom, shifting into something pale that moved with obscene speed. Slender white fingers locked around Tashan's wrist, jerking his arm and blade awkwardly across his chest.

"Stray cats always get into the strangest trouble." The bemused voice came from lips at Tashan's neck, those of a slim, dark-haired figure locked against the Osirian. The two froze like posing dancers, Tashan's sword folded between him and the stranger.

"Master!" Tashan sounded shocked—but only half as shocked as I was at hearing the word. Sensing my reaction, he twisted my way. The stranger intercepted his glance, though, locking Tashan's face forward with a rigid cheek. Green eyes narrowed over Tashan's shoulder, examining me.

"Landed yourself in prison." The stranger clicked his tongue. "I knew you'd find no end of trouble without me watching over you." The young man pulled back a step, freeing Tashan, but his eyes never left me. He smiled.

I'd seen that tight smile dozens of times before. It typically creased the faces of young nobles struggling to humor the lowborn—those that they couldn't command outright. Tousled hair gave him the look of some sheltered squire, but that innocence died in his mossy eyes. I could practically feel their cold. They didn't match with a face that made Tashan look experienced.

"I though you might have returned to the city," Tashan said, a soft twinge in his voice.

One of the stranger's thin eyebrows angled as he looked to Tashan. "Did that worry you?"

Tashan looked down, remembering the bundle that had clattered to the floor. It was our traveling cloaks wrapped around Tashan's pack. From one side jutted the lavender-wrapped hilt of my dagger. He unrolled the collection.

It wasn't all ours. Tashan held up a bulbous flask holding some tarry concoction, clearly marked with a tiny flame symbol.

Considine shrugged. "A few souvenirs I picked up in the armory with the rest of your junk. What's your little Pathfinder motto? 'Prepare, prepare, prepare,' or some such?"

It seemed to be good enough for Tashan. He stashed the bottle in his pack. Moving on to my possessions, he handed me my cloak and coin purse then extended my weapon.

"Just a moment there." With an upward sweep the stranger intercepted my blade, like a mother plucking a butcher's knife out of an infant's hand. "We're all friends here. There won't be any need for that."

He jammed the sheath into his belt, somehow finding space between the tight fabric and his narrow waist. He parried my frown with a charmless smirk. "Considine of Caliphas, the capital's foremost guide and garbage collector. And you," he wagged a finger at me, "are awfully popular for a priestess. All my best friends speak very highly of Sister Jadain."

He looked around the cell, pointing at opposite corners with an arc of his chin. "It looks like you've wooed your church fellows here as well." He toed the guard's corpse lying at his side. "This one took endless convincing before he agreed to introduce us."

If pointlessly murdering a man hadn't already left me disgusted, his disrespect for the dead would have.

"I doubt we have any mutual friends," I said.

"Oh, there's that famous Pharasmin charm!" He smiled, wrinkling his nose. "I bet you can make all the corpses blush. That's how you and Larsa became such fast friends, isn't it?"

"You know Larsa?" I gave him a second look. He had the arrogance I expected from agents of the crown. Could he be another accuser?

His closed-mouth smile stretched even farther. "Closer than blood for longer than years. And of course, our boy here as well. I'm Tashan's oldest friend."

The two shared a look, Considine looking very pleased with himself. Tashan shook his head.

"And now we're all friends!" The fop spoke quickly. "But alas, it's time to leave. So you should hand me your pretty little amulet and we should gather up Larsa and all be off before anyone notices the mess. Yes? Yes."

He extended his hand. The wooden spiral hanging against my chest made a single weak pulse.

"What? No." I couldn't imagine why he wanted my holy symbol. I'd whittled it myself, and I had no illusions about my skill with a knife. More than once I'd had my purse taken from me in

Caliphas. At knifepoint I'd been asked for my boots and belt, but never my amulet.

"I don't know you and I don't know why you'd want—" I choked.

Considine smiled wider. Even in the low light his white teeth glistened, his canines like snake fangs. Not the subtle points of Larsa's teeth, nothing that could be explained as a quirk of birth, they were scalpels cast in bone.

I grabbed the goddess's symbol. I might have offended the Lady of Graves. I might have been a poor student of her word. I might have brought shame to her church. Yet for all of my flaws, when faced with evil, it was for her I reached. I prayed that was something the goddesses valued.

I presented the twist of wood before me, a tiny shield against the undead.

"See, this is why," Considine said. "If you don't want to be friendly, I'm sure I can convince you." He nodded at the corpse. "Like I did him."

"Jadain, please." Tashan's empty hand motioned for me to lower the symbol as if I were holding a knife. In his other hand his drab blade was still drawn.

He was on the vampire's side.

"Tashan. What is this?" I said.

"Considine's a friend. He's rescuing us. We should get away from here."

Neither of them had moved any closer, but I felt surrounded. "You . . . you know what he is."

"Yes." Tashan nodded. "But he's like Larsa. We can trust him."

He sounded like he believed what he was saying, but something knotted in the pit of my stomach. Could this be what I sounded like to others—to Mardhalas—when I vouched for Larsa? Was I preaching the virtues of the damned? Was I trying to convince others my stray dog wasn't a wolf?

Maybe, but this was a bridge too far even for me. Larsa was half alive, and I believed that even a half-life was sacred. This thing, though . . . this Considine was unmistakably my goddess's enemy.

Tashan was still nodding. Next to him, the grinning vampire matched his nod.

I thrust the goddess's holy symbol toward him, presenting it with straight-armed conviction.

"Ugh. Truly?" Considine sounded disappointed, but took a step back. "Fine, then."

"Jadain! Please! We're on the same side!" Tashan looked quickly to Considine and back again.

Both of us ignored him. My arm stayed rigid and I took a step forward. The vampire matched my step, backing toward the door.

"This could go differently." His tone darkened. "This could go many ways differently."

I took another step. He edged back again, a sneer starting to twitch on his face. He was almost in the hall. Perhaps I could . . . I had no idea, but I had to do something.

"Considine." Tashan pleaded.

"Fine, fine." The vampire rolled his eyes. "For Tabby's sake, I'll give you a chance to fall in love with me."

"I don't—"

His eyes snapped to mine, his gaze seizing me like a physical thing. It was the reverse of a domineering look, one that forced your eyes away. I'd never seen such green as in those eyes. Even through the dimness of the cell, they were dark with intensity, promise, possibility. They were instant obsession.

He nodded at my symbol. "Now there's no need for that."

And there was no need for it. The amulet fell from my fingers, bouncing on its cord. My arm did the same, dangling from muscles gone slack.

Something small in me knew there was something wrong, but whatever its complaint, it was smothered by that twinkling, endless green.

"Good." He looked to Tashan and gestured offhandedly at me. Tashan still frowned.

"I promise I'll be gentle." He sounded like a child apologizing only because he'd been told to. "Now, any clue where they're keeping sister-dear?"

I should have shouted. I could have screamed until the guards came. At the moment, though, my mind knew only soothing green.

It was like the guard was trying to scream through water—no, through something thicker than water. Through soup. Tomato soup.

His breath lasted for longer than the others, but it gurgled to an end the same way. When he hit the floor he sounded like a heap of wet clothes.

Considine flicked his wrist and three short strands of neck-flesh hit the floor with a thwap. He moved on.

And because he had asked me to, I followed, addicted to his voice, to his eyes, to that snake-green hue.

Sometimes I had to step off that emerald trail to avoid heaps of once-people and growing puddles of blood, but that was a minor inconvenience.

Tashan had his sword drawn. He kept looking over at me. He seemed concerned about something. I smiled to reassure him.

We'd left the cell and wound through a hall of cells. People had reached out for us, had yelled for help. A devotee of Calistria had grabbed my shoulder, his thin hand with its painted nails just fitting through a barred window. He'd said he was going to be executed for something—"private lewdness"? It didn't matter. I was falling behind. I wriggled free and jogged to catch up.

The guards beyond the cells hadn't wanted us to go. Considine pushed them out of the way. They screamed, they bled, they fell, but not always in that tidy order.

We climbed. Tashan told Considine about our interrogation, the inquisitor, my excommunication. I felt like I should feel something, but I couldn't be distracted enough to truly care. Whatever the emotion was, it wasn't green.

There were more guards. I only noticed them as they tumbled down the narrow stairs. Once I looked back, thinking I'd noticed Pharasma's symbol embossed on one of their chests. Had all of them worn my goddess's mark? By the time I looked, the body had tumbled around the endlessly spiraling stairs, taking my curiosity with it.

I gained the final landing, passing through the already open door. Tashan and Considine had entered, laying red stains on my green path. Tashan drove his blade into the collar of a pudgy guard who managed to trip as he lunged for a nearby spear. Beyond him, Considine lifted two other men in deep-violet uniforms off their feet, pinning them to the wall. Two strong pounds, a sound like crumbling clay, and they were men no more.

This time I definitely spotted the goddess's symbol on their armor. I wondered if either of them had ever been to Maiden's Choir.

Once it was silent, attention turned to the narrow room's solitary door. It was a single wall of steel with two crossbars—one high, one low. Eight latches circled it and small locks studded the corners. It looked like the entry to some miser's vault. Whoever constructed it seemed to have made certain that not even a breath could slip through.

Considine threw off the crossbars, sending the beams clattering as though they were hollow. He tugged on a latch. It stuck fast. He forced harder. The metal slightly groaned, but didn't relent.

Instantly exasperated, he sighed.

Without warning, his hair turned stark white, along with the rest of his body and clothes. His body melted to the floor like he'd turned to wax. I was momentarily startled, then remembered what he did, all his kind could do—transforming into mist, calling upon low nocturnal beasts, controlling the minds of others.

I heard a small scream within myself. I tried to listen, but it drowned in an ocean of green.

The mist pooled against the base of the door. It roiled there for a moment, then climbed the edges. Fine tendrils explored every lock, vaporous fingers played over every seam.

"Miss Losritter! What have you done?"

I spun at the sound of my name.

Brother Abelard stepped onto the landing just behind me. Already his eyes were wide, fixed on the corpses slumped against the walls—particularly the one only inches from my feet. I hadn't noticed its blood seeping against the hem of my robe. I took a short step to the side.

Tashan spun, his blade flashing golden in the lantern light. The inquisitor hadn't come unarmed, though.

Four rapid snaps. Metal sparked off stone. Tashan grunted and hit the wall. A thin trail of blood followed him as he slid down the wall, three crossbow bolts bristling in a line from shoulder to chest.

I watched, distracted again by something in me screaming through that sea of green. It sounded more familiar this time, more urgent.

The inquisitor lowered his bulky mechanical crossbow, tearing off a case attached over its lath and replacing it with another. I'd seen such a thing before—the wooden cartridge fed ammunition into the weapon without the need for reloading. He brought it back up, leveling it at me this time. He held the crossbow like a trained hunter, but his grip trembled visibly.

"I see I underestimated you. I thought you were just an unworthy, but now I see you for what you are: a spider, a corruptor, a heretic sent to destroy our faith!" His attention moved from the corpses to me.

His hand tightened on the crossbow's trigger. "In the name of the goddess, I send you to—"

A black blur burst from a fog bank that hadn't been at my side a moment ago. Considine launched himself at the inquisitor, the red on his clawlike nails matching the holy man's robes.

Brother Abelard shouted a rickety, old man's curse and fell backward. His surprise took him an eyelash's breadth beyond the swipe of Considine's hand. Thin fingers clamped down on the crossbow's trigger. The weapon launched steel with a series of merciless metallic clicks.

The first caught Considine in the jaw, snapping his mouth shut with the sound of shattering teeth. The second sealed the lock, boring deeper holes into his face. Another heartbreaking bolt destroyed one of those endless emerald eyes. The fourth struck the ceiling. Considine was gone, a breath of mist dissipating into shadow and cracked stone.

"No!" I heard myself scream unbidden. I momentarily acknowledged that I hadn't shouted when Tashan fell, but the thought washed away on a murky tide.

The inquisitor landed on his backside with a full-bodied grunt. Something fell from his robes—it looked like a rosary, but made of tiny bits of sharp bone. Fumbling in his panic, he forced himself awkwardly back up. "Consorting with the undead! Goddess, forgive my tired mind and fading sight for not recognizing a witch!"

He trained his weapon back on me. "Jadain Losritter. The inquisition of Kavapesta finds you guilty of murder, heresy, fraternizing with savages, defiling sacred ground, consorting with the damned, and violations against the goddess. Your crimes outnumber all possibility of defense. I am bound by faith and holy oath to put an end to your corruption! In your final moment, to hasten your own passing, do you confess? Do you repent?"

There was a faint clink. The inquisitor's look shifted and he fired.

From his heap on the floor, Tashan had fished a fist-sized flask out of his pack and lifted it to throw. Abelard's bolt shattered glass and bone, spilling thick fluid down Tashan's arm. The volatile alchemical mixture burst into flames.

Tashan let loose a terrible noise, his pierced hand becoming a blazing torch. Most of the concoction splashed across the floor, oily smoke and the smell of burning meat clouding the room. Tashan beat his arm against his chest, panting out screams as he burned.

The sea of green drowning my mind parted in a moment of terrible clarity. Out of reflex I gripped the goddess's symbol and cast my heart out from myself, reaching for her ever-present hand.

There wasn't time to doubt.

"Lady of Graves, Mother of Souls, I ever submit to your judgment. Yet should your will guide me toward another fate, let my faith be a fortress to my soul and a dagger against my foes."

Her power enfolded me, cold and close, as if I'd woken inside a grave. For an instant it filled me, slowing my heart, chilling fingers tracing her holy spiral. I channeled that power outward. It burst forth in frozen blue radiance, manifesting as sharp as a blade of ice, a weapon of conviction and my own spirit.

Hovering, the spectral dagger twisted. Inquisitor Abelard's attention snapped toward the familiar light. He had just enough time for a shocked curse before the magical blade blurred and buried itself in his chest.

The crossbow dropped from his hands, a bolt firing aimlessly. A spectrum of shock and rage played over the old man's face. He stared at the mystical blade jutting from his chest, its light thrumming in time with my heartbeat.

"Mother, no." He coughed, blood flecking his gray lips. Then his eyes were on mine. "Tainted! Polluted soul! Blasphemer!"

A growing stain barely darkened his crimson robes. Despite the wound, he pushed against the shard of divine energy skewering him.

"You turn her power against her own children? Her power is not for you, heretic!" Wild-eyed, he took a step, but stumbled. Rather than falling, he flung his hands toward me. Too fast, a spidery hand clamped upon my shoulder. The divine dagger's cold light pulsed between us, under-lighting the old man's face, giving him a corpselike cast.

I tried to push away, struggling as cold hands sought my neck. Beneath that shock and exertion my concentration burst. The holy blade dissipated like sun-struck mist.

His own holy symbol, a spiral etched in steel, was in his hand. Full of outrage and condemnation, he shouted into my face. "Mother of Truth! Judge of Souls! I am your word given life! Fill me with your justice! Cast your verdict in flesh!"

My fist slammed against his chest. The bleeding old man clung fast, thin fingers clamping onto the back of my neck. Blue light flared around his metal amulet. Heedless of my struggling, he forced the icy emblem into my face. It found my right eye, its sharp edges digging deep, trying to blind me.

Screaming, I fell backward, but he followed, lifting his own voice. "Die, heretic! Die and be damned!"

The glow already blinding me exploded from an icy candle to a frozen sun. Heatless flame poured into my eye, searing my face, burning out my sight, setting my thoughts aflame. It wasn't truly fire—it was the goddess's absolute death, the stopping of all things, a ruin so intense it burned.

I didn't feel myself hit the floor or the hateful inquisitor fall on top of me. Animal desperation consumed me, made worse by my sudden blindness. I tried to make my writhing useful, kicking and scratching. Abelard's grip had slackened in the fall and I tore free, my own hands clawing for his sagging neck. Nails scraped loose skin. I clamped down, squeezing as tightly as I could. He choked, gurgling as he struggled, some of his strength having already fled. Tepid blood met my skin, dribbling down my fingers, becoming a stain spreading across my chest. We twisted desperately. I tasted tears.

His body was the first to give. He sputtered something as his body slackened, then collapsed upon me—the weight mostly from his robes rather than his birdlike body.

My face was numb. The green in my mind had almost totally dissipated, replaced by a seductive darkness. As I slipped into that starless dark, I was sure I knew Inquisitor Abelard's final strangled word.

Heretic.

23

A STAINED SOUL
LARSA

It took a long time to realize the noise was the cell door squealing open. My consciousness gradually bobbed to the surface, a slow journey that meant passing through a violent haze of spasms and pounding red pain.

Something was attacking—no, stabbing—my face. Kicking my mouth with pointed boots. My eyelids fluttered as weak as moth wings.

My arm was gone from my sight—I dimly remembered the shriek of it being yanked away. It was dark out there, beyond my own head. Nothing there was killing me, nothing outside my own face.

A silhouette stood in the dark, barely a different shade of shadow. I smelled blood on it—maybe mine.

Maybe this was death.

The throbbing callus of my skull muffled a new noise. I wondered over the strange sounds before remembering words and meaning.

". . . fetching in red, dear. Your choice of company, though . . . we'll work on it."

Yes. It was certainly death.

Thin arms were under me. Without caring or being able to prevent it, I let them take me.

The pounding had been bothering me for so long I only dimly noticed when it slowed. It wasn't an annoyance in my head or limbs, making it easier to ignore. A sharp slam brought me drowsily back.

It was still dark, but the cell was gone—or replaced. This one was smaller, too small even to lie down in. The ceiling was low and I could see windows in wood panels.

Someone was lying next to me. I tried to twist to see who. I expected the shriek of muscles still paralyzed by poison. I didn't expect my neck to actually move.

Jadain was heaped there, a pained expression on her face, her body bent awkwardly. She couldn't have been asleep like that—probably unconscious.

A shocked grunt came from nearby, followed by wet red strands splashing across the window—a carriage window? Almost immediately, the pounding below began again. Wheels rolled from dirt, to paving, then back to dirt.

As the carriage picked up, the clattering of wheels over road lolled me back to sleep.

Someone was vomiting. Worse, they were doing it near my head.

A chilly breeze blew through the open carriage door and I pulled the cloak around me tighter. Somehow it was still dark, but it wouldn't be for much longer. Already the stars were fading upon a navy backdrop. In the distance a whippoorwill repeated its roundabout call.

Leaning up stiffly, I could see outside. Tashan sat upon a fallen log, a lantern at his feet. He was working one open hand with the other, massaging the stiffness from it, examining it deliberately. Considine stood nearby, looking impatient as he glanced from his slave to the darkened tree line.

The barest drop of anxiety leaked into my chest, all my aching body could muster. Jadain. She'd certainly recognize him for what he was. Not that I was concerned for the arrogant ass, but rather Jadain. She'd been understanding of me, but Considine was another thing entirely. She'd be bound by her faith to at least try to return him to the grave—and I didn't expect the attempt to go well for her.

With my whole body throbbing, I couldn't bring myself to rush to anyone's side. Any death matches would have to be between them.

Where was Jadain anyway?

Another round of heaving and a patter of loose sick dribbled onto the ground, just on the other side of the door I leaned against. Ignoring the tightness, I worked my way into a sitting position, legs hanging out of the carriage.

"Breakfast is going to disappoint you, dear." Considine didn't even turn to address me—confusing Tashan, who looked up at him. "Unless you know any folksy recipes for pinecones."

"Just water," I choked, my mouth scabby. I coughed through it, tearing dry lips.

Tashan saw me, a look of relief turning apologetic. "We don't have anything to drink."

"Well." Considine arched an eyebrow. The Pathfinder frowned.

"You're up." Jadain circled around the front of the carriage, passing a pair of grazing sorrels I didn't recognize. Her voice was muffled by a scrap of robe she held to her mouth like a handkerchief.

She sounded weak and looked it. Her robes were torn, the misty purple hues darkened by stains. I could smell blood on her, along with a lingering sour reek. Fresh wounds appeared as she came into the lantern light, purple splotches climbing her neck and the right side of her face. Her eye was swollen shut.

She sat gingerly on the end of the same log as Tashan, facing me—her back to Considine.

"What happened to you?" I sounded like I was talking with my mouth full.

"Jailbreak. It wasn't pretty." She didn't elaborate, but wasn't trying to sound nonchalant.

"You came after me?"

"You weren't the only one they put in a cage." She gestured at the vampire with her eyes.

"I have a certain familiarity with cages, though I'm used to far prettier ones." Considine strolled closer, scrutinizing leisurely. "Speaking of 'prettier' . . . you're a mess." He pointed a finger into my face.

"Don't."

He ignored me, prodding my upper lip.

Jerking away sent spasms through my neck. Worse, the pain in my gums flared, a low burn I'd almost managed to ignore. A snarl made him retract the digit.

"This one's going to need your witchery next," he said to Jadain without looking at her. He walked back to Tashan. "Don't be long. The sun will be up soon. We've got a good lead on anyone who might be pursuing us, but it'll be up to you to get us out of the county."

"Where are we?" I asked, covering my lip with my fingers.

"About twenty or thirty miles northwest of Kavapesta. We're nearly at the border to Ardeal, so I can't imagine any local law following much farther." His hand gave a careless flip. "Angry clergy, that might be another matter, but all the more reason not to dawdle. The horses are fresh . . . *ish*. I'm sure you'll manage."

Considine collected a wrinkled bundle and dropped it next to me. The thousand old tears tattooing my body bristled, bursting with silent mockery as I realized they'd been mostly bare this entire time. I pulled my cloak tighter around me, grabbed my leathers, and slammed the coach door.

"Sorry about your ugly hat!" Considine's voice reached through the door. "It wasn't with the rest."

It didn't matter. I dressed quickly, pulling on my long shirt and traveling pants, not bothering with the armored bits. It still took several minutes with all the checking for rips and exposed gaps. It took longer to fight down the embarrassment filling my belly and push the door back open.

Predictably, Considine was the only one who commented. "Well, that's slightly better."

That fast, his attention swung away. "Now." He extended a hand to Tashan. "Someone said something about breakfast, and I just can't put it out of my mind."

The Osirian's eyes gave a tired roll. "You could have fed in Kavapesta. You left us there for two days, after all."

"One night! And can you really imagine me chatting up a goodwife taking in her laundry or some acolyte rushing home from evening prayers?" His look turned distant and lecherous. "Though . . . robes."

Tashan gave him a kick to the shin.

"Those people bless their water! Gods only know what they do with their blood." Considine's lips curled in a devilish grin. "Anyway, I always know I'll get a good fight with you."

"Please." Tashan snorted, pulling himself up with vampire's hand.

"Back in a blink," Considine said as he and Tashan walked toward the tree line.

Jadain shook her head, watching them disappear into the dark. "What is it between those two?"

I didn't try to sweeten it. "Slavery."

A pensive look knotted her brow. "I don't think so."

I shrugged, not interested in explaining all the ways Considine wasn't a romantic—or the end I expected Tashan was all-too-willingly running toward. "So what happened to you?"

She frowned. "It wasn't happenstance that we were stopped outside the city. Inquisitor Mardhalas told them we were coming."

"She told them about me?"

"She told them about *us*. She accused me of heresy."

She wasn't wearing her little wooden holy symbol. Despite her robes being tattered beneath her cloak, its absence was what made her seem undressed.

She went on when I didn't reply. "An inquisitor questioned me. He asked me about you. I thought he was trying to raise evidence against you, suggesting that you'd somehow enchanted me." She gave a hollow chuckle. "I apparently convinced him that my free will was intact, since he accused me of blasphemy and promised to excommunicate me."

"How'd you get away?"

"Your friend showed up." She nodded toward the shadowy trees.

I scoffed at her misread of our relationship, but let it pass. "He broke you out?"

She nodded.

"And you went with him?" I didn't hide my incredulity.

She didn't nod.

"It was terrible," she finally said. "He wanted you but didn't know where you were. He wanted us to come with him, but I knew what he was. I knew I didn't have a chance against him, but the goddess says . . ."

Her hand strayed to where her amulet wasn't, then dropped back into her lap.

"Then I was following him. He killed . . . many. Brothers and sisters of the faith. And I followed him, like he was the only thing I could see in a fog."

He'd dominated her—forced his will on her and made her his slave. I'd seen him do it countless times, usually to the drug addicts and waifs he entertained. Regardless of what Considine had claimed, I suspected Tashan was under his control, or had been for long enough that now he didn't know his own thoughts from his master's. That Considine had been able to control a priestess, and one sworn against his kind—that was surprising.

She went on, her voice surprisingly even. "We found your cell at the top of the tower. The inquisitor I told you about, he caught us there. He shot Tashan and managed to drive Considine off. He was going to kill me, but I held him off with the goddess's power. I prayed to the goddess to protect me, to hurt him, and she did."

She stopped to stare at the ground. It took her a moment to continue.

"He was furious. He called me a heretic and a witch." She forced open her swollen eye. "Then he did this."

At first I wondered how you could tear someone's iris—rip the color away without just blinding the eye. It wasn't a scar, though. Her iris hadn't been torn, it had been reshaped. Instead of a soft brown ring, the colored part of Jadain's eye twisted in a jagged spiral radiating out from a pupil turned misty. The shape was deliberate, Pharasma's spiral branded upon tissue and tears—but reversed. It wasn't the normal clockwise, outward-radiating swirl of the goddess's cometlike symbol. Instead, the spiraling star's head wound in on itself, spinning toward the pupil. It was an obvious corruption, an insult, like wearing another deity's icon upside down.

For a priestess, it must have been torture.

She closed the eye, rubbing it as though there were something caught inside. "I can still see, but I see everything through the mark. It's like holding a piece of glass over one eye: everything you see has the same flecks and flaws. But now the flaw is that blasphemy—the flaw is part of me."

She pulled her cloak tight around her. "I prayed to the goddess, begging her to heal it. She answered me—after all of this, somehow she still answered me. She closed my wounds and knitted my scars, but it felt like she didn't want to. I could feel her disgust and," she covered her eye, "she left this."

"Afterward, I was ill—so bad I nearly retched. The feeling didn't pass until I put her symbol away." She fished for something inside the remaining folds of her robe, but didn't withdraw her hand. "I thought it might have been a coincidence, but just before you got up I prayed to the goddess to heal Tashan's wounds. The Lady's healing came and restored him as it should, but so did that terrible feeling. I actually did vomit that time."

"I heard."

"But what's worst," she confessed to the ground, "what's worst is that through all of this, the blood, the killing, the accusations, the scarring, the goddess's curse—through it all, I've wanted to cry. I've felt it so strongly that at times I almost choked. But I haven't been able to. When I woke up in the carriage I tried—I must have spent an hour trying to squeeze out a tear. But I couldn't. It's like I've forgotten how."

I didn't know what to say. Anything I imagined sounded like a platitude or a lie.

We sat silently for some time.

Eventually the whippoorwill picked back up its call, jostling Jadain from her brooding.

"Sorry," she said flatly, looking back up. "He said you were wounded too?"

My lips tightened. "Yeah, but it's going to take more than a bandage."

"I can try calling on the goddess again. Maybe the nausea's a passing thing, or I'll get used to it . . . or we'll just have to do it fast."

I shrugged. It beat the alternative.

I opened my mouth, letting her see inside. Cool air rushed in, touching parts of my mouth usually shielded from the cold, making the twin holes where my fangs used to be feel all the more empty.

"Oh goddess." She tilted her head, looking inside. "That explains . . ."

I closed my mouth as she fished something out of her robes—a string of teeth, fashioned as a rosary. "Considine gave it to me—I think he thought it was funny. I think it was the inquisitor's."

"I've seen it." My voice cracked. I didn't look to see if any of the teeth there looked particularly fresh.

She stuffed it away and didn't ask any more. From another fold, she produced her amulet and, shutting her good eye, lifted it between us. She swayed slightly, but nonetheless began muttering a prayer to the goddess. It took a moment—certainly longer than other times I'd seen her commune with her deity—but surely enough cold light surrounded her hands. Lips moving slowly, brow clenched in concentration, she reached toward me with her goddess's blessing.

"Jadain." I backed away as best I could, still seated on the lip of the carriage cabin. "Jadain! Stop!"

When she didn't immediately halt, my boot came up between us. I hadn't meant to actually kick her, but my heel caught her in the abdomen as she leaned in. Her prayer ended with a gasp, the aura fading from her hands.

She rocked back. "The hells!"

"Your magic!" I had recognized her spell. It was the same power the priests channeled outside the city, the touch of the goddess that tried to burn out my heart. "That kind of healing. You know I can't . . ."

I'd been healed by magic before, but never by one of Jadain's order. Back in the Old City, beneath the cobbles of Caliphas, there were vampires who stilled prayed. Those who raised their voices to Asmodeus, the vampire god Ruithvein, or worse could weave the power of death to rejuvenate their vampiric kin. That same magic also worked on me. But for the living, death was death, and that which healed the people of the Old City would drain their life away—potentially even killing them. I'd assumed Jadain realized that. I'd also assumed that, as a follower of the goddess who stood at the border of life and death, she'd know which power to call.

The mix of puzzlement and anger on Jadain's face drained, her look turning distant. "Right. Her blessing burns you."

"Something like that, yeah. So reverse it. Make it not . . . burn."

She hid her amulet back inside her robes. "Call upon pain instead of healing? Pray for her to touch you with death instead of life?"

"Yeah."

She stared into the dirt. "I'm sorry. I can't."

It took a moment to realize what she was saying. When I did, it was my turn to stretch out the silence, only I was pausing to tamp down the heat rising in my chest.

Some of it broke through—maybe through the cracks where my canines used to be. "You mean you can, but you're not."

"I can't call upon the goddess's punishment and use it to heal you. It's . . ."

I finished her thought. "What? 'Unnatural'? '*Blasphemy*'?"

She squeezed her eyes shut.

I made a disgusted noise as I stood. "I've been waiting to see how far your open-mindedness about my kind goes. Don't worry Jadain, you're more like the rest of your order than you think."

I stormed into the dark, both out of annoyance and before I could say something nastier. The whippoorwill called and I let it be my destination, intent on silencing its obnoxious noise.

A dozen paces from Jadain, some part of me regretted speaking to her so roughly. I kicked as hard as I could, launching a stone into the mist, sending the thought with it. Damn her. I'd actually let myself buy into her talk. I'd let her convince me that she saw me just like anyone else, that she and I were the same. When it came to it, though, when she had to actually act on her claims, to speak to her goddess on my behalf, suddenly I was different. Suddenly I couldn't be healed, couldn't be comforted, couldn't be clean.

My march brought me to the tree line. I was hardly ten paces into the damp woods when Considine's voice drifted from just behind me. "You can't really be surprised."

I swung for his face. The blow nearly connected, but his smile flowed effortlessly out of reach.

"Did she call you 'sister'? Did you think she would?" His snakelike fangs glistened, mocking. "Did you think she'd call you something else?

Indulging my frustration, I kicked high. The blow came around hard and connected with his chest. He was surprisingly light, the blow knocking him from his feet. He never hit the ground, though. In the time it took to tumble he burst into mist. It drifted atop a fallen log, then rose back into a familiar shape.

"Sensitive," he said, brows high.

I walked away.

"They might bend the rules, but they never really break them. There's always an excuse." He hopped down, following. "They're ultimately very obedient things. Just look how eagerly she followed me."

"You controlled her."

I could hear the shrug in his voice. "I gave her an excuse to do what she wanted to."

"You made her kill her own people."

"Please, that little thing? I bade her follow along and she did. That she beat an old man to death, well—the young ones are such temperamental things."

She hadn't said anything about killing anyone. "The one who marked her?"

He confirmed with a hum.

Jadain wasn't a killer. As upset as she'd been over the death of the innkeeper's boy, I couldn't imagine the weight she'd feel over a death she'd actually caused—the death of one of her order, at that. Even to me, that sounded like betrayal. For her, it must have sounded like heresy.

"If my rescue educated your choirgirl on the harsher truths of survival, I don't require thanks for the lesson." He drifted next to me. "And if it broke her faith in the goddess of wasted lives, well . . ." He made a throwing-away gesture. "That's not really anything to begin with."

"It is when that was her whole life—if now she's too conflicted to do anything more than sulk." I wheeled on him. "I'd planned on having the support of a Pharasmin priestess while I hunted Rivascis. Now what?"

"Now you've got me." He brought his hands up in display. "We'll track down Father together and . . ." he swirled his hand, "*justice*, or whatever. We'll do whatever you want. It's exciting!"

"It's not exciting," I nearly shouted. "This isn't some holiday for me. My life is on the line for this! I disobeyed Grandfather in leaving the city—or, at least, he'll see it as disobedience. Even if I find Rivascis, even if I put him down, Grandfather might still decide to rip me apart just to make an example. He already sent you to watch."

A thought dawned on me. My eyes narrowed on Considine. "What are your exact orders anyway?"

"Hm?"

"Say we get to Ardis and Rivascis isn't there, or for some reason I can't kill him."

"Oh, darling. Always so—"

I tried to stay calm. "He sent you to see that I do what I said, but if I fail—if this was all a waste of Grandfather's time—you're supposed to *what*?"

I wanted him to say it. To tell me what was suddenly so obvious.

His bored expression only frustrated me more. "Well, whatever I'm supposed to, I'm not doing it unrested." He looked up into a sky empty of stars.

Fine, I'd say it. "You're here to kill me."

He gave me a look like I should know better, then a fake little laugh. "No, no of course not."

I glared, my doubt plain.

He shrugged deep. "Nothing in this world would pain me more, Sister-Dear, but don't start thinking you're anything special. We've all got Grandfather's nooses around our necks."

I shook my head. A reluctant executioner was no less an executioner. Maybe Considine wasn't due the entirety of my ire, but he was still Grandfather's agent, and who knew the larger game Grandfather was planning?

"Tabby will drive you on today—you should reach Ardis in just a few hours."

Surprise drained some of my annoyance. "We're that close?"

"I made good time last night. I move pretty fast when I don't have to waste time listening to nonsense." He glanced up. A familiar pale bat chirped in the branches above, alerting its master that the sky had lightened another shade.

"You brought that disgusting thing all this way?" I spared a scowl for the sickly creature. It hissed in response.

"Worry more about yourself and," Considine waved his hand generally, "this whole sad condition."

I rolled my eyes.

In the time that took he'd reappeared in front of me, intrusively close.

"What?" I tried to sound more annoyed than startled.

He'd acted fast in whatever dalliance he and Tashan had shared. I smelled blood on him.

"Consider it thanks, for so graciously letting me tag along." He leaned in, leading with his mouth. Crimson limned the corners of his lips.

My stomached lurched and I brought up my hands. The intensity in his eyes repelled me. Though I'd never noticed just how deeply green they were. Either that, or the scent of blood, made me hesitate.

Cold, thin lips closed over my own. His hands clamped onto the sides of my face, and his mouth opened.

I tried to yank away, but my body was still stiff and his grip unnaturally strong. He made a sound like a belch, blowing air that wasn't breath. Even through sealed lips I gagged.

Then came a wash of lukewarm blood.

I felt the warmth, smelled it, anticipated the taste in a single intoxicating instant. Not entirely unbidden, my lips parted.

Even secondhand, it was so much better than water, and it had been so long. The vessel didn't matter.

Pressing back, I drank.

24

THE UNINVITED
JADAIN

The sun rose across a green desert of rye. Oasis-clusters of small farmhouses sat far back from the road, purposefully discouraging visitors.

The hills of Kavapesta had leveled, leaving the horizon broken only by the Hungry Mountains behind and occasional marches of tangled trees—old growth left to divide the vast properties of local lords. Dual paths sped our travel, the hard-packed earth of the New Surdina's final furlongs, and—never more than a few dozen yards away—the steep banks of the Vhatsuntide River. The chilly water dashed in reckless white bursts over rocks and fallen branches, obviously just as eager to escape Amaans county as we were.

As the sun rose, the morning mists lifted. Gradually, a singular tower formed on the horizon, a lofty thing like a lance driven into the ground by its grip. I'd never laid eyes on it before, but I knew it immediately.

"The Palace Tower." I pointed ahead.

On the driver's bench next to me, Tashan raised his eyes and nodded.

He seemed underwhelmed, but he hadn't spent his entire life seeing it on nearly every pennant, crest, gate, and courthouse. The tower adorned the royal seal, being the pinnacle of Stagcrown Palace, the original home of Ustalav's royal court. Something between history and legend said that Soividia Ustav, the nation's first king, raised the tower so he could see across the lands he'd conquered and personally keep watch against the barbarians he'd driven out. The tower was a symbol of the king's protection, the light in its highest window reminding the people of their lord's endless vigil.

At least, that's how it was on all the royal crests.

In truth, the Palace Tower was much shorter than I'd imagined. Although still easily the tallest structure in the city taking shape below it, the tower probably didn't afford a view of more than a few dozen miles even at its highest point. Beyond the unrealistic physical possibilities, modern politics made the tower the symbol of a lost legend. Stagcrown Palace hadn't served as the capitol since the royal court moved to Caliphas more than forty years ago. Since then, the palace was maintained as a royal holding, but it didn't have any function I knew of. Certainly no light shone from the tower's height this morning.

The tower wasn't the only vacant structure. In the surrounding fields the homes of peasants gave way to manors surrounded by sprawling gardens and wrought-iron fences. I recognized these from the Caliphas countryside, the homes of nobles cleaving to the royal court. But even as grand homes clustered close, the countryside was no less empty.

We passed empty gatehouses and quiet fields. Gardens sought to escape over crumbling walls, often crawling to the very edge of the road. Many of the manors looked like they were sleeping—or worse—no glass reflecting from their window-eyes and ivy growing like the beards of vagabonds.

That's not to say nothing moved in those sad little empires. Armies of crows and pigeons bivouacked on roofs and between hedgerows, frequently skirmishing in both sky and field. Once a fox dashed in front of us—the pudgy thing certainly never having been chased by hounds or hunters. Saddest, though, were the houses half-collapsed on the muddy banks of the Vhatsuntide, but that nevertheless still puffed chimney smoke into the sky.

Obviously, the prestige of the old capital had departed, but not all had been able to follow.

Wind-shredded banners fluttered from the heights of Ardis's walls, their tatters faded from royal purple to shades of delicate lavender lace. Soot and crumbling gaps marred the battlements' sculpted antler patterns, while below an equally neglected bridge spanned a green-brown stream of mostly sewage. We slowed, but listless guards waved us across. Even at the gate, the soldier ignored our carriage in favor of interrogating a farmer hauling gourds to market.

Within the walls, drab people in patched woolen clothes went about the day's business. Shouts, coughs, and curses ricocheted from tightly packed statues and boarded-up civil buildings. Wagons clattered across loose cobbles, competing to be noisier than vendors barking impossible claims from cracked marble steps. Children summited stacks of crates spilling from alleyways. The capped and hooded people went about their business with downcast eyes, ignoring the neglected architecture and once-bold artistry towering above. Those pigeon-lined edifices seemed constructed by a different people—though from all the boxes and bundles weighing upon carts and backs, it seemed this crowd was only passing through.

"Which way?" Tashan asked as we came to an intersection with a nearly identical thoroughfare. In both directions friezes spattered by roosting birds stared from the pediments of empty-looking structures. To the west, the Palace Tower observed from over crowded rooftops—the statuary above outnumbering people on the street. Yet the unignorable structure offered no opinion.

"I'm . . ." I looked a second time, "not sure."

Tashan pulled on the reins, bringing the carriage to a halt mid-street.

"Pardon me, ma'am," I asked, leaning down toward a woman herding a gaggle of youngsters. "Do you know—"

She waved me off without even looking up, not even giving me the opportunity to finish. Not that I knew how I would have finished.

I turned back to Tashan, who was watching the crowd suspiciously. "Did Doctor Trice tell you where Miss Kindler lived?"

He looked at me flatly.

No help there.

I hesitated in reaching for the carriage door. Larsa had spent the entire morning with the curtains drawn, not making a sound. Not that she'd said a word since I refused to channel the goddess's killing touch. While, academically, I understood that Larsa's life ran a course unlike most, I couldn't bring myself to pray for death. The taker, the harvester, the cold mother—that wasn't what Pharasma was to me. We—her servants—killed to protect, killed as a mercy, but still, calling on death to spread death, to make it flourish, felt terribly wrong. Blasphemous.

Part of me resented her frustration. Was she actually angry that I *wouldn't* curse her?

I shook the thought away. I could empathize even if I couldn't entirely understand.

I made the first gesture, knocking lightly.

After a moment, a dark crack opened between the door and its frame.

"We're in Ardis. Do you know where Kindler's home is?"

Nothing changed in the dark. Then it sealed itself with a click.

I sighed—so much for the first gesture.

Tashan was looking at me expectantly.

"She doesn't know either."

Already we'd sat here too long. Every moment made us seem more like easy marks for shysters and pickpockets. Telling Tashan to wait, I hopped down from the carriage.

A pile of rags lay heaped in the shadows of a grimy alley. Only a chipped wooden bowl marked it as more than cast-off clothing.

Well, the bowl, and a beard long and stained enough to look like a patchwork quilt.

I knelt, placing a silver piece delicately in the bowl. "Sir," I spoke softly. "I'd like to buy your next meal."

The mound rustled, revealing old eyes beneath gray brows. He had a glassy, suspicious look. I knew from my time working with Caliphas's poor that he had every reason to be suspicious. Who knew who I was or what I might want? The lives of commoners were already cheap things to nobles and those tasked with entertaining them. The lives of those who wouldn't be missed, even cheaper.

"All I need are directions from someone who knows the city." I held up a second silver. It reflected in his dark eyes. "You don't need to take me there or do anything more. Can you help?"

He nodded, mostly a bobbing of his beard.

"I'm trying to find the home of Miss Ailson Kindler. I believe she's quite famous here as—"

"The writer," came a rich baritone from amid the bristles.

I tried not to sound surprised, but had to repeat myself when I told him yes.

He pointed toward the avenue heading east. "You want Bronzewing Row. Look for walls twice as tall as any others."

Thanking him, I deposited my second coin in the bowl. I crossed back to the carriage, where a street vendor was haranguing Tashan for blocking his place on the corner. The Osirian was looking at him blankly, as if he didn't speak the language.

"Bronzewing Row," I said, swinging back onto the bench. "Turn right here."

"What was that?" he asked, looking back at the man huddled in the alley.

"Nothing. I just asked a friend for directions." I smiled.

"You northerners." Tashan shook his head. "So fast to show your money."

"What?"

"You paid him. I could see it from here—as could anyone with eyes to see."

"So?" I frowned, not appreciating him raining on my charity.

He shook his head. "Just mind your purse."

I gave a dismissive sniff. "Not everyone's a criminal."

"That's exactly what criminals want you to think."

There were still some leaves on the trees lining Bronzewing Row. Most had fallen, heaping in gutters or piling against wrought-iron fences. Hedges circled the lots of small, smart houses, miniature manors with wide windows and bright curtains. Many had seen better days, stately appearances undermined by columned porches scabbed over with peeling whitewash.

One lot was a complete mystery. Its fence rose over eight feet high, its bars and sunburst finials embedding themselves in a dense hedgerow that grew even taller. A pine gate, just tall enough to admit a carriage like ours, interrupted the wall. Rivets and sturdy strap hinges made it look more like the entry to a fortress than to someone's home, an impression reinforced by a wicket set with a closed iron window. Upon the inset door hung a tiny placard carved with elegant letters: "No Readers."

"This place?" Tashan looked up at the peaks of several sharp gables staring from over the hedges. Their narrow windows were tightly curtained.

"I . . . suppose." It certainly wasn't welcoming.

I slipped down from the carriage, reading the dismissive sign a dozen times in the short walk to the door. Not seeing a bellpull, I rapped firmly and waited.

After a minute I repeated my knock. Then again.

On my seventh rap, the tiny metal window squealed open.

"What!" the man snapped.

My surprise carried me back a step.

"Sir!" My voice came louder and sterner than usual, but then, he'd set the tone. "We're looking for Miss Ailson Kindler. We're on important business."

Eyes rolled behind the grating. "Miss Kindler doesn't take visitors."

The tiny window squealed. Before it closed, I jammed my fingers through the narrow bars.

"Sir! Please. We've come all the way from Caliphas."

The gate hardly muffed his snort. "I'll save you some time, lady. We don't care how far you've traveled, how much money you have, or how many of her books you've read."

Tashan came up behind me. "Sir, we're here on the business of the Pathfinder Society. Our message comes from Venture-Captain Trice of Caliphas and is of pressing concern. Please admit us."

"Ooh." He drew the sound out mockingly. "The Pathfinder Society. You're the ones Miss Kindler said I could shoot if you showed up. Stay right here, I left my bow in the carriage house."

This wasn't the greeting I'd expected. If invoking the Society's name didn't help, then maybe Pharasma's would. I reached for my amulet, but immediately felt queasy.

"If only you'd let us speak to Miss Kindler for a moment. We're not admirers. We have serious business with her. Her life could be in jeopardy!"

The man beyond the gate didn't answer.

"Sir?"

I looked back at Tashan, not removing my fingers from the grated window. "Do you think he's still there?"

He took a step back. "I think he went to get his bow."

I hardly heard, looking past him. The carriage stood where we'd left it in the street. Only now, one of the doors hung open.

25

OLD LACE
LARSA

I landed amid a weedy garden of drooping pansies, clutching under my arm the thin parcel I took from Tashan's pack. From the look of the flowerbed, I wasn't the first to trample it, so I doubted my trespass would be noticed anytime soon. I checked the packet, trying not to further torture the letter from Doctor Trice or the records from Maiden's Choir. The trip hadn't been easy on the paper bundle, but the presentation didn't truly matter.

A drive of loose white stones and a yard dotted by decorative shrubs separated me from a miniature farmhouse. The building's flat-roofed porch gave it the look of a fat woman in a pistachio dress, her arms outstretched to steady herself. Not that the building looked unstable, just cautious. Windows peered from beneath severe gables and from beneath the porch's shade. Nothing moved inside, though. If anyone noticed me, they didn't appear to care.

A fit man with unkempt hair, dirty trousers, and his back to me disappeared into a small carriage house at the drive's end.

Not interested in meeting Kindler's servants, I hiked up the brown paper sheaf and didn't dawdle crossing the yard or climbing the stairs to the splintery porch. The wood smelled damp and more than one earwig lay dead between those floorboards paint didn't cake closed.

I didn't bother to knock. The door sagged in its frame, feeling slightly soggy, as though it were rotting beneath the white paint. I shouldered it open as delicately as I could. It grunted as it gave, but fortunately the soft sound didn't echo. I shoved inside, rumpling a faded mat.

Dust motes sparkled in the light from the door and several uncurtained windows off the entry hall. One beam illuminated a sideboard where the empty eyes of a basilisk's skull stared from between two pieces of wintery flatware.

I hesitated. Miss Kindler's sitting room was not what I expected from a woman in her seventies. Lace and cobwebs hung in near equal quantities amid delicate baubles and faded portraits. The memories on display were certainly not from a life lived delicately. A heavily framed picture of a grim palace loomed over the mantelpiece, four proud young men and women posing boldly amid its rose garden. An assortment of curios on the crackled marble mantel—slender crystals, a jade figurine of a Tian noblewoman, a brass Katapeshi lamp—partially obscured the painting, and that was just upon the room's most prominent shelf. If a wall wasn't covered by shelves, it bore some other display: a mounted bit of armor, piece of horn, scrap of skin, framed map piece, bit of woven tapestry, or less identifiable curiosity. Between a couch and chairs bearing the same faded floral pattern sat a delicate coffee table. All it held was a cup and pair of worn gambler's dice.

A creak from above interrupted my curiosity. It wasn't just the old house settling. I knew the sound of someone trying not to be heard.

The stairway rising from the entryway was a squeaky wooden affair. I climbed swiftly, but was hardly soundless. The short hall at its summit ran the length of the upper floor, its walls buried beneath more frames and small display tables. More dust stirred in the air. The soft wood of the walls and floors muffled every move. Together they created the eerie sense of being underwater, everything taking on a slow, weightless quality.

Eyes followed me down the hall, not just from portraits but from strange masks, mounted taxidermies, and the pale busts of somber strangers. One fishlike helmet of reeds and fronds only added to the hall's drowned aesthetic, its goggle eyes split between eyeing me and a more grotesque mask of cracked leather. I halted at the sight of that second mask, a jagged spiral slit stitched in ragged skin, just like we saw in the monk in mountains. There were differences, but it was definitely of the same revolting design. In the light it seemed a touch less monstrous, but whatever it was, it certainly wasn't some retiree's trophy. Trice had mentioned Kindler's adventuring days, but I hadn't expected to be touring a museum of her travels.

My list of questions about this woman grew longer with every step.

There was a fire beyond the door at the hall's end, obvious from the fingers of light slipping beneath. I tested the latch. It gave reluctantly and with an obvious clack.

Well, probably best not to seem too much like a housebreaker. I opened the door wider than I needed to creep through.

The musty smell of smoke and paper filled the miniature library. Books buried the walls. They even arched over the fireplace, where the largest or otherwise strangely sized tomes held places of curious prestige. Heaps of stray pages and unfiled volumes buried a rosewood desk, its slender legs carved with spritely figures hiding amid acanthus leaves.

Three chairs clustered around the fire, defended by a claw-footed tea table. Two were overstuffed affairs in smoky leather. The third was a lean, uncomfortable-looking contraption, wooden slats and wicker panels riding precariously upon narrow metal wheels. Of the three, it was the only one occupied.

The woman seemed held together entirely by her blouse's stiff collar and a tight bun that pulled equally upon silver locks and narrow wrinkles. Slim spectacles caught upon a upturned nose, threatening to dash themselves upon either the throw covering her legs or the tome of near equal size sprawled upon her lap. She nodded slowly, dozing in her reading.

Her? We'd come all the way from Caliphas for her? This spinster who had more in common with a dried turnip than an adventurer? I'd been assured that this journey wasn't just about stopping in on Trice's wet nurse, but now that I was here, I wasn't entirely sure. The very idea of my people's deadliest fugitive wanting anything to do with this woman seemed beyond ludicrous. That I had let myself be at all curious—that I'd at all hoped . . .

I didn't leave my responsibilities undone. I crossed the room just far enough to drop the packet on the tea table.

"Please let that be a death threat," came a drowsy sigh as I turned away. "Anything but another tawdry manuscript."

I drew myself up and turned. "It's from Doctor Trice of Caliphas."

She gave a bored glare, her eyes mere slits over her glasses. "Oh. That's so much less interesting than more of the countess's amateur poetry."

I didn't understand and stood silent.

One of her eyebrows rose archly, tightening lines across her face. She beckoned with her fingertips. "Well, give it here, child."

Ignoring her sharp tone, I circled in front of the fire and handed her the packet. She took it, but before she did, something slid into her sleeve. What did she have, a knife? I almost laughed.

She ran a bony finger from one corner to the other and slid the contents onto her lap, ignoring the folded letter and flipping open the folio. For a long moment she stared at the record's first page. She offered the remainder no more than a quick glance before closing the cover. With a jerk of her wrist she sent it sailing to land squarely atop the logs smoldering in the fire. Curious flames batted at the document's corners, then set to swift work consuming every page.

"Good riddance to that." She looked up at me. "Anything else?"

"Only that." I nodded to the letter left ignored on her lap.

"I thought it'd be rude to burn your venture-captain's note in front of you—it looks like you've had some trouble getting it here."

She might have just meant my stained clothes, or the fact that I'd broken into her home, but the swelling beneath my upper lip seemed suddenly conspicuous.

"I'm not one of Trice's grave robbers, so I don't much care what you do with it. Delivering the doctor's letter was only a courtesy."

"You broke into my home as a courtesy?" She made a bemused squeak. "Should I start expecting this from all proper ladies? How will they keep from wrinkling their gowns climbing over the eaves?"

I left her chuckling behind me.

It wasn't until I was at the door that she called after. "If you're not a Pathfinder, why did Beaurigmand send you with his letter?"

I didn't pause, passing into the hall where painted eyes and hollow sockets asked the same question.

"He thinks I'm your daughter."

26

CONDOLENCES
JADAIN

"It's lighter than I expected." Rarentz, Miss Kindler's gardener, gave Tashan's bronze sword a few lifts. They were on the porch, but I could hear them plainly through Miss Kindler's parlor window.

"It used to be heavier," Tashan said, "back when the blade was full. It shattered not long after I arrived in Caliphas and no one knew how to repair it in the traditional fashion."

"What, was it longer?" Rarentz had turned out to be quite an affable gentleman—after Miss Kindler shouted for him to put his crossbow away and let us inside.

"Yes, much. It had a curve like this." Tashan made some gesture I couldn't see.

"Huh. Like a sickle."

"Similar. We call it a khopesh." His voice turned wistful. "My parents gave it to me when I left Wati. It was my grandmother's, the one she used while serving as one of our pharaoh's Risen Guard."

He'd never told me that. Of course, I suppose that even after traveling together for over two week, I never asked much about his home. Now it seemed like a missed opportunity.

"That's quite a title." Rarentz sounded honestly impressed.

"It's a great honor."

A respectful beat passed between them.

"You just can't trust city metalsmiths," Rarentz said. "All they know is jewelry and how to sculpt angels onto bedposts. If you're planning on being around for a while, there's a smith named Foxthal who lives in Silversheaf—it's just outside the city, not an hour away. He's done good work for my family in the past. I'd bet he could reshape the blade there any way you like." The gardener interrupted himself with a surprised grunt. "I bet we could even find a proper picture of a—of your sword in Miss Kindler's library."

"Really? That would be a true blessing. Thank you."

Boys and their swords. I shook away a smile and turned my attention back to the business inside. The scrap of robe I'd been using as an eye patch slipped for the thousandth time. I retied it tighter, more than aware that it was the cause of a dull headache.

When I looked up with my good left eye, Miss Kindler had just shuffled back into the room where we sat. She focused on pouring water from a kettle into a porcelain tea set. Wingless dragons and herons circled the delicate cups, each inked in blue as faint as the veins on a princess's wrist. She'd forgone the convenience of her library's wheeled chair to serve us here in her parlor, despite our insistence against the bother.

Soon two cups were steaming on the low table, one within reach of my place on the sofa, the other just in front of Larsa, who leaned from a faded floral chair. She wrinkled her nose and sat back, looking no less ready to leave. The swelling along her lip didn't look any better.

Miss Kindler lowered herself into the chair next to Larsa, bringing her own cup to the table without the slightest clatter. She sipped deeply, picking up Doctor Trice's letter from the table and rereading it.

"You saw my sister after the attack on her home," the old woman said without looking up, her voice level.

Larsa nodded.

"How is she?"

"She's unharmed and resting safely," I said when Larsa didn't answer. "Doctor Trice is ensuring she receives the best care."

Miss Kindler's eyes lifted from the letter. She knew Havenguard wasn't just any hospice.

I relented. "She was obviously confused. She mistook Larsa for you."

"It threw her into a panic," Larsa added.

"I can see why."

"It wasn't just the trauma playing tricks on Lady Thorenly," I said mildly, meeting Larsa's darkening look.

"No, I shouldn't think so. I can see how our resemblance could have startled poor Ellishan. Especially," she nodded at Larsa, "if those gaps in your smile are fresh."

Larsa straightened in her chair.

Obviously she suspected that Larsa's incisors weren't just missing by happenstance. Even without them, the paleness of her skin, pointed ears, and tells I wasn't perceptive enough to notice could have betrayed her dhampir nature to a scholar like Miss Kindler.

"The wonder is that Ellishan noticed your vampiric heritage, too," Miss Kindler went on. "She used to be a smart girl, but that knife dulled years ago. She never had much of a mind for things more unsettling than politics."

She folded the letter sharply and set it back on the table. "But as unsettling as this is, I'm even more surprised by this visit. A state accuser, an emissary of the royal cathedral, and my most fretful former student all seem more interested in a coincidence of hair color than in who stormed my sister's home and murdered my brother-in-law." Age certainly hadn't stolen any metal from her voice. "There's something more here."

Larsa didn't hesitate. "When was the last time you encountered Rivascis?"

Neither did Miss Kindler. "I've never heard the name."

I caught a look from Larsa and took up our shared question. "That's a surprise. Doctor Trice said he remembered you mentioning him."

"Then he's mistaken. That's a rather distinctive name and I'm not prone to forgetfulness."

I nodded, uncertain whose memory might be at fault. This would have been a long way to travel if Doctor Trice had misremembered a detail.

"So who is my supposed acquaintance?" Kindler asked.

"The one responsible for killing your brother-in-law," said Larsa. "A vampire."

Miss Kindler considered Larsa. She took a long draw from her cup—I noticed the old woman's drink wasn't steaming like ours. "A vampire."

"His slaves were the ones who attacked Thorenly Glen."

She accepted it with a slow nod, not questioning the outlandishness of the claim. "Blake wasn't the reason—too dim to be involved with anything like that."

"No. No one at the estate seemed to have anything to do with the vampires' business."

"Why, then?"

Larsa told her what there was to know, adding a few particulars she hadn't shared with me—her visit to the manor, slaying the lesser vampires there, a grisly message. The old woman listened politely. Neither she nor her tea set seemed particularly scandalized by the gruesome talk.

"Where's this Rivascis come in?" Miss Kindler asked after Larsa finished.

"So far, he hasn't. Yismilla Col was important to Ardis's vampire underworld—her murder is tantamount to a coup. Sending her head to my superiors was a blatant insult. If Rivascis isn't involved, someone else in Ardis is. Since his name's come up, though, Trice sent us to you."

"Mistakenly," Miss Kindler noted. "Who are your 'superiors'?" Before Larsa could answer, she added, "Aside from Diauden."

The Royal Accuser's mouth tightened. She didn't seem used to the Royal Advisor's name tossed around as an afterthought. "I'm not permitted to say."

The old woman hummed through a little smile, nodding. "Well, it's a fascinating story, ladies. If I were even ten years younger, I'd be tempted to help you turn over every tombstone in the city to find my sister's attacker. As it is, though, I don't see how I can be much help."

"Well, there's another matter . . ." I trailed off. It wasn't really my place.

Both women stared across the table. The same cold blue steeled both their gazes—though Larsa's carried more of a warning.

"You mean my resemblance to Miss Larsa."

I nodded.

"I'm sorry to disappoint you again, ladies, but I don't have a daughter," Miss Kindler said with a shrug.

I blinked, taking a moment to compare the women's faces and frames. Wrinkles, the weight of age, and a prim dress disguised many of the similarities, but it was hard to ignore them—especially around the prominent noses and strong cheeks.

Miss Kindler noticed. "I don't deny a resemblance, and I'm not discounting the possibly of our relation, but if it's there, it's a distant one. Ellishan only has a son, and no other children. A branch of the family also lives in Taldor, so maybe there's some relation through them."

Larsa didn't look convinced. Miss Kindler's explanation was possible, I supposed, but it seemed fantastically unlikely—of course, no more unlikely than the woman simply having forgotten about having a daughter.

My eyes strayed to the painting over the mantel. I stood to take a better look.

"This is you?" I pointed at the five confident-looking travelers posing in a rose garden: a dark-haired man with a starknife and the symbol of the goddess Desna, a bald woman leaning on a pack dangling with bottles, an armored woman with a shield marked with a howling wolf, a blond man smiling as he posed with a crossbow, and Larsa, outfitted in a rider's duster.

Miss Kindler nodded. "And some of the best people who ever lived."

I leaned in. Even in oil, the resemblance was unmistakable. "Because it looks *so much* like her."

"I promise, no one is more aware of the similarity." Miss Kindler gave a less-than-subtle glance toward the seat I'd vacated. "It's been the better part of a century since I've seen that face, and then only in mirrors."

I took her suggestion and reseated myself. Both she and Larsa seemed to be going out of their ways not to look at one another.

"I don't know what else I can say. I don't have any explanation." Her expression hardened. "And I'm sorry if this insults you, Miss Larsa, but frankly I'm repulsed by what you're suggesting."

Larsa straightened, suddenly not shy about looking at her elder doppelganger. "What are we suggesting?"

"I hunted terrible things, I never laid with them. More than once during my career filthy-minded cowards tried to disparage me by conflating my enthusiasm with lust. It's ridiculous and, frankly, I find the thought disgusting." She turned to Larsa. "I don't mean this as any judgment on you, child. I think we all agree that the living and the dead shouldn't—"

Larsa lifted her palm, giving a single sharp nod like she agreed—or, more likely, like she just wanted the woman to stop.

"I had one other question." I sounded like I was changing the subject, though I wasn't entirely. "When we spoke to your sister, she said this was 'happening again.' What did she mean?"

Miss Kindler stood to refill her cup—not from the setting at hand, but from a crystal decanter on the sideboard. "No idea."

Larsa rolled her head. "You don't seem to know very much."

Miss Kindler ignored her tone, filling her teacup to the brim with some chestnut-colored concoction. "I don't know my sister's business and can't imagine what state she was in when you spoke with her. It could have been anything."

"I don't know." I couldn't help but sound more delicate than Larsa. "The church's records said . . ."

I reached for the folio, having thought I saw it with Trice's letter on the table. But it wasn't there.

"She burned them," Larsa said.

My look shot between them. "What?"

Larsa nodded.

"Why?"

"I thought I'd gotten rid of Trice's 'observations' years ago." Miss Kindler retook her seat. I could smell the alcohol in her cup. It wasn't subtle. "What's in my head and how I've needed help are no one's business but my own." Her voice turned firm. "And when such details run astray, it results in situations like this."

"Be that as it may, they were documents from my cathedral. They clearly recorded your time there."

The old woman deeply considered her drink. "Miss Losritter, I'm not a religious woman, so I don't know. Would you say your goddess protects her bookkeepers so well that no counterfeit could slip amid your cathedral's shelves?"

"Of course not." I rushed to add, "But I don't believe the records we brought were fake. I also don't know why anyone would want to falsify a handful of pages about your convalescence fifty years ago."

"When you live as publicly as I have, you become used to certain amounts of manufactured scandal. I have little patience for such things, and find it best to dismiss them outright. Anyway, fifty years isn't that long for some."

I snatched up her last words. "You understand how that sounds when we came to speak to you about something that refuses to die."

Miss Kindler looked out the window behind me. "The day's gotten on without me, I'm afraid, and our visit's put me behind on other errands." Placing her cup—already nearly drained—upon the table, she stood, a blunt suggestion that we do the same. "Thank you for your delivery and concerns. I assure you I'll keep them in mind."

Larsa and I shared a disapproving look.

"Certainly, Miss Kindler, but I don't know that we've made our intentions totally clear." I stood. "We've been asked to see to your safety as well as to track down those responsible for your sister's attack."

Laughter threatened to shake loose her tightly packed bun.

"I'm sorry, Miss Losritter, but I don't need any protection. I've managed to look after myself this long. Anyway, I don't keep Rarentz on hand for his gardening skill." She gave a thin smile. "And even beyond that, we have our sign on the gate."

"Something here in Ardis seems to have an interest in you and your family. You're going to need more than your gardener and an old gate," Larsa said, still not having risen from her seat. "I got in easily enough."

Miss Kindler smirked. "I have several wards protecting my home, most magical, some otherwise, and all quite effective. You might have slipped in today, but you didn't do so unnoticed. Had my protections determined you were an actual threat, you would never have gotten so far, and we certainly wouldn't have the pleasure of your company now."

Larsa's derisive puff went ignored as our hostess took a step toward the door. "Now, since you're new to the city, do you have lodging arranged?"

This had not at all gone the direction I'd wanted. Regardless, if we were being asked to leave, it was probably best to do so.

We'd given Miss Kindler a significant amount to digest. Giving her some time to consider the situation might make her more receptive to more questions later.

"No, not yet. We came here straightaway." I followed with small steps. Behind me, Larsa stood as well.

"Rarentz is a native. He'll find you something suitable."

"Thank you, Miss Kindler, for your time and hospitality."

"Of course. And try not to worry so much." She gave me a grandmotherly pat on the shoulder. "I know this all must seem terribly important now, but after a week things never seem as dire as they did in the moment."

I put on a flat smile. "I hope you'll let us visit again soon. I know we both still have many questions."

She mirrored my polite smile. "We'll see."

"Tomorrow perhaps?"

"We'll see."

Larsa was the first out the door.

27

HOME TO SHADOWS
LARSA

Think this will do for a few days?" Rarentz gestured at the ivory manor huddled amid ivy and mossy elms.

"What do you mean?" Jadain said, as we looked past the rusty gate we'd nearly walked by.

"Well, we could find an inn to overcharge you for a drafty room, or you could take your pick of drafty rooms for no charge right here."

"Who's home is this?" I glanced up at the prominent letter *T* worked into the gate. Even well back from the main avenue it was clear the house wasn't occupied, many of its windows boarded over like so many others we'd seen in Ardis. Even if the owners were gone, though, they hadn't necessarily given their home over to squatters.

"The Troidaises. They don't live around here anymore. I'm keeping an eye on the place while they're looking for a buyer." Rarentz produced a key and wrestled it into the lock. Even then he still had the give the gate his shoulder, the bars dragging gouges through the rocky drive.

"I check in every week or so." He smiled over his shoulder. "It's no palace, but it's warm and dry and you'll have plenty of space."

Jadain seemed unconvinced, looking down the street as if she expected to see constables coming to run us off.

Squat windows peeked through the weeds scaling the house. Too low for the first floor, the foggy panes likely helped light the basement. From the look of the place, probably a cold, musty basement at that. Perfect.

"It'll do fine." I squeezed through the barely opened gate behind Rarentz.

Neither Tashan nor Jadain rushed to follow.

"This is wonderful!" Jadain spun, face upturned toward the glowing crystal swans of the chandelier hanging in the foyer of Troidais House.

While the estate's walled grounds had been left to do what they would, the house's interior had waited for its owners' return patiently. Sheets filled quiet rooms with the ghosts of elaborate furnishings, colorful carpets stood rolled in corners, mantels and sculpted alcoves sprawled deserted. Dust and stray leaves collected along the baseboards, our unannounced intrusion interrupting their rest. The house seemed desperate for company, so much so that our steps echoed tenaciously, dancing up empty stairs and reverberating through unseen halls.

Despite the loneliness of the place, the chandelier had stayed lit.

Rarentz barely gave an upward glance. "It's the biggest pain about this place. Some cheap magic makes it glow, which sounds nice, but you can't shut the bloody thing off. And it's impossible to keep clean. It's a giant glowing dust trap."

"Well, it's lovely." Jadain's attention drifted back down. "You're sure the owners won't be concerned about us staying here? Should you ask first?"

"Oh, they don't live in the city anymore. It'll be fine." His boots clopped as he crossed to one of several heavy doors and pushed it open. "The kitchen's here. There's no food, but I can bring up some water and it'll be fit for cooking whatever you have with you."

The door swung as he dropped it. He crossed to the worn wooden stairs, pointing up them. "There're bedrooms upstairs if you want some privacy, but I'm afraid all the linens and mattresses are gone." He turned to Jadain. "There're still some of the lady of the house's clothes up in the master bedroom. If you'd like something . . . more, you're welcome to take a look."

The priestess grinned, suddenly mindful of robes stained by trail and knotted to keep their shape. Little of their original misty purple or ornamental swirls remained intact.

"If it's no bother."

"None at all."

She immediately made for the stairs, disappearing up them.

Rarentz turned to Tashan and me, still lingering near the entry. "Please. Make yourselves at home."

I wasn't interested in indulging his hospitality. I'd only come to Ardis for one reason. "Kindler said you know the city well."

"Yes." His look of pride faded.

"Criminals, smugglers, pesh dealers—where do those sorts collect?"

He frowned. "I'm not sure what you mean."

"Every city has an underside. Where's this one's?"

His look crossed to Tashan, maybe reconsidering us. "What are you looking for?"

"Who. I'm looking for someone."

"Some criminal?"

"A fugitive." I handed him my iron badge.

He didn't accept it, his eyes jerking back to my face. He'd recognized the seal as something more than just the identification of some royal messenger—I hadn't expected that.

"A traitor? Or some rogue noble?" Obviously he knew something about the sort of problems accusers solved.

"Something like that."

"Who?" He asked a bit too quickly.

"No one you'd know," I said, putting the emblem back inside my jacket.

"I've lived here my entire life. You might be surprised."

I lifted a brow. "By what? The criminals you know?"

His expression twisted, but he shrugged it off. "Spend enough time anyplace and you see things—sometimes you do things—most people have the sense to stay out of. You learn where to be to keep out of trouble and if you're looking for trouble?"

"So where do people in Ardis go when they're looking for trouble."

"White Corner."

"What's that?"

"It used to just be another neighborhood where a lot of regular folk lived. I don't think it was ever especially nice, but it wasn't a slum. It's mostly empty now."

"Why?"

"Ardis has been dying for as long as I've know it. White Corner is just one of the places that rotted out first."

"Why do you mean 'dying'?" Tashan chimed in.

Rarentz gave a sour grimace. "The royal court moved to Caliphas about ten years before I was born. Most of the most important families followed it south, but a lot of stubborn sorts stayed here to stick it out in the 'True Capital.'" He rolled his eyes. "And by stubborn, I mostly mean cheap or poor."

Rarentz might not have been old enough to remember, but I was. I wasn't working for the crown back then, but working for Grandfather alone wasn't really that different. On his deathbed, the last prince commanded the throne be moved from historic, geographically central Ardis to rich, metropolitan Caliphas. For Caliphas, the relocation meant even greater prestige for what was already one of the most important ports on Lake Encarthan. That wealth and clout had to come from somewhere, though, and apparently Caliphas's gain was Ardis's loss.

"Ardis has been emptying out ever since," Rarentz went on. "Without as much noble money in the city, many places hiked up prices and rents or got rid of workers. There used to be a lot of beggars on the streets. There still are, but growing up there were more. Who knows where they all went, but most came from places like White Corner. Practically overnight one family's little room turned into something three families could barely afford."

It was bad news, but from his detached telling it was apparently old news. I pushed him on. "And now?"

"The landlords eventually gave up—even they couldn't afford to live in their empty tenements. The people on the streets tried moving back in, but the gangs were already carving up territories. The watch tried to break things up, but eventually they gave up, too. It wasn't like the gangs were wrecking anyplace anyone important cared about. So now they just do what they please and anyone with sense avoids passing through White Corner."

"That's where I'm headed, then."

Turning for the door, I nearly ran into Tashan.

"We'll come with you," he said.

"Like hell you will. You'll stand out too much and I'm not wasting time keeping your ass out of trouble." I didn't care that Rarentz was listening. "And I don't need your master showing up to look over my shoulder."

The Osirian gave a detached blink, but stepped aside.

"Pass that along to Jadain, too. If she wants to help, remind her how useful her healing magic was this morning."

The door booming closed cut off any argument.

Just ahead, some street brat darted across the alley's mouth. He fired a look at me before running on, eyes wet flints amid a mask of rags. His footfalls sounded like crumpling paper. By the time I reached the next trash-heaped thoroughfare, he'd vanished.

But the whispers made it completely obvious where he'd gone.

The uneven alleys and staggering buildings of White Corner were far less abandoned than Rarentz had claimed.

262 F. WESLEY SCHNEIDER

I had no trouble finding the district. At any cross street, I merely headed the direction people were headed away from. Empty buildings were a common enough sight in Ardis, but few were truly dilapidated. As soon as that changed, I knew I'd arrived.

Trash heaped high enough to cover street-level windows. Congested gutters leaked brown streams across the cobbles. Scrawny mongrels scrapped with bloated rats—the rats regularly winning bloody victories. Over it all drifted a haze of plaster dust and the groans of diseased buildings. There were slums in Caliphas, but White Corner was a ruin.

If the city had a vampire population, this is where they'd hunt. It was just a matter of finding someone who'd notice nameless corpses and be bold enough to talk. Criminals were typically good for that sort of thing, the cockier and better organized the better. Those sorts weren't hard to find.

Usually.

Hours passed and the sun settled behind the city's jagged skyline. In the alleys, small fires attracted knots of voiceless strangers. Silent skirmishes over territory and food unfolded, the losers chased into the cold of the open avenues. Man-shaped rag heaps scuttled through the dark, hunting warmth, food, and their own hidden corners—all in pitifully short supply.

I kept my distance from the scavengers—they weren't the sort I was looking for. Junk lean-tos and trash palaces crowded the alley routes I favored. The inhabitants knew to keep their eyes to themselves, and only an occasional grumble marked my passage. At least, until it started getting dark.

A faint glow marked the veiled moon's climb. As it rose, the muttering became bolder. Noise echoed weirdly amid the urban ravines. Alleys inhabited only by lice seemed to sigh, given breath either by some trick of the wind or the murmurs of watchers in the windows above. I never made out an actual word, only the snipped cadence of complaint. Often voices sounded as though they were coming from just ahead, but every corner turned onto another silent street.

And I wasn't the only one to hear. Soon, every crowded flame reflected in dim eyes. The vagabonds hadn't just begun noticing me; the night simply made them bolder. I slipped from an alley and already eyes were upon me: three men around a heap of burning garbage, their lookout in a broken window, even a procession of conquering rats—they all had their eyes fixed on the shadows I kept to. I doubted the humans could even see me in the dark, but still they stared, and around them echoed that wordless mutter.

It seemed like I'd broken some law of the street, and White Corner had noticed. I reached to pull my hat lower, forgetting I hadn't had it since Kavapesta. I could feel its phantom weight nonetheless. With a sour groan, I dashed to the next alley. Hours had passed and I'd seen nothing of gangs or hideouts. I'd been listening for the screams or cruel laughs of slum warlords, but there'd been nothing. Only echoes murmured, without need of mouths or voices. I scoffed at Rarentz calling this place abandoned. Abandoned by civilization, definitely, but not by people. This place had become a wilderness, and something primal had taken root.

That's when the kid darted past. His deliberateness more than his appearance interested me, but he disappeared faster than I could follow. Tall flames burned at the end of the street he'd evaporated into, past a dune of broken furniture and whatever else sagging tenements had vomited loose. The fires crackled, sounding like steps or snippets of sharp curses. In the firelight, the empty buildings seemed to sway. It looked like any of them might collapse, silently and unmourned, at any moment.

The light also danced in staring, recklessly fearless eyes, several pairs watching from a rubble heap's slumped entry. If more glimmered in the street, I didn't notice. Even if I had, I'd reached the point where I didn't care.

My old approaches didn't seem to work here. Time for a new one.

The staring wretch didn't move as I broke from the shadows and didn't blink as I yanked it to its feet. Tangled sheets hugged its body, crusty onion layers of dirt and sweat as thick as leather. I slammed him against the crumbling plaster and couldn't tell where stained fabric ended and stained skin began.

I intended to speak—to demand, to threaten, to wring out the secrets of these zombie streets. But I smelled that familiar, rusty tang and felt a rising, racing pulse through my palms.

How long had it been since I'd fed properly? From the source? Considine's lukewarm charity had been irresistible in the moment, but after he vanished, the warmth in my belly soon followed. The reminder lingered.

Certainly no one would notice one less pitiful story in this place. I could easily convince myself this was a mercy if I even cared to.

I snapped the dirty thing's head to the side and bared my—

My nothing. My neutered, blunt, remaining teeth.

What did I really hope to do? Could I chew this hopeless, stringy sack apart? How long would it take dry gums to gnaw a vagabond bloody?

I dropped the uncomplaining, ageless, genderless collection of stains. It slid down the empty doorframe—still staring, still fearless. I struggled between rising disgust and the urge that gripped my dagger, ready to use it like cutlery.

When the whispers coalesced, they were close. "Miss Kindler."

I jerked at the proximity of the icy voice, my blade leaving its sheath.

Arms low, hands open, a leper princess stood mid-street— not at my back as it had sounded. A gown fashioned from sable strips wound across the stranger's body, every length pierced by precious baubles—punctured coins, mismatched earrings, dangling broaches, all crisscrossing her body in golden trails. She was thin, but the layers of her flayed dress disguised just how much so. What the decorative straps didn't cover hid beneath lacy black gloves and a matching veil.

I immediately suspected what she was—my people sometimes attempted to defy the sun in such heavy coverings. Her breast moved faintly. I reached out with the coldest parts of me, but didn't sense the tingle of death upon her. If she was one of my kind, she was taking pains to disguise it. Or perhaps the opposite, and she was failing at imitating a vampire.

"What did you call me?" I kept my blade between us. At my feet, the beggar had sunk back into its heap, having never even twitched.

"Miss Kindler," she repeated in a hissing accent, sounding as though she were speaking through clenched teeth.

"I'm not Miss Kindler."

"Of course," she said with cool deference. "If you'll follow me, my lord is waiting for you."

I checked the street again. She appeared to be alone, yet the firmness of her voice made it clear this wasn't a casual invitation.

"Your lord?"

"Yes." She bowed slightly, causing baubles to tinkle across her body. They hadn't made a sound a moment ago when she'd approached. "Your father."

This was not what I'd expected when I came here looking for the traitor. A hint, a whisper, a direction, yes, but never an invitation. "Rivascis?"

"If you'll follow me." She turned away without waiting for my answer, heading down the street toward the flames.

Again I scanned the shadows, even checked that the mass behind me hadn't twitched. Nothing disturbed the darkness. Even the faint whispers had ceased, as if they'd congealed into the shadow slipping down the street.

What choice did I have? Perhaps I could best this eerie messenger and learn what she knew with the tip of my blade, but something about her suggested I wouldn't have that chance. If she were leading me into an ambush, well, at least then I'd have some sense of what Rivascis was armed with. I trusted my experience to get me out of most trouble—or at least to recognize when I'd gotten in too deep.

The woman faded into the dark, trailing a gentle rhythm of soft chimes. With no better option, I followed.

28

FADED GLORIES

JADAIN

It didn't slam, but the front door's solid closing sent a pulse through Troidais House. I'd only just touched the banister at the top of the stairs when I felt the vibration through the wood.

Most of the rooms on the manor's second floor were like the ones below, given over to dusty floors and furniture costumed as ghosts. The master bedroom hadn't been hard to find, though, nor the wardrobe within. Many of the clothes were older fashions and had seen more than one alteration, but the fabric and design were lovely. Searching for something plain revealed dress after dress of Thuvian lace, wolf fur, fine sable, pearl clasps, and patterns fit to be display tapestries. In the end, I closed them back up, unwilling to threaten any one of them—grinning at the ridiculousness of dressing like a noblewoman.

Lady Troidais's husband appeared to be only a slightly less delicate sort. In a fine chest filled with a lord's attire for everything from receiving to riding I found a pair of well-worn pants and a plain, only slightly snug shirt. I ignored the faint unaired smell, and a few tucks and a tight belt brought together a relatively comfortable outfit.

My robes lay in a heap at the center of the plank floor, their violet swirls torn and muddy. Stripping out of them had been like peeling off a layer of dead skin. They'd take considerable work to mend and clean, if they could be saved at all. I didn't know if it'd be worth it, and wondered if it'd be better to merely toss them away. Either choice had a gulf of implications.

I tore away a roughly even strip of sleeve, replacing the loose bandage covering my branded eye. This one was deeper lavender and not nearly as stained. I balled the rest into my pack, then headed back downstairs.

Rarentz wore a sour expression as he and Tashan stepped from the manor's short entry hall into the chandelier's glow. Noticing me on the stairs, however, he brightened, bursting into full, honest laughter.

I halted, checking my outfit. Certainly it was unconventional, but not outrageously so.

"What?" I said sharply enough to be heard over his guffaws.

"Nothing!" He stifled his outburst. "I'm sorry, that's just not at all what I was expecting."

I looked down at myself again. They were work clothes, but they were still good quality—exceptionally good quality. They also didn't look like they'd ever seen a day of real work, and if they had, they'd been thoroughly scrubbed.

"I needed something that let me move around, not a dress for the opera. This works fine."

"It looks fine." He lifted his hands, apologizing. "It just surprised me."

Tashan's eyes had been working, looking me over, then Rarentz. "They're his," he said flatly.

Rarentz looked back at the Pathfinder with a surprised smile, but didn't say anything.

"What?" I wasn't sure if I'd heard correctly.

"All the lords in this country, they get old, they start looking like jugs of wine. So I doubt they belong to the master of the house." He gestured, tracing Rarentz's outline as if measuring. "But they're about his size, I'd say."

Rarentz gave an awkward chuckle. "You have a good eye for this."

"My father was a tailor." Tashan grinned. "I know something about fabrics."

"I'm sure I can find something else," I said, backing up a stair. Somehow it had felt less awkward wearing a stranger's clothes than those of someone I'd just met. I'd turned back up the steps before it struck me. "Hold on. Why are your clothes in the master bedroom?"

With another chuckle, Rarentz awkwardly rubbed the back of his neck. "Well . . . it *is* my bedroom."

A moment passed in silence.

"You're not just tending this house," Tashan said.

"No and yes," Rarentz said. "My family's been trying to sell our townhome for years. The trouble is, no one's buying. It was only supposed to be for a few months, but I've been keeping an eye on the place for almost three years now."

"Then you're Lord Troidais?" Tashan sounded skeptical.

"Really, that's my father."

"But you're still a nobleman," I said. "I thought you were in Miss Kindler's employ."

"Yes, well . . . that's a new development. She helped get me out of a tricky spot, so now I make sure her hedges stay trimmed and no one bothers her. I figure it's better than staying locked up here by myself or spending money I don't have." Open palms patted the air, trying to end the discussion. "So please, keep the clothes. To be perfectly honest, they're just what I wore whenever I had to muck out the stable."

It didn't really make me more comfortable, but what other choice did I have? I nodded my thanks and came the rest of the way down the steps. "What were you ever doing mucking horse stalls?"

"Oh, it's been a long time since my family had anyone to do our chores for us," he said with an easy shrug. "Our name might be noble, but the money's long gone."

He sounded remarkably reasonable about a situation that would have driven most of Caliphas's nobles past the brink. For a moment I felt sorry for him, but from the embarrassment coloring his cheeks, it seemed like he honestly didn't care.

I glanced down the empty entry hall, then to Tashan. "Where's Larsa?"

"She left," he said.

"Where'd she go?"

"Someplace called White Corner." Reading my expression, Tashan added, "She said not to follow."

"Why? What's there?" I sounded angrier than I meant to. Larsa had always had her own reasons for coming to Ardis, but I was still offended. I hadn't just traveled half the length of the country to stand by the wayside while she hunted down a killer.

"It's where the gutters dump the lowest of the low," Rarentz said. "She wanted to know where the city's criminals collect. I told her there. She went off after whoever she's looking for."

"And you just let her go?"

Tashan's steady gaze made me realize how ludicrous that sounded. I should have expected this. Her desire to hunt down this creature had been her only objective since Caliphas. Even the prospect of meeting her own mother never seemed to interest her. This had always been about finding her target.

I'd come with her mostly because I thought I could help. Secretly, I'd thought maybe the goddess led me to Larsa. That she wanted me to help put an end to something truly wicked. Now, though . . .

The mark beneath my bandage itched. I could feel the shape, the goddess's symbol corrupted. Worse than bearing that blasphemy in my flesh, though, was knowing that it was the closest thing to the goddess's emblem that I could bear. Even thinking about the wooden spiral hanging against my chest made my stomach reel. If that was what my connection to the goddess had been reduced to, what did I truly think I could do to help Larsa?

No wonder she'd left me behind.

I went to one of the windows by the manor door. Tashan said my name, advising me against following, but he didn't need to worry.

The overgrown lawn of Troidais House looked marshy and faded in the cloudy afternoon. Beyond the weedy gardens and ivy-snarled trees stood the manor's dark iron gate. A man was standing there.

He reached through a grizzled beard to grip one of the gate's rusty bars, his bearlike build unhidden even by heaps of rotting rags. He was too far away to be sure, but he looked like the beggar I'd spoken to earlier, the man with the opera singer's voice.

Had he followed us, first to Miss Kindler's and then here? Tashan's warning, which had sounded so uncharitable in the moment, took on an echo of truth. Was he looking for another handout? Did he need help?

I'd just resolved to approach him when his body jerked like he'd been startled. He glanced away, then back, giving the manor a long, suspicious look. Reluctantly, he set off down the street, shuffling away as though he'd been called.

29

BLOODSTAINS
LARSA

I f anything still played at the Mirage Theater, no one was buying
tickets.

The rickety neighborhood hall likely hadn't stood straight
even in whatever heyday it might have had, but now decorative
columns and the sagging marquee cocked at disorienting slants.
Broken seating and scraps from amateurish productions climbed
the theater's alley wall, heaped as if the junk had slid from an
askew upper story. The garbage seemed to be all that kept the
leaning theater from toppling against its neighbors and setting off
a cascade of giant, abandoned dominos.

We hadn't traveled far, just a few blocks, but the streets of
White Corner had grown notably less deserted. Grimy figures,
strangely ignorant of the cold, watched from empty windows and
trash-pile perches. No fires lit the alleys here, the moon's murky
light casting everything in still, frozen shades. Even the rats—so
brazen before—merely glared at our passage.

In our tour, the woman in black hadn't spoken another word.
She drifted down the center of the streets as boldly as a noblewoman through her own home, her bangles delicately announcing
her coming and trailing her in a procession of airy reminders. No
one impeded her passage.

Through the maze of crumpled apartments and trash barri-
cades she'd led me to the tired theater. Gliding into the alley, she
picked her way over the garbage heaps like they were palace stairs.

I'd been suspicious of the vagabonds on the street. They had some relationship with the woman, even if it was just being familiar enough to keep out of her way. The tight alley beside it, though, could easily be a killing ground.

I stopped well back from the gap's mouth. "What's down there?"

"He's waiting." She didn't slow her climb. A moment later she vanished over the heap.

Alone on the street, I cursed, searching the surrounding roofs and windows for any shift in the shadows. Nothing twitched, and only garbage rustled in the night breeze. Somehow the lack of obvious threats only made me more nervous. Still I followed.

Beyond the splinter mountain, a faint glow shone through the open backstage door. Stepping partway through, I kept my heel in the frame, expecting the door to slam behind me.

As it was, the woman stood there, her dark gown blending into the gloom, her trinkets pinned to shadows. They shone golden in the hint of light drifting down a short set of stairs.

"There." The metal glints pointed up the steps.

"This is why people always have to be reminded not to kill messengers. If I find anything other than what you said . . ." I wasn't subtle about drawing my blade into the space between us.

The ornaments hung silently.

Tired of her cryptic company, I made my way up the stairs.

Moldy, wine-colored curtains divided the stage. Harsh light leaked through their countless moth-eaten holes, the misshapen constellations doing little to illuminate the cramped backstage. Only the shadows of limp rigging moved, swaying across the bulging bricks of the theater's back wall.

A thumb-width gap slit the curtains. I parted them with the point of my sword.

Light flooded the stage, the footlights blindingly intense. Squinting and raising an arm, I pushed through, ignoring the baking sensation across my forearm.

Several dingy linens hung in straight lines and square corners, the legs of battered easels extending from beneath their frayed edges. A semicircle of hidden canvases transformed the stage into a gallery. It wasn't a particularly large display—only five tall pieces in total, and all of their subjects well hidden. All of them, but one.

Someone who looked like me smiled into the limelights.

Overly lush with light and blooming flowers, it was a portrait in oil, a red-haired maiden half-dancing through some imagined Elysium. Her face upturned to a springtime sun, she basked runty features that would never grow particularly feminine. I knew, since they were the same baggy eyes and pronounced nose that mocked me from every mirror. I'd never wear a lacy shift like the one hanging from her boy-shoulders, but I couldn't be too offended. Even though it was my figure, I doubted it was truly meant to be me.

A vagrant stood at the uncovered work, a muddy rainbow of pigments smearing his forearm. Fingers torn through tattered gloves directed a long brush in making adjustments. He assessed every dab and peck from multiple angles, pursuing some invisible perfection.

"There's plenty left to do." His voice cracked, as though he hadn't spoken in some time. "But I hope you'll help me finish."

Half-turning, he let a thin-lipped grin chisel his sallow face. He looked faded, blond hair bleached nearly to white, eyes worn to the barest gray. Beneath a bird's nest of unwashed hair, lean cheekbones and a sharp chin went to waste. He looked like a storybook prince, but after the fairy tale was well ended.

I launched across the stage.

What little there was of a smile faded from the stranger's face, but he didn't move to defend himself. He merely took a step away from the canvas.

My blade sheathed itself in his collar, dry skin splitting with the sound of tearing paper. He'd flinched as I struck, sending the blade into his neck instead of fully across it.

I yanked the sword free—its length as clean as when it entered—ready to roll away from his reprisal. But his hands didn't so much as twitch, still loosely gripping his brush. He studied me openly, head tilting quizzically on his half-severed neck.

I brought the second swipe across, intent on chopping the trunk of his neck from both sides. Faster than I could swing, he turned to watch it come, lowering his chin just enough to catch the blow on his jaw. Dead skin tore, steel screeched across bone. Despite the force of the blow, his head didn't move even a hair.

My sword snapped back, again ready to defend against what might come. His eyes followed the blade, but then merely returned to mine. He looked tired. Bored.

I snarled and struck again, hacking high. He shifted, the blade embedding itself in corded muscle. I wrenched back, not checking for his counter blow.

My sword bit again, widening his smile, feeding him steel.

And again.

Growing rage quickened every strike. Deliberate thrusts gave way to wild hacks. Not one did he try to avoid. Instead, he choose where each landed, guiding the steel into dense muscles, parrying with joints and thick bones. His expression didn't betray a hint of pain or anger, even as I hacked it to pieces.

What there was only stoked my outrage.

The swipes blurred together. I felt every bite, heard his bones splinter, but he never gave ground. I perforated arms, sliced clothes to ribbons, sent an ear slapping against the plank floor.

Screaming echoed around me. For an instant I thought I'd struck some organ inside him still alive enough to feel. Then I realized the shriek was my own. I channeled it into a word. "*Why?*"

With my off hand, I grabbed the sword's guard and heaved. The blade struck deep, and something inside him, muffled by muscle, gave a wet crunch. Slowly the sword forced deeper, sinking through the gristle of his bloodless heart.

I held it there, head close to the empty wound, hair spilling across the blade, the only sound my uneven gulps for breath.

I knew my sword hadn't harmed him. That silver symbol of my own impotence worked well enough against the slaves of vampires, but not vampires themselves. Had it been sharpened wood or properly blessed, it might have interrupted the foul force that gave his corpse life, leaving him helpless within his own husk. But I hadn't expected to face him tonight. I thought I'd have time to prepare, to gather the tools I'd need. I'd expected it would take weeks to track the rebel that had eluded Grandfather for decades. I hadn't expected his messenger, and certainly never should have followed her. Yet here he stood, unbreathing, unbleeding. Silent.

I'd come all this way, faced him as I'd dreamt for so long, and vented less than a fraction of a lifetime of outrage. I could hear Grandfather's voice, again and again: *If you must blame someone, blame your father.*

Yet the storm I'd brewed for decades hadn't budged him a step.

I anticipated his cold, dry fangs shredding my throat.

But he didn't move. Even as exhaustion caused my impaling blade to shudder, he didn't flinch. The smell issuing from his clothes and opened innards had a dry dustiness to it, like books in an attic. It wasn't altogether unpleasant. In fact, it reminded me of Kindler's home.

"I already gave you my life once." Rivascis's voice drifted from just over my head, calm and barely louder than a whisper. "Stay with me until dawn, and if you still wish it, I'll give it to you again."

I recoiled two or three steps, not bothering to struggle my sword free.

"You gave me your life?!" I screamed, barely resisting the urge to throw a manic laugh in his face. I could hear the tremble in my voice. "Is that what you think, you sick leech? What life did you give me? You left your daughter blind in a sewer, helpless and surrounded by corpses! Do you expect me to thank you for that? For a lifetime of nightmares?"

"Siervage calls you 'Granddaughter', doesn't he?"

I gaped and nearly sputtered. "Do you think that meant he raised me like some princess? That his servants treated me like royalty? You know what that made me!"

I tore off my glove and peeled my sleeve up to the elbow.

"I know the name of each creature that gave me these scars. Every bite and tear made by a tutor or nursemaid. If that hell's what your life's worth," I shook my arm toward him, "then it's not worth shit."

Eyes narrowing, he took a step toward me. I matched with a backward step, reflexively drawing the dagger from my belt. The blade was nothing compared to the silvered length still skewering his body, but its weight in my hand made me feel less helpless.

His eyes remained locked on my arm, even as he gripped the hilt of the sword jutting from his chest. Awkwardly, he dislodged the silvered blade, willfully slicing his palms in extracting it. The weapon freed, he twisted it in his grip and presented it back to me.

"Forgive me." His voice was barely a whisper.

"No," I said before I was even sure of his words. I snatched the blade out of his hands.

Rivascis's head bobbed in a single shallow nod. He turned away, returning to his easel. "It pained me to leave Caliphas, but I had disobeyed Siervage's will and killed several of his servants. To stay would have jeopardized those I betrayed him for—including you."

"Please. I've lived around vampires my entire life. You all think you're so tragic." I pointed with the useless blade. "I've gotten the gist of your story. You're not some wronged prince. You're a coward and a traitor."

He retrieved something from the lip of his easel. At first I thought the dark, enameled length was a brush, but it clearly had no bristles.

"*Traitor.*" He repeated the word slowly, as if it were a name he hardly remembered. "So you're my father's poetic twist? His ironic executioner? He's filled my daughter's head with his lies and then set her loose against me." I could hear his smirk. "Sounds like Luvick."

"I'm not here on his orders. I came to kill you on my own." It sounded like gallows defiance, but this was what I wanted. If I was going to die, I was doing it for my reasons.

He gave a casual hum, not bothering to glance up. With a word that sounded like a reptilian curse, he touched the polished stick in his hand to his opposite forearm, still crisscrossed with empty gashes. A minuscule storm of black energy rained from the wand. Wild but soundless, the lightless power filled his already healing wounds, knitting them at an even more unnatural speed. Even his severed ear, his rent chest, and a dozen other violations restored themselves. I'd seen this magic before. It was the same power Jadain had refused me just hours ago.

"So you're saying you left Caliphas without his leave? That's part of what saw me branded a betrayer." His eyes drifted back to me. His voice was louder—the magic had clearly reinvigorated him. "You know how they obsess over blood. The traitorous daughter of a traitor—it's a story they'll want to believe."

I knew it. It was the reason Considine was out there somewhere, watching and judging, his own fate hinging or whether or not I remained loyal. "Damn them, then. I don't care."

"If not your grandfather's orders, then you're here on my invitation?"

I spat. "I'm here because *I* want to put a stake in your chest." It took a moment for his words to seep in. "What invitation?"

"My dear—"

The point of my blade reinforced my sneer. "Don't you *dare*."

His apology was a slow wave of an open palm. I was tempted to strike the fingers off.

"I assume you received my men at Thorenly Glen."

"The thugs there were yours, then. You sent them there deliberately?"

His small gesture suggested a bow.

"They butchered the residents—a bunch of old folks." My sword's tip jerked between us, punctuating my disgust. "Brave."

"Not all of them, I hope."

"No." I glared. "One survived."

"Lady Thorenly." He nodded. "Good. I made it clear that I wanted no harm to come to her."

My blade drew back defensively.

"My coachmen were merely conveying Luvick's agent home," he said, as though such were a common errand.

"Yismilla Col's head."

"Indeed. But she had a message nonetheless. One you appear to have received." His eyes strayed toward the painting. "How is your mother?"

Could he have known I'd be ordered to Thorenly Glen? Undoubtedly both Siervage and Diauden would have interest in Rivascis's messengers. If Ellishan Thorenly was purposefully meant to be the only survivor, was our meeting and her reaction so predictable? And from that meeting, Kindler?

A thread certainly ran from one to the next, but that didn't mean much. Things like Rivascis too often claimed responsibility for coincidences.

"I have no idea," I said. "Why don't you tell me who she is and I'll tell you if I recognize the name."

"Do you really need my reassurance? You've just come from her home." He took a slow step toward me.

My grip tightened, lifting the point of my drooping blade. I didn't like the idea of him knowing where I'd been. "The lady doesn't seem to think so."

"Memories are fleeting things. Once you lose them they're very difficult to get back."

"Are you saying she just forgot?" I laughed. "She didn't seem senile to me."

"Did you tell her who you were?"

"I told her who everyone thinks I am."

"And?"

"And nothing. She insisted she doesn't have a daughter."

He nodded. "She recognized herself in you, though."

"Coincidence." I knew it was a hollow explanation, but I didn't have any better.

"I visited her." He glanced back at the portrait. "It was some months ago. She didn't recognize me, either."

I wasn't catching whatever he was hinting at. I didn't especially care, either, but so long as he was talking he wasn't ending my life. "Maybe she forgot you."

He leaned toward me with a slow smile, exposing one of his vicious canines. "Can *you* imagine forgetting me?"

The footlights' glow flickered across my steel, a broad swipe reminding Rivascis of its territory. "I've been trying to ever since Grandfather told me your name."

He seemed to take it as a compliment, smiling wider. "If you've been unsuccessful, then how could she just forget me— how could she just forget *us*? You may have only met her, but I promise, you've always been her greatest question. Even without proof of your parentage, you're too close an answer to simply ignore."

"It could just be a coincidence." I tried that explanation again, but knew those were more Kindler's words than mine. The painting hanging in Thorenly Glen, the portrait in Kindler's own home, the face staring across the stage, they all could have been me—but none of them were. Every one of them honored her with the face I wore.

"But you know it's not. And I'm telling you it's not. So is she lying?"

I shrugged. "You seem to know her so well. Is she?"

"You're a Royal Accuser, you deal with counterfeits every night. What does your experience tell you?"

"She convinced me."

"It seems she's convinced herself—that doesn't mean it's true. As you said, it doesn't seem likely she just forgot. I've known Miss Ailson Kindler for a very long time. If ever there was someone with a knack for defying the impossible, it's her."

"So what, then? So a woman I don't know doesn't know me. I'll save my outrage." I looked away, casually casting about for other ways out.

"You're still so young, and have so much you want to lose. In time, you'll realize how important memories can be—especially those memories whose burden we share with others. We're not just who we are, we're who we were, and who others remember us to be."

I rolled my eyes. "You know, that's the easiest way to tell your kind. You look young, but you always sound like old people."

"There's truth to that." He smirked. "Do you know why mirrors refuse to show our kind? It's because they only show what is, not what's happened. We're all just echoes of something past, memories stuck in time. Memories don't have reflections."

"Mirrors reflect me just fine," I said.

"And you find them generous? Have you charmed them so that they don't reflect your gap-toothed smile?"

My jaw tightened. Reflexively, my tongue worried one of the hollows in my mouth, releasing a dull pain. I tried to suppress a wince.

Rivascis noticed. From somewhere his voice stole a father's concern. "What have they done to you?"

His tone surprised me. I glared a warning, shoving away his mock distress.

He tried another approach. "When was the last time you drank?"

"I'm not like you," I fired back, hoping he believed the half-truth. Immediately I found myself trying to count the days since I'd tasted warm blood. Unbidden, I felt the pressure of Considine's mouth against my own.

"Are you sure?" He took a step toward the stage's footlights, their harsh glow dimming at his approach.

As the wall of light descended, the Mirage's airy hall coalesced out of the dark. Grimy chandeliers, each caught in a different stage of collapse, dangled over broken rows of sloping benches. Much of the seating was missing, shattered by vandals or torn away to feed alley fires. Those seats that remained were occupied.

Corpses, dozens of them, silent and staring, packed the theater. Most were grimy, matted things, tramps and scroungers as threadbare as their infested blankets. Plumes, bits of lace, strings of silver, and other glints of finery marked wealthier sorts. Coin obviously hadn't saved any of the assemblage from their fate. All sat propped in their places, unblinking eyes locked on the stage.

I'd never seen—never imagined—such a polite massacre. Even the crawling, scampering things I'd expect to revel in such a scene were completely absent. Not a chomping rat or buzzing fly interrupted the savage solemnity. In the entire crowded hall there was only Rivascis's steps echoing upon the stage.

He stood before the assemblage like a conductor about to make his bow. Clearly, he'd been the architect of this atrocity, but I couldn't guess at his work's meaning—I was too busy counting. The sea of faces faded into a rising tally, the body count growing less and less precise with every dozen.

Rivascis knelt at the stage's brink, reaching down to his attentive audience. My estimate shattered when a slender hand reached back.

With delicate force and a flutter of white aprons, Rivascis pulled a young Qadiran woman onto the stage. The maid's black-freckled skin did nothing to hide the pronounced red punctures high on her collar.

"What is this?" I took a step back toward the curtain.

"There was a time when I was an actor. I find I still do my best work upon the stage. Hence . . ." He gestured over the assemblage.

Leaning close, he cooed something into the maid's ear. As though he'd blown the seeds from a dandelion, she drifted toward me. Her dreamy stagger-sway reminded me of the vacant wards wandering the grounds of Havenguard, only here, it was clear no orderlies kept cautious watch. She halted only a half step away from me, close enough that I could see the shallow rise and fall of her chest.

But she was breathing.

I looked out across the theater of eavesdroppers, a self-conscious weight settling in the back of my mind. "They're alive?"

"Of course." With the lights no longer obscuring the hall, Rivascis's voice seemed louder, filling the theater. Clearly he noticed my rising irritation. "But don't concern yourself with them. They're mine to command, and they'll remember nothing of what they've heard."

He drifted to the maid's side. "You're famished, and she's yours. Drink as much as you like, however you like."

The girl wore her hair short, exposing her long, naked neck. It wasn't sympathy or stubbornness that kept me from opening one of her veins. I forced my tongue to keep its place, ignoring the feel of phantom fangs.

"No." I raised my open hand, ready to push her away if he forced the matter.

He turned his eyes away, looking as though that—of all I'd said and done—had wounded him. I knew he was centuries older than me, but proud in his rags, he looked like some nobleman cast into the streets. He seemed suited for better things, but his tatters bore no hint of what they might be. For a moment, I wondered if I'd mistaken him. Was this truly the father I'd heard so much about? The betrayer—not of my people, but of that girl surrounded by dead things in the dark—that I'd been so eager to destroy? Could this frayed thing really bear the burden of all the blame I'd been told to heap on him?

"I know I have much to atone for." His voice was soft. "But let me start by returning what you've lost."

The enameled wand was back in his hand. It seethed shadows, its length seeming to waver like a grotesquely long worm. He repeated a noise, more hiss than word. The shadows surrounding the wand congealed, a thunderhead brewing along its length. He extended it toward me.

Resentment rushed back. "Why would I accept anything from you?"

"Because you've traveled all this way to find me. To see what I have to offer—even if it's only my death." He took a step toward me. "And because I need your help."

My laugh surprised even me. "What can you possibly think I'd ever help you with?"

His earnest expression didn't flinch. "I need your help to save the most dangerous vampire-killer our people have ever known."

30

Siege on Bronzewing

Jadain

"Miss Kindler asks that you, Miss Larsa, and Mr. Essesh come immediately. It's a matter of some importance." Rarentz delivered his message from the frosty stoop of his own home. He looked serious, and his voice had lost much of yesterday's friendliness.

"I don't think Larsa's here," I said, pulling close the plum dressing gown I'd found upstairs. "Is everything all right?"

"I wouldn't wait for her if I were you." He turned abruptly and hastily made for the gate.

Light was only just starting to slip through the foyer's high windows, but the house was still cold enough that every breath hung in the air. I didn't have to wake Tashan, he was already perched on the landing overlooking the entry. He hadn't been as bold as I'd been in raiding the Troidais's wardrobes, wearing only his trousers and his bed's paisley quilt like a cloak.

"Cozy?" I couldn't hide my chuckle.

He grimaced. "You know, this is why they call you barbarians. If your people didn't have to spend so much time inventing ways to keep warm, just think what you'd accomplish."

"Who calls us barbarians?"

He looked like he wasn't sure whether or not I was joking. "Everyone with the sense to live someplace warm."

Ignoring the wounded expression I pitched him, he changed the topic. "That sounded like Rarentz."

"It was. Miss Kindler wants us, and apparently badly enough not to wait for a decent hour."

He nodded and, with an unintentional flourish of his quilt, paraded back to his room to get dressed.

"Of course it's not too early. You just drink it warm." Miss Kindler stood on her porch, looking down at me as though I'd just asked the stupidest question in the world.

She looked like she'd been up for hours—or hadn't gone to bed at all. The dusty lace radiating from her stiff collar had the look of cracking ice. Along with her wan complexion and the wintery shades of her tea dress, she looked in need of thawing out. I hoped her steaming teacup would help with that, but at the very least her tone seemed at no risk of melting.

"I'm hoping you can explain something to me." She picked her way down the porch's cracked steps, circling her teacup before her.

"I'll do my best," I said when she didn't elaborate.

With a doubtful hum she tried to walk through me, following the walk to the drive, then continuing on toward the carriage house. Tashan and I exchanged frowns, but followed.

As we neared, Rarentz slid out from between the carriage house's sizable plank doors, crossbow slung over his shoulder. His attention was obviously on whatever work he'd left inside.

"Go ahead," Miss Kindler called, attracting his notice. Dutifully, he hauled the first of the heavy shed doors open.

He was just crossing to tug open the second door when we came to the end of the carriageway. He didn't need to waste the effort. The reason for Miss Kindler's impatience was clear.

A body sprawled amid the dust and shadows of the carriage house. The slight figure lay crumpled against a rear wheel of the wagon we'd driven from Kavapesta, slumped like a dozing stableboy. I might have thought he was just sleeping, except for the length of splintered board skewering his chest. I recognized his vest's golden vines immediately. Larsa's vampire compatriot, Considine.

Miss Kindler was looking at me rather than the body. My mind fruitlessly raced to find some delicate explanation. Tashan's reaction shattered any hope of that.

"Sir!" His cry sounded honestly pained. He pushed past, sliding into the dirt next to the corpse. His hands went to the wooden spear skewering the vampire's chest, but drew back just as fast. He was clearly unsure of how to help, if there was anything at all left to do.

Rarentz came up next to me, a finger resting near his crossbow's trigger. He looked down on the other man without pity.

"You killed him," Tashan said, a snarled threat.

"He was already dead—try to pay attention." Miss Kindler shook her head. "Rarentz's quick work with the board only paralyzed him. I want to know why he was creeping around my home before we drag him out and let the sun do its work."

Tashan's jaw clenched, biting back words his vicious glare already conveyed.

"Well." Miss Kindler nodded, then turned to Rarentz. "Into the drive's center, please. It'll smell terrible, but at least he won't burn the yard when the sun takes him."

"No!" Tashan and I snapped at once. The Osirian had half regained his feet, his hand on the hilt of his sword.

But the old woman wasn't looking at him. She arched a brow toward me, mimicking a sardonic look I'd seen dozens of times on Larsa's face.

"I don't know the whole story, but his name's Considine." I tried to piece together what I was certain of. I suspected more, but there was no reason to darken the scene further. "He's a vampire who followed Larsa from Caliphas. He saved us in Kavapesta, when the inquisitors there imprisoned us. I don't know what connection he and Tashan have . . ." I didn't press the matter. "We knew he was following us, but had no idea when he might return."

288 F. WESLEY SCHNEIDER

"And you didn't think to mention this when I let you into my home?" Miss Kindler's tone remained level, but her wrinkles accented her frown, making it even more severe.

I took a moment's refuge in a long blink. Where the devil was Larsa to explain whatever this was?

"I apologize. I didn't think he was a threat—he saved our lives. But it does look like you dealt with the matter."

"Only thanks to a lifetime of being disappointed in what I can expect from common sense. My home's particularly well guarded against intruders, but it seems the more precautions I take, the more fools mistake them for invitations." She looked over the rim of her glasses. "And what sort of Pharasmin are you? 'I didn't think the vampire was a threat.' Ha!"

I sighed. "I've been asking myself exactly that quite a bit recently."

"Well, you have some heart, but not much in the way of sense." She patted my shoulder. "Trust me, my dear. That's a combination that ends in an early grave every time. Best to take care of this creature while we can."

Tashan was on his feet. "You'll not touch him."

"Come on, friend. Is it really worth this?" Rarentz adjusted his crossbow. It wasn't pointed directly at Tashan, but it would be with a twitch.

"He is." Tashan's words sounded like a promise. In the carriage house's shade, his blade didn't glimmer.

"Please." I stepped between them, calling for calm. "Considine has some sort of control over him. He's not himself."

"Jadain."

I looked over my shoulder. Tashan was shaking his head. "It's not that."

"Sensibility aside, I have to agree," Miss Kindler said, nodding at the Osirian. "I've seen plenty with their wits crushed by a vampire's will. That's not a slave's behavior."

Tashan responded to my confused grimace with a shrug. "My grandmother used to say, 'We don't choose what we love, otherwise we'd all be saints.'"

"Somehow I don't think your grandmother had corpses in mind," Miss Kindler murmured into her empty teacup.

Her frown deepened as the drive's fortress-like gate whined on its hinges.

At the opposite end of the white stone trail, a bald figure peeked toward the house, then took a cautious step on the grounds.

Miss Kindler's look ground into Rarentz. "This is why we always keep the gate locked."

"But I'm sure . . ." he said, mostly to himself. With his next breath, he snapped a brisk "Yes, ma'am" and was walking toward the intruder, his crossbow cradled in his arm. At least he wasn't pointing it at Tashan.

"This happen often?" I asked the old woman. Rarentz had just shouted some intimidating greeting.

Her head rocked noncommittally. "Doing favors eventually earns you a reputation." She was keeping a close eye on the intruder, who had clearly noticed the armed young man marching toward him. "People always want something, and never like to hear that you've retired from the favor-doing business."

The stranger stepped into the yard. He was a rough-looking sort, with a grease-smeared fur coat and mismatched boots. He was carrying a frayed burlap bag, choking it with one hand. Shapeless bulges dangled beneath his grip.

He wasn't alone. A woman with short-shorn hair and a bent chin cautiously followed. Her clothes bore enough mismatched patches to awe a harlequin. She openly carried a carpenter's hammer.

"Whoa now," came Rarentz's call.

"We're going inside." Miss Kindler clearly wasn't making a suggestion. I wasn't sure what was happening, but started with her back toward the porch, watching the strangers. Rarentz had stopped several steps from the gate, his weapon no longer pointed down.

Tashan didn't budge from Considine's side. "I'm not leaving him like this."

The old woman neither slowed nor looked back. "Do what you will."

The gate whined louder, opening much more than a crack. Ratty-looking men were pushing the door wide. There were more behind them.

"Hey! Who are you?" Rarentz's bow followed the first intruder.

"Who are they?" I asked Miss Kindler's back, fighting the urge to dart around the cautiously strolling old woman.

"No friends of mine. And friends of friends knock."

The stranger in the patched coat raised her arm and let her hammer fly. It skidded into the gravel just past Rarentz.

"Whoa!" he shouted again. "Turn around now or I'll shoot."

As if the woman's throw had been the signal, the other men streamed into the yard. They were rangy and tough, but their mismatched weapons made them look truly threatening. With brown glass shivs, chains, and clubs, they charged Rarentz.

He shouted again, gave a step or two, but finally loosed. Instantly one of the door-pushers fell, a bolt further tearing savaged breeches. He skidded into the gravel without so much as a yelp.

His fall did nothing to deter his fellow trespassers.

Rarentz was already reloading. The man with the sack was on him. Whatever the vagabond carried was heavy and the bag swung like a giant sap. Rarentz pulled the trigger again as he fell back farther, having to abandon the luxury of deliberate aim. The bagman dropped, a quarrel passing through most of his neck.

More grim-faced strangers appeared at the gate. Seeing Rarentz about to be overwhelmed, they charged to join the crush.

"Can you make it on your own?" I shouted ahead to Miss Kindler.

"I think I can navigate my own yard."

Eventually, I thought. I rushed toward Rarentz, the silver crescent of my dagger hissing as it slipped from its sheath. The elder priests said the blade's shape suggested the curve of Pharasma's holy spiral. Mine always looked more like a snake's fang to me, but countless nights of polishing and sharpening guaranteed it was far sharper than any tiny tooth. Pharasma wasn't just the goddess of death, but every member of her clergy was well trained in how to take life to defend life.

Rarentz swung his crossbow in a broad arc, only half successfully keeping five or six of the patchwork invaders at bay. A man desperately in need of an eye patch heaved a dismembered table leg over his head, his half-gaze intent on Rarentz's skull.

My dagger swept behind Rarentz's attacker, making the motion called the Rise from the Cliffs. Meant to sever the spine and send a body toppling forward, it was a favored death of many coast-dwelling Ulfen sailors. Swiping faster than was ritually advised, I judged about an eighty percent chance of the man experiencing a painless death.

The stranger's body tensed and collapsed forward rigidly. If there had been open air before him his plummet would have been a final moment of beauty. As it was, his club and nose crunched noisily as he toppled headlong into the gravel.

Rarentz swept his bow around, glimpsing the falling man's motion far too late to have saved himself. He was obviously shocked to see me, but his look lingered longer on the thin line of red glistening on my blade.

"May the River of Souls flow straight and swift, and carry you safe to the goddess's spire." Looking over Rarentz's shoulder, I dropped my solemn tone. "Watch yourself! The goddess doesn't play favorites!"

The flat of his crossbow caught a man wearing chalky makeup in the mouth, sending his head around too far and scattering his teeth even farther. Another thug lashed his chain at me like a whip. It was a drunkard's clumsy flailing and I easily skipped out of the way, then back as momentum twisted him around.

Although the positioning wasn't perfect, my dagger made the Poison Breach funerary incision—the first step in the somewhat dated Thuvian practice of replacing a corpse's bowels with packets of incense. I'd never preformed it before, but the stroke proved clean enough. A wet slurry splashed upon the ground and the man kept spinning. He looked surprised when his face came around to me, then he crumpled. Regrettably, his chances of experiencing a painless death seemed relatively low.

I approximated the Thuvian blessing. "Smoke to carry you into the heavens. Light to show you the way beyond the stars."

I wished I knew where to get some bukhoor.

"More friends of yours?" Rarentz shouted between curses.

"Mine? No. I thought they were fans of Miss Kindler's!"

"Heh! They do sound like bookworms."

It took a moment to understand what he meant. Makeshift weapons jangled and gravel crunched around us. Wounded men and women lay on the ground, struggling against smashed limbs to regain their feet. But Rarentz and I were the only ones speaking. No one else, not even the men I'd felled, had made a sound.

The woman with the dented jaw, one of the first trespassers through the gate, closed in. I could have slashed her forearm, driving my dagger up the pale path of her wrist like the most accomplished suicides.

"Hey!" I shouted into her face.

She didn't flinch or so much as look up. Her eyes were fixed on me, but it didn't seem like she was actually seeing me.

"Damn!"

"What?" Rarentz grunted through a pickaxe-like swing of his bow.

"These people aren't here. They're—"

The woman swung her hammer for my face. I pulled back just barely in time. The rusty head scraped across my collar, frighteningly close. Remembering my trainers' words, I didn't recoil. Lunging in, I perforated the arm of her patchy coat, making more incisions and pushing far deeper than I would if I were performing a simple bloodletting. The shallow cuts welled with blood and the hammer dropped from her hand.

She tried to slap me with her other hand. I met it with my dagger, the blade biting awkwardly and without design, but effectively nonetheless.

"They're not all here. I don't think they're doing this of their own will."

My opponent stared blankly at her bloody hand.

"So how's that make them less dangerous?" Rarentz walloped the woman over the back of her head. She fell slowly, like a sheet unclipped from a drying line.

"Just try not to kill them! This isn't their fault!"

"I'm sorry but—" he kicked a fat man who'd wrapped nine blunt fingers around his splintered bow, "I don't think they're going to give us that choice." He looked up. "Shit!"

Beyond the crowd pressing in on us, two youngsters in almost matching, grubby school uniforms ran across the yard. Her back to them, Miss Kindler was just now climbing the porch stairs.

"You got this?" Rarentz asked, slamming the butt of his crossbow into a doughy face with a crack, then abandoning the hunk of splinters.

"What? No." I fell back a step, but he was already running.

With a pack of empty-eyed killers facing me, the choice was easy. I sprinted after Rarentz.

The young nobleman crossed the patchy grass yard in a matter of seconds, tackling the faster of the two boys, smashing him to the ground. It was enough to catch one, but the second charged past, a sharp rock in his hand.

I was nowhere close enough to catch him. My dagger came up, ready to throw. But I couldn't. Even with Miss Kindler only a few steps ahead of the intruder, I couldn't do it.

"Ailson!" I tried to warn her. She didn't look back.

A round white rock struck the back of the boy's head with a crack, sending him reeling into the dirt. He skidded into the porch's stone stairs and didn't move.

Tashan was already halfway across the yard, not showing any signs of slowing. "Faster, please," he urged as he passed.

We helped Rarentz to his feet, and rushed after Tashan, who took the steps two at a time. At the top he turned, his sword glimmering golden.

We vaulted up the steps, aware of the voiceless noises closing in from behind.

Miss Kindler was frowning down at the youngster bleeding on her yard.

Flames roared over my shoulder. Shocked by the sudden light and heat, I pitched sidelong, sprawling across the porch.

Tashan was screaming before I could even twist to see why.

The jet of flame poured into him. It spread like water, defying gravity, drowning him in fire. When the flames reached his face, they did nothing to muffle his screams.

I think I screamed his name, but if I did, even I couldn't hear it.

The fiery jet's final pulse knocked him off his feet, sending him reeling. He collapsed against the doorframe, smoldering. Where he'd been struck, his shirt and chest were a single molten scar. His scarf was no longer yellow, reduced to a collar of ash around his neck. I forced myself to look higher.

His face, so sleek and proud only seconds earlier, made me want to cry.

He was alive, though. Despite the terrible scars, he was still alive. With a weak, confused hand he was trying to push himself upright.

"Pharasma, please." I was on my feet, already praying. I clutched at my chest for the goddess's symbol. My hand came back empty, forgetting I'd hidden it beneath my shirt so I wouldn't have to look, wouldn't have to feel that sick pain. With every second being vital, my discomfort felt unforgivably selfish.

It took more than a moment to fish out the twisted carving. That moment saved my life, but doomed Tashan.

The second jet of flame came lower, streaking across the wooden floorboards, sizzling dirt and old paint. Mercilessly, it struck Tashan, spreading faster and stiking harder this time. His outline blurred in the heat, each pulse of the burning jet causing him to convulse, as though relentless fiery fists beat him. His second scream was weaker, resigned.

Over it I could hear my own sobs. I reached out helplessly.

When the fire passed, Tashan lay still. My prayers turned bitter in my mouth. No words I could say, no plea I could make, would bring life back to the body lying amid its own ashes.

A blessing for the departed came reflexively to mind, but self-preservation forced it back. The yard had gone silent.

More than twenty desperate-looking men and women trampled Miss Kindler's grass. All were sad stories, their bottle knives and trash swords weapons of directionless revenge. They formed a semicircle around their leader, as if even in their stupors none dared come close.

She was a graveyard shadow, thin and macabre. Her dark veil and gown of black sashes couldn't disguise her gaunt figure. She might have been dressed like a mourner, but nothing about her suggested sympathy. Gold jewelry studded every one of her dress's tightly wound wraps, each a morbid collector's piece. The most gruesome, though, she held like a fencer's foil: a length of red metal, its tip red hot and faintly smoking.

"Miss Kindler, please come with me." She spoke slowly, in an accent that I didn't recognize, but that sounded cold and wet.

"The hell she—" Rarentz started. A touch from Miss Kindler cut him off.

"I assume we're going to be out late." Her voice was obscenely calm. "If that's the case, you should know I don't go out at night without my shawl."

She looked at Rarentz and gestured at the door. "If you'd be so kind. It's the blue one on the rack."

Rarentz nodded. He seemed calmer all of a sudden, sparing me a quick look as he and took a step toward the door.

My wordless warning came too late. He turned only enough to make things worse. Spinning end over end, a bottle struck his temple. Mossy glass exploded and rained across peeling paint and ashes. Rarentz followed with a shudder that shook the porch's old timbers.

Cursing, I knelt as quickly as the cheap glass allowed. Shards and blood matted his hair, a series of fresh gashes pouring red across his eye.

"That was uncalled for," Miss Kindler said as I picked away the sharpest green shards.

"You'll come now. No tricks." The woman in black's tone left no room for debate.

The old woman didn't relent. "You've proven you have the upper hand. I could have asked for any of a hundred magical trinkets, but I don't wish to see anyone else harmed. However, none of that changes the fact that I'm old and get cold easily. You can, of course, take me by force, but I'm clearly more fragile than I once was. So if you want to risk my going to pieces in your mob's gentle hands, by all means, send them. Otherwise, I'll have my shawl."

I worked while Miss Kindler spoke. Rarentz's wounds weren't deep, but they were still bleeding. I worried for his eye. His lids were cinched shut, as though, even unconscious, he was squinting through the pain. Tiny bits of glass glinted at the corner. I worried there might be more inside.

This time, when I reached for my holy symbol, it was there. As soon as I grasped it, a wave of nausea poured over me. My own eye, the one the inquisitor had left his scar upon, filled with cold light beneath its bandage, the eerie blue of Pharasma's power. My lips, parting to speak a healing prayer, snapped closed, just barely holding back an acidic surge of stomach juices.

Damn it. I'd hoped this would pass. Twice now I'd silently prayed that the sick feeling had been a reaction to what happened in Kavapesta. That Brother Abelard's death was too fresh in my mind, that it was compounding the doubts I was already having. Maybe it was. Or maybe the goddess was denying me. Was I suddenly sickened by the goddess's touch? Or was she sickened by mine?

My amulet dropped from my hands. It bounced on my chest. Rarentz still bled.

"Priestess." The dark woman's voice sounded like she'd whispered in my ear. "Get the old woman's shawl. You have ten seconds."

My surprised look darted from the shadow in the yard to Kindler's expressionless face. I scrambled up, forcing myself not to look down at Tashan, and struggled with the door. I was in and out as fast as I could manage, emerging back onto the porch with a gaudy thing of robin's-egg silk and sky-blue beads. It didn't look very warm at all.

"Thank you, dear." Miss Kindler accepted it and wrapped it around her shoulders. She spared a soft glance at Rarentz. "I trust you'll look after him. Good help and all."

Not waiting for my reply, she turned to the mob. The shawl was longer in the back than I'd thought, falling down her back like a short cape. It fluttered lightly as she started down the steps, taking them even more slowly than before.

"Lead on, miss," Miss Kindler said as she descended. "Though I do hope you've brought a coach. I'm afraid I don't go anywhere especially fast these days."

I could feel the frown beneath the stranger's veil.

A long finger in mourner's lace extended toward me. "Her as well."

I started. Immediately, my knife was back in my hand. At least one part of my faith hadn't abandoned me.

The army of beggars moved as one, their cacophony of jangles and clomping starting anew. Over the noise I could hear Miss Kindler. "You surely didn't come for her. Take me and leave the girl be."

"Our lord has a taste for the ironic. He will certainly have a use for a death priestess."

The mob reached the bottom of the weathered stairs.

"Get back!" I shouted, rising to my feet with a wide slash, knowing the worthlessness of both warnings.

"Call them off, or your master will be terribly disappointed." Over the press of stained hoods and matted hair I could see Miss Kindler arguing with the shadow. The woman in black was clearly ignoring her, her eyeless gaze on me.

My blade worked fast, using my higher ground to the best advantage I could. It worked the incisions of a Nidalese Eye Darkening, taking one pair of eyes, than another—as, in Nidal, the honored dead are granted the gift of eternal darkness. Hands clamped on my arms and I shrugged them off. One more swipe almost claimed another eye, but clammy palms prevented me from completing the ritual cuts. My struggling began with shouts to the goddess, but gave way to desperate kicking and curses.

Through the quiet throng I could still make out Miss Kindler bargaining with their leader for my life.

"Well, if you won't be civil about this, then when you see your master, do tell him that I said to piss off." With that, Miss Kindler laid a finger on the clasp of her shawl and popped like a soap bubble.

The woman in black turned abruptly, twisting at strange angles. Her veil searched, but all that was left of Miss Kindler was a faint trace of blue smoke.

I flung my head around as best I could, searching to see where the cagey old woman might reappear.

But there was nothing. The yard, the porch, the house's blank windows—all were empty. It was just me and the strangers.

The woman's voice gave no hint of disappointment or annoyance, which somehow made it seem even more lethal. Her command was simple and severe. "Silence her."

I struggled harder, focusing my shouting on her blank veil, but her will-less slaves followed their orders swiftly.

I barely heard whatever struck me, but distinctly remember the sensation of falling into that black, bottomless veil.

31

POISON

LARSA

S top that," Rivascis said, not taking his eyes from his easel.

I ignored him, running my tongue over the half-familiar points in my mouth. "They don't feel like before."

"They're better than before. Unmarred." He dabbed at the palette of colored oils he'd smeared upon his forearm. "In time, you won't notice."

I gave an unconvinced hum.

He'd been painting while we spoke. It hadn't all been civil, but I hadn't stabbed him again. I'd asked him where he'd been, why he'd left Caliphas, why he hadn't returned. He told me the beginnings of several stories, but insisted that the details of his reasons and travels come later, saying there'd be time to explain everything. I wasn't so sure.

Over the course of the evening I'd paced the Mirage's stage more than an entire troupe of actors would during a performance night. The stage's dressing remained the same, except for the Qadiran maid curled up against a proscenium arch. She was breathing shallowly, recovering. He'd laid a blanket over her.

"You're soft on the humans," I said, nodding at the sleeping girl.

"Am I?" He didn't turn. "Does that surprise you?"

"None of the Old City's vampires would waist a moment on most humans—much less worry about whether or not they're cold."

He made a small, curious noise. "And how have Caliphas's vampires faired since I left? Arrogant, posturing things. Are they the lords of their city?"

He was baiting, but not necessarily me. "You know they're not."

"No. They keep to filthy, hidden places and claim themselves rulers of the night, when, in truth, they're nothing more than parasites. They feed on the scraps of human society and flourish in the places the living forsake. Their own blind arrogance sets them apart, propping them up as rulers upon thrones of dung."

"That's a grim way of viewing it." I was a bit surprised that he'd leapt to the topic with such casual nimbleness. I knew there was bad blood between him and Grandfather, but he seemed quick to criticize. "They keep to the truce Luvick and the city's rulers forged."

"That's exactly the problem. There's 'Luvick,' and then there's 'the city's rulers.'" He casually mixed pigments upon his forearm, sounding slightly bored. "Your grandfather, for all his posturing and manipulations, has made his people no better than sewer rats. He's turned Caliphas's vampires into a nuisance the humans consciously, willingly endure. He's legitimized a divide between the people we are and the people we were."

I'd never heard anyone speak out against Grandfather like this. Were we in Caliphas, I'd be backing away, expecting Grandfather's assassins to emerge from the shadows like dark, avenging angels. "So this is the talk that branded you a rebel."

He gestured with his brush as though offering a toast. "A piece of it."

"So what's your solution? Outright war with the humans? Becoming the monsters they fear?"

Shaking his head, he clicked his tongue. "The game's not all black or white, all peace or war, ruler or slave. We could be governing the humans, and making them love us for it. With a bit of subtlety, the patience to use our gifts effectively, and a modicum

302 F. WESLEY SCHNEIDER

less arrogance, we could convince them to serve. Just look at what I've built here." He gestured to the enthralled audience.

A theater full of living zombies stared at me.

"Like a storybook," I said flatly.

"Give it time. White Corner has come to heel since I've arrived in Ardis. While Yismilla Col worked Luvick's will here, there was lawlessness in these streets, useless squabbling and wasteful violence. Now things are calm. The rest of the city hasn't noticed yet, but they could be made to. Ardis could be my city, in time. And those who worked with me, who followed and obeyed, would be treated well."

"Like this?" I gestured at the dozing girl. "Like a pet?"

"The comparison is crude, but you're not incorrect. They need guidance. Guidance our people have the perspective, experience, and time to provide. All our people would need is a leader to help them control their hunger and nudge them out of their crypts. We might be people of the night, but the shadows need not make us anonymous."

"Your grand rebellion barely sounds different from Grandfather's web-spinning."

"Maybe, but that would hardly make it the first war to start between parties that fundamentally agree on all but specifics."

"So a world where vampires openly work with and rule over humans." My mind had wandered to my own position in such a place. "Is that why you took Kindler as a lover?"

Suddenly he didn't have some quick response.

There was a long silence.

"You should go soon," Rivascis said, prodding a white rose upon the canvas.

That seemed to have touched a nerve, but he was right. Colorful figures had just begun to appear high in the theater's balcony, abstract harlequins capering across a triptych of stained-glass windows. They looked like they'd been ripped apart, only illuminated in scattered slashes where light slipped through the board coverings outside. Dawn light.

"Where are you staying?" I asked.

"Still hunting?" He gave me a sidelong grin. "Perhaps I'll tell you . . . next time." He cleaned his brush in his mouth, setting it deliberately on his easel's ledge. "For now, though, I have a measure of tedium to take care of before I rest."

He turned to the corpselike crowd.

As the light in the theater had faintly risen, it was easier to pick out individual audience members. They remained unnaturally still for such a large gathering, but dawn seemed to be melting the frozen audience. Some were starting to slightly fidget in their seats. Somewhere toward the back, a woman cleared her throat.

"Your control over them is fading." I recognized the signs. Like so many other vampires, Rivascis could force his will upon the living, but it wouldn't last forever.

"Indeed. In a matter of hours they'll revert to their own short-sighted devices, but there's still plenty of time to remind them of a better way."

"Of your way."

He gave me a patient half-smile.

"Seems like a lot of effort for street folk."

"That's Luvick's pride talking," he said with a sharp gesture. "The view from the street is no less accurate than the view from the tower. Even more so if you're looking for things in the shadows." He nodded to the crowd. "My servants see everything and go willfully unseen. I've replaced their despair with purpose, and should one of them go missing, I will know why."

I wasn't buying it. "They're bait."

He turned slowly, facing me fully. "Go on."

"Vampire bait." I walked toward the stage's apron. "Yismilla Col had her entire cell here. You dispensed with them, but how could you know how many of them there really were?"

The audience's eyes didn't follow me as I paced. It was a strange feeling to be ignored on stage. "You also know Grandfather will send a reply to your package eventually. If his messenger is one of his other children, they'll be hungry, but won't want to attract any notice."

"These people aren't bait. They merely are what our kind always treat them as: victims." He stepped to center stage, and the audience took note. "The difference is that now they have someone watching over them."

I doubted he could hear me roll my eyes. "I'm sure you and all your subjects are looking forward to the day when crushing their will is just a formality."

"Indeed." He acted as though he'd missed the jibe. "I could have one of them see you to Troidais House."

I frowned, not having told him anything about where we were staying. "I think I can manage."

He nodded. Crossing to the slit curtain I'd entered through, he held his arm high to open it.

I took one more long look at the covered canvases and silent audience, then followed gradually, not interested in jumping at even one of his unspoken suggestions.

"My work might keep me indisposed for a time," he said as I came close. "When I call again, will you come?"

Looking into his face, I tried to analyze his intentions. His sheer, calm expression hadn't changed, and there was no command in his tone. In any other creature, I would have said he sounded lonely. In one like him, though . . .

"Maybe." I kept my voice level. "But I have my own work to attend to."

One of his brows lifted slightly, but he nodded.

I passed under his arm and into the dark of the backstage area. A gray rectangle at the bottom of the short stairway opened into the cold morning.

"If you see your mother," Rivascis's voice rustled between falling curtains, "speak well of me."

I walked across half of Ardis, ignoring the city coaxing itself into another overcast, unremarkable day. With the dawn, White Corner's ghosts had abandoned their haunts. The quarter appeared deserted.

The sun dissolved the morning fog, again making me mourn losing my shady riding hat. Nonetheless, I followed an aimless path, sometimes with my eyes closed to keep out the glaring sun. Over miles I repeated the night's conversations, growing increasingly frustrated. Rivascis hadn't been the monster I'd expected, that for years I'd quietly been fashioning and revising. Was it actually the most ironic of a lifelong string of paternal disappointments that my father couldn't even live up to my resentment? That certainly didn't make me want to forgive all he'd done and hadn't done. I still wasn't sure if that made me hate him less or more.

In my head, I heard Grandfather's voice over and over again, exhorting me to blame my father.

For the first time ever, I didn't know that he was worth the blame.

I was still working it all over when I reached Troidais House.

I didn't announce myself and didn't expect to be greeted. Nevertheless, I'd anticipated something besides dust and silence. My footfalls echoed far beyond the entry's verdigris-colored tile. No board creaked or hinge squealed.

A folded page waited on a wobbly pedestal table, a single line of precise script inside. *Called on Miss Kindler. Join us when you can.*

I had hoped for nothing more than finding a dark, quiet place to doze in the house's cellar. I considered letting them wait.

I didn't know much about Kindler, but I was certain of something: she wasn't the type to post a sign and an armed guard, then leave her front gate open.

It was only ajar by an arm's width, but even that seemed outrageous. Jagged splinters dusted the ground. The lock had been wrenched out of place.

I held still, listening. Nothing so much as whispered beyond. I slipped inside.

What I saw didn't make me want to slow.

The bulwark of hedges cast heavy shadows across the grounds. I kept to them, skirting the yard, watching for movement. Nothing twitched, either amid the trampled flower gardens or in the quiet house beyond.

I slipped behind the carriage house and waited for some sign I'd been noticed. Still nothing.

The scents were still fresh—churned earth, blood, ash. The discarded lay still, wounds already drying.

The faces were hard and unfamiliar, their clothes little more than scraps. Thieves, perhaps? Or maybe a gang audacious enough to prey on an old woman? That seemed unlikely considering the makeshift weapons. They were the sort of things someone might grab off a junk pile, the weapons of . . .

Oh gods.

I didn't recognize any of the faces from the Mirage's audience, but one group could have passed for the other. Not because of the obvious poverty, but because of their expressions. Death surprises most humans. Those who aren't surprised are typically too distracted by pain. None of the bodies looked surprised, or the least bit pained. Every blank expression looked bored by death.

My teeth ground against unfamiliar fangs. I hadn't seen a mirror yet. When I did, would these new teeth look like Rivascis's straight smirk? Would he be laughing at me from every shiny surface? I had the sudden urge to tear them from my head.

I pushed the thought away. I didn't recognize any of the bodies. That pushed me on. There were more than a dozen corpses littering the yard. If Jadain and Tashan had been here, they put up quite a fight.

I checked the nearest cluster of corpses. One had his neck cracked, his face smashed by a heavy blow. Another had been felled by a single stroke from behind. More had met similar ends, their deaths staining the drive's ribbon of white stones. I glanced through the open carriage house doors. The fighting didn't appear to have spread into there.

Another group had fallen on the porch stairs.

Straight, even slashes gave way to wilder cuts. Dark trails dotted the ground where some of the wounded had walked away. Fire had scoured the stone steps, carrying with it the smell of meat left on open coals. It wasn't from the bodies scattered there now—they had come later. The smell was worse on the porch's dirty timbers. A streak of cinders stretched from the stairs to a blackened—

Tashan's bronze blade had captured some of the fire. He'd polished it every morning of our journey, chasing off dew and the night's shadows, but I'd never seen it shine with such luster. The eyelike pommel, though, was crusty with ashes.

I vaulted the bodies on the stairs. The yellow threads around the corpse's neck gave it away. Its features had withered in the flame, but it was definitely Tashan. Whatever had happened, he'd caught it head-on, the back of his arms and neck still showing stripes of sunny skin. The rest was ash. After a glance at his face I didn't look back. But it was too late. The sight lingered beneath my eyelids.

Turning away didn't help. One of the corpses on the porch was Kindler's man, Rarentz. He was sprawled facedown, his face a half-mask of glass and drying blood.

I knelt, finding a pulse easily enough. He was unconscious, but the puddle of blood beneath him didn't look like it was still being fed.

Maybe I wasn't too late to be of some help.

Something scraped the timbers overhead as I heaved Rarentz onto the couch in Kindler's sitting room. I'd heard it before, sounding from Kindler's library. Apparently the place wasn't as deserted as I'd thought. I adjusted Rarentz's head at an angle that hopefully wasn't pushing glass shards deeper into his face and recovered my sword from the coffee table.

The floorboards seemed quieter than before, the eyes of the masks in the upstairs hall wider, more alarmed. It seemed like the house had witnessed what transpired outside and was still gripped by shock.

The library's glow had faded, leaving it as hearth-cold as the rest of the crowded rooms. But something was out of place. At first, it seemed that the walls had somehow been rearranged. It wasn't the walls themselves, though, just the bookcases. Behind the desk several shelves had swung away, like a door on unseen hinges. The lowest steps of a hidden stairway were just visible in the dark opening. Only a step away, Miss Kindler leaned over her desk, a cornflower shawl draped over her shoulders. She held a dip pen in one hand as she riffled through a drawer like a thief in her own home.

The door creaked as I pushed in.

Faster than I would have thought possible, her attention was on me, a straight white stick appearing from nowhere to replace her pen. I halted. What was that, a wand?

She recognized me quickly enough. "Are you late?" She slid the length of wood back up her sleeve with a practiced flick and recovered her pen. "Or are you here to finish the job?"

I stepped fully inside, tightening the grip on my sword. "What?"

She didn't look at me. "Where were you?"

"White Corner. Learning the streets."

"That's a coincidence, all of White Corner came for a visit while you were gone." A glare shot over the brim of her glasses. "They killed one of your friends, maybe both."

My jaw clenched. "Who sent them?"

"How should I know?" She returned to her search. "Everything was quiet before you showed up. You come talking about monsters—something I haven't had anything to do with for years—and the very next day I find a vampire in my shed and have my home invaded by sleepwalkers."

"What vampire?" She couldn't mean Rivascis. Considine?

She ignored me. "I haven't lived this long believing in coincidences. What have you brought with you? What haven't you said?"

"What did I bring with me?" My voice shot higher than I'd meant. "I didn't have a thing to do with any of this until I got caught up with your family. I came to you looking for answers and all I've heard are contradictions."

"Well, you've been up to something." She aimed her quill at my face. "Those don't just grow back for your kind."

The stranger's teeth in my mouth pricked my tongue. There wasn't any reason not to tell her.

"I didn't come all this way just to look in on you. I came to put an end to a fugitive. A vampire." I sheathed my sword. "One you supposedly knew."

"The one hiding in the shed? I've never seen him before."

"I don't think so—and your shed was empty."

Her lips made a stony line. "I left all of this business behind. Monsters and spirits and young people running off getting themselves killed, that's all past. Whatever this is, I want nothing to do with it."

"I don't think you're going to get that option. Don't the bodies outside prove that?"

Her eyes narrowed.

I hurried on, not having meant to insult her. "The vampire I'm after, he's my father."

She blinked, her gaze drifting away. Several moments passed before she began drumming her pen on the desk.

"And you think I'm you're mother."

"I don't know," I answered honestly. "But he does."

The creaking noise she made sounded annoyed. "That has certain . . . implications. You're sure?"

"He told me."

"You know him, then? You've met him before?"

I tried to think of some way not to make it sound damning. "His name's Rivascis. I've known about him for—for all my life. But I only met him last night."

The pen clicked rapidly. "You found him?"

I nodded.

"On your first night here?" She shook her head. "He wanted to be found."

"He's not the first vampire I've tracked down," I said, suddenly defensive. She was right, though.

"He wanted to be found. The smart ones only reveal themselves when it's in their best interest."

The mask of ashes crowning Tashan's corpse leapt to mind. Had Rivascis just been keeping me out of the way?

Her clicking stopped. She gently put down the pen. "So you found him, but it sounds like you both survived."

There had been a moment while I was uselessly carving up Rivascis that I realized I'd failed, that I'd come all this way for nothing. As he and I had talked, that feeling had faded. Now it rushed back, just as intense as before.

"Yes."

"Why?"

I didn't answer.

Not just that, I couldn't find an answer. Questions had been winding through my mind since I'd left the theater. I'd struggled with them through miles of the city's cold streets, but every time I thought I'd caught even the least of them, they slipped away.

"Why?" she repeated more forcefully.

"I tried to kill him." The tired frustration of a hundred wasted blows settled back into my arm. "He was too fast."

"Then why aren't you dead?" She gave voice to the question that I'd already repeated hundreds of times this morning.

"He never struck back." I was almost whispering. "He could have at any time. I don't think I could have stopped him. But he didn't."

"He just let you go?"

It hadn't been like that. I shook my head. "I'm sure I could have left, but he wanted to talk."

"And what did he say?"

"He apologized."

"For what?"

"For leaving me in Caliphas. For never coming for me. For all the things they did and made me do."

Her head shook so slightly that, for a moment, I mistook it for a tremor of age. "He would have said anything. That's how they win you over. The most dangerous know the best slaves are the ones who serve willingly."

"Why would I help him?" I threw up my hands. Some dam inside me broke, but I didn't care. "I've obeyed corpses all my life. Every time I've defied them they've dragged me back and made sure to remind me that I'm just a tool to use how they please—to break if the whim takes them. This—coming to find you—it's given me a reason to escape. This is the longest I've gone in my entire life without crawling through shit to take a corpse's orders. But even now I know it's going to end. Some night soon they'll lose patience and take me back. Or I won't be worth the effort, and that'll just be the end. In either case, for a few days I have a life, and I'm not spending it as someone else's slave."

My last words rang, fading into the library's pages. Those books looked more receptive than Kindler, whose face remained an arrangement of flagstones. I sealed my mouth, realizing what an untrustworthy thing it was.

Kindler gradually worked her way around the desk, holding its edge for support. Her voice came slower, softer. "It sounds as though this Rivascis told you things you've waited a very long time to hear. He's giving you a choice, and you're choosing to defend him."

Was she pandering to me? I ground my teeth together. After a long breath, I spoke deliberately. "He's one of the only people who's known what I am who didn't treat me like either a slave or some curiosity. He's the only person since Jadain who—"

My frustration with Kindler had completely distracted me. "Where's Jadain?"

The old woman's expression didn't change. "I haven't a clue. The woman leading those thugs said their master might have some use for her."

"What woman?"

"The sort you'd notice on the street. All in black, a veil—"

"Gold pinned to some atrocious dress?"

Kindler frowned. "You've seen her?"

Something heavy filled my stomach. Like that, everything I said about Rivascis sounded incredibly naive. Hopes I didn't want to acknowledge tore free, flotsam snatched away by a wicked tide. I dropped into one of the lounge chairs, staring nowhere. "She led me to Rivascis."

"Who is she?"

"I have no idea."

Silence hung there for a moment.

"She knows something about magic," Kindler said. "Fire, in particular."

I looked over, confirming what she was suggesting. She gave a sad nod.

I hadn't known Tashan well, and certainly hadn't trusted him after what happened in the mountains, but he deserved better than that.

"They killed Tashan, beat Rarentz, and took Jadain." I stated facts. "But somehow you managed to get away?"

Kindler waved my halfhearted accusation away. "The veiled woman wanted me to come with her. It's not the first time someone's tried to take me somewhere against my will." She adjusted her shawl. "I've had this little treasure with me a long time. Just a whisper and," her snap sounded like a breaking twig, "I'm someplace else."

She gestured to the bookcase passage opened behind her. "In this case, my writing room."

"You left them, then."

She frowned. "No, but I did manage to escape. I was readying to call the guard when you arrived."

That didn't sound like "no" to me, but I didn't press the matter. What could I have expected the old woman to do?

"I don't think the city watch is going to be much help." My fist clenched, feeling empty without my sword's grip in it. I pushed myself up from the chair, the weight in my stomach hatching into anger. "If it was Rivascis who did this, I know where to find him."

Kindler glanced to a curtained window, a dismal glow at its edges. "Truly? He showed you where he rests during the day."

She was right. I knew where he'd been, but in truth I had no way to know where he was hiding.

"He was painting at the Mirage Theater in White Corner. It might not be where he keeps his coffin, but it's a place to start."

"Painting?" She looked doubtful.

"Yeah. It looked like he'd been at it for some time." I hesitated, but couldn't think of any reason not to tell her. "It was of you."

Disgusted deepened every wrinkle.

"You in your youth," I clarified.

She leaned back on the desk and was quiet for a long moment.

"How old would you say?" she finally asked, her attention straying across the room.

I shrugged. "I don't know. About as old as I look."

She nodded gravely. "About as old as I would have been in the file you gave me?"

The question made me suspicious. "I suppose."

Kindler crossed to a bookcase near the fireplace. Reaching high, she pulled upon a set of dusty books. The matching bindings slid from the shelf as one, their covers a solid whole. Taking the set in both hands, she set it carefully upon a side table. Bony fingers traced the edges of the nearly square set, producing a series of metallic clicks. The last noise was the loudest, and a hidden lid popped open.

Kindler reached inside and produced a folio of crumbling pages. She flipped the cover back and handed it to me.

I recognized pages before taking them: a record from Maiden's Choir. More than that, I realized upon reading only a few lines, it was Kindler's record. The exact file I'd delivered to her the day before. The record she'd burned.

"How?" I flipped through the file. It was all here. In fact, there was more.

"It's from Havenguard. Supposedly I stole it years ago."

"Supposedly?" That was concerning. I'd scoffed at the possibility of the retired explorer's senility, but this sounded like the beginning of a confession.

She reached into the box of books and produced a wrinkled old traveler's journal. She didn't open it, just handed it to me.

I set the file down, then took the charcoal book and unwound the leather strap tying it closed. I skimmed the first page, then the next.

"What is this?" I didn't look up, flipping through the first dozen pages.

"A warning. Read."

I nodded slowly, not understanding. The handwriting subtly changed every few pages. The messages were all short and similar, but in different ink.

"But who wrote them? And who are they for?" When I looked up, she was watching. Her expression was something between worry and doubt.

"Read."

Choosing a short message several pages in, I read aloud.

"Ailson. You've always known knowledge is your greatest weapon and strongest shield. You've also known it can be a responsibility, that it can inflict wounds of the deadliest kinds. You know things that could change the lives of those who mean the most to you—rarely for the better. You've kept such secrets, because what you know could be a poison.

"I'm sorry, I know you will not fully understand, but you are poisoned, Ailson. Fortunately, I have a cure. It's not brave, but I beg you to believe what you read here and on the pages that have come before. The cure is forgetfulness, and even now you benefit from its balm.

"Do not do as I have done. A future in doubt is better than a past you cannot change."

It was signed at the end with a simple "A."

"Is this . . ." I pointed at the signature.

She nodded. "It's mine. The message is from me."

32

BURIED ALIVE

JADAIN

Voices. I recognized the noise before I could understand the words. The combination of nausea and a throbbing headache didn't make interpreting them any easier.

Something else was off.

The voices were close. Close enough that I was sure I didn't recognize them.

A sudden crack startled me fully awake. Through slitted eyes I watched a shadow topple, sprawling to the ground with a clatter like a handful of coins. But the ground was clearly situated in the wrong direction.

I was suspended upside down.

The figure in the black gown lifted herself from the dirt floor.

"Don't presume you know my wishes," a man's sneering voice came out of the dark. "Do as I say, exactly as I tell you. Anything else is failure."

"Yes, Lord," the woman said, speaking through clenched teeth. "But, if you will . . ." She waited for approval. I couldn't hear or see any hint of permission being given beyond the dim ring of lantern light, but she nodded nonetheless.

"Her eye." The gesture toward me made my already unsettled stomach lurch. "She's been cast out."

The woman on the ground had called him master, but in his tattered clothes, he looked more like a prisoner. His face was all angles, sharp and severe with a jaw for etching marble.

Thin brows were razor lines over a statue's eyes, his irises the color of slate in rain. He was striking, but in some antique way. It felt like being attracted to a portrait of someone a thousand years old, both surprising and morbid, as there was no doubt he was dead.

I shut my eyes as he approached, trying my best to feign unconsciousness. It didn't matter. He wrapped my shirt collar into a fist and pulled. I rose, a chain clanking above. Something cold and sharp barely touched my cheek. The linen bandage covering my eye fell away.

"Show me." His voice was inches away from my face. I tried to remain still, praying he wouldn't notice the gooseflesh prickling my neck and arms.

"If I open them, you will never close them again." His voice was carelessly calm. "Show me."

I opened my eyes.

His colors had faded, leaving his skin sickly and dagger-cut hair like sun-bleached straw. There were wrinkles, tallies along his thin lips and crow's feet edging eyes only inches away. The passage of breath didn't disrupt his frozen features. His attention fixed on my right eye. The perverted symbol there prickled as though a fly's steps circled toward my pupil. Despite the revulsion, I dared not blink.

"She travels with your daughter," the dark woman said, her jewelry complaining as she regained her feet.

"Indeed." The dead man's face was close enough to mine that I could feel the air carrying his words. I smelled like ashes.

"Tell me, priestess, are you responsible for this?" He twisted his grip, turning me in the direction opposite to my past view.

Several layers of dark canvas lay across the ground. At their center stretched Considine, still bearing a sharpened board through his chest.

The fist at my throat shook me.

"No." I coughed, my mouth dryer than I'd expected. I wondered how long I'd been unconscious.

"Then you won't have any objections." He dropped me. Chains clattered, a beam above groaned, and for a sickening moment I swung freely.

My captor crossed to the other corpse, knelt, and yanked the stake impaling Considine. The crunch of spilt bones caused my teeth to clench, but the wood came free. He snapped the board and sent the pieces skittering into the dust.

Considine thrashed, but his lips moved most desperately. "Intrusion? My, no! I have nothing but the utmost respect for your mistress. You see, I've read all—"

The remembered moment passed, his head lifting in confusion. His curiosity settled on me first, then drifted to the man standing over him.

"Oh." His body gave way to misty eddies. They swirled upon the ground, ready to drift in any or all directions at once. Reluctantly, the vapor rose and dissipated. The lanky, truant academy boy vampire stood there, fingering a sizable tear on the left breast of his wine-colored vest.

"Father." He looked up with a wide smile. "It's been too, too long."

"I am not your father," the man said sharply.

Considine made a little pouting noise. "Hurtful. I'd call you 'master', but you freed me of those duties so long ago. What they call you in the Old City just doesn't seem polite. And 'Rivascis', hmm, I just don't think I could get used to—"

"Quiet."

Despite refusing to call him "master," Considine's mouth snapped shut.

Rivascis turned to the empty dark. "Did Luvick send you after me?"

Considine guffawed, then made a show of trying to stifle it. "My, no. Grandfather goes well out of his way to keep me from any matter that ventures too close to being meaningful."

"Then why are you here?"

"Watching after your daughter, that's all—can I call her your daughter? Do you call her that? You *have* met, I assume." Considine looked to me. "You seem to be taking an interest in her friends. I might have misjudged your paternal instincts."

"Larsa brought you?" Rivascis kept a strict, level tone.

"In a manner of speaking, yes."

The space between the two blurred. When my eyes caught up, Rivascis's claws were where Considine's face had been. Considine's fog was reforming into features, a step behind where he'd been standing.

His mouth seemed to manifest first. "Grandfather did send me, just not after you. A friend conveniently comprised the third part of Larsa's little trio. That he didn't tell anyone about inviting me to make it a quartet didn't come up until we were nearly here. Sister-dear didn't appreciate me tagging along uninvited, but she has a soft spot for her big brother."

Considine turned to me, and my stomach pitched. As if feeling my discomfort, he smiled, his thin fangs obvious. "Right, Jadain?"

Rivascis's glare unhurriedly passed between us, settling back on Considine. "You allowed yourself to be staked by an old woman."

"By an old woman's wolf of a gardener," he corrected. "But I'm not the only one to have his intentions undone by Miss Ailson Kindler. Tell me, are the rumors true? Has she single-handedly kept you from launching your rebellion against Siervage for all these years?"

"The years have made your tongue even looser." Rivascis looked over Considine's once well-tailored clothing. "I won't hear any talk of revolution from a thing that survives on the scraps of the living."

Considine reached for a tatter that might have once been part of Rivascis's coat. "Are we really going to compare scraps?"

The elder vampire jerked away.

"Why would I want a revolution anyway? Apart from inconvenient disruptions like this, I'm quite content in Caliphas. I've a fine room in what amounts to a palace, with the means to indulge my every curiosity." Considine gave a bitter little laugh. "I don't see the outrage."

"Your lord's dwindling ambitions infect you. He'd see you all rot beneath the capital rather than rising to control it. He clings to a memory of power. Tell me, little prince, who can you feed upon in Caliphas?"

"I don't want for blood." Considine shrugged. "Warm or cold, taken screaming or given willingly."

Rivascis scoffed. "You take what you're told you can take. Whatever watered-down dregs Luvick and his human masters dole out. Taking the blood of the weak has made you weak. I didn't give you immortality to see you continue a wasteful, wanton life."

"Oh? You're going to lecture me about clinging to life now? How many years have you spent playing your perverted game of kiss-chase?" The younger vampire gave a nasty laugh. "I hear she's not the beauty she once was. What were you—"

Considine wasn't fast enough the second time. Rivascis's claws tore into his throat, the lines of claws bulging beneath the younger vampire's pallid skin. I choked back a gasp, doing my best to stay forgotten. Considine just gave a schoolboy smile.

"I haven't decided what to do with you yet. Unless you want to hasten my decision, control your tongue." Rivascis's voice was a harsh whisper. He looked around the island of lantern light, from dirt floor to the sagging crossbeam ceiling. "I can't hold you, so you're free to go about whatever business your master sent you on. But Ardis is mine now. If you leave, I'll have to assume you're working against me. That will make our next meeting far less . . . civil."

Upon speaking that last word, he drummed his claws beneath the flesh of Considine's neck.

"Should you stay, though, perhaps there's a place for you besides at the end of Luvick's leash."

Claws slipped cleanly from Considine's flesh. The ragged wounds flapped as Considine bent his neck, as if stretching away a morning's stiffness. The gaps had mostly sewn closed by the time he finished.

Considine gave a noncommittal nod. "Well, I do prefer to keep my options open."

"I remember," Rivascis said, taking a step into the shadows.

At the edge of the lantern's ring, the woman in black was visible only as faint golden glimmers. She stepped to follow her master.

"Stay and consider your failings," Rivascis said without turning. "I'll call when you're necessary."

She halted, hundreds of bangles clattering disappointment.

"Don't kill the priestess. I will find use for her." Rivascis's voice drifted back from the darkness.

I released the breath I felt like I'd been holding since the vampire had grabbed me. This might have been a nightmare, but at least it sounded like it wouldn't be my last.

His casually courteous voice snaked back again. "Otherwise, feel free to drink your fill."

I wondered if I'd be able to tell the difference between one nightmare's end and the next's beginning.

33

REMINISCENCE
LARSA

I knew what she'd forgotten.

"Me." It was harder to say than I'd expected.

Kindler looked guilty but defiant, like a criminal with convictions. She didn't try to defend herself.

"How?" I paged through the battered journal. It was old, but its wear didn't appear to be from regular use. Rather, its back cover was ripped and one corner was badly damaged. It looked like it had been thrown more than once.

Kindler produced a handful of what looked like sticks from the box and scattered them across the tea table. Some were stripped wooden lengths with scattered scars, like the trunks of miniature birch trees. A few were more unusual: a cylinder of rose-colored crystal, a rod of intertwined silver and bronze, an overlong finger bone etched with eel-like symbols. None were more than a foot long.

Wands. Though there was no way to know at a glance what sorts of magic such a collection contained.

"They're expended." Kindler picked the remaining few from the box and placed them with the others. "Every one used up."

"What did they do?" I idly picked up one of the white wooden ones.

"Made you forget."

I nodded. "How much?"

"This many? Drained in their entirety? Could have been years."

"Do you not remember years of your life?"

"I don't know." She gave a little shrug. "Do you remember the things you've forgotten?"

"I might realize a year had gone missing."

"Maybe. Years don't seem that long when you get to be my age." She ran a finger through the heap. There must have been at least thirty of the mismatched lengths. "But no, nothing stands as an obvious gap. There are certainly things I don't recall well, but I believe that's normal. Any obvious incongruity would probably make the magic fail."

"What do you mean, fail?"

"This magic doesn't erase your memories, it just prevents you from remembering them. The records are still there, they're just locked away."

Kindler took the journal back from me. "I woke up one morning in this chair with this journal open in front of me. The message on the page was clearly from me—it was in my hand, even used ink from my desk—but I didn't recall writing it. My first instinct was to examine myself, to see if I was being affected by any sort of enchantment. I have enough experience with that sort of magic that it wasn't difficult. Sure enough, I was under the effects of dozens of spells, all manipulating my mind. You can imagine my distress. Fortunately, I have tools packed away to deal with just that sort of thing. But then I read the rest."

She paged through delicately. "Every page is a warning, written by me, to me. On every page a me from a different day tells the me of today that there's something I can't stand to remember. There are eighteen different messages—eighteen, because seventeen times I unlocked the block on my memory. There are years between some of these. The ink changes, so does my hand. But in every case, I chose not to live with whatever it was. Each time, I replaced the block."

Her finger traced a line of smeared ink on one page, the words spattered by water droplets. "I remember terrible things—friends dying, terrors proving the gods aren't kind. But there's something worse." A bony finger tapped her temple. "Something that a whole younger, stronger court of myself judged they were better off without."

She began replacing the wands in the disguised box. "So I didn't peel back the magic. I don't travel anymore, I don't cause much trouble. I write my stories and pen letters to friends who won't threaten to visit. I keep to myself and am finally reading the library I've spent a lifetime assembling and neglecting. I am retired. And I've decided that I deserve a little happiness."

The Havenguard file was next. She gently closed the journal, winding the cord back around it. "So I packed it all up, stowed it on a high shelf, and made myself a cup of tea. And when that wasn't enough, I fixed myself something stronger."

The lid sealed with a click. "There have been days I wondered— days I thought of nothing else. I've spent weeks cleaning records and sorting old correspondence, hoping to find even some hint of what it might be. Something that might make not knowing easier. But either there's nothing, or I've been terribly thorough."

She crossed to the desk, one hand sliding along its edge as careful steps carried her behind it. "I purchased a few new wands from a band of Varisian tinkers, not too long ago. Most of the time such wanderers are frauds, but their leader had a few years on me. She seemed like the sort who knew what she was doing. I think she recognized me, or at least, something about me. We compared stories for a bit. Eventually, she offered to sell me several sticks she'd found in the west, touting them as magic to counter magic. They were expensive, but I have money. I bought them. I told myself I did it to fund the band's travels, and just in case I run afoul of some wizardly sort down the road."

She rolled back her wheeled chair and took a seat behind the piles of old books. "I never used them, though."

I crossed to the opposite side of the desk. She looked small and tired behind it. "How does this help us find Jadain?"

Kindler gave a resigned nod. "Maybe it doesn't. But the fact of the matter is that everyone else seems to have some hint of what's happening, and I haven't a clue. One of my most reliable colleagues thinks you're my daughter. You say there's a vampire lurking in the city who's fixated on me. Even I can't deny the resemblance you and I share. I'd happily dismiss this all as some terrible trick if there weren't a heap of dead strangers in my yard."

"It's not a trick," I said flatly.

She nodded. "It's a mystery, then. And we're likely the ones with something to lose if it isn't solved."

"Where do you suggest starting?"

She leaned low and opened one of the desk's bottom drawers. "Not far from here." She dropped another wand on the table. Rather than a length of birch, it seemed to be a slender shard of old, gray stone—like some piece of a larger sculpture. A frayed silk ribbon wrapped it, its length a rainbow of gaudy colors.

"When I bought this, the Varisian woman said it would keep my family from harm. When I told her I didn't have a family anymore, she just smiled."

Kindler peeled back the ribbon. The tip of the wand gripped a clear glass shard.

"I should have suspected then what trouble I'd be in for." A faint smirk bent her lips.

I felt out of place and stepped for the door. "How long will you need?"

"I'm not sure." She picked up the wand, rolling it between her fingers. "It depends on whether you know how to use this or not."

34

DEATH MASK
JADAIN

A nd what's this?" The woman in black's breathy voice climbed as though she'd made some risqué discovery. Fingers in silk slid beneath my shirt.

Every beat of my pulse felt like a punch to my skull, the result of hanging upside down for who could say how long. Through it, I could still feel a familiar weight against my neck, caught in a pocket created by my collar.

The stranger's gloved fingers felt filthy, like the touch of something covered in dust. They lifted away the goddess's symbol.

"This looks familiar." A rapid, throaty chuckle shook her veil. Her yank caused baubles to clatter across her gown, but failed to break my amulet's cord. The second attempt failed as well.

Somewhere at the light's edge Considine gave a short, nasty sigh. He'd been pacing endlessly. Twice I'd tried to speak to him, but he'd ignored me both times.

The woman jerked the cord down over my head. It tugged my nose roughly, but slipped off.

She lifted it, spinning, close to my face

"But this isn't right . . ." She pinched the emblem close to my face, comparing the goddess's spiral to my brand. "Your mark goes the other way."

The symbol, close enough to be little more than a brown blur, filled my vision. Hanging had been uncomfortable, but the darkness beyond my tormentor began to crawl. It felt as though I spun, bodily following every twist of the goddess's spiral. The air thinned, hardly filling my chest. Something in my guts began to fail and a burning sensation ran up my throat. I squeezed my eyes closed, shutting out the sight of the goddess's symbol. It hardly helped.

"Fascinating." She pressed the warm wood against my cheek. It barely added to my discomfort.

She made a lilting noise. "Does this offend you?" Her gloved hand pressed against my cheek and brow. Even through the grimy silk, her fingernails dug into my skin, peeling the lid of my cursed eye open.

She displayed my amulet plainly, and the weakened dam in my stomach shattered.

Being upside down made vomiting even worse. I arched my neck and heaved as forcefully as I could, my thoughts being only to keep it out of my nose. I succeeded to some degree, but wasn't spared some hot, bitter splash.

A thousand metal ornaments clattered like a collection box. The noise emphasized my tormentor's sucking gasp and sudden withdrawal, suggesting I hadn't suffered my sickness alone. The shouting that followed was clearly cursing, but I didn't understand a word. Every noise she made was a shocked pop or throaty gurgle, like what I'd just heaved up had been given voice.

Considine's impish laugh sounded from behind me.

The veiled figure's head shot up at the noise, her arms lifted in disgust. Some of her ornaments jangled with distinctly soggier notes. I couldn't see her eyes, but the blank fabric fixed on me, as though I were the one mocking her. Avoiding the puddle seeping into the dirt floor, she slid back toward me, one sooty glove extended.

"Careful," Considine said. "Remember what your master ordered."

The stained wraith halted, her eyeless gaze looking beyond me. "Your master, too."

Considine gave a short, indecisive hum.

"He only said not to kill her." Damp fingers settled around my neck.

The vampire scoffed. "Your master's come a long way if he's taken to seeing the charm in pedantry."

She considered. Gradually, slimy fingers slipped away.

"This unsettles you?" She knelt close, her veil opaque even from inches away. She lifted the spiral back into my sight. I pushed as far away from it as my bindings would allow. "Pitiful thing. Maybe you won't be as useful as he imagines."

She pressed closer, the goddess's symbol backed by her shroud.

Again my stomach rolled, but it didn't have enough energy for another full-on revolt. I pushed away farther, but still she pursued. There wasn't much I could do, but there wasn't nothing.

I threw myself forward, swinging in my bindings. Craning my neck as far as I could, I snapped my jaw.

My teeth caught something more than I'd expected. I twisted. Fabric tore. Something beneath, something loose, tore as well. She screamed, flinging herself back, clutching my amulet.

I held her veil in my mouth. It was wet and . . . full. Something was inside. I gagged and spat my mouthful into the dirt.

On the floor, the veil unfolded like butcher's wrapping. Something glistened there, square and slimy, a moist scrap.

Not thinking better of it, I twisted to take in my tormentor hissing on the floor.

By the goddess, what had I done? My jaw trembled. A sudden oily taste coated my tongue. I spat again and again.

I could see her eyes, red as embers, burning into me, gazing from bony sockets. Every vein, every muscle strand, every pale bone of her face was entirely visible. How? What had I done?

"Disgusting," Considine said, as though he'd noticed a dung pile.

"Filthy beast!" Gloved fingers knotted over her mouth, barely muffling her scream. Something like half-dried ink oozed between her fingers. Pulling back soaked hands, she looked into dripping palms. Doing so revealed her leaking mouth. Her chin, somehow, was even more grotesquely bare, even more exposed than the rest of her skinless features.

No, not skinless. Something, some curse or cruel disease, had afflicted her skin, making it transparent. It was little more than a thin, wet film, veins and oily masses pulsing beneath a sheath like frog eggs.

Pulsing. Whatever passed for blood in her corpselike body still flowed. Flowed enough that it was almost imperceptibly darkening the front of her gown and the cracked earthen floor.

She was on her feet, gore-soaked hands reaching. I twisted violently, trying hopelessly to wriggle loose.

"Careful, now." Considine rounded to just the corner of my sight. "Wouldn't want to lose a finger next."

She spared him nothing more than a short hiss and wrapped a damp hand around my neck. Any hesitance had left her grip. She squeezed.

Silk hissed and she dropped a glove away, revealing a hand just as transparent as her face. One of its half-visible fingers traced a cold line across my skin. It started at the corner of my vision and circled, following the spiral marring my eye. It felt like a slug's trail. I flinched, but the sheathed hand at my throat held me still.

She brought her face close to my ear. "You're going to regret that, you little scag." Her voice sounded wet, and she swallowed down whatever leaked into her mouth. Her gasping accent made sense now. Her mouth, too wide and full of thin sharp points, had no lips.

I didn't have any other choice. My eyes strained, my sight reaching out as nothing else could. "Considine!"

330 F. WESLEY SCHNEIDER

The vampire didn't seem to move, yet his outline became even more indistinct. He faded into the shadow.

I shouted again, trying not to choke, but he was gone. My eyes squeezed shut, trying to hold back desperation and something more.

"Does this mark offend you? Disgrace you?" She rolled a fingertip and a needlelike nail pierced my cheek.

I focused on trying to keep my breathing even.

She pushed deeper, her claw a scalpel scoring my cheekbone. "Does it?"

"Yes!" I screamed, my eyes bursting open at the same time.

She gave a soft, satisfied murmur. "Good."

With her thin, sharp nail she elaborated on the goddess's perverted symbol, gouging it into my flesh.

35

FINAL MOMENTS
LARSA

I mouthed the awkward word again, the noise that was supposed to call out the magic. "*Cevash*," or something like it.

"Don't hold it in your mouth," Kindler instructed. "Draw the noise in, shape it, then release."

Not that I had any idea what she was talking about. I knew a bit about magic, but actually casting spells, that wasn't for me.

I tried, and nothing—then again. Even the third time, I wasn't sure it had worked. I hadn't done anything different, just gestured and spat some nonsense. I was shaking the thing when Kindler eased back in her chair and closed her eyes.

"It began with my sister then as well."

Kindler's voice surprised me, as much the words as their dreamy distance.

"We lived just outside Caliphas. Our parents had never been rich, but we had grounds and name enough that people still thought of us as nobles. That reputation was enough to get Ellishan enrolled in classes at the Quarterfaux Archives, back before it was just a museum."

She smiled at whatever played out behind her closed lids. "I was so jealous of her, getting to live in the city, explore, meet so many new people."

"Father worried about her going off and insisted she come home twice a month. He even paid for a coach in advance to ensure it happened. Ellishan complained, but there was never any chance she'd win."

I took a seat on the lip of the desk. This didn't sound like it was going to be a particularly sudden revelation.

"Things went well. Ellishan would come home with books and news and sometimes little gifts. Mother loved it—they'd gossip about good families and little scandals for hours. Father would just sit and shake his head, but never disapproved. He was always just happy to have her home.

"After our parents went to bed, I'd make Ellishan tell me everything—what she was learning, about the city, everything. It was all becoming commonplace to her, but I made her draw me maps, point out who lived where, and explain step by step how to flag down pay carriages. She was only a few months older, but I felt like she was turning into a real lady—growing so worldly, living her great adventure."

Kindler's lips straightened. "It didn't last."

"The coach arrived hours late. When it did finally arrive, no one emerged. Father was at the coachman's side before he even slid off his bench. I remember Mother putting her arm around me like I was a little girl. I was confused, not just because the driver had come without Ellishan, but because my parents seemed to know something I didn't."

"The coach driver was a good man who'd worked for Father for quite some time. He said that Ellishan hadn't been at her dormitory. He'd spoken with the housemother, but even she hadn't seen my sister for days. Not knowing what else to do, he came to tell Father straightaway. He drove us back to Caliphas that night."

"You went with him?" I instantly regretting blurting out the question, afraid it might break the spell.

Kindler's eyelids didn't so much as tremble. "Father didn't want to bring me—outright refused, actually. When insisting didn't work, I tried something like reason. If Ellishan was missing, one of her dorm mates probably knew what had happened, or maybe she'd left some note with a friend. They certainly weren't going to let a man, even a concerned father, interrogate a dozen young noblewomen in their girls-only dorm. Me asking a few questions, though . . .

"He still didn't like the idea, but he'd worked with the Caliphas constabulary and knew the bureaucracy involved. He grabbed me by the arm and gave me a hundred stern orders, but I didn't hear any of them. All I knew was that I was going. The circumstances were dreadful, but I was going." She shook her head.

"On the drive, I kept trying to be worried for Ellishan. I was too excited—to see the city, to find out what had happened, to have an adventure. I'd already convinced myself that she'd slipped off to some handsome sculptor's studio, someone with bad parentage and good hands. I knew father would be furious, but between that eruption and now I'd get to see the city as Ellishan had."

"It turned out to not be that easy. We . . ." She trailed off, slowly opening misty eyes. "It gets hazy from there."

I flicked the wand, but didn't call on the magic. "These memories don't seem helpful—or particularly traumatic."

"There's more, but it's . . ." She shook her head. "It's like waking and having a dream fade, only in reverse."

"I could just wave this a few more times and get to the meat of the matter."

Her glare snapped up. "You will not. If there's a bandage on my mind I'd rather not just rip it away. We'll ease through this, if it's all the same to you."

"Fine. But let's not make memory lane longer than it needs to be."

She closed her eyes and settled back in her chair with a frown. I pointed the wand and flicked the noise off my tongue. "*Cevash.*"

Kindler choked. Once, then again, convulsing like she'd been punched.

The wand appeared to have more to do with it this time. The glass tip wasn't clear any longer. It looked slightly crazed, like a piece of frozen fog.

"Don't . . ." Kindler gasped, ". . . use that again. Not until I say."

I didn't argue.

Several minutes of slow, deliberate breathing passed before she continued. "Things in Caliphas didn't go at all as I expected. Father hardly spoke. He obviously wasn't imagining the same romantic conclusion to our trip that I was—or maybe he was. In any case, we went to the Quarterfaux dorms immediately and spoke to the housemother, but she didn't seem terribly concerned. She humored Father, but then tried to explain the ways of young students, big cities, and candlelit cafés. He wasn't interested in modern romance, though. I'd never seen him like that. He cut her off, explained his expectations firmly, quoted quite a bit about local legal procedure, and demanded to see Ellishan's room. It got things moving, but not far.

"Ellishan shared a space with a girl named Caileen. While Father and the housemother tossed my sister's room, I found her roommate in the dormitory parlor. She was a naturally proud sort and didn't seem particularly interested in chatting with her country roommate's younger sister, but Ellishan had told me enough stories to loosen the little princess's tongue.

"Apparently Ellishan *had* met a young fellow, a supposed poet named . . ." Kindler stopped for a moment.

I brought the wand up after a moment's silence. "Do you need another—"

"No. It doesn't matter." She waved me off. "The two had apparently met almost every night at a nearby café called the Ember Rose. I went to tell Father, but he'd worked himself into such a state that I couldn't get in a word. We left, retiring to a small rented room, intent on going to the constabulary the following morning.

"Neither of us slept much that night, Father out of worry, but me out of increasing concern about Father's reaction when Ellishan reappeared. By that point I'd concocted some elaborate story about my sister and her handsome beau, and wasn't eager to see their fairy tale shattered." She shook her head, chiding a past self.

"The following days were all waiting, conversations with bored constables, and my Father growing more distraught. I learned the stretch between our room and the Whiteshaw Constabulary, even picked out the Ember Rose café along the route, but father refused to leave me unattended. On our fourth night, we waited on Whiteshaw's hard benches for a report on the guards' daily rounds. My poor father had slept so little over the prior days that he'd dozed off. Thinking more of my sister than his worry, I slipped away."

Kindler began massaging her temples, causing me to wonder if there was a physical effect to the magic—magical scabs being torn away from a fragile mind. If there was, she bore through it. "My plan wasn't a plan at all, it was just a destination. I didn't know who I was looking for or what I'd do if I found him, but the only lead I had was the Ember Rose. So I went."

"I don't think I truly expected anything to come of it, but I found him there—or he found me. I was sitting and watching, drinking the same cup of bitter tea, concocting lies to tell Father upon returning. He approached from behind me and crouched like a satyr in some bad romance, grinning like he wanted to share some joke. I immediately didn't like him." The wrinkles about her nose deepened.

"He knew I was Ellishan's sister, said he could tell by my hair. I asked all the wheres and whos I'd been mustering. His answers were short and now obviously vague, but they had hints of familiarity. He claimed to be a former suitor of Ellishan's, but that their relationship ended when she took up with some handsome foreign gentleman. He said he'd followed them one night and it'd be his pleasure to show me where the stranger stayed."

Her chuckle was dry and utterly mirthless. "I was such a fool."

"Where was it?" I wanted to place things in the Caliphas I knew.

"I don't know, but we didn't go far. The place had been impressive once, but it wasn't any more than a tenement now. More people seemed to be sleeping in the halls than the rooms—rough sorts. I did my best not to look frightened by their looks and comments. My cheerful guide helped keep them at bay. We came to the ground-level apartment where my sister and her lover had denned up. No one answered our knocks. The romantic fantasy I'd created was fading, but I clung to it, for both Ellishan's sake and increasingly my own. Part of me wanted to run back and get Father, but my guide urged me on."

She sighed. "No bohemian dressings, no fuming incense sticks—inside it was nothing like what I'd imagined. I'd seen more romantic work sheds. The pitiful little apartment wasn't entirely empty, though. Light shone up from a trapdoor. I wondered why a place like this would have a wine cellar. I was so . . ." She shook her head, but this time she didn't stop. "I shouldn't have looked."

"Hands yanked my feet out from under me and tugged me down. The stranger watched me fall and only smiled. His teeth were fangs. I screamed and something carried me away."

Even with fifty-some years between then and now, she was clearly describing an entrance to Caliphas's borderlands. There was the New City above, then sewers built amid the foundations and old basements of the city's forgotten structures. Those were the remnants of the city built centuries ago, the one that burned, sank, and was forsaken: the Old City. Few in Caliphas today imagined that the courts of their ancestors still lay somewhat intact just below—or that they were far from deserted. It wasn't a proud place, but it was vast and hidden from the light. Little surprise that Grandfather and his kind had claimed it. There was a part of me—a part I hated—that thought of it as home.

Kindler stiffened, sitting straighter in her chair. "When the candle sparked, it wasn't the flame I saw first, but deep gray eyes. They seemed surprised to see me. Behind them wasn't at all the stranger I'd expected. Not some gutter lord or monster, but some out-of-place noble, like a prince in hiding. There were hands on me, but all I saw was him and those misty eyes. He wanted my name. I wanted to give it to him, and I did. I also wanted to ask for his, but all I could do was stare."

I didn't wait. "Rivascis."

Kindler nodded. "I don't think he ever said as much, but it was like I'd always known."

Her wistful voice made it sound like some fated connection, but I doubted it. He'd likely subverted her will at first sight.

"He wasn't alone. There were others, but they were less. He ignored them, and I tried to do the same. He asked why I'd been in his rooms, and I told him that I'd come looking for my sister. He knew who I meant immediately and asked if I wanted to go to her. I worried about what that could mean, but told him yes. His hand was on mine, cold and as dry as parchment. He wanted to lead me away, but something in the dark interrupted."

Her arms wrapped around one another. "It was the voice of the darkness itself. It came from all around us and sounded like dirt crumbling through your fingers. I remember its accent, but could never place it—formal, as if each word were being read from some ancient book. It thrummed through me, every sound a tremble. I didn't fear it until Rivascis called it father."

I was starting to place things. In the dark, she'd likely been dragged past the Porphyry Stair into the depths of the Old City. Whoever had abducted her had dragged her before its betters. She never knew it, but her meeting with Rivascis likely transpired before dozens of silent, thirsting judges and their ancient creator.

Grandfather wasn't truly the shapeless presence Kindler remembered, but in the dark, in the ruined Sarenite sanctuary that was his audience hall, his voice might as well been that of the Prince of Darkness himself.

"The darkness pronounced a sentence I didn't understand." Kindler's brow tightened. "Their plans hadn't accounted for family bonds. Disruptive variables couldn't be permitted. I had to be removed. The voice said that—'removed'—but it was clear what it meant. I thought to run, wanted to even, but a calm I couldn't understand locked me in place. Rivascis defended me. I didn't understand why, but he claimed I had qualities my sister lacked, favorable traits for something known only to him and the blinding dark."

She shook her head. "It didn't go well. The dark's decree was no better, calling for my disposal. Rivascis turned to me. There was an apology in his eyes, but something urged me on. The calmness tamping down my fear broke. I yelled. I don't remember exactly what I said, but I begged them to let Ellishan go. I told them that if they did, I'd replace her. Having no idea what it meant, I told them I'd cooperate so long as they set her free."

A grim obstinance crept across the old woman's face. "There was only the stuffy, black silence. It felt like I'd drowned and drifted to the bottom of some stifling tropical sea. Eventually I thought I picked out whispers, but they were so faint I might have imagined them. When the dark spoke again, it had a simple choice: leave but never see my sister again, or stay, know that my sister would leave unharmed, and never see her again. I answered immediately."

"You stayed to save your sister?" I tried to keep my opinion out of my voice. She couldn't have known the fate she was choosing. I'd spent decades in the Old City's dark. If I could trade that nightmare with anyone, I'd do it in a moment.

She nodded. "I was so terrified, but Rivascis stood there with me. He helped me save my sister's life."

From the sound of it, all he'd done was release his control on her. I couldn't be sure of any of that, though, and didn't bother trying to explain. I was more curious about why a vampire—any vampire, but especially one of Grandfather's own children— would defend one lost noble girl over another. Blood was blood, and mortal lives were short and not worth bargaining over.

There was also a more obvious question. "How'd you escape?"

"I remember the dark closing in, but it grows foggy from there."

Without asking, I flicked the drab wand. "*Cevash.*"

Kindler's head jerked. She starred at me through old memories. Her jaw quivered. Arms and papers scattered across the desk. When her body slammed against naked wood, I wasn't sure which would break her apart: the force of the blow or her trembling scream.

36

MERCIFUL DEATH

JADAIN

Blood blinded my right eye. The smell of copper overpowered that of the bile spilled below. Streams of hot tears tried to erase the slimy trails of the fleshless woman's finger.

She pulled her hand back, admiring the heresy she'd carved into my skin. The goddess's inverted symbol burned on my face. I could feel the inquisitor's touch again, feel his outrage working its mark on my face. It was a stain marring my soul as much as my flesh. But she—with nails like a tattooist's needle—had turned the stain into a scar.

My throat, already burned by vomit, was raw from screaming.

"Do you think I could peel it away?" she casually asked. "It's loose now. The skin-shape would probably come away in one strip."

Considine's voice, drifting from the darkness, sounded just as nonchalant. "I think your master's already going to flense you, so why not make it worse?"

The threat of more caused the pain burning my face to flare.

I could see her bare hand. She held her forefinger extended like a brush—one over-soaked in red pigment, the paint falling to the ground in fat drops. My blood did more than her transparent flesh to hide the disguising bone below.

"He invited us to feed. I wouldn't turn down his generosity." She took a step back toward me. The gold upon her gown clattered like chains.

I could already feel her impossibly wide mouth on my neck, her stingerlike teeth on me. Although no amount of thrashing had loosened my restraints, I still struggled. Chain bit deeper. I could feel bruises spreading. It felt like the metal was scouring bone.

The cord binding my feet to the ceiling jerked and my shoulders hit the ground before I even realized I was falling.

"What are you doing?" The woman in black sounded more angry than confused. My feet were free, but my wrists were still bound—hands numb from being crushed beneath my body. I kicked myself away from her voice, heels digging furrows in the dirt.

Whatever I struck wasn't a wall.

"You've wasted enough." Considine's voice came from just above. He took a soundless step back, extracting his legs from my back. "Keep still," he said, a moment before my wrists jerked free.

Gaining a sitting position, I tried to rub feeling back into my hands. I thought to say thank you, but the pain searing my face burned away that reflex. It was too late to thank Considine for anything.

The woman slinked to the edge of the lantern light, her blank red eyes locked above me. "The master will know you're the one who freed her."

Considine made a dismissive chirp. "I'll tell him myself."

"If you weren't his son—"

"If I weren't," he interrupted in a friendly tone, "I promise that right now I wouldn't be so curious about how blood from the Darklands tastes. If you'd like, though, I'd be happy to disown my father for fifteen minutes or so."

The semi-visible woman gave a breathy growl and withdrew completely from the light.

The vampire's voice turned to me. "You should heal yourself. The smell is distracting."

"I can't," I snapped back, refusing to look at him. Blood ran from my cheek into the corner of my mouth.

"Your amulet. She has it." He sounded apprehensive. Unsurprising. As uncomfortable as the sight of the goddess's symbol recently made me, it was nothing compared to the revulsion a thing like Considine experienced. I couldn't expect him to fetch it back from Rivascis's servant for me. "Hmm."

"It's not just that." I felt his expectant look, but didn't elaborate.

A linen handkerchief fluttered into my lap. It seemed clean enough. I pressed it to the right side of my face.

I sat in silence for some time, exploring the ragged edges of my wound. It was consistently deep, but superficial. I wouldn't lose my sight or much mobility in my face over this, but it would need healing soon. If not by the goddess's grace, then it would need many, many small stitches. In the latter case, there would be a scar—an unignorable one.

I bit my trembling bottom lip. *Not in front of these things.*

After a time, Considine went back to pacing.

I watched with my clear eye. In the sad yellow light it was hard to pick out the bloodless tint of his skin or the predatory points of his nails. His messy hair hid the points of his ears. Except for the tear in his vest exposing the unmarred skin over his heart, he might have been any sheltered noble stumbling home from a night's carousing. I was reminded of the heartsick young man I'd counseled at Maiden's Choir weeks ago. Could he have been secretly just as much a monster? I had urged him to follow his heart back into the world, knowing nothing of his lusts or what he could have been capable of. Mardhalas, rather, had pointed him toward the path of cold, reflective prayer. I'd thought that so inhuman, so tragic at the time. But was that truly the safer course? Was I so blind to the monsters around me?

I nodded into the dark. "What is she?"

"That one?" Considine's eyes fixed on something I couldn't see. "A parasite."

The shadows gave a breath like a hiss.

"They're called urdefhan. They live deep underground and usually have the sense not to aspire to better things. I've only ever seen one before, but that one was also bargaining to become a vampire. They don't seem attached to life in the same way as things that live under the sun."

I glared into the dark. The weaknesses of being a vampire must seem far less dire, for a thing born underground. Stakes and burning light didn't seem so concerning in a world without trees or sun.

I looked back to Considine, curious without really knowing why. "You called him father."

His heel took a moment longer to fall than it had the step before. He spun a barely patient grin my way. "A bad joke."

"It sounded like one he'd heard before."

"It's been some time, but he never did have a sense of humor."

"You call Larsa your sister as well."

"Oh dear, are you trying to analyze me?" He chuckled. "Here's a secret to take back to your scholars—if you ever get out of here. When you die, sicknesses of the body never need worry you again. Sicknesses of the mind, though—whew. Nothing, nothing, *nothing* makes you more neurotic than being dead." He was grinning and shaking his head when his course looped him back into view.

"Fortunately for you, my dear Miss Losritter, my own personal exorcist, I'm one of the sane ones."

"I'm not your personal anything."

"Oh really?" He halted, cocking his head. Emerald glinted in his eyes, like a stray sunbeam spearing a single stained-glass frame. A tide washed into the edges of my sight, a suggestion of irresistible green sea currents. I slammed my eyes closed, but the invasive shade tinged even my most private darkness.

"Stop." I said it like a prayer. "Stop, please."

The tide ebbed. I could hear the smile in his voice. "Whatever do you mean?"

I held my eyes closed until I was sure I couldn't see anything at all.

"Oh, you've been a good sport." He was behind me, circling again. "Yes, yes, one big happy family. Sister, brother, father . . . well, no need for mothers. Neither Larsa nor I would be walking this world if it weren't for dear Father. I'd be bones in a hole somewhere and she'd be nothing at all."

"You're not a dhampir, though. You're—"

"A full-blood."

"I don't . . ."

"I know, it's very complicated." He was obviously enjoying this. "Every vampire's born a slave of his master, the one who created him—you know how all that goes, yes? Biting, but not feeding?"

I nodded, not that he waited.

"Some will never be anything more than slaves—our spawn. Good for servants and pretty, useful, temporary things, but not the sorts you want to bother with a decade later. They have some of our tricks, but they'll never, ever be true vampires."

"But Larsa's a dhampir. How's she work into all that?"

He gave an unsure hum. "She's a delicate topic. Some say she's something like a spawn, but without the least of our blessings or obedience. Other's say she's a special case. Either way, it doesn't make her popular."

"But . . ." I wasn't entirely sure how to politely phrase the question. "How?"

A thin brow and a corner of his lips rose as one.

"She's alive, though. Right? How can a . . . dead man sire a live child?"

"Miss Losritter," he said with a few clucks of mock surprise. "I'd always heard Pharasmins are crypt-cold about sex."

Pain helped keep my face impassive.

"If you *must* know, consider . . . let's see . . . a riverside mill. The water flows, the wheel turns, grist becomes meal." His hand mimed each step of the process. "But say, one day, the river dries up. The water stops flowing, the wheel stops turning, the grist lies unground. It's a sad state of affairs"—his voice dropped—"but one we all have to deal with.

"Fortunately, there are ways to divert water back into even the driest riverbed. The water might only flow for a time, but that can be enough to get the wheel turning again. Barring mechanical problems, that can be just long enough to grind a few more loads of grist . . . if you take my meaning."

"Yes. Quite. Thank you." I regretted asking.

He nodded with a wide, helpful grin.

"So, if Rivascis is truly Larsa's father, then do you know her mother?"

He shook his head. "You *do* pick the cutting questions, don't you? As a matter of fact, I—"

Iron hinges squealed in the dark.

"Speak of the Archdevil and he shall appear."

"Considine," Rivascis's voice whispered from the shadow. It echoed strangely, coming from all around us at once.

"Coming, Father." Considine winked at me, then disappeared beyond the wavering ring of light.

Hinges complained again, then it was silent.

For just a moment, I was relived to be alone. Then I remembered.

From beyond the lantern's reach, red eyes opened. Twin embers from the depths of Hell itself stared fire into me.

37

COFFINBORN
LARSA

I didn't know what to do. I'd seen people with sucking wounds suffer less violently. For some reason Jadain popped to mind. What had she done in Ulcazar when that innkeep was howling?

I put my palms on Kindler's shoulders hesitantly, not sure of how much force to apply. Her sobbing didn't change, but one of her hands came up, trying to trap my own between it and her bird-like shoulder. My instinct was to yank my hand free. I thought it might be better not to, though. She certainly couldn't harm me.

I stood there and let her sob.

It was some time before the noises stopped, but longer before her breathing evened. I took her soft pat on my hand as a cue to finally take a step back.

I busied myself collecting the desk's stray contents, too embarrassed to look her in the face. A monogrammed handkerchief was dabbing her eyes by the time I finished. Her face had more color than usual, a shade of washed-out pink. It perhaps wasn't flattering, but it did make her look more alive. How long would it last?

She cleared her throat, but took a moment more to compose herself. "Thank you, my dear."

But her look wasn't what it had been. She stared at me.

"What?" I asked when she didn't say anything, speaking mostly to break the silence.

She gave a small, tight smile. It looked like she might tear up again. Instead, she just asked, "Where was I?"

I returned to the desk, retrieving the wand. Its point hardly looked like glass anymore, more like a piece of polished stone.

She started slowly. "I don't know how much time passed in the dark under the city. I had to assume they'd released Ellishan, as I never saw her. I imagined what she'd do. She'd find Father soon enough and tell him what she knew. The two would rally guards and family and fill these tunnels with torchlight. More than once I was certain I heard my name, echoing through the subterranean distance. I'd shout replies into the dark, but no familiar voices ever answered. Those that did were never comforting.

"I wasn't alone in that hot, piss-smelling dark. They kept me in a cell—a cage, really. I could feel the bars upon the floor and just reach the ones over my head. There were other occupied cells around me. I learned the names and imagined the faces of some, but others were incomplete presences, collections of repeating whimpers or soft shifting noises—like something trying to convince even itself that it wasn't there. There was Maddie, a merchant's daughter; Shar and Eaven, a young couple with Northern accents; and poor, lost Oloura, who never overcame her fear of the dark. More came and went, but their names have faded or I never learned them."

I didn't mention it, but I knew the place she was talking about. A half-crumbled space with cages that made it more like a kennel than a prison. The people of the Old City kept unexpected guests there, but rarely for long.

"But our captors were more real. They'd enter through a door that ground across the stone. Sometimes it wouldn't open for what might have been days, sometimes it opened and you couldn't hear its rumble over someone's sobs. The crying ones were the ones most likely to be taken away, so many of us learned to keep quiet. In any case, the jailers would slip between the cages and only make noise if they wanted to. Sometimes they'd whisper to us, horrible things about our smell or blood or bodies. They didn't hide what they were. With their cold skin and sharp touches, we all knew. None of us believed it at first, unwilling to accept that such things really existed. We all overcame our denial in time.

"Our vampire keepers came for one of two reasons: either to bring us stale food and warm water, or to take someone away. Sometimes those taken never came back. Sometimes we only heard from them once more, when their screaming reached us even through the prison door. Other times, they returned, but never spoke of what happened. That sparked my fascination even more than my dread. What could they be doing that would make us co-conspirators in their work?

"It was probably weeks before I learned what was behind the door. I woke to the sound of my cage opening. Invisible hands grabbed me. I tried to struggle, but their grips might as well have been iron bands. I bit and clawed, but whatever had me only laughed. I heard the door growl open and we passed through halls and more doors in complete darkness. They only released me to throw me over a rough table, chortling as they faded back the way they had come.

"Had the lantern light been turned down any lower it would have been snuffed out. Even as it was, I could barely look at it. Its intensity gradually increased. There was a chair, but I remained standing, stretching my body for the first time in I couldn't say how long. Marks covered my arms and my clothing was starting to show serious wear, but I was still what I remembered being. That was a surprising relief.

"There was a hand on the lantern and a voice asked if I was being treated well. I recognized Rivascis in the rising light. He was still a stranger, but he'd been all the kindness I knew in that place. I didn't know what he wanted, but at least I didn't think he would harm me. He said he couldn't tell me everything, but he'd explain what he could.

"He told me we were being poisoned, in a sense. The meals we were given, the food we never saw, was laced with the ashes of dead royals. There were legends among his kind that drinking the blood of true royalty could bestow incredible power. Rivascis's father, the voice in the dark, was seeking a way to artificially create a supply of such noble blood. We were experiments in creating that supply."

I'd never heard such a thing. That certainly wasn't to say it wasn't true, but the idea of the deathless deriving power from any corpse—regardless of its former station—sounded suspect. Regardless, I let her continue.

"I remember tasting the ashes in my mouth. I wanted to vomit, but hadn't eaten in so long I couldn't muster more than a few raw gags. Rivascis apologized profusely. He gave me a pear and handful of almonds, begging me to eat what I could and to hide the rest for later. He lamented that he couldn't help all the captives, and worried aloud about the guards finding out. I asked why he was helping me, why he cared. He didn't say. Soon the guards returned and took me back to my cell.

"That was the first of several meetings with Rivascis. Every few days the guards would take me to him. He'd asked after my welfare and smuggle me more food. He never said there was risk to what he was doing, but he insisted that I not let either my prison mates or the guards know. We talked while I ate. I had many questions about where we were, what was happening, and his role in it. He answered what he could. Occasionally he'd ask about my family and my life above. Inevitably, though, the guards would end our discussions too soon.

"Still, those moments with him became the only time I was certain I was still alive. With him, I could see, speak and be spoken to, and, in time, even let myself feel safe. I knew what he was, but that came to mean less over time. There were the things in the dark, and there was Rivascis.

"During one meeting he seemed particularly agitated. I asked why, and though he seemed surprised, he told me about his discontentment under his father's rule. When the guards came for me, he sent them away. We spoke for hours. After that, our meetings changed. I learned more about him and his sunless world. It made me less afraid. During another meeting, I kissed him. His skin was cold, but it wasn't what I imagined a corpse's skin to be like. He seemed surprised, and soon after returned me to my cell.

"Rivascis didn't visit me again for a long while. I worried that I might have offended him—that maybe the touch of the living revolted him as much as I expected touching a corpse would repel me. In the dark of my cell, I wrestled with my feelings.

"Eventually, he did call again, though. Over pear slices and wine he told me how I fascinated him, how I was the only one who the darkness hadn't broken. He marveled over it and wanted to know why. He speculated on my psychology and family history. I told him it wasn't any of those things. He asked politely, and I let him put his arms around me.

"From then on, I was still a prisoner, but he no longer felt like my captor. He told me about his people and what they were. He explained how they were monsters, but also like normal, living people. He claimed to remember what it was to be alive, and even shared his hopes of a world where vampires and humans worked together. There was a grimness to it all, but also a lonely sort of hopefulness. It made me believe the dead still had dreams.

"During our discussions, he mused on ways to smuggle me away and told me of plans he was setting in order. More than once, he came with news of thwarted hopes. I tried to hide my disappointment. We tried to comfort each other. There was a simplicity to our relationship, even as it grew more physical. I didn't know if he felt the way I did, or even if he could. On some level, I didn't care. If this was my world now, I would embrace whatever happiness I could find."

She paused, swallowing hard.

"Things changed when the woman in the cell next to me began shrieking. Maddie had been here longer than me, a span that must have been approaching at least a year. She'd become morose in the past weeks and had been taken away more than once. Like others before her, she didn't speak of what happened beyond. A change in her screams made it clear the guards had come, and they dragged her away. We heard Maddie howling for a long time, even after the door grated close.

"Who knows how long it was before they cast her back into the cage next to mine. We pressed her to tell us what happened, but she didn't answer. Somehow we all knew this was something different, but she ignored our questions.

"She slept a long time, and we left her be. Hours passed. I don't think she wanted us to know she was awake, but eventually I heard her sobbing softly. I whispered to her, pleaded to know what had happened, and finally she told me."

Kindler drew a long breath. "They had taken her child." The old woman's look was full with the confession. "I couldn't say a thing. I couldn't even console her—not even if I had words for such loss. I was paralyzed. Not by shock or sympathy, but by a truth I hadn't let myself acknowledge. That's when I was sure, though. That's when I became convinced something was growing inside me."

I brought back Kindler's water in a teacup with a ring-shaped whiskey stain. She accepted it with a nod.

I picked up the stone wand—it seemed heavier than it had before. "Again?"

She shook her head. "Maybe in a moment. There's still more." She didn't look at me.

I knew pieces of the next part of her story, but I didn't rush her. She didn't look like she could take being rushed. Something of the steely spinster I'd met only a day earlier seemed thinner, as if the memories were wearing her away. I was starting to understand forgetfulness's appeal.

Finished with her drink, she settled back into the desk chair, folded her hands, and closed her eyes. It took a moment and a long sigh before she reluctantly continued sifting through her memories.

"Maddie was only the first. In the dark, several of us had felt it. But no one had dared say anything. Not only did none of us want it to be true, it felt like a betrayal—of our desperate little group, and of ourselves.

"After Maddie, we spoke openly of what lay beyond the growling door. The cause had been different for each of us. Whispered rituals and bitter alchemical draughts featured in several tales. The timid woman named Shar claimed that she and her lover Eaven had been left alone for days in a pristine glen. Not long after they'd finally thought themselves safe, the illusory world faded and she was returned to her cell. Eaven hadn't been seen since."

She swallowed as though it were a challenge. "I didn't volunteer a tale. When they realized I hadn't spoken, I repeated some of what I heard. I didn't dare tell them the truth. Of them, I was most the traitor. I was the one who thought she was in love.

"I was confused, but that changed to something far darker. Everything Rivascis had said, it had all been a lie. I doubted the food had ever been tainted—it was likely just a ruse to convince me to literally eat out of his hand. From the beginning, I'd been his experiment. It was so clear. I was such a fool."

Her voice slowed to little more than a whisper. "I wanted to hurt him—thought even to hurt myself, but . . ."

Her mouth worked, but nothing came out. Even through closed lids something glistened at the corners of her eyes.

"You don't have to . . ."

She stopped me before I could finish.

"It happened to all of us." In the time it took to lower her hand and dab her eyes, her voice had lost much of its tremble. "Not everyone survived. For some it was worse than we'd imagined. Oloura had twins."

"Even I had my time. I didn't scream, and neither did it. I hardly remember it, just another blur of darkness and pain. What slipped from me was cold and quiet. I couldn't be sure that it drew breath, but I was certain it moved. A nursemaid I never saw carried it away. I think I struggled with her. I don't know what I was thinking, but then I didn't think anything for a long time."

She was still. Whatever she thought or saw, she kept behind closed eyes.

I set the wand on the desk and stood. That was enough.

Kindler obviously didn't think so. "Nothing was the same after that." A firm timbre, strengthened by anger, crept into her voice. "They still needed us . . . for a time. We were fed better, and twice daily they brought in the things they called children. They let us feed them. But they took more than normal children. After just a few weeks they had sharp little teeth. We grew used to the bites. None of us were ever sure we were nursing our own. Eventually, they stopped coming—the guards, the children, even the food. By that time there were only six of us left, and none of us were well." Her jaws worked slowly, grinding together as her head gave a grudging twist.

"The shouting began as soon as the light slipped beneath the prison door. Most of us thought it was some hallucination. Some probably mistook it for death—those who did hadn't made much of a mistake. Our guard looked like she'd never seen the sun. Veins like fractures covered her bald scalp and she moved like a lizard. For some reason she carried a single lit taper as she moved from cage to cage, unlocking them. I laid eyes on my cellmates for the first time. They were matted, skinny wretches. I'm sure I wasn't any better. None of us looked one another in the eyes. Not that we had much opportunity to. Our hissing jailer herded us out of the room, into shadows filled with more claws." She lifted her hands, miming the grope of thin white clutches. "I realized the light was to light our way. We were leaving."

"We stumbled as we went, unused to standing, less used to walking. Cold, sharp grips pulled us along. They didn't even bother to curse us when we fell. But we could hardly resist. It was clear we were being led up, maybe toward the surface. None of us dared ask, or even hope. Poor Oloura, she broke into a fit when she realized it. She'd suffered more than most of us and refused to be parted from her children. When she tried to flee back to her cell, they dragged her . . . screaming."

Kindler released a long breath. "We stopped nowhere in particular, just a tunnel with a trickle of sludge. Words hissed ahead, irritated noises. Rivascis emerged from the dark. It was the first time I'd seen him in maybe months. I remember something in my chest leapt, but whatever it was, it burned away in a sick surge. I wanted to scream, to charge and beat him down. My handler must have sensed it, and nails dug into my arms. My eyes tore him apart, but he didn't notice. He informed our herders they'd be taking a different path. Several complained, but none defied him. He led us on.

"We climbed as we limped along, winding gradually up. Our guards seemed more irritated than before. Rivascis moved among them, occasionally snapping in a language I didn't understand. Every time he passed I looked into his face, searching for some answer there. His eyes never met mine.

"After what seemed like miles, we came into a true sewer tunnel fixed with rungs climbing to grating above. I could feel cool air, smell more than just running rot. That's when one of the vampires challenged Rivascis. The guard didn't believe the elder vampire was leading them wherever he'd claimed. For his part, Rivascis didn't argue. He vanished. When I saw him again he was yanking the rebellious guard's head from her neck."

A hand crossed to her shoulder, holding her body. "The other vampires set on him. He moved with a devil's speed. It was like the shadows themselves had turned on those coarse, lesser creatures.

He channeled them back down the tunnel. Soon he was standing between us and them. I stared, as we all did. Finally, his eyes found mine. When he shouted to climb, everyone but me obeyed. The others dragged themselves up the nearby ladder. I could feel the cold air above. The night seemed fantastically bright."

Her hand gripped her own shoulder roughly, threatening to tear her lacy collar. "He was at my side, then, his cold hand on me again. I almost screamed and tore away. His face was covered in gore, but his eyes still faked having a soul. His voice sounded noble's—like a prince's. 'I never wanted to lie to you,' he said. 'And I never will again.' That's what put me past the brink. That's when I knew for certain that he'd always been a monster, just one who'd deluded himself into believing a mask of humanity was his real face. He was a monster that had no idea what a monster he was. I screamed, and not caring if it was hopeless, I put my fists and broken nails to his face."

She squeezed her eyes tighter, then released. "I know I connected—know I caught him off guard. Something in his look changed, then he was gone, vanishing in a breath of black fog. As fast as I could, I scrambled up the ladder and onto the plaza above, not stopping until I was far from the grate."

Her eyes opened mere cracks, as if adjusting to the library's dull light. "When I came to myself, I was in a plaza of black and white tiles. Above us, Pharasma's spiral glowed from beneath a forest of steeples. Two priests in violet were already hurrying down the cathedral steps. A warm hand touched my shoulder, and it all gave out."

Kindler stared at the desktop. "The Pharasmins cared for me and the other survivors for weeks. I was reunited with my family and eventually returned home. But I didn't stay long."

Picking up the wand from where I'd left it, she stared into the now-foggy crystal. "I couldn't stand the thought of staying near Caliphas, knowing the city was just a scab over that other,

356 F. WESLEY SCHNEIDER

nightmarish world. I left soon after, staying with family and attending school in Andoran. I had terrible nightmares there. More than once I even thought Rivascis had come after me. I couldn't forget what had happened, and when I realized that, I obsessed. I sought out all I could about vampires and terrible things like them. I did many things I regret to learn what everyone warned me I shouldn't. Even when I was expelled from Almas University I hardly noticed.

"It wasn't until I met members of a local explorer's league that I realized my scholarly addiction could actually be put to use. I joined them and, eventually, the Pathfinder Society. I traveled and learned more than I could at any university—not just how to fight but how to think in a fight." A smile might have flickered at the corner of her mouth. If it did, it was gone in an instant.

"Eventually I returned to Ustalav. I said it was to root out the things hiding in its shadows. I claimed that I wanted to use my stories to spread warnings and methods of challenging the things that haunted my homeland. But none of that was entirely true. I wanted Rivascis. What he'd done, what he'd told me—the truth and lies didn't matter. I wanted to drive a stake through his chest. I wanted to avenge the girl who wandered into the dark searching for her sister."

"That hunt became my entire life." Her eyes strayed to me. "And I failed."

38

TRIAL OF FAITH
JADAIN

It's that you're all, *always*, leaking." The voice owned by those scorching eyes spoke as though I'd answered their question. Beneath them, points of gold glinted, false stars twinkling in the endless night.

"All of it. Blood, words, bile, obvious little lusts—it's repulsive." Her colorless wrapping overbore the lantern's frail glow, the light giving ground before her. "And it all leaks down into our world. Your frailties, your sins, are our rain."

"You're welcome to return to . . . wherever." I tried to sound bold. I couldn't feel the edge of the lantern light, but I knew my back was against the shadows.

"Oh, I will, once I have what the master's promised. A vampire's kiss holds no terror in a world without light. What your simpering people call a curse, I'll accept like a crown."

"So it's like that? 'Be my slave and I'll make you a queen'?" Already properly screwed, I didn't have any reason not to speak my mind. "I'm sure that'll work out just fine for you."

A dull bit of jewelry caught the light. It didn't glitter as it hung from a bloodied but still transparent digit.

"'Be my slave and I'll protect you'? 'I'll make you strong'? 'I'll keep you safe in death'?" The goddess's symbol swung on its cord. "What was your bargain? How did it end for you?"

My guts began to squirm. I looked away, eyes retreating from the spiral's dizzying curves.

The scrap of wood struck me in the face, the shock of its touch hitting me harder than the physical blow. It clattered to the dirt. That alone, letting her symbol touch unsanctified ground, was an insult to the goddess. Before I could even reach for it, nausea caused the ground to roll like a ship's deck. Again, I had to look away.

The light shone up through the urdefhan's skin, under-lighting a skull barely masked by wormy veins. Rows of thin teeth clenched in a predator's smile.

"Your friend did you no favors cutting you down." She took a silent step closer. The baubles on her gown seemed suddenly sharp, glittering like fangs. "I can't allow you to run free."

There was no escape. There was only this island of light. Who knew what might be in the dark beyond? A door? Certainly, but not an open one. I hunched anyway, ready to run, even knowing I'd be caught.

"Leaving?" She gave a crackling, back-of-the-throat chuckle.

I grabbed Pharasma's symbol out of the dirt. Ignoring my stomach's complaint, I brandished it like a miniature shield.

Her throat noise became more violent, rising higher and faster. "Your gorge won't save you again."

I squeezed my eyes closed. My body spun, the spiral etched into my face spinning as well. The sickness, the hesitance, the pain all twisted in that scar. But even tainted, it was only flesh. I pushed it away, and prayed. *Lady of Graves, I know I've not been worthy. I know I've questioned. I know my faith has been stained with doubt. But please—*

The rough wood in my grip vanished, turning colder than ice. In my hands burst Pharasma's own blazing blue-white comet, its light brilliant even through my cinched eyes. The ghostly wave crashed over me, churning my insides more violently than ever. It felt like I was falling, but I didn't loosen my grip. I clung to the goddess's frozen symbol.

I opened my eyes just as the wave struck the woman in black, flinging her back with a shocked, inward-sucking shriek. Divine light seared her and momentarily burnt away the surrounding shadows. She looked frail and ragged, and this prison was just a cellar. The dark's lies drifted away.

Just as fast as the Lady's light erupted, it was gone.

Illness gripped me. The goddess's symbol was still cool in my hand. Cold as the grave.

Why now?

The thing in the darkness spoke cruel syllables.

I threw myself sidelong, plunging into the darkness. Flame roared out of nothingness, scouring the lantern-lit island. A whiff of a terrible scent invaded my memory: Tashan burning—twice.

I rolled hard, scrambling desperately. The fire followed, a second tongue of hellfire devouring my path. Across the room the flames emerged from an outraged constellation of flickering gold, the metallic stars crowned by a muscle-draped skull.

Something shifted under me as I scrambled across the dirt floor. My hand closed on wood. A splintered board—the stake that split Considine's chest. It was garbage, but it was sharp. I grabbed it.

Flinging myself through the shadows, I closed on the after-image of gold and bone still burnt into sight. Vicious noises, like a serpent trying to speak, slid through my near-blindness. I rushed toward them, holding the stake low and in both hands, pressing my amulet against it.

The thrust I made mimicked the first of two stomach cuts doomed Brevic nobles called spirit-tying, a murder-suicide for lovers. The splintered wood blindly tore thin fabric. Weak flesh relented like a worm taking a hook. The wood sank in, but in the dark I couldn't gauge the slash's effectiveness.

I smelled a gasp of wet, onion-reeking breath. The vicious noises slowed, but relentlessly ground on. Heat rose between me and the vaguest golden outlines, as if the borders between reality and Hell's infernos were ready to shatter.

Goddess. *Please.*

Fire and light exploded forth once more. I was falling, spinning. My body no longer felt no longer whole. My soul was ripping loose from my body. I didn't feel any pain. I hoped the goddess would judge me mercifully—even knowing death's justice knew no mercy.

The scream that followed wasn't my own. My eyes sprang open to a wintery vision of blues and white. The cold radiance fountained between us, emanating from the emblem pulsing in my hands. It spread to every corner, bursting in tides over the bony claws grasping for my face. The lidless eyes behind them were unable to shut out the goddess's light, and the monster jerked away.

To the light was a familiar calming cold. Yet the urdefhan writhed, her tainted soul wracked by the waves of holy energy. A screech escaped chattering teeth, cutting off her savage spell-shaping. Her body tugged at the stake still in my grip, undoing her impaling. Trying to cover her face, she fled, her jewelry rattling wildly, some tearing away to shatter upon the hard dirt.

The hinges of a sagging door howled as she ripped them open. In my palm, the goddess's light dimmed, but not before the last glimmers of the urdefhan's gold darted away.

I released a long breath. My throat unclenched and I heaved violently. Fortunately, I didn't have anything left to vomit up. I breathed slowly. The sickening sensation was real, but for the first time I was sure of its source. The goddess still accepted me when I reached for her. The sickness and doubt, it was all in the brand twisting my face. The curse didn't stem from the Lady's symbol— it was the dead inquisitor's mark, a malediction of zealotry and obsession disguised in the words of scripture. I hadn't been worthy in his twisted estimation. I'd thought that meant Pharasma had judged me unfit as well. The icy bit of wood in my hand promised that wasn't the case.

I swallowed the nausea. It was fantastically uncomfortable, but I could bear it. I swept the amulet over my head. The spiral fell over my heart, holding fast in that familiar place. I laid my hand there. Even through my shirt it still felt cool.

"Thank you, Lady."

I grabbed the lantern, adjusted my grip on the wet stake, and went to the open door. The Lady of Graves was just, but she was not merciful.

39

BLOODTHIRSTY

LARSA

I leaned on the warm, slightly sticky railing of Kindler's porch and sighed. The air tasted cold and coppery in the worst way.

The whole day had passed while I'd been inside, coaxing memories from Kindler's self-inflicted amnesia. Even after uncovering her experience beneath Caliphas there were still endless intersections between her life of monster hunting and her obsessive search for Rivascis. We meticulously picked them free, but I hardly heard many of her later tales. I humored her, waiting for the account of her return to Caliphas to learn more about her missing child. Yet when the wand's magic revealed no more, that story hadn't trickled forth. I left the old woman dozing in her library, exhausted by the weight of returned years.

The sun had already fallen behind the hedgerows. In the yard, corpses in rags still lay amid shrubs and mismatched little gardens. Nothing had disturbed them. Even with the gate clearly open no one had bothered to investigate or, more reasonably, alert the constabulary. Spoiled blood seeped into the grass, the drive, the porch's boards, all wasted like cheap wine left out overnight. My mouth was suddenly dry.

Pharasma—maybe less a prig than I'd thought—saw fit to tap the veins of fate. A heavy breath escaped from a facedown body sprawled on the porch stairs.

I yanked him up by oily curls and gnawed through ruddy skin, trying to ignore the feel of moles on my lips. The resulting gush was slow—he was obviously almost spent—but he still had pulse enough to keep his blood warm. He was already dying, so I allowed myself to be decadent.

"Does vintage mean nothing to you?" The voice surprised me, but not enough to stop. Only once the gush slowed to a cool leak did I pull away with a gasp. For the moment I wasn't thirsty, but I certainly didn't feel satisfied.

Considine leaned against the house at the far edge of the porch, condescending with a slow headshake. His anemic rafter-rat fluttered to the top of the farthest column, staring at me with buggy black eyes.

I wiped my mouth with the back of my hand. "Where have you been?"

"Visiting with our dear father." He rubbed something between his fingers, exaggerating his nonchalance.

I rolled my eyes. "I've seen him as well."

"Finally had the reunion you always dreamt of?" He'd heard me fantasize about taking Rivascis's head more than once.

"Yes and no."

"Seems like more 'no' than 'yes,' to me."

"Nothing to report back to Grandfather about yet." I hadn't forgotten the reason he'd been sent to keep watch on me. "One conversation doesn't mean I've forgiven him for a life of slavery."

"Slavery," Considine piped. "So dramatic."

"What about your visit? Should I be concerned about you returning to his service?"

He shrugged. "He made an offer."

"And?"

"And he made an offer." He shrugged as he turned to survey the yard. "You've been busy. Who are they?"

"It wasn't me. Sounds like they're Rivascis's thralls. They came with a foreigner in black and tried to carry off Kindler."

A brow arched. "You don't say? So your traveling companions did all this?"

364 F. WESLEY SCHNEIDER

"Seems like they did the best they could. Jadain's missing. They beat Rarentz nearly to death—"

"No shame there," he interrupted.

"And Tashan . . ."

I had his attention. Eternal youth made it rare that any sort of gravity weighed on Considine's features. But for an instant, he was a man of his true age, the frailties of his hundred years obvious in his darting eyes. It so surprised me that all I could do was nod.

Considine followed my look to the body-shaped pile of ashes heaped against the doorframe. A bronze sword lay next to the heap, the pommel's eyelike design sealed beneath a lid of soot.

Something in Considine's continence quivered, then burst.

Mist tumbled across the porch. It seeped between slats and wafted against my boots. The fog was thin enough to see the mossy floorboards through by the time it washed around Tashan's corpse. It thinned further.

There was no distraction in the yard-turned-battlefield. Beyond the city's austere spires stars were just beginning to appear out of the deepening dark. I watched a dozen blink open, then a dozen more.

Most of the light had faded by the time a column of fog soundlessly built itself at my side. Considine's thin shoulders froze in its midst. Wood screeched as his nails dug into the railing.

We stood not speaking for a while.

"You tore your vest." I finally ventured without turning.

"Yes . . ." His voice sounded just as casually bored as usual. "I'd grown especially fond of it, too. My favorite for quite some time, actually."

I nodded.

"Someone's going to pay for that." Turning away, he headed for the far end of the porch. "I've something to show you."

I rounded the side of the house just as Considine squeezed a heavy chain in his palm. It burst, its loops falling away from the cellar door's handles. The flimsy wood panels clattered open and he vanished inside.

"I took it upon myself to see if our hostess had any conveniently dark places hidden away." His voice descended the rickety steps. "As it turns out, she does . . . and better." The stairs that barely squeaked at Considine's passage groaned under my steps. For not the first time I considered the wisdom of following a vampire into the dark.

Kindler's basement was much as I expected, filled with the shapes of dusty boxes, old furniture, and the like. Considine touched a lantern and gave an impatient command. Light sprung from it, though no flame burned within.

A broad circle etched the flagstone floor, its cultic geometries traced in crimson wax. That was something of a surprise.

Not the only one either.

I'd spent the day listening to Kindler recount tales from her travels. Although they were filled with mysteries and strange explanations, they were still an old person's stories—epics to her but meaningless episodes to anyone else. They'd already blurred together in my mind, but here they became real.

"This is all from Kindler's travels . . ." There was plenty to take in.

Brushing dust from the lacquer surface of a portable Pharasmin altar, I avoided the pieces of silver cutlery impaling the wood. "She just told me about this. It's from the failed exorcism of House Beumhal. Three priests died trying to expel a knocking spirit from the hostel's kitchen."

I slipped deeper, between stacks of crates to a leaning coffin-like box. Although its iron surface was fixed with a dozen padlocks, its doorlike lid lolled open. Desperate scratches scarred the interior. "She imprisoned the ghoul-mayor of Clover's Crossing in here. The thing starved inside for a month before it gave in to interrogation.

"And these are likely some of Ramoska Arkminos's failed cures for vampirism." I ignored Considine's snort, pulling a lengthy red vial from a full wine rack that clearly didn't hold a single vintage.

"Even this." I strayed back to the room's center, kneeling at the sinister diagram's edge. "Kindler and her colleagues summoned the devil Abeixul right here, and convinced it to return the soul of Istan Calmeyer's nephew."

When I looked up, Considine was watching me. "What?"

"Sounds like you've joined the old woman's church." Suspicion tinged his voice.

"Quiet. I've been listening to this all day."

Not that he was wrong. I was definitely more than a little impressed. Tales I could have written off a moment ago proved far more impressive with the realities—often grim ones—collected before me.

"Oh, then I suppose you won't be interested in these." He toed open a chest's lid and nodded, purposefully keeping his distance. "Look familiar?"

They did.

The chest's padded quarters brimmed with glass flasks, mirrored squares of silver, mummified bulbs of garlic, sturdy lengths of sharpened hawthorn, and stranger paraphernalia. Most were tools I was well acquainted with and, from another perspective, so was Considine.

"Been snooping?"

"Simple curiosity." He shrugged. "And I'm glad I did. I was set to make this my temporary residence before seeing these. I'm not terribly interested in being the boar that fell asleep at the butcher's."

Kneeling, I tested the weight of one polished stake. Something inside shifted. I barely felt the hidden seam and, twisting the tip, dumped the contents onto the floor.

Considine was past me in a breeze of chilly mist, reforming quickly. "Watch that now!"

The water pooled, clear and plain. Considine's reaction answered my question as quickly as it entered my mind. Holy water. Handy.

Nodding, I replaced the stake with the others, noticing in doing so that all the others were not stakes. Discarded among the wood was something far more elegant.

The dagger was light, as if carried by the spreading wings that formed the hilt. A carved bird skull stared from the intersection of blade and grip, its hollow sockets encrusted with dust. The residue made it look like it had just woken. Even in the dimness the silver blade practically glowed.

Silver, which with the right incantations . . .

"Ensorcelled?" I asked, holding it up for Considine to examine.

He rocked back, but something caught his attention. Muttering without words, he leaned in to studying the thing.

"Oh," he said after a moment. "Oh, that's nasty."

"What?" I pulled it back, looking into its eye sockets.

"Whoever made this had a grudge." He gave a dark chuckle and nodded at the knife sheathed at my hip. "Cut me."

My look told him not to dare me.

"Really. Do it." He gave his cockiest grin.

That made it easy. The familiar edge gleamed, arched for his forearm, and bit. Not deep, though, as there suddenly wasn't anything for it to slice but spreading mist. Considine reformed a step away, the nick on his arm already healing.

He ignored my "So what?" look, nodding at the other blade. "Now with that—and nothing fancy."

Was that worry in his voice? I repeated my stroke with the winged dagger. The blade pierced and slid effortlessly. Before I could jerk it back, it had transfixed the vampire's arm. We both made surprised sounds, Considine's through gritted teeth.

I yanked the dagger back. It made a sound like it was being drawn from a sheath. "Why didn't you dodge it?"

Considine clapped a hand over the gouge piercing his wrist. The first knick was already gone, but this looked like it would take longer to heal. "Like I thought—nasty thing." He nodded at the dagger's dry blade. "Something locked when it touched. Not quite as bad as being staked, mind you, but truly an unsettling feeling."

"You couldn't change?"

He shook his head. "I really don't know how you manage, always having to drag all that weight around."

I pointed the blade back at him and he lifted his hands in surrender. This was already proving useful. Reaching back for the dagger's sheath, I found something better. The dagger's twin was a perfect match. Hefting one in each hand, I found their weights to be identical. These were true treasures.

I fixed the sheaths onto my belt, but kept one dagger drawn. "Why are you showing me these?"

His head made a bored roll. "I haven't had to bother with Father's delusions of justice and deservedness for some time. I've recently been reminded that I prefer things that way."

"So you want me to use these against Rivascis?" I didn't take to the idea of being his cat's-paw.

"What you do with them is your business. Visit the Royal Opera, perhaps. I just came from there, it's quite a lovely building—if you don't mind rats. Or Pharasmins."

Pharasmins? "Jadain?"

He closed his eyes and again showed his palms. "I merely want to ensure you have your full range of usual options."

"Right."

"You've always called your particular brand of stubborn nonsense 'justice.' Here's a box full of it. Share as you please."

I scoffed, sheathing my new dagger. "If that were the case, do you really think you'd benefit?"

"Normally, no." He flipped back another box lid and shook out a long cloak of dark leather. It was patched, but well kept, with a severe style. Unlike the one I'd lost in Kavapesta, this was obviously tailored for a woman.

"You're trying to buy me off with a cloak?"

"Of course not, dear." Grinning, he reached back into the case and withdrew something equally severe. "I know you much prefer hats."

40

MONSTER HUNTER
JADAIN

Having teeth doesn't make you a wolf, little lost priestess." The unveiled creature's voice slipped between moldy wood crates. "Even mice can nip."

The empty cellar room where I'd been held opened into another basement room, this one crowded with all manner of crates and stranger shapes. It felt larger, despite the junk, but I couldn't be certain.

"I once treated a drunk who had his fingers eaten off by rats," I said into the dark. "When I told him I needed to take his entire hand, he didn't sound half as worried as you."

I raised the lantern high, illuminating a leprous giant's skull. It gaped from atop a stack of musty banners, its eyes red sequins, its parchment-bone crumbling. Beyond stood row after uneven, awkwardly stacked row of crates, scrap timber, and enough hanging garments to shame a queen's wardrobe. Pulleys and rigging dangled from the rafters, casting tall shadows amid so much that already resembled half-hidden figures. The garish colors and strange shapes made it look as though someone had locked away an entire carnival down here, then forgot it entirely.

I began cautiously down one aisle, choosing the one crossed with the fewest torn banners and stray limbs. The lantern light seemed to spread farther than it had in my prison, a mixed blessing as buttons glistened and shadows swayed with every step.

The sharp wood in my grip twitched every time I thought I saw a glint of gold.

"Are you hunting me, blind little mouse?" The voice came from nowhere in particular, echoing off stone here even while musty gowns swallowed it there. "Do you want to meet your goddess so badly?"

Dull pain burned my face. "You had your chance for that. It's my turn to return the favor."

Her ugly rattle-laugh drifted above the clutter. "When I die, the Horsemen will tear apart and devour my soul. A feeble thing like you won't be what sends me to them."

"Then why hide?"

Silence.

Could be she didn't have a quick retort. Also could be I was getting close.

I stepped through a row of fallen polearms with blunt wooden heads. They were props, like so much in this basement. Beyond them, collected bits of set dressing matched in shades of black and crimson, repeating patterns of horns and flames. Exaggerated suggestions of red-faced devils leered out of the dark. The wooden head of a single massive fiend loomed like a gate, so tall its fiery brows scraped the ceiling. Its mouth gaped wide enough to consume the damned three abreast, and mirrored eyes glinted as I approached.

Slipping between the hellmouth's blunt teeth led me into a cramped corner of the room. Battered wooden representations of torture devices lined the walls while heavy curtains hung in tight bunches. Grim-faced iron maidens surrounded a long pine box. Whatever performance these were all for, I had no interest in seeing it.

Gold danced at the edge of the lantern light and my scrap of wood jerked up. It felt desperate.

Fortunately, the metal wasn't affixed to a familiar gown. Rather, it was a brooch hanging from one of the corner's bundles of dark fabric. The piece of jewelry was far from alone. The entirety of the curtained mass sparkled with mismatched trifles, glittering earrings, sunburst brooches, a Sarenrite's ankh, gold foil twisted around iron bands, and more. Individually, the tiny decorations would have been entirely unassuming. Set on somber fabric in their haphazard collection, they openly betrayed their owner.

Something behind me dripped.

I spun, a prayer on my lips—but again, nothing was there. A muffled drop sounded once more, water splashing into water. I knew my captor was wounded, but surely not badly enough to be sopping like that. The noise was faint and close. I held the lantern toward it, raising it to the box at the makeshift room's center. Not a box at all, I realized with a second look, but another exaggerated recreation, this time of an overlarge coffin. If this were the urdefhan's den, it made some sort of sense—a fake coffin for a would-be vampire. At least she was practicing.

The goddess's symbol, tangled in my grip with the stake, spun as I drew closer. Its shape—seeming more familiar than it had in days—reassured me even as a mild nauseous tide rocked my insides. I pushed past the sensation and whispered a prayer, calling on the goddess to reveal evil even where I couldn't see. I didn't expect the magic to pinpoint the creature, but it would let me know if she were close.

The hint of evil was a bitter taste in my mouth. I circled the wooden case, wary of what might lurk within. The sensation grew stronger, not in the direction of the coffin, but toward the wider room.

She was behind me. Maybe I could use that fact to draw her out.

So softly I could barely hear my own words, I called upon the goddess's aid again. Once more she acknowledged my prayer, her touch a cold, depthless constant far beyond the sickness that momentarily welled up as I whispered. The air around me grew cold, like a cloak left on the line overnight. The goddess's protection might have been invisible, but if she willed, it would protect me against any evil. Once I might have hoped it would be enough to defend me. Now I knew it either would, or I would soon stand at her side. Neither option was mine to choose, though both agreed with me if such was the Lady's will.

I threw off the coffin lid as dramatically as I could. "Ha!"

I didn't have to feign surprise as it flipped high and crashed awkwardly, the wood proving far lighter than I'd anticipated.

"Indeed." Her voice was close.

I spun. She was there, standing among the devil's fangs. With a hiss she threw fingers of black and gold toward me. Noxious green light burst from her palm in a crackling, grasping limb.

Familiar words were on my lips. If there was any chance the goddess held me in disfavor, this was sure to fail.

The light's point coiled and dove for my neck.

I sped through my prayer.

With neither sound nor burst the fetid light vanished.

"What?" the urdefhan shouted over the final word of my prayer. Shock turned to rage. She rushed forward, eyes blazing, fangs naked, a vision of damnation clattering through the hellmouth.

My prayer rose on a scream, becoming a condemnation. Between us, light froze in shades of chilling flesh, icy shards forming a radiant dagger. I felt it like it was tethered to my heart, an extension of my conviction manifested by the goddess's might. It sought my command.

The urdefhan saw the blade and twisted past. Across her rags, every dented bauble glared hatefully. Claws rose for my face, not to grip, but to skewer.

A dozen terrible ends came to mind—the Nidalese Quiet Death, the Qadiran Kiss for a Traitor. I pushed my training aside. Whatever this moment was, it would be mine.

"Take her!" I didn't need to speak. The blade, sensing my desire, pivoted and struck like a winter gale. Dreary ribbons tore, gold ornaments rained and shattered. The divine dagger slashed lines of frozen light, vicious and impossible to follow.

A terrible noise, less a scream and more the rattling of alien organs, escaped her. The woman in black stumbled. Fleshless hands came up only to be slashed to the bone. She twisted to keep her invisible attacker in sight and turned her back on me. As firmly as I could, I grabbed her by the arm and heaved. Shock visibly reverberated through fleshy spindles in her transparent neck. She seemed hollow. I heaved, toppling her into the coffin. She landed with a crack. The impact repeated an instant later as the dagger slammed down, piercing her chest, pinning her into the false casket.

The dagger's cold light illuminated her from the inside, shining out through the slashed gown and skin like a sea creature's.

"Master . . ." The gurgle sounded like a word. "You promised."

Then her life leaked away.

With the slowing jerks of black veins, the dagger's glow faded. A moment later it too was gone. In the lantern light, tarnished jewelry glimmered indifferently.

Something dripped, louder now and more steadily than before. I lifted the light over the corpse. The coffin's bottom was stone—or rather, the coffin had no actual bottom. The floor beneath was visible, along with a sewer drain barely large enough for a rat to squeeze through. A rivulet of blood wormed into that darkness, each drop's plummet marked by a steady "tap" into some deeper pool. The sewer, from the smell.

The urdefhan's lips lay less than a finger's length from the drain. I'd thought her final words were merely a dying regret, but as something heavier than a blood drop splashed below, I wondered if I wasn't the only one who heard.

41

STAGE FRIGHT
LARSA

I couldn't trust Considine, so I went to White Corner first.

The Mirage Theater was empty and looked like it had been for years. The stage was dark, and not even rats bothered to provide an audience. Still, I searched the place, checking for any hint that Rivascis might return. There was nothing. Even his paintings were gone.

I suppose it made something like sense. If Rivascis really had been an actor in life, he wouldn't keep to the same copper-a-ticket theater. He'd have higher ambitions.

Maybe I'd misjudged Considine.

It was well past midnight by the time I reached the Royal Opera, so I didn't expect the gate to be open. Still, it swung with hardly a touch, iron acanthus leaves giving with ghostly silence.

The Ardis Royal Opera posed beyond, a temple of sculpted columns and arches crowned by angelic musicians. If Considine hadn't told me otherwise, I would have thought the playhouse ready for all the pomp and drama of the city's elite. Supposedly, the opera had closed its doors a decade ago.

Tonight, no one had reminded the lamplighters.

Delicate lanterns shimmered in rising ranks upon hundreds of unwashed pillars. Gigantic twin braziers, their flames caged beneath bands of wrought-iron ivy, lit arching staircases at the end of the stony drive. The only shadows allowed to linger settled between great doors etched with heavenly scenes in tarnished bronze. The opera's entryway stood open, but seemed far from inviting.

I felt like I was spoiling someone else's entrance.

Instinct and habit urged me away from the light. Perhaps there might be some side entry amid the willows and footpaths winding around the place.

I caught myself. Why waste the effort? Supposedly, I was welcome here.

The lanterns stared, critiquing every step as I crunched down the gravel road. If anything other than flames watched from the columned balconies or rows of slim windows, it didn't make itself known.

No footman met me at the stairs, no host watched the doors. I passed inside.

The domed interior seemed every bit as open as the grounds beneath the cloudy sky, and I felt no less exposed. Somber flames stood stiffly upon somber tapers, a thousand matching candles set in lush iron candelabra. Sculpted ivy and more black acanthus wound up bony marble pillars to a broad mezzanine. Shadowy steps formed twin stairways, built to channel patrons toward the rows of theater doors above.

My every step was a drumbeat on the domino-patterned marble. Constant reminders to myself that I was welcome here didn't make it less unsettling. If Rivascis was to be trusted, I shouldn't have anything to fear. My wariness spoke semiconscious volumes on that topic. Still, I climbed. Our last meeting had taken place on a stage, so I sought another.

Entering the theater proper was like passing into the heart of some gigantic beast. The place practically bled, velvet seats descending in a crimson cascade, rows of darkened boxes like chambers ready to pump. The balustrades lining the balconies interrupted the gory motif with polished walnut carved in the shapes of stags, knights, and unrecognizable crests. The sculpted figures froze in their race toward the proscenium arch, the stage's sweeping frame carved with a lofty battle between broad-shoul-dered knights and crumbling skeletons. At its apex, the royal crest, with its stars, antlers, and tower, shone in gold and red stones. But it was far from the theater's centerpiece.

The footlights beamed. Center stage hunched a row of five funeral biers, each draped in dour cloth and strewn with flowers, as though the caskets they bore held the bodies of fallen royals. Above each hung a great, full-body portrait, furthering the impression of a royal funeral. Each painting flattered a noble figure: a man with a butterfly amulet and black ponytail hiking some idyllic mountain trail; a spectacled woman without a wisp of hair working diligently over books and beakers; a victorious knight with golden hair that gleamed brighter than her sword and a shield emblazoned with wolves; a dashing fellow laughing as he offered a toast from a warm-looking taproom. I'd seen them all before, posing in the portrait in Kindler's parlor—her former adventuring companions.

The fifth, central piece I also recognized. It was Rivascis's portrait of me, of Kindler—who could say. Apparently completed, it hung like the others in an ornate brass frame that looked heavy enough to crush a horse. Unlike the others, it did not hang over a casket. The bier beneath was empty.

"Do you like them?" Rivascis's voice boomed from the stage, filling the auditorium. He hadn't changed since last night, still dressed like a lord thrown from his horse.

I strode down the aisle. "What am I looking at?"

I could hear his smile, the grin of an artist invited to talk about his work. "Simple reminders."

He adjusted the wild flowers overflowing the casket beneath the portrait of the dark-haired man. All of the coffins were full with them, though none of the arrangements were the same—wildflowers for the first man, rhododendrons and foxgloves below the bald woman, snowy lilies and red tulips beneath the last two. The central bier was bare.

I tried to keep mindful of the open space, not eager to be eavesdropped on by an entire audience again. All the theater's seats seemed empty this time. The balconies and boxes above, I was less sure of. "You've certainly chosen a dramatic spot."

A sweep of his hand encompassed the whole auditorium. "Where better to draw the curtain on a performance that's gone on far too long?"

"Whose performance?" I had to shout to be heard.

"I've lost count of the full cast, but the major players have always been myself and the woman who used to be your mother. Yet when even the antagonist stops caring about the plot, it's time to draw things to a close."

"What plot have you stopped caring about?"

"Me?" A grimace almost locked back his chuckle. "I'm sorry, my dear, you have me all wrong."

He strolled past the plain bier at center stage, dragging a finger across its surface. "No, I'm afraid Kindler has always been the motivation behind all this. She's been the one to force scene after scene, even when others were content to let the past fade away."

I rounded the orchestra pit and climbed onto the stage, avoiding the heat and glare of the hooded lamps. Standing, I saw the corpses.

None of the flower-filled caskets held flowers alone. Wasted skin and bare bones served as beds for the lavish gardens. Each looked old, one being little more than a shattered skeleton.

"So you're going to add her to your collection here?"

"Oh, this isn't my collection. It's hers." His wave encompassed them all. "Each a fine soul buried by her recklessness."

He slipped to the bier occupying stage right, placing his hands at the head of the casket beneath the portrait of the traveling man. "Jaivin Whilwren followed Ailson into the woods outside Chastel. He recovered bodily from being savaged by wolves, but they say the curse of the beast has no cure. Ultimately, your mother cut his throat."

He moved to the next. "Oralo Viacarri championed reason and the sciences, but Ailson ever dragged her toward the precipice of insanity. Your mother abandoned her in the catacombs of Rozenport, where libraries and prisons are one and the same.

"Aleidamor Graydon. A knight who died believing Kindler had saved her from a life of ball gowns and perfume.

"And Duristan Barlhein." He rapped the final corpse's forehead. "This one so wished he could have been your father. He fell to a creature your mother mistook for me."

His stroll ended just past Duristan's bier, only steps away from me.

"Each one of these idealists was swept up in Ailson's obsession, her quest to reveal the world's dark places. She convinced all of them that daring was somehow a shield, and they followed her places she had no right to lead. They believed she was a teacher, a beacon against fear and ignorance, but she was easily the most broken of any of them. None knew how often her cases, her explorations, followed my travels. They died never knowing they were pursing me."

His arrogance was plain and I didn't care to indulge it. "So what? You're saying her reputation's a lie? That she's not some famous monster killer? You can't tell me all her work is just a side effect of chasing you."

He shrugged. "If you don't believe me, then believe her. She's won quite a name for herself: Ailson Kindler, lady of the haunted page. She's made no secret that her tales spring from her own deeds, her characters just masks disguising her and her compatriots. Her stories are gory trifles, but I assure you, her every ink drop equates to ten times that in spilled blood. So why would she pay such a high price? Why would she let students, allies, and friends fall by the score? For truth? To help strangers? Armies don't die under those banners. But for passion, obsession, revenge . . . ooh."

If he could still be aroused, I was sure I'd see gooseflesh prickling his marble forearms. "She could have just hated you and everything like you. Crusaders have banners, after all."

"Exactly! That fire, that thirst! She bent her life, her mind, her world to hunting me. And she was close—so often, so close. More than once I barely escaped her. She lit the sewers of Karcau alight just to drive me into the dawn—in all my centuries, that's the closest I've come to true death.

"Surely you know how hard it can be to feel alive, truly alive. How much more difficult do you think it must be for those of us who don't draw breath? For decades, Ailson Kindler made me feel alive, made me struggle to continue being, and reminded me I'm not truly dead yet."

He shook a tight fist. When it unclenched, I could clearly see the dark holes his nails dug in his palm. The four bloodless gashes knitted closed almost immediately.

"But all of that faded." His hand dropped. "I don't resent her aging, I resent her burning low. When truth and revenge proved too elusive, she settled on fiction and coin. And when even that didn't satisfy, she packed it all away. That beacon that these souls gave their lives for, that so often managed to sear me, chose to snuff itself out. You've met the woman in that moldy house. I told you she was your mother, and once that was true. Now, though, that place is only home to Ailson Kindler's shadow."

I looked back over the hall, just to be sure. It still appeared empty. "What's all this, then? Will you call your audience when it's time to kill her?"

"I hope it doesn't end as plainly as that. I don't want to kill her." He followed my look out over the absent crowd. "I want to restore her, to rekindle what she locked away within herself. I want to set her free."

"Really?" If he'd set Kindler as the villain of his story, his tone convinced me he thought of himself as a hero—a savior. I nodded to the caskets. "With these? Her dead friends?"

"There's no door to the prison she's created, but I'll break it open with a chisel and mallet if I must. This—" He retrieved a slender length of dark wood from where it lay upon the central bier: another wand. I suspected its powers were similar to the one I'd used. "This is my chisel. And these," his arm arched past the four corpses, "my hammers. I don't expect my work to be clean, but it will not fail."

Certainly he didn't realize I'd already restored Kindler's past. I doubted he'd react well to learning his performance was spoiled, but the vampire's fury was preferable to putting Kindler through this. I still heard her pain, the wail and small sobs that nearly broke her. Those had just been from the memories. Revisiting a lifetime of loss with the grisly results . . . I couldn't fathom how Rivascis could plan such a thing and still call himself hero. "You understand you're bringing back the darkest parts of her life. All her sorrows."

"Not the darkest parts, I assure you. But in part, yes." He didn't sound sympathetic. "I need strong moments, memories that will fight to return. Those I've brought here, they're scars on her soul. No magic can just erase them. I will show her the mirror, but I'll also guide her through the pain."

"You? She hates you. Even if she's forgotten, that's sure to come back. Do you really think she'll be grateful?"

He twitched. Certainly that thought couldn't have surprised him. "I have been the passion of her life. She's known no greater challenge, no greater love than me. I am the thread that connects all of these events," his hand traced a path, then fell open toward me, "all the way back to you."

Of course. The realization was like climbing stairs and *then* noticing the shit on your boots. "I'm one more corpse in your gallery."

"I need you here. You're family. She could never forget family."

"I was never her family!" Vague frustrations growing since Kindler's library crystallized, then cracked. "If she *ever* wanted me, she didn't once she realized what you were. I've never been anything to her—to either of you."

His expression narrowed. "What would ever make you think any of that?"

I cursed. I'd said too much. He certainly hadn't told me about Kindler's days beneath Caliphas. That anyone in the Old City would have known the particulars of his tryst seemed unlikely. I snapped my jaw shut. Unfamiliar fangs scratched my lower teeth.

Seeming to see me for the first time, he took a step closer. "You're wearing your mother's clothes."

I fought the instinct to grab the winged daggers beneath my cloak.

"You look so much like her in them."

I took a step back. "You know she'll never be the woman she was. She's never going to hunt you again. She's old now. She spends most of her time in a wheelchair. That happens to them—to us."

He shook his head. "There's still life in her. The chase isn't over yet."

"Even if you bring back her memories, she's not going to be the woman you remember. She's not going to stalk you across the world."

His jaw tightened. "Then perhaps it will end here. If there's nothing left of what she was, then our affair might finally, truly be over." The words ground out grudgingly, as though this were the first time he considered them. "If that's the case, I'll look her in the eyes one last time, and then end it. Even then, I'll have my loss. Either way, I'll have something." He put a hand to his still chest. "Something here besides cold time."

This wasn't just about Kindler. "You're not trying to take Grandfather's throne. You're trying not to become him."

The vampire stopped short. The suspicion in his face faded. He stared past me.

When he spoke again, something in his voice sounded like Kindler, remembering. "He offered it like a gift: never wither, never die. I was just past being young. My audiences loved me, my rivals envied me—why would I ever want it to end? What did I know?" He let something invisible fall away. "I leapt at the chance."

His lips drew a bitter line. "It took years to see the lie, but I saw it in him first. Whatever Luvick is, he *has* withered, and he has died. Life simply doesn't flourish in corpses. It might linger, but it leaks away in time."

Rivascis shook his head. "I felt it in myself. Every emotion became like a faded picture. There was thirst and distractions from the thirst, and I knew I'd eventually tire of distractions. I considered watching a sunrise.

"Before she came, I'd mused that there might be another way. Luvick and the others never truly took me seriously. Maybe I never did either. But when Ailson came, something stirred. I didn't recognize it at first, and even once I did, I wasn't sure. I realized I wanted to protect her, and then, I wanted to protect what I felt for her. For a moment, she didn't care what I was. For a moment, I was alive again. You came from that moment." He looked through me. "I couldn't leave her with Luvick, so when I could, I set her free. I asked her to come away with me. It was too late. What I'd done, following my supposed-father's schemes, had turned her against me. I was only a monster to her."

His look settled back into the present. "That's when I left. That's when they branded me a traitor, not just to Luvick's selfish rule, but to his dead, pretentious vision of what our kind should be. I traveled far, not just to avoid my sire's grip, but in hopes of recreating what I found with Ailson. Yet nothing ever bloomed. But it didn't matter, because she eventually came back to me. Her feelings for me might have changed, but not mine for her.

She chased, I fled, and I was alive again." His gaze lifted. "Then it ended."

His voice didn't carry for long. The hall drifted back into silence.

I spoke slowly. "This was never about you and Grandfather You've never been the threat Caliphas's vampires made you out as. You left to chase Kindler, then to be chased by Kindler. And now, all this—it's still about her."

And, like always, I'm just a pawn in it all.

My crumbling sympathy sounded Grandfather's voice. *Blame your father.*

"You won't just leave her be, will you?" It was a simple question, and I asked it as such.

An incredulous brow climbed. "If the fire that drove me across the world for the better part of a century has died, let it be dead. I won't be haunted by ashes."

"She isn't dead yet."

"Exactly, which is why I wanted you here to meet your mother, to remind her of what was. But Considine, I needed him to be my errand boy one last time."

"Considine?" I already knew I shouldn't have trusted him. "What's he have to do with any of this?"

"As much as I've hoped such wouldn't be the case, I'm forced to accept that you might be right. I might have to end the life of my last great love. If that's the case, then I won't let it be a waste. Considine will carry what happened here back to the corpse-nobility of Caliphas. He'll tell them that I did what Luvick never dared—that I put an end to the greatest vampire-killer of our time. You're right, I'm not the rebel-demon Caliphas's vampires make me out to be. But there's still time for that."

I almost laughed. "You'd rely on Considine? Fickle, unreliable Considine? Melancholy, hates-you-for-making-him-your-slave Considine?"

He ignored my humor and simply nodded. "No flattery is more true than your enemy's."

Considine might be a joke in the Old City, a pariah who'd only escaped execution so he could be tormented. Yet despite his nonexistent status, everyone knew he'd been Rivascis's slave—even though he'd refused to follow after his master's betrayal. He'd been lauded for his loyalty to Siervage, even as he was denounced for betraying his creator and prince.

"He won't be so easily manipulated. Knowing Considine, he wouldn't speak a word of this just to spite you."

"I've known Considine for far longer than you. He is my son, after all." His fangs showed as he smiled. He nodded toward the back of the theater.

Past the footlights' glare, standing halfway down an aisle of red, Considine stood smirking. He awkwardly adjusted a limp body over one shoulder, a frail gray frame trimmed in lace.

Considine had sent me here. Then he'd abducted Ailson Kindler.

42

SHADOW PUPPETS
JADAIN

The rickety steps whined like a dozing animal as I climbed two at a time. Fortunately, I reached the cupboard-sized door at the top before the doubtful things decided to pitch me off.

I pressed my back to one cold stone wall, alone with my breathing and the dark well below. Listening, I stared back the way I had come, expecting the jangle of metal or a sinew-draped skull. Yet my own ragged breathing was all that disturbed the shadows.

It took several tries to look away from the stairs dropping away below. Each time I was convinced that I'd glimpsed something just as I turned away, that I was about to miss the last thing I'd ever see.

Damn this. I barged through the door and threw it closed behind me. The latch snapping shut was an incredible relief, dispelling images of slug-white fingers bursting through the narrowing gap. When nothing slammed against the closed door, I fell against the opposite wall—the close and surprisingly comfortable opposite wall.

Cushions, each a satin square perfectly sized for an individual bottom, stood in roughly even, waist-high stacks. Hundreds ran down the hall and out of my lantern's light in both directions. I leaned for longer than I should have, letting the quiet softness comfort me. I had no more sense of where I was here than below, but the air didn't pile upon itself like the inside a crypt. I breathed, remembering the ache in my face, the tortured skin throbbing at my wrists and ankles, the blood crusting my hair. As urgency faded, the pain rose.

A prayer of healing came to mind and, squeezing my amulet, I ignored the familiar sick sensation and spoke quickly. The goddess's breath rose as I called, blowing across the worst of my wounds, tingling my abused joints and face. The numbing cold faded quickly. My hand went to my face. The gash was lessened, but still there.

I couldn't linger, wherever this was. It would have to be enough. Lifting myself from the soft heap, I picked a direction and pushed on.

It seemed like a servant's passage—close, with a low ceiling and unadorned walls. Eventually the stacks of cushions ended, replaced by tall rolled awnings or banners. More short doors appeared, some opened. Inside, my light picked out sewing tables and mountains of thick fabrics, but only high, narrow windows. Perhaps this was some sort of workhouse.

The hall finally ended in a corner room of benches and short cubbies. Red coats with tasseled epaulettes dangled in several of the alcoves, uniforms long employed only by moths. I barely paid them a glance, going immediately for the door. With the flip of a latch it opened and the night flooded in.

The vastness froze me. I'd expected some alley or muddy yard, not the endless sky and racing water. Garden hedges slid away in gentle slopes, slender trees posing alongside as they tumbled toward what looked like a tear in the night sky. Above, clouds blew like tattered pennants before a vague patch of moonlight. Below, the night had crashed to the ground, growling as it sought ways back aloft. Several stars had been dragged down with it, bobbing unsteadily as they sought to keep their places. Only faint lanterns on distant piers brought sanity to the view of three mighty rivers meeting and careening through the dark.

The structure I'd barely set a foot from stood undaunted by the great rivers beyond. A cliff of blind arcades climbed over me, regularly interrupted by dark glass and friezes of wan angels. I felt the gazes of shadowed celestials, but not only theirs.

The garden wasn't empty. Dozens of bodies lay scattered across untended lawns and stained benches, a small army of tin knights cast aside by some divine child. But it wasn't a battlefield. While I couldn't be sure in the moonlight, none were obviously wounded or bloodied. They would have looked like they were merely sleeping, except that none had their eyes shut. Dozens of heads lazily rolled to look at me.

Squat stairs led from my door down to a path slipping away around the temple-like building. The way was scattered with bodies. I'd lost my fear of corpses long ago, but these . . .

I eyed the mound of rags sprawled across the bottom of the steps. The heap stared back from beneath heavy white brows, any suggestion of a face lost amid deep wrinkles and a beard of bristles. I recognized it all the same.

Careful not to disrupt the lulling rush of the rivers, I crouched on the stairs. I reached out to the old man, checking for some sign of life. I didn't dare more than a whisper. "Sir?"

His watery eyes didn't move. Maybe I imagined it, but now they seemed to see, fixing *on* me rather than through me.

"Sir, are you . . . all right?" Of course not, but I couldn't think of anything else to ask. Still, he didn't respond.

Uncertain, my hand danced in the space between us, reaching, drawing back, reaching. Finally I touched his shoulder, something between a comforting pat and rousing jostle.

The rags toppled and spread, cracking and rustling as they pushed themselves up. Beneath those damp, dark eyes, a gap in the beard fell open, his face and mouth rising as though he meant to swallow me.

I leapt back as he gained his feet, his form lost in a patchy heap. There was nothing in those eyes, no recognition, no intent. I'd seen the dead walk, seen corpses strung with foul powers into magical marionettes, but this was different.

"Sir!" I filled the whisper with all the severity I could. Sharp wood dug into my palm. The desperate sensation was becoming familiar. My shiv came up.

He ignored it, stumbling up a step. I had to give ground just to avoid stabbing him.

"Sir, please!"

His mouth worked like a fish, toothlessly gumming the space between us. With a muffled clop, he climbed. I fell back farther. In the yard, more of the fallen took note. Heads rose, hollow eyes narrowing on our scuffle.

Even if I did overcome the old man, even if I could bring myself to silence him with a crusty splinter, how long before those others were on me? I could feel their coarse hands already. Was this the half-dead mob that had dragged me from Miss Kindler's?

It didn't matter. This couldn't be the way.

I grabbed the door handle and pulled hard. A thick glove came up. His eyes said nothing, but as the door slammed, I realized what was half hidden within his stained beard. That mouth opening and closing, hidden lips repeating again and again: "Help."

But I didn't know how.

The door quaked under a heavy blow. I flipped the flimsy-looking latch and backed into the hall I'd just followed. The door quivered under another slam, the bang echoing, but it held.

For how long, though? My only choices were the long dark hall I'd already followed, or on through the dressing room.

Someone else made the decision for me.

An indistinct voice reached me. I couldn't make out the words or the distance, but it definitely came from back down the hall.

It could have been Rivascis returning, growling orders after finding his minion dead. That would have been fast, even for an accursed thing like him.

Another slam upon the door shook the whole wall.

I couldn't stay. The mindless thing outside wasn't as easily deterred as I'd hoped. I tried to make out more of the voice. It came again, but offered no reassurance. It was too far off, too indistinct.

At least it was someone, in a place perhaps better used and lit than these forsaken halls. If nothing else, I'd seen what lay behind the structure. Perhaps the front would offer an easier escape.

I rushed back the way I'd come, moving as fast as I could while keeping somewhat silent. Behind, wood splintered. Ahead, the voice grew louder . . . and more familiar.

43

MALEDICTION
LARSA

Considine." I spoke as evenly as I could through clenched teeth. "Put her down."

He brushed the words away, strolling down the aisle with the old woman slung over his shoulder. "Oh, it's quite all right. She weighs almost nothing at all, and I've already brought her all this way."

Rivascis was already watching when my look shot to him. I closed on him quickly, steps resounding like blows upon the stage.

He answered my unspoken question gently. "I told him to."

It all seemed suddenly familiar: Kindler, swooning over Considine's shoulder, like any soon-to-be bloodless victim. Rivascis, arch and arrogant, so like the creatures of the Old City he claimed to loathe. They looked like the garbage I'd spent years scouring from Caliphas's streets.

"Tell him to put her down." I drew Kindler's dagger, its whisper sounding like a slow, eager "yes" as its silvered blade slipped free.

Rivascis's head tilted a single surprised degree. "No."

The blade practically flew for his chest.

Even surprised, Rivascis likely could have darted away, avoiding the lunge entirely. Maybe he expected another violent tantrum. Maybe he wanted to further remind me of the threat I didn't pose. Regardless, he was wrong, and didn't move.

Silver sizzled in his chest. Dead flesh hissed around the gleaming metal, the wound's edges shriveling, turning rotted

392 F. WESLEY SCHNEIDER

and black. The shock of one who'd entirely forgotten a sensation contorted Rivascis's expression. His look snapped to his chest. I drove the blade and whatever toxic blessing it bore into his ageless husk.

His growl seemed to emerge from the wound before slipping between bare fangs. Too late, he surged backward. The speed of his retreat yanked the blade from my hands, but the dagger—a veteran of who could say how many slayings—refused to let its prey escape. It clung fast, burning the vampire's core.

Traversing half the stage in a blink, Rivascis yanked the dagger free. The wound's withered edges hung dead, making no sign of knitting closed. He sneered at the clean, gleaming weapon, strangling it in his grip.

"This was to be *our* moment . . . if needs be, our revenge!" There was more in his voice than just anger. "She would have remembered and we'd be what Luvick never let us be, or she'd die and we'd have the closure we both needed."

"I didn't come here to be a part of your stage show." The dagger's twin drew just as eagerly. "You almost made me forget why I traveled all this way to begin with. But your tirade reminded me. I came here to kill you, and damn it, I'm going to do my job."

He spat. "A killer for humans that fear you and dead things that resent you."

"Maybe. Or maybe I've just decided to make sure there're fewer reasons to be scared of the dark."

Whatever hopes remained in Rivascis's eyes froze and died. "So be it." He threw a clawed hand toward me as he shouted, "Take her!"

Hours of preparation were instantly ruined. Precisely arranged petals cascaded, hands rotted into claws drawing four corpses awkwardly from their coffins. Dead eyes, or the darkened absence of eyes, turned my way. Nearest me, the remains of Oralo Viacarri scrambled to extricate herself, violet-stained claws scoring casket wood. From between fangs fell an obscenely long tongue, as plump and bruised as if she'd been strangled.

My dagger spun from the vampire to the thrashing thing. As soon as I split my attention, Rivascis's form tore itself apart. I cursed, but couldn't follow as the ashen smoke wisps slithered from the stage.

Viacarri's hungry husk burst free in a whirl of broken nails and teeth, and three equally ravenous corpses followed.

44

CHARMING THE DEVIL
JADAIN

It was a theater, and the stage was far from empty. Coffins, giant portraits, and hundreds of flowers framed the production already in progress. Larsa brandished a dagger at the monster who'd left me prey to his servants. Their words boomed through the hall—the not-so-empty hall.

Midway down one of the wide, crimson-carpeted aisles stood the only member of the audience. The only two members of the audience, I realized as my eyes adjusted to the low lights.

Miss Kindler lay wilted over Considine's shoulder, her normally tightly packed hair falling down the vampire's back like unraveled lace. She looked smaller than last I saw her, facing down intruders on her lawn, and didn't move.

The funeral bier positioned at center stage was empty. Was she bound for it?

I hesitated, and Hell's gates tore open.

Larsa's blade disappeared into Rivascis's chest, a blow that momentarily pinned time in place. Stillness reigned for an instant, a crystalline quiet I feared my frantic pulse might shatter. Unstoppering his bloodless wound, Rivascis freed the dagger, along with the breathless moment. The shouting upon the stage turned to growls and orders. Larsa was armed again.

Closer, Considine rolled his head impatiently.

The rich carpeting masked my footfalls, but I didn't presume he wouldn't hear me coming. The pathetic piece of wood in my hand made a desperate weapon, but it had already pinned Considine once. If it needed to, it would make a fine threat.

The vampire turned a cheek toward the hall's unlit chandelier, addressing the ceiling. "You didn't leave a mess downstairs, did you?"

"Someone cut me free. I was bound to defend myself."

"Well it smells like you reveled in it." He turned, training his cynical consideration on me. "Ugh, did you skin her?"

"Please put Miss Kindler down." I adjusted my grip on the makeshift stake.

He cooed, as if over some decadent dessert. "Did you get a taste for killing in the dark? How your church charity group will gossip."

"I don't want to hurt you. Just let me take her out of here."

He drew himself up. "Can you hurt me? Can you bring yourself to do it? My favorite servant?"

He winked, and his eyes glimmered emerald.

The color of the ocean welled up at the edge of my sight, the hall's crimson sinking into the murky shade. All around, the glint in the vampire's eyes seeped in, soft and calm, unavoidable and certainly lethal. It seemed like the color poured into the room, but I knew it was all in my mind. That shade, an intruding reflection of Considine's eyes and whatever unspoken will lurked behind them.

I clenched my eyes shut just to avoid drowning, whether in the vampire's gaze or the silent waves eroding reality. But the rotten green didn't fade. Even behind my eyelids the color spread like ink from an idle quill. It looked so much like deep water that the drowning sensation felt natural.

I gripped the goddess's symbol, clinging to it like a buoy. The sinking sensation lessened, but not because of the cool calm of Pharasma's power. The goddess's dead chill was there, but it was merely a wisp amid the whirl of nausea that swept through my body. The spinning sickness, so reminiscent of the spiral clenched in my palm, forced out everything else. The lapping emerald tide rippled and faded, like a flood scattered by a hurricane.

The sensation was hardly comforting, but at least it was familiar and came from inside me.

"You are not welcome." I glared at Considine down the length of my outstretched arm, across the soft blue glow that spun in my vision. "Not in my mind and not in this place."

"Oh dear, now you're starting to sound like a Pharasmin." He flexed his neck. "Do you abjure me? Do you condemn me to some untidy hell? Oh, I know—"

"Perversion of life and the Spiral of Souls, in Pharasma's name, I cast you out!" The goddess's symbol flared as I thrust it toward him. Pale light and cold air burst forth, and suddenly the amulet wasn't a mere thing of twine and wood, but a door to the chill halls of Pharasma's immortal court. The touch of death—true death—was in that cold caress, a solemn promise to the living but, to a thing like Considine, a harsh reminder of his false immortality.

His wan features withered as if scoured by flame, and his words died on a tongue that wasn't there. I drew my amulet back, gasping. I'd meant to rebuke the strange vampire—the dead man who'd, after a fashion, saved me at least once—not burn him to ash.

His shape billowed, a dank mist riding the crest of the luminous wind. Nothing more than vapor, he surged back and scattered like a ground fog retreating from the dawn.

The rustle of Miss Kindler's skirts was louder than the slap of her body as she struck the ground, facedown. Forgetting Considine, I rushed to her side. Maybe she was made of tougher stuff than it looked. Maybe every bone had shattered without bothering to make a sound.

"Goddess willing, this isn't your time," I muttered, checking her arm for breaks. Finding none, I rolled her over. She gave a weak but heartening noise. "Ailson? Are you all right?"

"Call me . . ." her eyes didn't flutter, her voice was barely a whisper, "Miss Kindler."

She'd survive. The goddess either loved or loathed the salty ones. In either case, she never rushed to collect them.

Something cracked. I was momentarily weightless, then skidded on my back a dozen feet up the aisle from Kindler, all before I even felt the impact. The force of the blow left me gasping. I struggled to get my elbows beneath me, gulping to recover my air. My chest felt somehow loose. I could feel the bruise radiating out, slow and warm.

Rivascis's bent over Miss Kindler, his grip sinking into her sleeves. Yanking her from the floor, he spun her to face the stage. There Larsa gave ground before a quartet of corpses. The hanging portraits were idealized reflections of the sagging flesh and moldering clothes below.

"Do you see them? I found them all. The ones you called family. The ones who died for you—because of you. Do you see? Do you remember?" Rivascis's every word sounded like an accusation.

The old woman could barely struggle in the vampire's grip but turned her head away as best she could.

"This is your doing! You spent each of their lives chasing me, and now what? Do you even recognize them? Are they even worth a memory?" He shook her, his voice fierce. "Do you even remember *me*?"

He twisted her to face him, leaning closer with every word. "I knew you'd never love me, not after you learned the truth, but I made do with your hatred. All those years, I accepted every failure and sting knowing they were ours to share. But what you've done . . . locking it away, discarding all those years. Everything it meant! Everything we were!"

He pressed a bloodless cheek to hers, forcing their shared gaze to the haunted stage. "I won't let you forget. All of them, they're here to make you remember. I've restored the only friends you ever had, found the daughter you never knew. I've brought it all for you." His growl balanced on the edge of tears. "And by every dark space between the stars, I swear, you *will* remember, you *will* be that relentless angel once more, or I will scatter whatever embers you've left behind and mourn the ashes."

Miss Kindler stared blankly back at him, her eyes wet, her hair falling in dusty ribbons. She showed no fear, but also no recognition.

The vampire read the same and sneered into her stranger's face, his thin lips pulling back from vicious fangs.

I tried to shout for the goddess, but the words caught in a fit of violent coughing.

Rivascis leaned for Miss Kindler's throat, a lion intent on helpless prey. I could barely breathe, much less move.

But Miss Kindler's salvation was far closer at hand.

45

REVENANTS
LARSA

Oralo Viacarri's jaws chattered for my hand as it drove into her shoulder. Stretched flesh tore beneath my fingers. I shoved, narrowly avoiding the claws scrabbling to dig into my skin. She flailed, still grasping, as she toppled from atop her bier. Her engorged tongue—easily as long as my forearm—lashed amid a dust storm of flaking, dead skin.

Falling, she became entangled with the creeping corpse of Jaivin Whilwren. Not being particular, the other corpse sank teeth like broken glass into her shoulder. She didn't scream.

It would take a moment for them to untangle themselves. I spun, bringing my dagger up defensively. Steel and bone rattled as the skeleton of Aleidamor Graydon lowered herself from her bier. With a deliberate, fleshless hand the armored bones reached back into her coffin, lifting from it a fire-scarred sword seemingly made to cleave foes in half. With a strength freed from sinew, she hefted it with one bony claw.

The dead knight had to wait, though, as I realized why Duristan Barlhein had lingered in his coffin. I knew the man only from his portrait and Kindler's wistful comments on his charm, tight bottom, and skill as a marksman. The former two had most certainly rotted away, but some hint of the latter remained. His tongue, like a half-swallowed garden snake, slid salaciously up the quarrel he aimed from his dirty rosewood crossbow.

I dove behind the unoccupied central bier, landing amid a rain of splinters. Just behind me, a bolt slick with corpse juices embedded itself in the neighboring coffin. Beyond that, the hissing ghouls still wrestled to untangle themselves.

Iron-shod bone marched closer. My cover wouldn't matter for long, and there were too many to take down one by one. I cursed myself for having seen the corpses and assumed that was all they were—one moment was all it would have taken to sense the undeath in them. Self-condemnation would have to wait if I was going to survive to bully myself.

Dispatching the two ghouls as they struggled apart was sure to earn me a quarrel in the back, as was attempting to retreat offstage. Chasing down the crossbowman would win me the same, and I'd have to avoid the knight's mountain-cleaver. This would have to be fast.

I snatched one of the hollow stakes from inside my cloak, snapped off the tip, and stoppered the cavity with my thumb. A bolt whispered through the air, sailing above my cover. Another, louder whoosh followed. The gigantic blade screeched as it struck, spraying the stage with sparks. As I flung myself away, my hat caught on something. I looked back to see Graydon's sword embedded in the marble bier, pinching my hat's brim between stone and steel. She hadn't bothered with the slow march around the marble slab, but had tried to go through it. Over the split stone lip, her skull's sockets bore their darkness into me.

I kept low against Viacarri's bier, but in rounding it came within full view of the thrashing ghouls. Their tongues noticed me first, bloated worms blindly sensing my pulse. Their sunken eyes caught me and their struggling took on renewed vigor as they fought to extricate limbs, claws, and mismatched teeth from one another.

I dared a quick glimpse over the stone. Fortunately, flighty Desna, goddess of bad plans, smiled down on me. I'd guessed my position closely enough. The armored corpse fought to reclaim her weapon from the marble. With no muscle to flex or breath to grunt, she froze, straining in one unrelenting tug. Behind her, the deathless marksman frothed, his view—and more importantly, his aim—blocked by the knight's rust-pitted frame.

Momentarily shielded, I let the other corpses come. Possessed by jealous hunger, they scrambled one over the other, their claws etching furrows in dry skin, jaws tearing loose clothing and hair. My stake swept through the space between us, and I slipped my thumb from its tip. The arc of holy water sparkled in the footlights.

It caught Viacarri full in the face and chest. Where it struck, the blessed water meted out years of denied decay. Dead flesh sizzled and fell away in curling flakes. The nightmare thing's seared tongue recoiled behind her shattered teeth, stifling the hiss-shriek escaping her withered lungs. Frantic claws bailed the water from the pits of her eyes, destroying whatever lingered inside. She crashed backward.

Still teeth came. The holy water had barely spattered Whilwren. He leapt his former companion's convulsions, nails and tongue outstretched. I fell back toward the stage's rear curtains, remembering my narrow band of cover and the dead marksman too late. Cursing myself, I grabbed the hungry corpse's wrists and spun. Almost immediately my grip slipped, his flesh sliding like a loose sleeve. Whilwren's anxious tongue slapped my neck, teeth chasing after. Before they could tear away my throat, the ghoul jerked, a spray of bone fragments dusting my face. Limp, he crashed against me, and I heaved him back. The corpse fell upon Viacarri, a quarrel jutting from the back of his head. Blind and thrashing, Viacarri furiously attacked the corpse, indulging her hunger on dead flesh.

With a rumble like the opening of temple doors, Graydon's titanic sword slid from its stone prison, dropping my hat to the ground. Though far less nimble than the fleshy dead, the skeleton took a rattling step back from the marble, then toward me.

402 F. WESLEY SCHNEIDER

I slipped the silver dagger in and out of Viacarri's neck with neither effort nor sound. The dead woman gurgled and her torment ended.

Obviously some memory infused the skeleton's bones, her sword rising in the stance of a veteran soldier. Keeping distance from her and out of sight of Barlhein's crossbow forced me back out from between the biers. Nothing separated Graydon and me now. With her every step, bones clattered against steel, sounding like the tramping of an entire legion. It made her sound invulnerable. I could easily out maneuver her . . . if I wanted to catch a quarrel like Whilwren.

She came on. I backed to the edge of the stage.

I darted forward with my blade, little more than a dinner knife compared to her head-taker. With surprising speed, her sword arced. I dropped to me knees to avoid it. The slab of steel shattered one of the footlights, sending brass and sparks exploding across the stage. With a bound, my feet were back under me. I rose fast, bringing my dagger up at the same time. It scored Graydon's breastplate and, skipping over her gorget's lip, slid across her utterly exposed skull. Silver hissed on bone, but left nothing more than a fine white line on chin, teeth, and cheek.

Limned in sparks, her sword rose, but her bony claw came up faster. I leapt back too late, and she caught the front of my cloak. The leather stretched between us, too tough to tear or twist out of. Gritting teeth at the gamble, I spun to the side, letting the leather fan between us. The skeleton's skull, claw, and sword followed as I darted from behind her.

Barlhein's crossbow snapped. The quarrel hissed. A coin-sized hole appeared in the stretched flap, hardly a breath from my chest.

With only a moment, I slammed my dagger into the thin bones of Graydon's hand. Whatever foul power gave them motion didn't give them unnatural durability. Finger bones shattered and

I was away. The air stirred with the passage of her gigantic blade even as I raced across the stage.

Barlhein was already reloading his weapon, his clawed fingers twitching as they worked, his tongue pointing like a stray digit that didn't know how to contribute. I launched myself into his coffin just as he brought his weapon and attention back to bear. I slammed my dagger into the bow. He fired. The taut string released, but caught on my blade. The loaded quarrel sprang from its track, toppling into the coffin.

The undead thing hardly seemed to notice, his nails already grasping for my throat. One set of broken claws clamped onto my shoulder. They dug through my thick cloak, into my skin. The corpse's touch was death itself. Instantly I was aware of every vein in my body, every current of warmth beneath my skin infected with a gripping cold. My joints stiffened.

I was back in Kavapesta. Back in that cell. Back in the prison that was as much my own body as a thing of stone and burning light. I tasted blood in my mouth.

Barlhein's tongue—just as bloated and wild as the other ghouls'—lashed my cheek as he leaned in, his jaws opening over my face.

Not again. My growl sounded through my teeth, resisting from somewhere deep. I wouldn't be a prisoner again.

Shaking with deathly cold, my hands shot up. My left snatched the ghoul's wriggling tongue. My right gripped my dagger.

The ghoul tumbled back, out of the coffin, trailing clumps of congealed gore. His severed tongue thrashed in my grip like a decapitated snake. Tossing the disgusting thing away, I followed the hissing corpse. He had landed awkwardly on his back and twisted to right himself. Black spatters flew as he hissed.

Rivascis said this man had wanted to be my father.

My boot came down on the neck of Kindler's onetime lover with the sound of a rotted branch snapping. I ground my heel through the former hero's wormy spine.

Far too late for all that.

I'd been aware of tromping bone and steel, but I started as the next clang landed so close. I spun. Graydon was there, her skeleton jaw lowered in a soundless battle cry. Her sword was already falling.

The light was blinding.

46

PENITENCE
JADAIN

A length of twisted yew slipped from Miss Kindler's sleeve and angled toward Rivascis's face. She spoke a word, clear and strong.

The wand erupted with a geyser of light. Radiance, harsh and dawn white, exploded between the woman and the vampire. Rivascis's face glowed in a moment of stark under-lighting, his gigantic shadow splashing across the ceiling. Just as quickly, his sharp features seared like parchment over flame.

Only the first syllable of a scream echoed through the hall, the rest cut short as the vampire vanished into a plume of pyre smoke. As if propelled back by his own scream, Rivascis's smoky cloud toppled down the aisle in a shadowy avalanche.

The light from Miss Kindler's wand faded, but still she tracked the smoke's densest part, aiming another blast of smuggled sunlight. Faster than any natural smoke, the vapor tumbled into the orchestra pit.

Turning her aim to the stage, the supposedly retired monster hunter commanded her wand once more. Another brilliant beam cut through the dismal theater. On stage, its sharp swath illuminated a single battered coffin, a pair of gleaming footlights, and a fleshless figure in antique armor. The skeletal knight froze, its gigantic sword hefted like a headsman's axe. Some caliginous stain tore loose from the corpse, burning away in the harsh light. Bones and armored plates shuddered, then crashed to the stage in

406 F. WESLEY SCHNEIDER

a battlefield hail. The massive blade was the last to fall, striking the decapitated helm with a defeated clatter.

A step from where the swath of light faded, Larsa removed her elbow from her eyes. Her cloak was ripped, but she kept her feet and collected her hat from across the stage.

"Are you all right?" I asked at Miss Kindler's side. She took my arm before I'd offered it, pulling herself to her feet with a creaking sigh.

"I'll pull through." She was already descending the aisle, white wand still at the ready.

Larsa perched on the stage, overlooking the orchestra pit opposite us. Trim chairs, music stands, a conductor's podium, and the like collected in the recess. It was dim, but there wasn't so much as a wisp of smoke.

Miss Kindler frowned.

"He could be anywhere." Larsa checked about her, dagger still in hand. I did the same. Every seat, box, and balcony was filled with shadows.

"Yes, but he won't be back here. You've spoiled his performance." Miss Kindler nodded past Larsa. Flowers, broken lighting, coffin splinters, and old corpses littered the stage. "He's a perfectionist. He won't try again until everything's in order."

Her nonchalant commentary surprised me. "I thought you didn't know Rivascis."

"Your friend helped me remember."

"He's retreating." Larsa ignored my curious look. "This wasn't his plan. If we're going to finish him, now's our chance."

"He's wounded and it's almost dawn," Kindler said. "He'll retreat to his sanctuary."

"I found him holed up in another theater in White Corner. It might be there."

"Maybe, but he would have been taking a risk meeting you there. He's smart enough to know you'd think to look there, so I doubt it."

Larsa rose, ready to move. "I'm not losing this chance. If we hurry, maybe we can spot him leaving."

"He won't just run through the streets, either as a man or mist. It's too near dawn and too obvious."

"Then what, that's it? It almost sounds like you want him to—"

"Under the theater," I interrupted. "There's a coffin down there. A grate underneath leads to the sewer."

A touch of surprise lifted Miss Kindler's brow, followed by the barest hint of a smile.

"Show us." Larsa vaulted off the stage. I was already rushing back up the aisle, Larsa only steps behind.

"I'll stay here, if it's all the same to you." Miss Kindler took a seat in the front row.

I halted. "I don't think that's wise, ma'am. He could be back. And there's a mob of his servants outside."

"All the more reason not to leave." She didn't look back. "Unless you expect me to crawl through some sewer with you?"

Larsa passed me. "She can handle herself. Come on."

I hesitated, but didn't argue, following Larsa. I spared one more look as we dashed from the theater. Miss Kindler sat still in the front row, staring at the portraits still hanging over the stage.

The coffin in the cramped basement storage space hadn't been disturbed—a tangle of limbs wrapped in a somber gown overflowed the lip, just as I'd left them. Larsa kicked the coffin. "This is it?"

Slow black blood dribbled through the metal mesh at the casket's bottom, each drop echoing in some hidden cistern. The grate was even smaller than I remembered.

Through her transparent skin, the dead urdefhan clenched her teeth, grinning wickedly.

I didn't bother to answer.

Larsa nodded at my amulet. "Can your goddess get us through, or track him, or . . . ?" She made a frustrated gesture.

I shook my head.

She cursed loud enough for it to echo.

"Such a lady." Considine's voice preceded him into our lantern light.

My hand was already around the goddess's symbol, but Larsa was faster. She bounded across the coffin, following her silver blade.

"Careful! Careful, now!" He straightened, practically levitating as Larsa's knifepoint edged beneath his chin.

"Why?" she shouted into his face. "Why tell me where he was? Why give me these—" her blade jerked, "if you were working for him?"

He grimaced against the razor hissing at his neck. "He told me to fetch you and bring the old woman. He didn't say anything about giving you an arsenal and setting her loose when it was most opportune."

I shook my head. "He only dropped Miss Kindler after I burned him."

He shrugged, keeping his eyes fixed on Larsa. "Just keeping up appearances. Plausible deniability and whatnot, in case things went sour."

"You're trying to play both sides. Like always." The winged blade hissed louder, etching Considine's chin.

His neck craned. He talked faster. "Why would I help him? You know how he left me. What I've endured since."

Larsa had none of it. "I know you're a liar and a selfish coward who can't be trusted."

Considine's eyes widened by little more than a hair, but the surprise was there. His mouth worked, as if fighting to swallow a bite of bad meat. It took him a moment, but when he spoke again his voice was cold. "You were there. You saw the ashes."

Tashan.

She held his eyes, looking for the lie. "Why should I believe that one, out of all your pets, mattered?"

He didn't have an immediate response. "I don't know." He managed to shrug a hair higher. "I don't know if we get to pick the ones that do."

She looked like she was already regretting it, but she pulled the dagger away. "You can get through." She nodded at the grating.

His lip curled, but he didn't push her. He nodded. "I can."

"Can you find him?"

"It'll be a maze down there. Even if he did pass through, he wouldn't have left a trail." He turned his nose away from the rusty bars.

"He did. I can feel the chill from his passage, but it's already fading. You can track him the same way if you put your magic to it."

"Through a *sewer*?" His pursed lips wrestled one another. Larsa's face was steel. "You're going to owe me for this."

"I didn't stab you." Her nail clicked on her dagger's tiny skull, emphasizing how quickly that could change.

"Hardly a favor."

She rolled her eyes, but nodded.

"Vris is getting fat off mosquitoes in the courtyard. He won't be hard to spot. Once he starts circling, follow him. He'll be able to tell where I'm headed." Considine didn't wait for Larsa's nod. His fog circled the grating like water in a drain, then was gone.

Finding the bat was easy enough. Following it through the Ardis night seemed next to impossible.

Before I could complain, Larsa was off at a run. I chased after, trusting in senses I certainly didn't possess to lead us. Not that she was much easier to follow. Even with her eyes locked on the fluttering thing, she still outpaced me. I struggled to keep up, but didn't bother to call out. I knew she wouldn't slow.

The opera's courtyard was empty except for shadows cast by struggling braziers. Either the vagrant army only bivouacked at the theater's rear, or it followed its master into the dark. I didn't waste the time to finding out. We were through the opera's gates and into the empty streets before any of Rivascis's slaves made themselves known.

Only a faint night mist wandered the streets. If anyone else strolled Ardis's avenues in the earliest hours of morning, they knew subtler—and likely safer—routes than we. Vris led us east, unsurprisingly toward the abandoned district called White Corner. As we neared, the blocks huddled together, tightening in sloppy, uneven shapes. Larsa slowed to a jog, struggling either to follow the bat between mismatched roofs or to split her attention with the increasing number of cluttered alleys. Gradually, I managed to catch up with her.

"I saw Tashan," Larsa said as I came alongside, her eyes remaining fixed on the empty black sky. "How'd it happen?"

I tried to keep the panting from my voice. "One of Rivascis's cronies. A monster disguised as a woman."

Though it was hard to tell while running, I think she nodded. "The thing in the basement?"

"Yeah."

"Your work?" She spared a quick glance.

"Yeah." I said matter-of-factly.

Larsa maybe nodded again.

Almost an entire block passed before she went on. "I'm sorry I wasn't there."

I'd never heard her apologize. I suspected she didn't often, and probably wasn't practiced at it. The trace of guilt was obvious in her voice. I tried not to make it worse. "You couldn't have known what Rivascis had planned."

"I could have. I knew what he was. I shouldn't have run off."

Something rote came to mind, something about the goddess and everyone having their time. I had counseled enough survivors to recognize the vague "would'ves, should'ves" of those who went on living. But Larsa sounded as though she were stating pure fact. Maybe she should have known.

"Then you owe Rivascis." I didn't meet her look when her head turned. "Probably we both do. This isn't just your revenge anymore."

She didn't say anything, but that time I was sure she nodded.

White wings swept low across the cluttered street. We both ran on into the slum.

The sickly bat circled a tavern crushed between two larger buildings. The two-story wreck looked like the keystone of the entire block, being the smallest structure but also the only one sound enough to stand on its own. A stained signboard shaped as a coffin bore the name "The Boneyard." A salaciously alert, wood-grain skeleton sat upright in the coffin, staring down and grinning with too many teeth. Unhinged doors stood jammed into a heap of garbage and wooden wreckage spilling through the entrance. The place looked empty, but I supposed that made sense.

I stared at the heap of street junk blocking the way in. "We'll have to make some noise to get through."

Larsa's hat bobbed. "Likely the point."

"Worth trying to find—"

"He's got nowhere else to go." Mounting the junk heap, she gave one of the doors her heel. It shuddered. A few more solid kicks and it cracked, toppling through a gap tall enough to crouch through.

It was completely dark inside. Larsa didn't wait for me to relight the lantern. She drew her dagger and disappeared from the misty street.

It took a moment to rouse the lantern flame back to life, but when I did, the light seemed small and useless. Fortunately, I wouldn't need it much longer. Already the barest hint of color was creeping into the sky. Morning wasn't far off. I just hoped I'd get to see it.

Holding the lantern high, I clambered over the waist-high junk pile and followed Larsa inside.

I worried about making too much noise when the cold floorboards squealed beneath my boots. Less so when Considine's body crashed down from above, a silver blade skewering his neck.

47
WHAT THE GRAVE
WON'T HOLD
LARSA

It wasn't just a tavern. The Boneyard was a box house, something akin to a bar, a brothel, and—true to Rivascis's form—a theater. Vampires were all predictable in their own ways. More than once I'd wondered if imagination was a trait of the living, if new ideas could take in dead ground. In any case, Rivascis never abandoned what he was in life, refusing to venture far from the stage.

Not that this wreck at all compared to the Royal Opera. The Boneyard's day was years past. Waves of looters had hollowed out the taproom, leaving little more than the raised stage. The platform abutted a bar that could have served as a promenade. Hollow personal boxes lined the walls, once offering lounge seating for those seeking more discreet performances. Yet despite the stripped furnishings, no looters had been daring enough to risk the half-collapsed catwalk dangling in the theater's middle space.

Miles of ropes ensnared rickety slat walkways; tangled cords gripped sandbag clusters mid-fall. Among them dangled cockeyed curtains, iron trapezes, even a pair of coffinlike dancing cages— heavy-handed callbacks to the morbid house name. The full extent of the deathtrap's convolution faded into shadowed rafters, but it shifted and groaned like an animal left to starve in a snare.

Rope twangs and clattering chains preceded what I expected to be a crashing metal landslide. Leaping back, I narrowly avoided Jadain following a weak light through the door. The body struck with a meaty slap—a body in a torn red vest. The twin to the dagger in my hand fully pierced his neck, its point bloodlessly emerging from the opposite side.

I'd expected to have more of a hunt ahead of me than this.

Tugging the dagger free, I expected Considine to dissolve into fog and blow away somewhere safe—he'd be aware of dawn's approach even more than I. But he didn't. Once extracted, the blade's magic should have released his full suite of vampiric tricks. Still, he didn't so much as smirk. He might as well been a corpse . . . more a corpse.

"See what you can do." I tossed Jadain the winged dagger. "And if you need to, use this. It won't stop Rivascis, but it will slow him down."

She nodded, already dropping to Considine's side.

I leapt the body, snared a chain dangling almost to the floor, and climbed. Rivascis had that dagger when he fled the opera. He was up there.

Hand over hand, I swung up, alert for the sounds of bending metal or tangled scaffolds tearing loose. Whatever the chain was attached to slid, giving a lazy metallic yowl, but it held. At its top, I found myself at the center of the web of damp rope and rotting boards. The dark didn't hide much from me, but countless slack ropes and stray timbers obscured dangling shapes. It was like I'd slipped into the wreckage of some hovering shipwreck. I pulled myself onto an angled length of catwalk, a small island amid the knotwork maze.

"So whose slave are you really?" Rivascis's voice drifted from nowhere in particular. "I recognize your mother's daggers. Did she convince you that you're not one of us? That there's a place for you in the light—among the living?"

The catwalk creaked as I inched down its length. He was speaking, which meant he had to be solid. *Keep talking.*

"There's not, you know. They'll never understand. You'll always be their monster."

"She didn't convince me of anything."

"Then you're really nothing more than a slave. I assume Luvick's—you couldn't honestly consider Diauden master."

I swung off the catwalk, pulling myself toward another island of knotted chains. "You're so concerned about my employers. I've got plenty of my own reasons to want you dead."

"You've imagined enough."

"Did I imagine all those years under Caliphas?"

"Dear," he pandered. "We only met yesterday—never before. Anything you expected of me, anything you think I owe you, you've concocted for yourself. I've done nothing but heal your wounds and tell you the truth."

"You killed Tashan. You tried to kill Miss Kindler." I tested the strength of a tangle of sandbags. Two slipped free, falling soundlessly then bursting upon the bar below with heavy sawdust thuds.

"The slave of your master's dog and a woman you also only met yesterday. I'd never have expected such a sensitive soul to bloom in Luvick's charge."

I sucked my teeth and slid past the sandbags onto a thick beam. Past it hung more thick ropes, off-kilter lights, and one of the coffin-shaped cages. The cage was closed, but wasn't empty. Inside, almost as tall as the cage itself, was a plain box, a pauper's casket.

Rivascis's casket.

His ultimate retreat. He hadn't hidden it underground, where the light couldn't reach and where a hunter might expect. He'd hidden high, someplace pursuers wouldn't think to check and where, if they did, they might break their necks trying to navigate.

Three slow, chiding clicks sounded through the rafters.

"Kindler didn't try to use me as part of some twisted revenge parade. If I'm a romantic, I'm taking after you." I grabbed a chain supporting an iron chandelier and, giving it a cautious tug, swung onto it, closer to the coffin.

The light fixture dropped. My stomach lurched, my breath bursting out in a sound of wordless shock. The floor rushed up.

The iron snapped and swung, throwing me to my knees atop the chandelier's mismatched arms. I grabbed the suddenly taught chain at its center. Forcing my eyes away from the floor, I looked up into the rigging for a safer place.

Rivascis reached from behind the angled strut I'd just stepped from, one hand holding the chandelier's rusty chain beneath a broken link. The entire contraption, with me on it, dangled from his grip.

The feather pattern on the dagger's grip dug into my palm. He was so close.

He stared down. "Careful."

I stood cautiously. Kneeling, he extended his free hand down to me. "I knew it would be dangerous to be my child. I know that doesn't make up for what you've suffered."

I took his hand and he lifted me up. The chandelier dropped away, its crash shattering metal far stronger than bone.

"Perhaps I can find a way to make up for those years. Perhaps together—"

Still suspended dozens of feet above the stage, I lunged, jamming the bird-skull dagger into his chest.

He didn't drop me. Despite the surprise, then wrath that cracked his stony expression, he didn't let me fall. His grip tightened and I expected to hear my wrist crumble, yet he didn't lash out. The dagger might have pierced his heart, but even with its magic, it wasn't a stake. It wouldn't paralyze him, just lock him in one shape.

He spoke calmly, eyes darkening. "I warned him, warned Siervage, that servants would be less troublesome than children."

I sneered, reaching for one of Kindler's stakes even as I snapped some retort. But my mouth refused to open. My jaw was numb, my tongue dead. Still his eyes darkened, growing unfathomably deep.

They looked like a sea on a moonless night, a vast body in which no light could survive. Those dark waters slipped the banks of his eyes, surging on the tide of a will that defied even death.

It crashed over me, and I began to drown.

48

AN ENEMY'S ENEMY
JADAIN

I almost screamed when Larsa fell. My heart lurched, and when a white claw caught her wrist, it didn't return to its place.

I looked for an answer in the corpse sprawled in splinters in front of me. Considine was dead. I just couldn't be sure of *how* dead. His wounds had knitted closed, but he hadn't moved. He wasn't ashes. If he were truly dead, I was fairly certain that age and decay would have caught up with his body, leaving nothing but a heap of stale salts.

That hadn't happened, and that was my conundrum.

I knew how to reduce him to that, how to burn the blasphemous life out of him. The prayers to do it were at the forefront of my thoughts. The memory of his emerald eyes crushing me against the back of my own mind was also at hand. I'd burned him with the goddess's light once and he fled. If I burned him again, he wouldn't have time to escape.

Larsa kicked in Rivascis's grip, finding nothing but open air beneath.

"Damn it." A healing prayer leapt to mind, but I pushed it aside. The blessing of life wasn't want the vampire needed; it would only sear him. Even after all I'd seen, the thought of calling the goddess's death-dealing touch still sickened me. I refused to call upon her to pervert life, to make the unnatural flourish, even for such a dire cause. So the wicked riddle shouted through my head: how do you bring death to the dead?

Blood.

He lay there, mouth slightly agape, thin fangs barely exposed. Could he have just overexerted himself? Could he just need a few drops . . . ?

If I couldn't bring the goddess to him through my prayers, maybe I could restore him myself. I brought Larsa's dagger to my wrist and took a deep breath.

"No need for all that now." Considine gave the barest smirk, his eyes still closed.

In relief, I slapped his chest with my damp palm. "Are you all right?"

He feigned a gasp. Mossy eyes peeled open and he wiggled his fingers. "Well enough, considering my father just stabbed me and broke parts I'd forgotten I had." He gave an earnest pout. "I'm starting to think I'm not the favorite child."

"Larsa is up there with him right now. She needs help."

He followed my eyes, arching to look back over his own forehead. He rocked with his small nod. "Seems like it."

My eyes bulged. "She needs *your* help!"

He drew out an unmotivated hum.

"She's your sister! You have to help her."

It sounded like his shrug creaked. "I say that, but—you know—not by blood."

I gaped. He really wasn't going to do anything. "Even if so—please."

"Sorry, just don't see the odds in it." He sat up on his elbows. "Better that we get out of here—the city, I mean—before Rivascis wakes up from the nap he's about to take."

Larsa's body had gone rigid. I couldn't see her face or the monster that held her in the shadows.

I jammed the silver dagger into Considine's leg. The goddess's blessed spiral was in his face before he could complain. "I could burn you right now. Help her!"

Hissing, he recoiled. I was too close, though, and the dagger's magic did indeed seem to be slowing him down. He jerked his face away. I considered forcing my amulet against his cheek, burning the Lady's mark into his alabaster skin.

"Considine. Please." I pulled the painful symbol back.

"Desperate!" Turning back, he bared his fangs in a smile. "I'm impressed. Fine, fine, get off me."

I leaned back, giving him space, pulling the dagger free at the same time.

He twisted, looking up at Larsa and the catwalk above. "You're going to owe me for this."

I nodded.

For a moment I thought he was talking to me in another language. The rhythmic noises he muttered sounded older than words, arcane syllables utterly different from my prayers. An oily shape congealed between his hands. His fingertips caressed it, molding it into a globe. With a rush of light and heat, the conjured shape ignited, and in the next instant exploded forth. The ball of flames streaked like a comet, burning back shadows as it careened directly at Larsa.

This time I did scream.

49

BLOODLETTING
LARSA

Every muscle numb, every thought suffocating beneath the crush of Rivascis's will, I barely noticed the noise and burning light suddenly filling the rafters. Rivascis looked past me, then everything blurred.

My back slammed against a horizontal beam. The vampire was over me, a slab-cold layer pressing down. Even through the haze of his presence, I had enough control of myself to rail, to scream, even if that thrashing only raged within my head.

He was going to drain me. He would tear open my neck, my life would leak out, and he would live on for an eternity more. The one end I always expected, the one end I dreaded most, was now.

I could still feel the dagger in my grip. Even though I couldn't move, I could still feel it biting into his body. This might be the end, but at least I could delude myself into believing I would die fighting back.

The roof beyond exploded. Fire erupted around us, raining down from above in a hellish storm. The beam beneath me cracked, slipping a span as all around the web of knots and platforms gave way. Splinters like arrows plummeted from the ceiling, falling along with burning shingles. Amid the firestorm, the dark tide in my mind receded. Rivascis's will slipped away.

My body burned. My legs especially felt seared. Even beneath my cloak, my skin throbbed. Miraculously, the falling debris had avoided me thus far. Snapping my neck to either side, I realized I was still a prisoner.

Rivascis's claws, smoldering in seared rags, dug into the wood to either side. He held himself over me, staring into my face—I avoided meeting his eyes again. Embers rippled across his clothing. Through his side jutted a metal jag the length of a small spear.

He could have avoided that. My dagger stared from his chest, buried in him up to its steely bird skull. That wasn't preventing his escape, though. If he'd dropped me I probably wouldn't have realized it until I was bleeding out on the ground. He could have fallen himself, then walked away without a wound a moment later. Still, he stayed.

The air sizzled. He burned. It smelled like chemicals, like sulfur. The flames crackled, but died soon after exploding. Despite that, the light they brought didn't die.

I shifted and sunlight blinded me. A hole tore through the roof, angled to catch just the crest of the dawning sun. It fell over me, hazy and cold. Yet where it touched Rivascis, the vampire burned. He twisted away from me, away from the light.

I didn't let him.

Both my hands closed on the dagger skewering him, holding him in place. It wouldn't take long.

His claws were on me, peeling away fingers. His nails scraped skin, but I held tight. He was so much stronger. I couldn't hope to overpower him, but I didn't need to. Pain shot through my hands as something snapped. I held tight.

"Larsa." He said my name like a command, but there was a desperate stitch. I ignored it.

More pain. Unbidden, one of my hands dropped away.

The smell of sulfur intensified. The stony shade of his face began to char, pristine marble blackening to shale.

At least two of my fingers refused to move. I ignored the pain, even as he broke another finger gripping the dagger. I groped inside my cloak—I didn't have long. My thumb twisted backward. I screamed when it gave way.

Not just from the pain.

From the depths of my cloak, I heaved the last of Kindler's antique wooden stakes, forcing it up with an open palm. It struck just higher than the silver blade inching from the vampire's chest.

But it didn't enter. He'd caught it between us.

"Larsa." His eyes met mine, gray and dusty. "You can't blame me . . . for wanting to feel alive."

Gritting, I hammered against the flat of the stake. "You're not worth blaming anymore."

My palm struck, bone cracked.

His grip slipped, and the stake drilled into his skin. Faded eyes widened and a centuries-old body trembled. The convulsion passed in an instant. His thin lips stretched in a smile—one that hid his fangs. "Ailson . . . I knew you'd always follow."

"I am *not*—"

It didn't matter. Whatever fire the sun set within his kind did its work. His features sparked, skin crisped, then it all silently burned. In withering eyes, something pooled then slipped. As the cinders of his face fell, one charcoal-strained tear caressed my cheek.

His body lost its shape, his clothes sagged, and from empty rags my father's ashes buried me.

50

ASHES
JADAIN

Oh, don't fuss, I can do it—I *can* do it myself!" Considine sputtered as I dragged him by the leg away from the single ray of sunlight piercing to the box house's floor. He might have said he could, but I wasn't so sure the way he'd whimpered when the stray crack of dawn-light splashed over him. Regardless, I released him into the shadows.

"Thank you!" He tried to reclaim his dignity, standing with a frown and brushing down his outfit—particularly the pants leg I'd just released. A splinter had torn a considerable gash. "Well, it was already ruined, I suppose. This has turned into a surprisingly costly night." His expression turned wistful, and he quietly turned away.

I thought better of it, but asked anyway. "Are you okay?"

Was I trying to comfort a vampire? I'd pray for forgiveness later.

The dead man chuckled dismissively. "Of course." He followed it with a sidelong smirk, but it faded fast. "You know . . . you could have put an end to things back there. Using that dagger again, that was a nasty trick."

I scanned his face, mostly his eyes. They were green—not even a particularly spectacular shade—but in the moment they looked sincere enough. "Yeah. And you just laid there after Larsa took it out the first time. You could have turned into fog and slipped away. Why didn't you?"

"Just curious, I guess."

"About what?"

He grinned. "Whether or not you'd try and burn the *wicked* out of me, I guess."

I didn't return his smile. "I thought about it."

"But you didn't." His grin widened enough to show one of his sharp canines. "Doesn't your goddess insist you destroy things like me—abominations, life and death, all that? But you didn't."

I nodded.

He gestured toward my scar. "Brand's starting to suit you, eh? We are what we wear."

For the first time in days, I'd forgotten the mark. I traced it gingerly. It was tender, but didn't burn like it had. "Everyone's a heretic to someone."

Were he a devil straight from the Pit, Considine couldn't have given a more insidious smile. "That's why you're my favorite. Which reminds me . . ." He waggled a finger. "You owe me a favor."

Now he *sounded* like a devil, too. I supposed I had agreed to get him to cast his spell, even though I doubted he'd have honored such a tenuous bargain if our positions were reversed. Regardless, I waited to hear my sentence.

"Well, I could . . ." A sharp nail tapped curling lips—he was drawing it out. Eventually, he just shrugged. "I'll have to think on this. I've never needed a favor from a priestess, but now that I've got one, I'll have to come up with something worthwhile. You're off the hook for now."

Somehow that made it worse.

I turned to the heaps of rigging and catwalks piled in the bare taproom. Thick dust filled the air, drifting through beams of sunlight piercing the perforated ceiling. It piled in ashy drifts across the floor, creeping into every crack and floorboard. I could just make out Larsa, sitting with her back against one of the rafters above. Even from our vantage below, it was clear what had happened to Rivascis.

426 F. WESLEY SCHNEIDER

"You all right up there?" I called, immediately covering my mouth afterward. The thought of breathing in vampire ashes made my soul nauseous.

She didn't answer, didn't move at all. Understandable, I suppose.

"We should give her a few minutes, but I think I might need your help getting her down."

"That, my dear, is your problem." Considine straightened his tattered vest. "Right now, I deserve a drink."

I turned my frown on him, but the wisps of ground fog were already dispersing.

51

DUST
LARSA

The frame of Kindler's front door was thoroughly charred and in need of much more than a fresh coat of paint. But it wouldn't need the attentions of Jadain's fellows in the clergy. When we returned to Kindler's home, any evidence of Tashan's corpse was gone. Considine was the only suspect in the disappearance, but somehow that seemed fine to both Jadain and me.

Kindler had found her way home as well. She offered us tea at the door and didn't ask any questions. Jadain gave her all the answers she could have wanted. Neither asked me to say anything. I closed my eyes and leaned back in one of Kindler's hard armchairs. I hadn't meant to fall asleep, but when I started at Jadain's touch it was well after midday.

We returned to Troidais House. For the next two days, I kept to the cellar and mostly slept. Jadain oversaw Rarentz's recovery, treating him like a patient in his own half-empty home. I could hear them talking and occasionally laughing softly in the kitchen above.

I expected to have unpleasant dreams. I expected Rivascis to repeat himself behind my eyelids, to try and make amends again— but he didn't. Vampires cast neither reflections nor shadows, but I wondered what other impressions they didn't make. Somehow I was already having trouble remembering his face.

More than once, I took the length of twisted black enamel from my pocket. It had been the only thing that hadn't blown away amid the dawn light. For nearly anyone else, Rivascis's wand held a curse, the hand of death frozen in its tight coil. It was the only mercy Rivascis ever granted me. I used it to heal my shattered hands, but after that I just stared at it. His ashes encrusted its cracks and whorls.

In my ledger of scars, I knew one kindness didn't undo years of torture. Still, it felt like a parting gift, an apology that came too late. I accepted it—at least for now.

I decided to tell Jadain I was leaving for Caliphas. I wasn't obligated to. Our partnership—as tenuous as it had been—was over. Her agreement with Doctor Trice to look after Kindler was fulfilled, as was whatever part of it I'd accepted. But she'd earned the courtesy. More than that, she followed when I chased Rivascis into the dark. I owed her.

Rarentz was there when I came into the kitchen. They stopped their conversation.

"How are you feeling?" Jadain asked over her patient's shoulders. She was wearing more of Lord Troidais's work clothes.

Rarentz twisted at the table. A bandage covered his eye, but nothing elaborate—he seemed like the sort to have a brush with death and emerge with nothing more than a dashing scar. He offered a polite nod and an empty seat.

I declined the latter. "Well enough to travel. I'm headed back to Caliphas."

A beat passed.

"So soon?" Soft surprise tinged Jadain's voice. Her bandage *was* elaborate, masking most of the right side of her face. I shifted my stare, but it was too late. She turned her head a self-conscious inch.

I nodded. "Tomorrow."

"The coach is still at Miss Kindler's." She turned to Rarentz. "Would it be too much of a bother for you to prepare it for us?"

The nobleman gave a dismissive sniff and touched his bandage. "I don't think that settles our account, but I'd be happy to."

She'd misunderstood something. "You don't need to come."

Her bandage shifted as her brows went askew. She turned to Rarentz. "Would you excuse us for a moment?"

He nodded and slipped past me, out of his own kitchen.

After he was gone, the priestess motioned toward his empty seat. I settled my hands on the back, but didn't sit.

Worry was plain in her eye. "Why are you rushing back?"

"It's been two days. It's hardly a rush."

She just grimaced.

What did she expect from me? "Why would I stay?"

"You've never had anything pleasant to say about Caliphas, or your people there. This could be something new—a fresh start. You could stay here, get to know Miss Kindler . . . she'd probably like that."

"I don't think so."

"Why?" It was clearly an accusation—one I'd been considering quite a bit over the past few days.

I swallowed my annoyance. I wasn't good at this, but Jadain had earned an answer.

I pulled out the chair and crossed my hands on the table. "Rivascis called me a slave for serving both the Royal Accusers and Siervage. But it was easy to brush off. I knew there was more to me." I stared at my fingers. "At least, there was while he still ran."

Only Jadain was in the room, but I felt like I was in front of a jury. "Hunting him, I did for myself. I hated him since before I knew him. I made him into the monster I blamed for every terrible thing in my life. The promise of ending him dragged me through so much. But now that he's gone, all that's gone, too. I've finished him, but part of me wants him back."

Jadain put her hand out, not touching mine, but close. "You're mourning your father. That's only natural."

I laughed at the ludicrousness of it. "I didn't realize you could mourn someone you killed. I've wanted to put a stake in him my entire life. Now that I've done it, I'm . . . empty. I'm nothing."

"You're not nothing. You're free." Her voice was soft, but steady. "He hurt you, and you've struggled with those wounds for a long time. For the first time ever, now he can't hurt you anymore."

"But that's all I was. I let them think I was their tool to kill vampires, but I wasn't. I was my tool to kill him. Now he's gone and my use for myself is over. Now I'm just someone else's pawn." My hands clenched. "I am a slave . . . just like he said."

"Don't be ridiculous."

I glared up.

"You're the most determined person I've ever met." She pitted a smile against my grim look. "Maybe, in a way, that did make you a slave, a prisoner of your own hate and bad memories. You set a gigantic, terrible task for yourself, but somehow you've achieved it. That doesn't mean your life's over, it means now it's really yours. Those old pains aren't gone, but you don't need to be dragged along by them anymore. What's next is up to you. It's finally your turn to make your life mean what you want it to."

"Like what?"

"Like whatever you want. That's the hard part. We've got a long trip back to Caliphas, though. I'd be happy to help you figure it out along the way."

She still didn't get it. "Our job is over. You don't have to come with me."

"I know." She said it as though it'd been obvious. "But it's my calling to comfort the mourning and help those searching for their fate—doubly so when they're friends." She patted my hand.

I fought back the reflex to yank away.

Her touch was light and warm.

It wasn't so bad.

Both Jadain and I had stops to make before heading to Kindler's home in the morning. I didn't ask after hers and she didn't intrude on mine.

My business took longer than I anticipated, and it was approaching noon by the time I reached Bronzewing Row. I'd planned to be well out of the city by then. Nevertheless, I found myself staring at Kindler's door, and not just because of the man-shaped scorch mark. If my life was going to mean what I chose, I couldn't bury just half of my past. I swallowed and shouldered through the sagging door.

Kindler's home was perpetually dusty—somehow it seemed even more so than before. From the lounge stared all her memories—tiny keepsakes, curios, books, other treasures. Over the fireplace stared a woman who looked like me, and the living faces of four monstrosities I'd destroyed myself. It was unsettling to look at them again. It must have been worse for Kindler. I didn't linger.

Upstairs, the door to Kindler's library was open a crack, enough to see she'd already lit the fire. I knocked lightly. When no one answered, I pushed inside.

Posture rigid, attention fixed, Kindler sat at her desk conducting a quick quill across a page. I approached softly and watched her write. She looked like Diauden, channeling her face's intensity into scratches of ink. I wondered if my abrupt departure from the capital had inconvenienced that scheming old spider. I hoped it had.

"Bound for home, then?" Kindler didn't look up, her pen going through the motions of a polite conclusion.

"That's right."

"It won't be out of your way to deliver this, then." She nodded to the page.

"Maybe. It's a big city." I'd had my fill of errands and letters.

"It's for Trice—a firm reminder that I'm retired. Also a warning about the arcane wards I'm adding to my gate and what they'll do should any visitor even so much as whisper the word 'Pathfinder.'"

432 F. WESLEY SCHNEIDER

I looked over the page. The salutation read, *To my worst student.*

"I can make sure it finds its way."

"Thank you." Her signature was merely a dash followed by an "A" that was more flourish than letter. "And what about you? How sure is your way?"

"I suspect we'll be avoiding Kavapesta on the way back, but that shouldn't make the trip too much longer."

Brows pinched apprehensively over the rim of her glasses.

I puffed, dismissing the look. "It's a bit late to start being motherly."

The look vanished as she placed her glasses on the desk. "I suppose. Still, even at my age, there are days I could do with a bit of mothering."

As proud and proper as she was, I couldn't imagine Kindler wanting help from anything more than a servant. Even the admission seemed like a confession. "It's just not something I'm accustomed to."

"Me either, it seems. I suppose you're right, and we're too late for all that anyway." She gave a small smile. I appreciated that she didn't sound wistful.

I nodded politely. "About a lifetime too late."

She saw her letter into an envelope, pressed a candle-flame-shaped seal into wet wax, and stood, presenting it to me. "Here you are Miss . . ." Her own words distracted her and she let the letter slip back to the desk. "I hate that you don't have a last name. Just 'Larsa' seems so improper."

"There are too few of us in the Old City to need surnames. Siervage's ilk choose their own names, which tend to be distinctive enough."

"Yes, yes." She waved with the letter. "It's not just a name, though, it's a sign of esteem—and sometimes more. You're certainly deserving of a bit of respectability every now and then."

I'd never thought of it like that.

"While you could always come up with your own, I can't see mine going to much more use. I certainly don't expect to be around long enough to tarnish it more than I already have. If the sound suits you, you're welcome to use 'Kindler' if the occasion requires."

I stared at the straight-backed old woman. Her look was hardly warm, but it was polite—welcoming, even. She might have been extending a stranger an invitation to tea—but I wasn't used to even that.

"I'll think about it." I gave a little nod. "Thank you."

She handed me the letter and I found a place for it in one of my cloak's deep pockets. My fingers bumped something smooth.

I cursed to myself. I'd almost forgotten—some part of me wished I had. But I'd already gone this far.

"I have something for you as well."

She gave a well-mannered hum.

"Something to return, actually." From a pocket I drew a twisted length of silver and bronze. I placed it on the table.

She leaned close, replacing her glasses. "A wand?"

I nodded.

"This is one of mine." She picked it up, rolling it in her hands.

"It is. I took it the other day, when we were . . ."

Kindler nodded. "You've . . ." She looked up from the wand, expression pained. The lace veil of formality quickly swung back into place. "You've restored it."

"I paid a local for the service and he completed the work this morning. I'm afraid I didn't know the original command to active it, so I used the same one as your dispelling wand."

"So, it has its original power to repress memories." She stared past it. "Why?"

"I owed you something for all your help—especially for saving me at the opera. A return to your peaceful retirement seemed like the least I could do."

It was only half a lie.

She didn't flinch. Neither did I.

Finally, she nodded. "I see. Thank you." He voice was tighter than it had been a moment ago.

I returned the nod with a touch to the brim of my hat. Before she could say more, I was tugging the door shut behind me.

I stood in the hall, freeing the breath I'd held while leaving. At least that was over now. I'd come here hunting my father, not running home to my mother. That had been incidental.

Now we could both get on with making our lives our own.

Jadain held the horse's reins as I climbed onto the carriage.

"Everything all right in there?" She must have read something on my face.

"Fine." It sounded weaker than I'd meant, but I didn't try again. The priestess watched me, but didn't press the matter. I appreciated that.

Something was different. "Your brand is . . . lighter." I couldn't say "gone"—it was far from that. Her pupil had regained its natural shape, but the purple-blue marks that had so clearly marred her face had faded to a lighter, pink scar. It was still grim, but less so than it had been.

She patted around her eye. "I spoke with my brethren here and explained what happened—well, most of what happened. It sounds like they've had their own tensions with the penitents in Kavapesta. They were outraged to see the goddess's curse on one of their own and gladly helped me remove the spell."

"Not the scar, though?"

She gave me a droll look. "You're lucky I've decided not to be sensitive about it."

I opened my mouth, then promptly shut it.

Jadain laughed. "I've decided to keep the scar, at least for now. It's something of a reminder—of this journey, of my faith, of the things I've suffered, but most of all, that there's always another view, another way. I'm sure my sisters at Maiden's Choir will have many questions, and I look forward to answering them."

That surprised me. "So you're returning to the church. Even after what the High Exorcist tried to do?"

"Oh, I plan to expose what Mardhalas tried to do—as best I'm able. But even if I can't muster the proof . . ." She stood and fished something out of a pack behind her, producing a handful of sharp teeth. "I picked up a few souvenirs this morning: the teeth of a whole crypt worth of corpses, and an urdefhan's fangs. And if anyone ever wants to claim I'm too soft to serve the Lady of Graves, I'm going to make them choke on these."

I blinked, surprised—and a little impressed—by the scarred priestess's new fire. There were more teeth in her palm than just the ghouls' and urdefhan's, though. Two shiny, slightly oversized canines looked particularly familiar.

"Are those . . . ?" I couldn't quite bring myself to finish.

"They are." She looked defiant. "I'm even thinking of stringing them all together—I got the idea in Kavapesta."

I leaned away from her, suddenly wary. "You're keeping my teeth?"

Jadain grinned. "We've got a long trip back to Caliphas. Think of it as a warning—just in case you get thirsty along the way."

ABOUT THE AUTHOR

Editor-in-Chief at Paizo Inc. and co-creator of the Pathfinder Roleplaying Game, F. Wesley Schneider is a writer and game designer obsessed with horror and dark fantasy. This is his second work to feature the irascible vampire hunter Ailson Kinder, the first being the novella *Guilty Blood*. That tale, along with his short story "Shattered Steel" and his comics set in the Pathfinder world, can be found on **paizo.com**.

As a game maker and world-builder, he has a hand in nearly every Pathfinder RPG offering, but is well known for scripting the unnerving Carrion Crown Adventure Path, writing the fan-favorite adventure *Seven Days to the Grave*, and populating Pathfinder's various hardcover bestiaries. He's also the creator of the gothic nation of Ustalav, the Pathfinder RPG's realm of terror and the setting of this novel, which is extensively detailed in *Pathfinder Campaign Setting: Rule of Fear*.

Wes and his husband live just outside Seattle with an unlucky black cat and an endlessly expanding collection of frightening books, films, and video games. You can follow Wes on Facebook, Tumblr, and Twitter (@FWesSchneider), and at **wesschneider.com**.

ACKNOWLEDGMENTS

My deepest gratitude goes to my husband, Russell, for tolerating me for the eon it took to write this book. Considerable blame for this effort goes to James L. Sutter, who encouraged me to write it in the first place. Additional thanks then go to him and veteran editor Christopher Paul Carey for their eloquence and patience. Dave Gross, James Jacobs, Erik Mona, and Jessica Price all have my thanks for the counsel and wisdom that made this a far better story. For their wit and creativity, I'm also grateful to the entirety of the Paizo team. Finally, thanks to my parents, Fred and Susan Schneider, and my grandmother, Marie E. Ritter, for their boundless enthusiasm and encouragement.

I couldn't have written this without all of you.

GLOSSARY

All Pathfinder Tales novels are set in the rich and vibrant world of the Pathfinder campaign setting. Below are explanations of several key terms used in this book. For more information on the world of Golarion and the strange monsters, people, and deities that make it their home, see *The Inner Sea World Guide*, or dive into the game and begin playing your own adventures with the *Pathfinder Roleplaying Game Core Rulebook* or the *Pathfinder Roleplaying Game Beginner Box*, all available at **paizo.com**. For a closer look at the nation of Ustalav, where this book is set, check out *Pathfinder Campaign Setting: Rule of Fear*, also by F. Wesley Schneider.

Amaans: Hilly county in southern Ustalav.

Andoran: Democratic and freedom-loving nation far south of Ustalav.

Archdevils: Powerful devils second only to Asmodeus in the rule of Hell.

Ardeal: Formerly powerful county in northern Ustalav, now in decline.

Ardis: Former capital of Ustalav, now fallen from prominence and full of abandoned homes.

Asmodeus: Devil-god of tyranny, slavery, pride, and contracts; lord of Hell.

Avalon Bay: Section of Lake Encarthan that includes all of Ustalav's ports.

Avistan: The continent north of the Inner Sea, on which Ustalav resides.

Barstoi: Backwater county in northeastern Ustalav.

Brevic: Of or pertaining to Brevoy.

Brevoy: A frigid northern nation famous for its swordplay.

Caliphas: Capital of Ustalav and that nation's largest port, located in the southernmost county (also called Caliphas).

Calistria: Also known as the Savored Sting; the goddess of lust, revenge, and trickery.

Chastel: Farming town in central Ustalav.

Darklands: Extensive series of subterranean caverns crisscrossing much of the Inner Sea region, known to be inhabited by monsters.

Desna: Good-natured goddess of dreams, luck, stars, and travelers.

Devils: Fiendish occupants of Hell who seek to corrupt mortals in order to claim their souls.

Dhampirs: Rare humanoids born of unions between humans and vampires, possessing some vampiric traits but remaining living creatures (rather than undead creatures like vampires and their magically created spawn).

Elysium: Outer Plane where good-natured, freedom-loving souls go when they die.

Flayleaf: Plant with narcotic leaves.

Full-Blood: Vampiric slang for a true vampire.

Ghouls: Undead creatures that eat corpses and reproduce by infecting living creatures.

Great Beyond: The planes of the afterlife.

Horsemen: Nihilistic, godlike entities of pure evil that rule the plane of the afterlife called Abaddon.

Inner Sea: The vast inland sea whose northern continent, Avistan, and southern continent, Garund, as well as the seas and nearby lands, are the primary focus of the Pathfinder campaign setting.

Inquisitor: Religious warrior empowered by divinely granted magic who hunts enemies of the faith.

Isger: Nation far south of Ustalav.

Karcau: Mysterious Ustalavic city famed for its opera.

Katapesh: Mighty trade nation south of the Inner Sea. Also the name of its capital city.

Katapeshi: Of or related to the nation of Katapesh.

Kavapesta: City in central Ustalav notorious for its extreme devotion to Pharasma, particularly a sect known as the Pharasmin Penitence.

Kellids: Tribal human ethnicity native to the lands north of Ustalav, often regarded as uncivilized and barbaric by southerners.

Lady of Graves: Pharasma.

Lady of Mysteries: Pharasma.

Lake Encarthan: Massive lake in central Avistan that touches Ustalav's southern border and facilitates trade.

Lastwall: Nation dedicated to keeping the Whispering Tyrant locked away beneath his prison-tower of Gallowspire, as well as to keeping the orcs of Belkzen and the monsters of Ustalav in check.

Leland: District in Caliphas.

Lepidstadt: City in Ustalav noted for its university.

Nidal: Evil nation in southern Avistan, devoted to the worship of Zon-Kuthon, god of pain, after he saved its people from extinction in the distant past.

Odranto: Militant border county in northern Ustalav.

Old Capital: Ustalavic slang term for Ardis.

Old City: Vampiric slang term for the secret city of vampires located beneath Caliphas's sewers.

Osirian: Of or relating to the region of Osirion, or a resident of Osirion.

Osiriani: The native language of Osirion.

Osirion: Ancient nation south of the Inner Sea, renowned for its deserts, pharaohs, and pyramids.

Pathfinder: A member of the Pathfinder Society.

Pathfinder Society: Organization of traveling scholars and adventurers who seek to document the world's wonders.

Pesh: Narcotic drug made from a type of cactus.

Pharasma: The goddess of birth, death, and prophecy, who judges mortal souls after their deaths and sends them on to the appropriate afterlife.

Pharasmin: Of or related to the goddess Pharasma or her worshipers.

Pharasmin Penitence: Extreme sect of Pharasma's church that believes pain and hardship in life will result in rewards in the afterlife, and thus advocates an ascetic lifestyle.

Prince of Darkness: Asmodeus.

Psychopomps: Immortal servants of Pharasma who guide souls into the appropriate afterlives.

Qadira: Desert nation on the eastern side of the Inner Sea.

Qadiran: Of or related to Qadira; someone from Qadira.

Risen Guard: Elite Osirian military unit dedicated to guarding the pharaoh, every member of which has died and been brought back to life by magic.

River of Souls: Unending procession of recently deceased souls traveling from the mortal world to Pharasma's realm for judgment.

Royal Accusers: Ustalavic investigators and secret police reporting directly to the prince and his advisors.

Rozenport: Port city in southern Ustalav.

Ruby Prince: The current pharaoh who rules Osirion.

Ruithvein: One of the first vampires to come into existence, now a powerful devil worshiped by many vampires.

Sarenite: Of or related to the goddess Sarenrae or her worshipers.

Sarenrae: Goddess of the sun, honesty, and redemption. Often seen as a fiery crusader and redeemer.

Sarkorian: Of or related to Sarkoris.

Sarkoris: Former nation just north of Ustalav, destroyed and overrun by demons long ago.

Shelyn: The goddess of art, beauty, love, and music.

Shelynite: Of or related to the worship of Shelyn.

Sinaria: Mysterious, swampy county in northern Ustalav.

Sleepless Agency: Private investigation and security firm based in Ustalav.

Sothis: Capital city of Osirion.

Spawn: Lesser vampires created when true vampires drain their victims to death but choose to grant them an element of their own undead nature. Not as powerful as true vampires.

Taldane: The common trade language of the Inner Sea region.

Taldor: A formerly glorious nation that has lost many of its holdings in recent years to neglect and decadence. Ruled by immature aristocrats and an overly complicated bureaucracy.

Thuvia: Desert nation on the Inner Sea, famous for the production of a magical elixir which grants longevity.

Thuvian: Of or related to Thuvia.

Tian: Someone or something from Tian Xia, the Dragon Empires located far east of the Inner Sea region.

Ulcazar: Small, mountainous county in central Ustalav.

Ulfen: Human ethnicity from the cold nations of northwest Avistan, particularly the Lands of the Linnorm Kings.

Undead: Dead creatures reanimated and given a semblance of life by magic.

Urdefhans: Malicious, half-transparent humanoids who live deep underground in the Darklands and worship the Horsemen.

Ustalav: Fog-shrouded gothic nation of the Inner Sea region once ruled by the Whispering Tyrant. Though now ruled by humans, it still bears a reputation for strange bests, ancient secrets, and moral decay. Rife with superstition and often said to be haunted.

Vampires: Undead humanoid creatures that feed on blood and possess a number of magical powers.

Varisia: Frontier region at the northwestern edge of the Inner Sea region.

Varisian: Of or relating to Varisia, or a resident of that region. Ethnic Varisians tend to organize in clans and wander in caravans, acting as tinkers, musicians, dancers, or performers.

Vauntil: Pastoral farming town near Caliphas in Ustalav.

Venture-Captain: A rank in the Pathfinder Society above that of a standard field agent but below the group's ruling Decemvirate. In charge of directing and assisting lesser agents.

Vigil: Capital of Lastwall.

Wand: A sticklike magic item imbued with the ability to cast a specific spell repeatedly.

Wati: Osirian city famed for its necropolis.

Whispering Tyrant: Incredibly powerful lich who terrorized Avistan for hundreds of years before being sealed beneath his fortress of Gallowspire a millennium ago.

White Corner: Mostly abandoned slum district of Ardis.

Turn the page for a sneak peek at

PIRATE'S PROPHECY
by Chris A. Jackson

Available February 2016

7

PERILOUS PROPHECIES

Torius mounted the quarterdeck steps, yawned in a great lung full of sea air, and smiled. *At sea again . . .* The motion of the ship, the wind in his hair, and the creak and groan of the rigging never ceased to ease his nerves. Beneath his feet, the deck barely heeled. The seas were running about twelve feet, but *Stargazer* bore it easily, steady on a beam reach, stabilized by her full hold and towering canvas. A glance aloft confirmed that nothing had changed since his last watch; all plain sail with a reef in the main and forecourse. Since becoming privateers, they'd run with the usual white sails at all times, forgoing the black sails they formerly used at night while pirating. Though it made checking the sails easier in the dark, it also made Torius feel a bit like a bug on a white tablecloth. *One of the trade-offs for being legitimate, I guess.*

"Nothing on the horizon, Captain." Thillion met him with a casual salute and a smile. "Not a single light nor sign of a ship. Snick worked the bugs out of the compass, and we're on course."

"Good." A glance around showed only one thing missing. "Where's Celeste?"

"She went below." The elf shrugged. "She asked if I needed her, and since we're headed for open sea, I said that I didn't. Kortos was off our port beam at sunset, and we've been on a rhumb line for Sothis since then."

"That's odd. She usually waits up for my watch."

"She's not in your cabin? I thought . . . well . . ."

Torius waved off Thillion's unease. The whole ship knew that he and Celeste often reserved the early evening watch for private time. "No, she's not there, and I didn't see her in the galley." He glanced around the middle deck, but didn't spy her distinctive white hair. He grew uneasy. *She's been acting strange lately . . .* "Would you mind staying on watch for a few more minutes, Thillion? I'd like to find her."

"No problem, sir."

"Thanks. Oh, and you can ease off to the west a few points. We're not going to Sothis."

"Yes, sir!" The elf grinned. He knew that meant that none of the Stargazers had decided to jump ship.

Torius went to their cabin first, wondering if he might have missed Celeste curled up on her pillows in the dark, but she wasn't there. Nor was she in the galley or reading in the spare stateroom. The main hold was dark, so he lit a lantern and started exploring among the barrels and crates of herbs and spices, the scents of rosemary, sage, and other exotic herbs overpowering in the close confines. The cargo was well secured against the motion of the sea, and Snick's babies were stowed away, but no Celeste. There was nothing forward on this deck but crew quarters, and he knew she wouldn't disturb the sleeping sailors.

A great, dark hole opened before him, the open hatch to the lower hold. A cool breeze ruffled his hair from above. As was their usual practice when the weather was good, the main hatch had been replaced by a grating for ventilation. Moonlight filtered down through the gaps, the checkerboard of pearly light sweeping back and forth with the roll of the ship. Torius shone his lantern down into the lower hold. There weren't many places to hide aboard a hull only a hundred feet long. He descended the ladder and peered into the gloom.

Over the ship's creaks and groans, he caught a faint sound of scratching. *The ship's cat chasing a rat?* Torius worked his way forward, shining his lantern into the narrow gaps between the stacked crates of cargo. When he reached the forepeak bulkhead and the hatch to the storage locker, he heard the scratching again over the rush of the sea past the hull. Definitely from inside the locker.

What the hell? Torius hung the lantern on a hook, quietly drew his dagger, and reached for the latch.

Scratch, scratch . . . *Like a pen on parchment, or . . .*

He pulled open the door. "Celeste?"

The soft lantern light spilling into the storage locker illuminated the naga coiled among the canvas and cordage. Turning toward him, she hissed and blinked at the light. The pile of translucent, scaly skin beneath her confirmed his suspicion. Celeste was shedding.

"Go away, Toriusss."

"What's wrong? I've seen you shed before. It doesn't bother me." In fact, she usually shed her skin in their cabin. Instinct drove her to seek a safe haven until she could rid herself of the sloughing scales. It was inconvenient, but passed quickly. *So why is she hiding away in the bowels of the ship?*

"I . . . I don't want you . . . to come any closer. Please. Just go."

"No." Something was wrong, and Torius was determined to find out what it was. He grabbed the lantern, stepped inside the cramped locker, and shut the hatch behind him. Looking closer, he saw patches of dry skin still clinging to her body. That was unusual; her skin usually shed in one complete piece. Only once had he seen her looking so splotchy . . . chained in a slaver dungeon when he first met and rescued her. Later she had told him that stress adversely affected her ability to shed well. From the looks of it, she was pretty stressed right now. "Tell me what's wrong. You've been edgy lately, but this is over the top. What's bothering you?"

"I don't . . . I can't tell you." She turned away, hiding her face in her coils. "You'll think I'm crazy. By the stars, *I* think I'm crazy!"

"Crazy? What are you talking about, Celeste?" Torius gently ran a hand down her cool scales and felt her shudder. "What's happened?"

"I don't *know*! I saw . . . something that can't be real!" She writhed her coils, scraping more of the old, dry skin off her tail with a distinctive scratching sound. "It *can't* be . . ."

"What can't be real? What did you see?" He knelt down and ran his fingers through her hair, trying to ease her nerves, though her behavior had him truly worried. He'd seen her upset before, even to the point of hissing and spitting venom, but this was different. Judging from her wide eyes and twitching tail, she was terrified. Her natural reaction to a threat was anger, not fear.

"I saw . . . Snick, but it wasn't Snick. It was like the whole world stopped around me, then she . . . changed." Her head rose from her coils and turned to him, blinking hard against the light, tears glistening in her eyes. "She spoke to me . . . in my head, and then she changed into . . . a butterfly. Into *Desna's* butterfly!"

"She . . ." Torius swallowed his initial skeptical response. If Celeste said Snick turned into a butterfly, then he believed her. He'd never known her to hallucinate or have delusions. "What did she say?"

She fixed him with a hard glare. "You think I'm crazy, don't you?"

"No, I don't think you're crazy, but I don't know what happened either." He ran his hand through her hair again, and she leaned into the caress. At least she still trusted him. "This could be some evil trick, or it could be exactly what you thought. It could have been a waking dream sent by Desna. She is the goddess of dreams, you know."

"Dreams . . . But why would Desna talk to me, Torius? What did I do?" Celeste shook her head. "I've never prayed to any god in my life!"

"True." Though Celeste wasn't an atheist, she tended to rely more on astrology than any divine influence for her answers. She believed the entire universe was a single immense consciousness, and that the motions of the planets among the stars sent messages to those willing to pay attention and listen. But that didn't mean one of the gods might not take an interest in her. "But you did spend weeks at her shrine. Maybe you . . . caught her attention."

"But I don't *want* her attention!"

"Why not?" Torius smiled, relieved to think there might be a simple, albeit astounding explanation for her vision. "I pray for Gozreh's attention all the time. It'd be nice to know that she was actually listening! Besides, you couldn't have picked a better deity than the goddess of stars."

Celeste slapped her tail against the hull. "But I *didn't* pick her!"

"No, but maybe she picked you."

"But why?"

"Who knows? Because you already look to the stars for guidance, maybe? Now, maybe you can just ask Desna."

"But that's just it, Torius. She said . . . that I had to find my *own* answers."

"She did?" Torius considered for a moment. "Actually, that sound exactly like something a deity would say. What else?"

"She : . . touched me." Celeste's eyes lost their fearful look and assumed a far-off, wonder-filled sort of gaze. "And for a second, I had the answer to everything, every question I could ever think to ask, but now . . . I can't remember."

"Well, I'm glad of that, anyway!" Torius laughed.

"What?" Celeste looked horrified. "Why?"

"What would be the fun in living if you had all the answers? No more exploring, no more discovery, no more adventure!" He shrugged. "Kind of like knowing the end of a book you just started reading."

"But . . . I think she does give me *some* answers." At Torius's befuddled look, she explained. "That slaver galley, Torius. I was wondering if we should fight, and suddenly . . . I just *knew* we'd win. At the time, I didn't understand how I knew, I just *knew* I was right."

"You did?" He grinned at her and laughed out loud. "Well, that'll come in handy!" A sudden memory came to him of Celeste shrouded in starry light. "What about that cloak of starlight during the battle? I didn't recognize it as one of your usual spells."

"I don't know. I didn't . . ." Celeste closed her eyes for a moment, then opened them wide. "Maybe I did! I . . ." She blinked, and starlight shimmered around her. She looked down at herself in amazement. "Torius! I did!"

"Holy . . ." Torius bit his tongue. Blaspheming in the presence of a divine manifestation didn't seem wise. Reaching out a hand, he felt a cool pressure against his palm before his fingers penetrated the radiant aura to brush Celeste's scales. "How did you do it?"

"I just . . . asked." She closed her eyes again and the luminous barrier faded.

"Did you send it away?"

"Yes."

"Can you summon it again?"

"I . . . don't want to." She writhed her coils again, her agitation returning.

"What's wrong, Celeste? If these are gifts from Desna, you should use them."

"But I'm not a cleric! I don't worship Desna! I've got my own faith, my own beliefs. Why would she give me anything unless . . . she wants something in return?" Celeste bit her lip and shook her head.

"But Desna's a good—"

"It doesn't matter! I didn't ask for it." She looked stubborn. "You don't give someone a gift out of nowhere then ask for devotion in return. It's . . . *rude!*"

"This isn't like gifts at a birthday party, Celeste. Just because we don't know *what* you did to earn her thanks doesn't mean you didn't do something worthy." He pondered, wondering how he could help her, and realized that matters of religion weren't really his area of expertise. "Maybe you should talk one of Desna's clerics, or at least someone who knows more about faith than a pirate."

"Maybe." Celeste took a deep breath and shuddered down her entire length. "I guess it couldn't hurt."

"You'll probably have to wait until we get back to Almas. I don't remember seeing any shrines to Desna in Ostenso."

"What about Sothis? Aren't we stopping there?"

"No." He smiled broadly. "No need; the crew all decided to stay. We've already come off to the west, and I'm going to make our turn to the north early, since Trellis is in such an all-fired hurry for us to deal with this Chelish weapon."

"Thank you for telling them all the truth." Celeste slithered forward and brushed his cheek with her own. "And thank you for helping me sort this out."

"I didn't do anything." Torius ran his hands through his lover's hair and held her close, her glossy new scales cool against his shirt. "I just listened."

"Sometimes that's enough."

A surge of urgency twinged along Vreva's nerves. *Mathias . . .* She cast her spell, and looked down to check her disguise: the rough-skinned hands of a sailor, feminine yet muscular arms, and the canvas trousers and wide-collared shirt of a Chelish sailor on shore leave. *Perfect.* Without a mirror, she'd have to assume her face resembled her chosen foil—one of the sailors she'd seen on her way to Ronnel's cabin. She wasn't worried; dusk was deepening and in the dark one sailor looked pretty much like another.

Another empathic surge thrilled up her spine; Mathias was close. Before she could step into the open, she caught sight of him, a black blur dashing into the shadowed alley. He leapt up into her arms and nuzzled her neck.

She's coming up the street. She looks like the same Chelish sailor she did last time, skinny with brown hair, missing one front tooth, and a scar on her cheek. He bonked her chin with his forehead, mewing in apology when she winced.

"Don't worry. It's healing." The bruise was from the armrest of the settee in Ronnel's private cabin. He had turned out to be what one of her earliest instructors called a rough trick. The admiral wasn't really a sadist, but made love like he was fighting a battle: hard and fast, no mercy, no surrender. Vreva had given as good as she got, though, and he had a few bruises of his own.

I don't know why you didn't just kill that bastard outright! Mathias mewed quietly. *Without him, this whole plan to start a war falls apart. On second thought, let me go with you next time. You slip knock-out toxin into his wine, and I'll chew off his balls.*

Vreva stifled a laugh. Her familiar tended to be protective, and hadn't liked it at all when she returned from the dalliance sporting bruises. "As tempting as that sounds, I can't kill him. Anguillithek could be the kingpin behind this, and if Ronnel ends up dead, the devil will know something's up. He's still a good source of information."

He's not that good a source. You learned that they're targeting Augustana, but nothing about the weapon.

"For some reason Ronnel didn't like to think about it, and it's a difficult subject to work into pillow talk. But if Bushatra's actually guarding the weapon as you said, delving into her mind might give me all the details I need." Vreva peered around the corner and saw a Chelish sailor striding up the street—skinny, brown hair, and scarred cheek. "You're sure that's Bushatra, and not a real Chelish sailor?"

I'm sure. Same bad leather smell. The only way she could lose me is to lose that corset! I had no trouble following her the other night. His ears twitched. *But then, I'm a cat. You should probably be careful!*

"Always." Dropping Mathias, Vreva peered around the corner again and cast her charm spell. Winning the woman's trust was essential before she started reading her thoughts. Between the magic and her disguise as a fellow sailor, she hoped to get Bushatra thinking about things more important than just what she was planning to have for dinner.

Vreva felt her spell wrap around the woman's mind, then fail, some interposing force brushing her magic aside. Vreva wasn't too worried. She cast the spell again, and once again it failed to take hold of the witch's mind. *Damn!* Spell failure was common to new casters, but Vreva prided herself on her arcane skills.

"Something's wrong," she whispered, ducking back into the shadows as Bushatra strode past her hiding place. "She's resisting my magic." Vreva watched carefully, worried that her attempts might have been detected, but the witch walked on without a glance, her steps fast, evidently intent on her destination.

Losing your touch?

Vreva shot her familiar a glare. "I'll have to try without the charm." She cast her thought-reading spell, and stepped out of hiding. Instantly, numerous minds—astute, dull, and indifferent—flickered into her perception. Concentrating, she identified Bushatra's, a keen mind indeed, which might explain the witch's ability to shrug off Vreva's charm spell. Hastening her steps, Vreva affected the raucous manner of a Chelish sailor on shore leave.

"Hey, shipmate! Hold up there!" She slurred her words as if tipsy, and fished a pipe out of a pocket as Bushatra turned to face her. "Got a light?"

"Bugger off! I'm busy!" The witch turned away and continued up the street.

Vreva tried to delve her thoughts, but didn't get past a haze of irritation. "Too busy to light a shipmate's pipe? Well, that's friendly for ya!" She lengthened her stride to keep up as she focused on the woman's mind. She could feel it, but couldn't penetrate through to hear her thoughts. "Come on, mate. I lost my matches. Just a light."

The witch turned, glared at her supposed shipmate, and uttered a single arcane word. With a snap of her fingers, a spark ignited the bowl of the pipe. "There's your light, now bugger off!"

"Whoa, nice trick!" Vreva puffed and blew a smoke ring. She slowed her steps and tried one final time to pierce the haze of Bushatra's mind. Nothing. "Thanks, mate!" She raised her pipe and grinned, but the witch didn't even look back.

"What a *bitch*," she muttered under her breath as she strolled off the street. Mathias joined her in moments.

I told you she was a piece of work. Mathias rubbed her leg as Vreva tapped out her pipe. When she'd tucked it away, he hopped up into her arms.

"Yes, you did, but something's wrong. I can't seem to get any magic to work on her."

Maybe she's just tough. Mathias lashed his tail, and she felt his revulsion for the witch. *Or maybe her magic is stronger than yours. She *is* a witch, after all.*

"Maybe . . ." Vreva stiffened her resolve. If she couldn't get information about the weapon from Bushatra's thoughts, she'd find another way. "Where did you say she goes?"

A house up on the hill. She meets some people there. Last time she stayed half the night.

"A coven, perhaps," Vreva mused. "Well, then, I think I need to check out her little circle of friends. But let's take a roundabout route. And hurry. I'd like to get there before she does."

Mathias squirmed in her arms, and she dropped him. *Follow me!*

Vreva cast a quick spell to render herself invisible and hurried after her familiar. A cat running up the streets wouldn't draw attention, but she didn't need curious eyes following her. She was breathless by the time they stopped, hunkering in the shadows of an alley in an unassuming neighborhood.

Right there, across the street.

"That's it?" The house didn't look like a witches' lair. With lacy curtains, a low wrought-iron fence, and white-painted gingerbread moldings, it looked more like someplace a grandmother would bake cookies.

What did you expect, a spooky mansion with bats flying out the windows? Mathias's sarcasm tweaked Vreva's temper, but he was right. Witches weren't often the stereotypical hags that most people thought they were. *There she is!*

Still looking like a Chelish sailor, Bushatra approached the house. She pushed through the creaky gate, climbed the steps, and knocked on the door. A moment later, the door opened, and Bushatra dispelled her disguise. A tall blond man let her in without a word. Shadows passed the windows in the front of the house as the two figures were backlit by the lamplight.

There's another one.

A man in a merchant's jerkin strode up the street carrying a satchel. He, too, went to the door, knocked, and was let in by the blond man.

"How many are there?"

Four, including Bushatra. Mathias lashed his tail. *The last one's a woman. Short with spectacles and curly red hair. I don't see anyone else coming, so maybe she's already inside.*

"There's one way to find out. Stay here." Vreva cast her invisibility spell once again. There were few people out and about, but the street wasn't deserted. She hopped the low fence to avoid the creaky gate, and slunk up to the window. Through the tiny gap between the drapes she spied a comfortably furnished room. The man who had brought the satchel was pouring wine into glasses and distributing them to two of the three people who sat around a low table. The redheaded woman was there, but she wasn't the one who caught Vreva's eye. Vreva got her first close look at Bushatra.

Mathias wasn't kidding. She's a piece of work, all right. The woman's hair was wild, and bone jewelry pierced her nose, ears, eyebrows, and lips. Her deep tan and the livid scars that marred her face and arms confirmed her Kellid ancestry, the flesh bearing the evidence of a hard life. Yet all of that was nothing compared to the closely fitted leathers that Mathias had claimed smelled unmistakably like human skin. Vreva suppressed a shiver of revulsion as she spotted strange tattoos inked here and there upon it. No wonder the woman only left the ship in disguise. She would draw unwelcome attention in Ostenso.

Lips moved among the group inside the house, but Vreva couldn't hear a word. *We can fix that.* She whispered a complex spell, and bent her concentration on the room beyond the window. Shortly, their voices sounded in her mind as if she stood among the coven of witches.

"—lovely vintage, Tyfuss." The blond man lifted his glass and sipped daintily. "Are you sure you won't try some, Bushatra? I daresay it's better than the swill they serve aboard *Devil's Trident.*"

"I'm not here to sip wine and trade pleasantries, Pothario. I'm here to learn magic from the rest of you, and give you magic in return. Your ridiculous social interactions don't interest me."

"Well, I hope you don't mind the rest of us being ridiculous." The red-haired woman held out her glass for Tyfuss to top up. She pushed up her thick spectacles with a flick of her wrist, the gold charms on her bracelet jingling with the motion. "What else are we supposed to do while our familiars exchange spells? Remember, *you* approached *us* with this offer of collusion. Besides, what's your hurry?"

"*Fate* hurries us on, Keah. *Robust* is due to arrive any day, and I need to learn as much as I can before I have to go."

"Relax, Bushatra." Tyfuss picked up the bottle and poured a measure into the empty glass on the table. "Have some wine. We've made excellent progress in our spell exchange, and there's nothing for us to do while we wait for our familiars."

Bushatra grasped the glass and drained it in a single swallow. "Sour grape juice . . . You should learn to make archi. It's better than this."

"No way am I going to drink fermented yak's milk." Keah wrinkled her nose and pushed up her glasses again. "I don't even like beer."

"*Chelish* . . ." Bushatra made a disgusted face.

"Why do I get the feeling I'm being used?" Tyfuss narrowed his eyes at Bushatra, possibly put off by her opinion of the wine, or his country. "So far, you've benefited from this interaction more than we have. Why should we believe that you'll ever come back to give us what you promised?"

"Because I've *shown* you what you'll receive. Once I've fulfilled my promise to the Chelish and escape the destruction of Augustana, Ronnel will take over as provincial governor and grant me lands and a title, not to mention enough money to make you all rich! Don't worry; you'll all get what you were promised!"

A title! So that's the price of destroying a city. Bile welled up into Vreva's throat. *How can they so blithely consider killing thousands for their own gain?*

"Or, you could be filling our heads with delusions of grandeur," Pothario said.

"I would *never* betray my coven!" Bushatra glared him down, her dark eyes flaring with spite and her pointed teeth flashing. "Enough blather! I'm here for magic, not talk." Bushatra flung her glass aside. The crash elicited a hiss and a squeak from a corner of the room hidden from Vreva's view.

Keah leapt to her feet and glared at Bushatra. "If you hurt my Woobles, I'll—"

"You'll *what*?" Bushatra bared her filed teeth in a gruesome sneer. "I have more magic than any of you, and I'm offering to make you all *rich*. All you have to do is help me see far enough into the future to make sure my plans are still intact, and you'll get your reward, so just shut up and finish your rotten grape juice. I want to cast another vision tonight."

"You've already shown us all our futures." Tyfuss drank more wine, seemingly unintimidated by the witch's rant. "Why try again?"

She can see the future? Vreva revised her assessment of Bushatra. She might be revolting, but she wielded some serious magic if she could see farther than a few days into the future. Of course, if she would risk a shouting match with a drowning devil she was either powerful or insane. *Maybe she's both . . .*

"The future's always changing. Even as the course of a river may change with the rains a hundred miles away, the course of a prophecy may be altered by seemingly unrelated events. I want to make sure all is well with *Robust*. If something has gone wrong, your futures will change."

"You said nothing *could* go wrong," Pothario protested.

"Once the weapon's aboard *Robust* and we're under way, I'll be in control of the situation and nothing *can* go wrong. Until then . . ." Bushatra shrugged.

Vreva's mind spun with potential plans of action. Perhaps she could contact Torius by dream spell. If he could waylay *Robust* before the ship reached Ostenso, it might buy them more time to discover what the weapon was and how to destroy it. Or it might tip off the Chelish Navy and blow *Stargazer's* cover. Laying plans against someone who could see the future was a paradox waiting

462 CHRIS A. JACKSON

to happen. *Am I altering their futures just by listening in on their conversation?*

"I don't get why they can't use another ship. I mean, the navy's got dozens, right?" Keah's petulance drew Bushatra's glare.

"It has to be a merchant ship, Keah, not a warship. How else can they sneak the weapon into Augustana harbor? A naval ship would never get past the Gray Corsairs. Besides, it's the captain of *Robust* that Ronnel wants more than the ship itself. Apparently, Ronnel holds some dire threat over his family. Caught him cuckolding some count or something. If he doesn't go through with this, Ronnel will ruin his entire family name. They're not likely to get any other volunteers."

"Oh." Keah sipped her wine and heaved a gusty sigh. "Well, you can read my future again if you want. I never get tired of seeing myself rich and powerful."

"Good! Finish your spoiled juice and we'll go down."

"Let me set the wards first." Pothario put down his glass and stood. Withdrawing a tiny bell and silver wire from a pocket, he positioned himself carefully and began to chant. The bell chimed as he cast the spell, and the wire glowed and vanished in a shower of silvery sparkles. Quickly, Vreva cast a spell of her own. To her dismay, she discerned a subtle magical aura that centered on Pothario and encompassed most of the room, including the front door and window. Several other items among the coven glowed with brighter auras, the most powerful coming from Bushatra's tattooed leather corset.

Maybe that's why my spells failed.

"Pothario, you're so paranoid!" Keah finished her wine and stood.

"It keeps me alive." Pothario tucked the little bell away and gestured deeper into the house. "Shall we?"

"Yes." Bushatra stalked out of Vreva's view and the others followed, exchanging glances behind her back.

Vreva slipped over the fence and hurried back to Mathias. "Well, that was interesting."

What? He hopped up into her arms.

"Their familiars are exchanging spells, and Bushatra's using the others to look into the future."

Their familiars get spells? Mathias sounded hurt. *How come I don't get spells?*

"Because I'm not a witch. I'm more worried about the look-ing-into-the-future thing. How can we thwart them if they know what we're going to do?"

But if you know they're looking, can't you plan for that?

"What do you mean?"

If Bushatra sees their futures, make them see what you want them to see. Mathias flicked his tail. *Make it look like—*

The loud slam of a door drew their attention back to the house. Keah hurried through the gate, clutching something close.

The door opened again, and Tyfuss called after her. "Keah! Don't be ridiculous! I would never—"

"Let her go, Tyfuss." Pothario grasped his arm to keep him from running after the fleeing woman. "What she saw is between the two of you. Don't let it interfere with our plans." Tyfuss pulled him back into the house. The door closed, and Keah hurried up the street without looking back.

What the hell was that about?

"I don't know, love, but I think it just gave me an idea." Vreva dropped Mathias and prepared a spell. "Stay here, and follow Tyfuss back to wherever he lives. I'm going to follow Keah."

You're not going to kill her, are you?

"No, but I need to find out what scared her so badly." She cast her spell and vanished from sight. "It may give me the edge I need to outwit Bushatra."

Mirian Raas comes from a long line of salvagers—adventurers who use magic to dive for sunken ships off the coast of tropical Sargava. With her father dead and her family in debt, Mirian has no choice but to take over his last job: a dangerous expedition into deep jungle pools, helping a tribe of lizardfolk reclaim the lost treasures of their people. Yet this isn't any ordinary dive, as the same colonial government that looks down on Mirian for her half-native heritage has an interest in the treasure, and the survival of the entire nation may depend on the outcome.

From critically acclaimed author Howard Andrew Jones comes an adventure of sunken cities and jungle exploration, set in the award-winning world of the Pathfinder Roleplaying Game.

Beyond the Pool of Stars print edition: $9.99
ISBN: 978-0-76537-453-0
Beyond the Pool of Stars ebook edition:
ISBN: 978-1-46684-265-6

PATHFINDER
TALES

Beyond the Pool of Stars

A NOVEL BY Howard Andrew Jones

Rodrick is con man as charming as he is cunning. Hrym is a talking sword of magical ice, with the soul and spells of an ancient dragon. Together, the two travel the world, parting the gullible from their gold and freezing their enemies in their tracks. But when the two get summoned to the mysterious island of Jalmeray by a king with genies and elementals at his command, they'll need all their wits and charm if they're going to escape with the greatest prize of all—their lives.

From Hugo Award winner Tim Pratt comes a tale of magic, assassination, and cheerful larceny, set in the award-winning world of the Pathfinder Roleplaying Game.

***Liar's Island* print edition: $9.99**
ISBN: 978-0-7653-7452-3

***Liar's Island* ebook edition:**
ISBN: 978-1-60125-4264-9

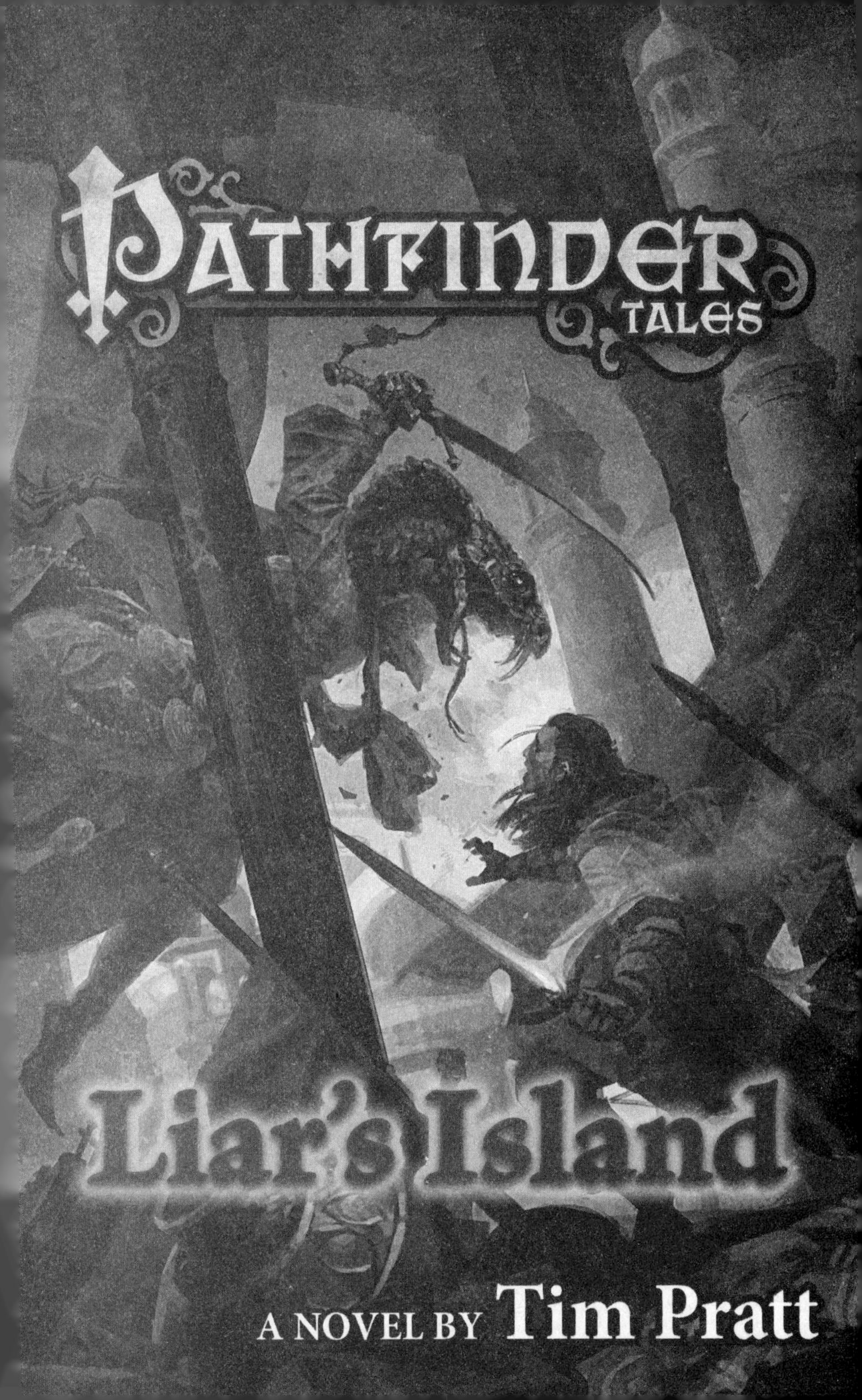
PATHFINDER
TALES
Liar's Island
A NOVEL BY Tim Pratt

Count Varian Jeggare and his hellspawn bodyguard Radovan are no strangers to the occult. Yet when Varian is bequeathed a dangerous magical book by an old colleague, the infamous investigators find themselves on the trail of a necromancer bent on becoming the new avatar of an ancient and sinister demigod—one of the legendary runelords. Along with a team of mercenaries and adventurers, the crime-solving duo will need to delve into a secret world of dark magic and the legacy of a lost empire. But in saving the world, will Varian and Radovan lose their souls?

From best-selling author Dave Gross comes a fantastical tale of mystery, monsters, and mayhem set in the award-winning world of the Pathfinder Roleplaying Game.

Lord of Runes print edition: $9.99
ISBN: 978-0-7653-7451-6

Lord of Runes ebook edition:
ISBN: 978-1-4668-4263-2

PATHFINDER
TALES

Lord of Runes

A NOVEL BY Dave Gross

Years ago, the dwarven warrior Akina left her home in the Five Kings Mountains to fight in the Goblinblood Wars. Now at long last she's returning home, accompanied by Ondorum, her silent companion of living stone. What she finds there is far from what she remembers: a disgraced brother, an obsessive suitor, and a missing mother presumed dead. Yet the damage runs deeper than anyone knows, and when Akina's brother is kidnapped by ancient enemies from the legendary Darklands, she and Ondorum must venture below the surface—and into danger as old as the stones themselves.

From debut novelist Josh Vogt comes a tale of love, redemption, and subterranean battle, set in the award-winning world of the Pathfinder Roleplaying Game.

Forge of Ashes **print edition: $9.99**
ISBN: 978-1-60125-743-7

Forge of Ashes **ebook edition:**
ISBN: 978-1-60125-744-4

PATHFINDER
TALES

FORGE
OF
ASHES

JOSH VOGT

Jiri has always been special. Found as an infant in the ashes of her village, she was taken in by a neighboring shaman and trained to be a powerful jungle druid. Yet when Aspis Consortium mercenaries release an ancient evil that burns her adopted home to the ground, Jiri must gather a group of her own to uncover the secrets of a lost nation and stop the fire spirit—and the greedy treasure hunters trying to leash it for their own ends—before it lays waste to the entire Mwangi Expanse.

From acclaimed short story author Gary Kloster comes a tale of revenge, lost cities, and unlikely alliances, set in the award-winning world of the Pathfinder Roleplaying Game.

Firesoul print edition: $9.99
ISBN: 978-1-60125-741-3

Firesoul ebook edition:
ISBN: 978-1-60125-742-0

PATHFINDER TALES

FIRESOUL

GARY KLOSTER

Torius Vin is perfectly happy with his life as a pirate captain,
sailing the Inner Sea with a bold crew of buccaneers and
Celeste, his snake-bodied navigator and one true love. Yet all that
changes when his sometime friend Vreva Jhafae—a high-pow-
ered courtesan and abolitionist spy in the slaver stronghold of
Okeno—draws him into her shadowy network of secret agents.
Caught between the slavers he hates and a navy that sees him as
a criminal, can Torius continue to choose the path of piracy? Or
will he sign on as a privateer, bringing freedom to others—at the
price of his own?

From critically acclaimed author Chris A. Jackson comes
a fantastical tale of love, espionage, and high-seas adventure,
set in the award-winning world of the Pathfinder Roleplaying
Game.

Pirate's Prophecy print edition: $9.99
ISBN: 978-1-60125-664-5

Pirate's Prophecy ebook edition:
ISBN: 978-1-60125-665-2

PATHFINDER TALES

Pirate's Promise

CHRIS A. JACKSON

Raised as a wizard-priest in the church of the dark god
Zon-Kuthon, Isiem escaped his sadistic masters and became
a rebel, leaving behind everything he knew in order to follow his
conscience. Now, his unique heritage makes him perfect for a
dangerous mission into an ancient dungeon said to hold a magical
weapon capable of slaying demons and devils by the thousands and
freeing the world of their fiendish taint. Accompanied by companions ranging from a righteous paladin to mercantile mercenaries,
Isiem will lead the expedition back into shadowed lands that are all
too familiar. And what the adventurers find at the dungeon's heart
will change them all forever.

From acclaimed author Liane Merciel comes a dark tale of
survival, horror, and second chances, set in the award-winning
world of the Pathfinder Roleplaying Game.

***Nightblade* print edition: $9.99**
ISBN: 978-1-60125-662-1

***Nightblade* ebook edition:**
ISBN: 978-1-60125-663-8

PATHFINDER TALES

Nightblade

LIANE MERCIEL

PATHFINDER
CAMPAIGN SETTING

THE INNER SEA WORLD GUIDE

You've delved into the Pathfinder campaign setting with Pathfinder Tales novels—now take your adventures even further! *The Inner Sea World Guide* is a full-color, 320-page hardcover guide featuring everything you need to know about the exciting world of Pathfinder: overviews of every major nation, religion, race, and adventure location around the Inner Sea, plus a giant poster map! Read it as a travelogue, or use it to flesh out your roleplaying game—it's your world now!

EXPLORE YOUR WORLD!

paizo.com